RIPPLES

SHARE YOUR THOUGHTS

Want to help make *RIPPLES* a bestselling novel? Consider leaving an honest review on Goodreads, your personal author website or blog, and anywhere else readers go for recommendations. It's our priority at SFK Press to publish books for readers to enjoy, and our authors appreciate and value your feedback.

Our Southern Fried Guarantee

If you wouldn't enthusiastically recommend one of our books with a 4- or 5-star rating to a friend, then the next story is on us. We believe that much in the stories we're telling. Simply email us at *pr@sfkmultimedia.com*.

RIPPLES

SFK
PRESS

EVAN
WILLIAMS

The Thomas Paine quote from the introductory page is taken from *Age of Reason*, by Thomas Paine, Part First, Section 11. Scriptural references are taken from the 1611, King James Version of *The Holy Bible*.

ISBN: 978-1-970137-91-0
eISBN: 978-1-970137-92-7
Library of Congress Control Number: 2019930076

Cover design by Olivia M. Croom. Interior by April Ford.

Printed in the United States of America.

RIPPLES owes its parentage to the 2013-2015 group of instructors and students involved in the Queens University of Charlotte's Low-residency MFA Program for Creative Writing.

To Fred Leebron, whose telephone call inviting me into the program became the true beginning of my serious writing career.

To David Payne, author and instructor extraordinaire, whose guidance has proven priceless.

To Jonathan Dee and Pinckney Benedict for their ceaseless encouragement.

To the ongoing support from fellow alumni, a true family of writers who express vicarious joy in the successes of their Queens peers. Too many to list are those who have read, advised, and critiqued sections of this book.

Special thanks must be given and dedication extended to the members of my first work group, Linda Miller, Richard Patrick, and Steve McCondichie, who each, after having read an early version of the fishing trip story, now paraphrased in Chapter 11, asked the question, "What happened after Ben and Granny returned home?"

That question inseminated this novel.

"And I moreover believe, that any system of religion that has anything in it that shocks the mind of a child, cannot be a true system."
—Thomas Paine

CHAPTER ONE

"And a man's foes shall be they of his own household."
—*Matthew 10:36*

Aloneness clung to Ben Bramley. Any hope for a normal life had been kicked out of him before his first shave.

College diploma in hand, he retreated to the wild lands, distancing himself from society before it could disappoint him further. The only exception to his voluntary exile came in the form of psychiatric therapy from Dr. Joyce Mendel, a Manhattan native, new to the mountains of Western North Carolina, and beyond foreign to the culture.

"THIS IS DR. MENDEL SPEAKING. How may I help you?"

During their first session he had told her that his life could be summed up by a book title, *Chop Wood Carry Water*—a reference to the daily regimen at the remote cabin atop Cut Laurel Knob.

In contrast to the physical demands on his farm-muscled six-foot frame, solar panels, a hydro-electric generator, and satellite internet service softened the self-imposed quarantine, along with the company of Smoky, a marbled-gray Maine Coon.

"Listen, Doc. I'm in a real bind. My dad's had an accident. May not make it. I'm headed to Abundance."

"Oh, my! When?"

"Right now. I needed to speak to you before I cross over the ridgeline and lose signal."

"Ben, I'm so sorry. At least swing by my office. We can talk."

"No time, Doc. And if I stop, I might not start again. Also, I wanted to let you know I probably won't make my session this week. And if I can't reach you by phone, in case I have a meltdown, let's say, will you keep an eye on your e-mail?"

"Of course, Ben. Did you remember to take your running shoes and clothes?"

"First thing I packed. Tell me again what you call that *run-until-I-can't* disorder of mine."

"You're too smart to have forgotten."

"Maybe. Could be I just like hearing you say it."

"Alright, I'll indulge you. In clinical terms, you present as 'an obsessive, frenetic runner, using the exhaustive aspect of physical activity as a primary coping skill.'"

"That's what I love about you, Doc. You can make crazy sound sophisticated. Thanks for keeping an ear out. I better get off the phone before my better judgment puts a halt to this insanity."

"Take care, Ben."

Pressing the END button, he stared at the phone.

Stop, and think. This is a classic sixth-commandment situation—Honor thy father and mother. This is your big chance to atone. Maybe your last chance.

The instructive voice inside his head belonged to Charlton Heston, from his role as Moses in the epic movie *The Ten Commandments*. Ben's waking hours included frequent King James Bible interjections from Moses. But unlike the plagues on Egypt, which came and went, Ben remained hardwired to see the world framed in the religious training of his childhood.

THE ODOMETER ELICITED AUDIBLE SIGHS as miles registered. To break the cycle he resorted to one of his many mind-shifting tricks—lists. They came in handy during sleepless nights in bed. Lists of his twenty favorite books, favorite movies, movie stars, favorite everything.

"Favorite song," he began, "'Losing My Religion,' by R.E.M."

Having cheered himself with that blasphemous admission, he decided to enumerate a general list of his favorite things: "reflections, falling snow, shadows, shelves full of books . . . moonlit snow, arched bridges, waterwheels."

Pausing after each entry, he savored the recollections before moving ahead. By voicing his list aloud, Ben prevented Moses or any negative self-talk from occupying his thoughts.

"Twilight, anything without time limits, people watching, serial-killer psychology, distinctive voices," as he edged into a more inter-personal realm, he opened that door wider to include, "the tattoo of approaching high heels, an almond-shaped face with prominent cheekbones, tan lines, sunlight through a white-linen dress, long hair (especially wavy or curly), sizeable nipples sprouting from bumpy areolae, sex without debate."

The sporadic sex he had enjoyed since hermit-hood involved booking hotel rooms in Boone, then trolling bars where App State students hung out. Pretending to be a tourist, come to enjoy the scenery or take in some snow skiing, he invited women to join him for dinner and champagne at the finest hotels. False names and backgrounds guaranteed him anonymity, *to preserve my reputation*, he told himself—a holdover from his small-town upbringing—though he often questioned what reputation, if any, needed preserving.

Whether the forays into Boone pacified or agitated his mental state, he had not managed to resolve. Poor substitutes for meaningful relationships, the casual sex bypassed all possibility of extended coupling. Coupling would have been in direct violation of his vow of solitude.

In truthful moments he could admit that the sexual encounters were more to him than the normal biological impulse or the compulsion for conquest in the name of masculine confirmation.

Got to talk to Mendel about that one day, after we get past the bigger shit. If we get past the bigger shit.

One-night-stands also eliminated the possibility of a self-proclaimed eventuality.

No sane woman would hang around for the uncensored version of Ben Bramley. Hell, I'm too much for my own self most of the time.

THREE AGONIZING HOURS IN THE driver's seat left him two-hundred yards short of a right turn onto River Road—*their* road—prompting a field of red flags to flash across his mind's eye, fabric snapping in the sharp wind.

In response, Ben's left hand dug in his jeans pocket, pulling out a plastic cowboy. Monochromatic, tan colored, though he preferred to think of it as *burnt sienna*—a more dignified designation. Cowboy's curved legs were designed to sit astride a horse, now twenty-four years gone. Though the plastic figure had originally belonged to James, his younger brother, Ben had laid claim. This was back in the day when James had to play the role of Davy Crockett. Ben got first choice, Daniel Boone—who was also the namesake for Ben's adopted home town.

"Stop!" he warned himself, pulling the black Acura SUV into the Abundance Post Office parking lot—four meager spaces, all vacant at the late hour.

What are you doing? Moses asked.

Ben paid no attention, engrossed in Bret Michaels's vocals, pouring from the radio. The music escaped the vehicle's open windows, to reverberate off the brick face of the post office. Unable to resist, he accompanied Brett for the final refrain of the rock ballad, "Every Rose Has Its Thorn." The hit single had debuted in 1988, fall semester of Ben's freshman year at Duke University.

A faint remnant of freckles bunched closer when he grinned at the thought of hearing his beloved song on an Oldies Rock station, two years into the new millennium, and two years into his own third decade.

"Not getting any younger, just like this town," he said to the empty intersection.

He was being generous with the title *town*. Abundance fell more under the category of a *community*, and, more to the point, a community of lives lived too safely. Imagination, innovation, and brilliance were not in great demand, with each cog in place and working to the general satisfaction. Where worshippers sang, "Give Me That Old Time Religion," and meant it, by God.

Born of a family who considered cinnamon toast to be gourmet fare, Ben longed early on for more than simple circumstances could provide. Wrong time. Wrong place. Wrong relatives. Though he had worked hard to fit in, followed the rules of home and church, he remained a multi-hued boy, cast in the black-and-white world of Abundance.

While the byway lacked dreamers, it excelled in natural beauty. Surrounded by ascending ridge lines in graduated hues of blue, its boundaries lay at the bottom of a bowl of gently rolling land, a crazy quilt of working farms and woodland borders. Topographically fortressed against the outside world, the area found that change came slowly, or bypassed it altogether.

As he exited the SUV, Ben's soles skidded on fine gravel atop the asphalt lot. Staring at his past, he killed the radio to wrestle with the family crisis, minutes down the road.

The October sun's last light stretched long shadows across the terrain.

"No progress in fourteen years," he observed, the landscape idling in neutral.

Abundance School—decrepit when he attended—didn't have the capacity to look any older. Potato-chip–sized paint flakes peeled from the prominent Federal-style trim encircling the two stories that housed grades one through twelve. The innovation of kindergarten had been blocked. "Budgetary reasons," they said.

Generations of Bramleys, and Etters—his mom's side—claimed alumni status from that cyclical institution, where graduating classes bore identical surnames from one year to the next in perpetuity.

Between the school and post office stood Uncle Stan's gas station with its two-bay garage. Three vintage pumps stood sentinel in front. None accepted credit cards—an inconvenience store.

Beyond the school, the Abundance Growers' Packing House spilled soft, yellow light onto the highway. A silhouette of flatbed trucks laden with apples awaited their turns to unload. Forklifts buzzed around the perimeter to disappear inside the building, where dozens of worker bees graded and packed fruit. In a few weeks the packing house would lapse into a coma, until resurrected by the influx of next summer's produce.

And in the center of the crossroads cluster loomed Redeemer Baptist Church, absolute authority oozing out of the mortar joints, which forever locked the clotted-blood-colored bricks in their place of prominence.

A church sign identified Redeemer—a low-rent, changeable-letters kind of sign, the kind often found occupying any roadside strip of crabgrass. Underneath the church's name, a solemn message: "Visitors Welcome. Members Expected."

Noticeably lacking were any of the standard warnings—"Turn or Burn," "If You Died Tonight, Where Would You Go?" Rather, it quoted scripture: "Behold you have sinned against the LORD: and be sure your sin will find you out. Numbers 32:23."

Ben shuddered at the divine guarantee of exposure, though he daily assured himself that his faith had eroded to nothingness.

Craning his neck, he looked up at the righteous-white steeple, illuminated by a column of light reaching to the heavens. Monday night. No church service. Safe enough to avoid being spotted by the locals. He reminisced, stalling.

"You cannot escape the steeple! The Great Eye sees all!" he bellowed, double-checking for listeners before adding, "Agnostics rule! Baptists drool!"

Though Ben was delighted with his jab, the hollow noise fooled neither himself nor the God from his youth.

Unsettled by his human's strange behavior, Smoky jumped from his curled position on the front seat to the safety of the farthest corner of the cargo area.

"That's not true," Ben recanted. "The Great Eye can't penetrate closed doors or dark nights where husbands beat wives, or wives screw somebody else's husbands. It doesn't stop the teenager breaking into a widow's home, or the teen's little brother getting his ass kicked at school." He hesitated. "No witnesses. Didn't happen. A lie agreed upon."

With each word, his fury grew.

"You steeple people, you couldn't leave Mama alone!"

Feet wide apart, as if preparing for a slugfest, he went silent when his better senses caught up, acknowledging he had been screaming while a frustrated fist beat the innocent air.

"Damn! Less than two minutes here and I'm losing it."

He pulled the cell phone from his pocket, speed dialing number one, for Dr. Mendel. *Out of Service Area* appeared on the screen. "No bars," he conceded. "That figures for this hick town."

You understand your mistake.

"What do you mean?"

You didn't run far enough. Stayed in the same state. Kept in contact, too.

True, he had not lived outside of his home state after graduating from Duke University. "The Harvard of the South," insecure Southerners called the noble institution, stuck in their post–Civil War, self-esteem issues. The same second-hand title had also been applied to Vanderbilt, Emory, and Davidson, maybe more—all evidence of the pandemic insecurity.

"I couldn't abandon them." Ben responded to Moses, in the same tired excuse millions of other Southern boys had mouthed, frightened to venture north of the Mason-Dixon, or west of the Mississippi.

"They're my grandparents, and he's my dad, if only in name. He might die."

He might die, but you being here isn't going to change fate. The greater threat is maintaining your stability. That's what's at stake, and you know it.

Ben had no response.

In the real world, he had drawn sympathetic listeners, humored by his assertion of growing up not only in the Bible belt, but in the actual buckle. His sardonic tirade would continue: "It's as if God took a handful of Protestant Brand super-phosphate fertilizer, and spread it across the mountains and valleys, causing churches to spring up in profusion. Southern Baptists and rural Appalachia go together like hookers and street corners. And you can pretty well find a church ready to service you on every block."

Turning from the church, he glanced across the highway to a row of connected buildings the locals called "the business district." A combination grocery and general store dominated the sad grouping. Attached to the south end of it was the Abundance Café, the only eatery for miles, in a community where the structures, other than the church, all had "Abundance" within their name.

The café's neon sign glowed a red *OPEN*.

"Well I'll be damned. They used to serve the greasiest, thickest cheeseburgers around."

Learn more about Ben's tormented relationship to the Baptist faith by subscribing to Southern Fried Karma's YouTube channel, Fugitive Views.

CHAPTER TWO

"As a dog returneth to his vomit, so a fool returneth to his folly."
—*Proverbs 26:11*

A parting scowl at Redeemer Baptist's steeple preceded Ben's return to the driver's seat. The need to run overtook him—a go-to mechanism when his brain could not process a reality overload.

He checked the hour glowing on the radio.

"Not enough time."

Every bodily cell screamed *abort* in a message of self-preservation. Only the power of childhood indoctrination could countermand the urge.

"Therefore to him that knoweth to do good, and doeth it not, to him it is sin"—one of many Sunday school memory verses that had earned him a silver-cross lapel pin.

He wrestled the vehicle onto River Road, the Bible imperative odiously weighing on his mind. Left of the road the Unolama River churned. In avoidance, his eyes riveted on the two parallel yellow stripes on the road. His fingers found the main window control. He put all four up tight, and set the radio screaming to mask the presence of ploughing rapids.

The name, Unolama, anglicized from the original Cherokee, *unole ama*, meant "thunder water."

Legions of gray boulders littered the waterway, tumbled down from the mountains that traced the river's southern edge. Angry whitewater alternated with calm pools, masking sucking currents underneath. Snags lurked near the false safety of the banks, where trophy trout baited fishermen to waters prepared to take life.

"A mean river," Pop had often called it, and local references to specific sections—Widowmaker Bend, Cow-Kill Falls—confirmed his assertion.

Widowmaker Bend got its name when Charles McCallister didn't return home from a fishing trip, though some folks quietly speculated he might have escaped an unhappy marriage on foot.

Cow Kill Falls earned its infamous name when a Mr. John Turner, in the early 1800s, decided the calm waters above the falls presented the best option for a cattle crossing. With most of the river festered with boulders, his choice made sense, on the surface. Underneath, a vicious current sucked his entire herd over the falls, throwing them on the jagged granite at the base.

"Helluva way to tenderize beef," Pop often joked, after checking to make sure Granny couldn't hear his lapse of language.

Sam and Lily Bramley's property extended to the Unolama for a significant length. Turbulent and oxygen rich, the river drew them fishing; the family coveted the native brown trout and stocked rainbow trout thriving in its cold waters.

Boyhood Ben had orders to never go fishing there alone.

A MILLION DANCING SPARKLES OF moonlit water caught Ben's peripheral vision. The river refused to be ignored. An unrelenting pull of shared history had long ago lodged between his ears.

The speedometer climbed to sixty-five miles per hour as he tried to outrun his past.

At sight of the Bramley home Ben's foot punished the brake pedal. Four Michelins grabbed the pavement, and left the vehicle askew in the road.

The combined odor of burnt rubber and brake pads overtook his nostrils.

"Definitely hell. I smell the brimstone."

Less-than eager to move, he sat parked.

"What's the deal God? Years I screamed at you. Off by myself, in the woods, my voice echoing back at me. Masturbatory prayer. No answers. Nothing resolved.

"I deserved better. So did Pop and Granny, the poster-couple for Christianity. Church every Sunday, pay their tithe, and publicly give you the credit for each breath they draw.

"Ignoring my suffering is one thing. Ignoring Pop and Granny proves that you suck at being the supreme deity. Not that you care about the opinion of one un-born-again Baptist. And why am I bothering to talk to you when I'm not even convinced you exist?

"Ancient habit, I suppose, with the shock of seeing the family farm, and scared to set foot outside this SUV.

"So it's been what, twenty years since you've heard from me? High school, maybe earlier, when I officially gave up on you fixing my life? Anyway, I survived, without a shred of help from you."

A head weighted with enormity dipped to his sternum.

"I couldn't make sense of your works-in-mysterious-ways plan. And through the critical lens of family tragedy I came to see that everyday life didn't comply with what they taught in Sunday school. Sermons either."

As if in answer, the night air carried the distant rat-a-tat-tat of a fully loaded truck's Jake Brake, as it eased down the steep grade at the west end of Valley Road.

"Maybe I think too much. Went off to college, and got my mind turned with all that worldly knowledge. But we both know you lost me long before I got out of Abundance. And we both know the reasons. Fourteen years of freedom interrupted by one phone call, and, like a porch dog, I come running. Back here where the people are so far up your ass, no way the light of reason can penetrate. All part of the phantom umbilical cord that tethers me to this patch of planet. And any minute now, when Pop or Granny see my hi-beams, it's sayonara to my carefully crafted little world.

"Speaking of which, there's a shadow in Pop and Granny's living-room window. What's behind curtain number one? Well, Ben, if I had to guess, that small silhouette belongs to Lily Bramley.

"I hate myself for still trying to be the good boy, all that do-the-right-thing crap they shoveled in Sunday school class. And for my longshot at redemption I've gotten myself into a scenario which cannot have an upside.

"Hate to vent and run, Almighty One, but I better pull in the driveway. She's already out on the front porch. Nice talking at you. Hope it proved as useful for you as it was for me. Let's try to get together more often.

"Here goes everything!"

"Ben, is that you?" She yelled with the volume of a contestant at the state hog-calling contest.

"Yes, ma'am," he hollered from the driver seat.

His reluctant right foot eased back from the brake, but it could not be convinced to apply gasoline to the predicament. Tires inched forward almost imperceptibly as the vehicle idled its way into the driveway of his youth—the homeland that had scarred him to the bone.

Before he got out, Ben's green eyes performed a hair inspection in the rearview mirror, his curls the same orangey red as the clay found on the farm. Not the same as the lighter-colored clay on top of the ground, but the color when a shovel brought a solid wedge of soil to the surface, sticky enough to stay affixed to the tool, then pried off by a boyhood Ben, who found it ideal for creating clay animal shapes to dry in the sun.

Unable to passably arrange the unruly locks, he concluded, "She'll say I need a haircut, and she'll be right."

Lily Bramley had been "Granny" since Ben started forming words. Her abiding interest in his welfare included his personal appearance. Following the telephone call demanding his return to Abundance, Ben's first act had been to take scissors to a lumberjack beard and the longest of his belligerent curls. He shifted his gaze to the right. No light shone at his dad's house. There was no sign of life. Yet still came the creak of hinges, the unmistakable sound of a screen door snapping shut, followed by a small shadow framed against the starry horizon racing across the front yard, running out of sight down River Road. Ben blinked, and tried to rub the familiar clip from his eyes. *It's started already.*

GRANNY WAITED ON HER COVERED porch. Behind her, Ben could see the silhouette of the old two-seat swing hanging from the porch ceiling. She used to transform it into a little boy's flying carpet, traveling anywhere in the present or deep into her storied past.

The remembrances from Granny's childhood weren't ones of shiny new toys from the Sears Roebuck catalog. No toys at all unless she and her brother and sister made them, so the thrill of a family hog killing led to her brother blowing up the animal's bladder for a homemade ball.

Ben latched onto her every word while seated next to her in the swing, its flaking green paint oxidized to almost turquoise by the slanting rays of 10,000 evening suns.

"Ben, where do you want to go today?" she would ask.

"How about to Florida to see Uncle Lucas?"

Pushing her feet off the porch surface, Granny would set the journey in motion.

For what seemed like hours in child-time, they swung while she described the scenery on the travel route, pointing at pretend people and objects.

"How about we stop at that gas station up ahead? Get us a cold drink."

She would pause the swing for a moment as they washed down make-believe peanut butter crackers with their make-believe sodas. Ben helped her check for oncoming traffic before they pulled out onto the imagined highway.

For that brief period back then, his relationship with her felt magical. And in spite of inflexible exile, his mental image of home continued to be Granny and Pop's house, fifty feet of grass between it and the childhood bedroom he shared with his brother, James.

"THIS PLACE IS AN ASSAULT of memories. Even the happy ones aren't going to help me now," Ben predicted, planting a size-twelve foot on the driveway. "Baby steps."

Granny waved across the darkness. "Do you need us to help you with unloading anything?"

Her voice . . . and he forced a smile, though it pricked his heart with the disingenuousness.

"No thanks," he yelled back. "I've got one suitcase and my laptop . . . my computer," he said. "That's all. Except for Smoky. I'll come back and get him."

"Must not be planning on staying long if that's all you brought," she fired.

He took her volley and kept marching forward. Out of habit, his left hand sought his pants pocket, fingers finding the plastic burnt-sienna Cowboy.

"I'm going to stay as long as it takes."

He sped his gait to close the gap between confident words and inner uncertainty.

"What's a Smoky?" Granny asked mid-hug. Ben marveled at her scrawny body's stabilizing power.

"My cat," he replied, in no rush to release his hold. "Smoky is my cat. I couldn't leave him behind with no one to watch him."

The unmistakable smell of a recent permanent rose from Granny's hair. *She still adds color,* he noted, appreciating the small sameness of her perpetual brown-gray shade. Similar instances of comforting sameness resided within him, though he actively resisted their pull.

For someone who thrived on her hugs and doting, he limited his opportunities for them: at six-month intervals, he would meet Granny and Pop for lunch on neutral ground—anywhere other than Abundance or the Bramley farm. Each occasion he took great joy in presenting them with gifts: a new pipe or a bulging, foil bag of exotic tobacco for Pop; another Hummel figurine for Granny's collection, more of her Sunday perfume; and a fresh brick of hundreds from his sizable bank account.

Squeezing him harder, Granny said, "I love you a million bushels."

Her signature phrase never failed to work its miracle on Ben.

"I love you too," he said, grasping at sincerity.

His inner self had long cast about for substance, the presence of anything that could pass for love. With the exception of lingering hurt, his searches detected only unsettling emptiness, at which he had concluded, *I'm like one of those candy Easter bunnies I used to beg for: bigger than all the other chocolates, but hollow inside.*

Unsure of being lovable or able to feel true love for others, much of his desire not to claim love centered on his imperative to be guiltless of what he considered the most damnable infraction—hypocrisy. Did he have the capacity for love? Did it rest in an unopened puzzle box, deep within his being?

"Hey, son."

Pop had appeared in the light coming from the open front door. His two words, each rounded with softness, conveyed a mountain of emotion.

With the older man as his model for manhood, the desire to be like Pop began early for Ben. At three-years old, Ben had informed Granny, "I want my hair cut like Pop . . . with a hole in the middle."

Pop had on his glasses, an indication that he had been

reading. Likely one of two books—the *Farmer's Almanac* or *The Holy Bible*—both forever resting on the lampstand within reach from his favorite chair.

"I've read through the Bible four times," he often told guests, pointing to the cracked and frayed volume, the gold-embossed letters reflecting the lamplight. "Old and New Testaments both, and I'm working on my fifth round."

The short, unassuming farmer epitomized the God-fearing man of the soil, to Ben's mind. Easy to picture Pop in the standard faded overalls, chambray shirt, and lace-up work boots. At the moment he wore a scaled-down version of his Sunday attire from having visited the hospital earlier in the day.

"Hey, Pop. It's sure good to see you."

Ben rested his hand on the old man's shoulder, looking deep into the safety of watery-blue eyes, reconnecting.

"Same here, even if it took your daddy's fall to bring it about. The good Lord sure does work in mysterious ways."

"What exactly happened, and what's the latest from the doctor?"

Ben dealt in facts. Speculation regarding the *Lord's* involvement in life-threatening accidents for the sake of a family reunion, edged toward insanity.

"You explain it to him, Sam."

Granny had begun fidgeting at the vocalization of her son's dilemma.

Pop explained.

"Early this afternoon Jason was trailing behind the pickers, getting some of the apples they had missed, figuring on us using them for cooking during the winter. Since the help had all the ladders, he took to climbing the trees for some of the higher fruit. Reckon he slipped and fell. Landed smack dab on a big, old root sticking up out of the ground, and with the extra weight of a picksack full of apples, he snapped his back in three places."

"When is he going to have surgery?"

"That's the thing," Pop continued. "There's so much swelling around his spinal cord. They can't operate until it goes down."

"So what are they doing?"

"Keeping him pumped full of painkillers. Enough to keep him from moving. He's knocked out. You'll see tomorrow, when we go."

"You're here now," Granny said, patting Ben's arm. "Everything's going to be okay. Let's get inside."

Steeling himself, Ben stepped into a room where little had changed since he fled to college. He glanced at Pop's worn recliner, duct tape covering the worst wounds. On the television, The Kingsmen Quartet crooned the Southern gospel of their Asheville beginnings, with Ray Dean Reese belting out bullfrog-deep notes from "This Old House."

A tiny voice inside Ben spoke up for stability. His grandparents and their home constituted one of the few anchors in his world, along with the seventy-five acres that made up the Bramley farm—the land Pop had taught him to love, the land Ben later decided not to love.

Why could he not drop his guard and admit to feeling secure in a living room with the same mismatched lamps, the same pedestrian artwork on the walls as when he was a child? Not that his grandparents were tacky; rather, they were Depression-era folks, hard-pressed to part with any item possessing the slightest whiff of functionality—practical to a Spartan degree.

Granny regained his attention. "Your room's ready if you want to put your things away."

Ben shook off the transfixed state and acknowledged her.

"I'll do that and go back for Smoky."

Thankful she didn't follow him up the stairs, he ascended with a clinched jaw, and feet that required severe encouragement.

My room, he repeated silently, rejecting the notion. Granny said it matter-of-factly, as if nothing had changed.

The magnitude of anxiety, the shallow, rapid breathing, had his head floating adrift from his body. Alerted by the early warning signs of stomach upheaval, he fell up the last few steps, commando-crawling through the bathroom door.

Soon reprocessed cheeseburgers and fries floated in the commode, evidence of a drive-thru stop one-hundred miles earlier.

"You okay?" he heard from below.

Wiping his mouth with the back of his hand, he forced a calm response.

"I'm fine. Be back down in a minute." He closed the door to keep future odd noises from wafting down to Granny's ears.

Standing up, supporting himself with the sink, he looked in the mirror at a face on par with mugs shots of meth addicts. A double handful of water splashed in his face left him nothing more than shivering and wet.

Wow! What's the old saying? "The anticipation rarely lives up to the realization." Guess I disproved that theory.

The battle far from over, he walked the short distance to his former bedroom door, coaxing the handle.

Lady or tiger?

Round two of nausea threatened as he glimpsed, then closed his eyes on, the photograph-like image. The bedcover had been updated, maybe nothing more. The disarray from his rush to pack and leave for Duke remained preserved like one of the period displays he had seen at the Smithsonian Institute on his Junior Beta Club trip.

"The Twilight Zone Meets River Road." That's what we'll entitle this episode.

Granny hollered again, "You must be hungry after your drive. What can I get you to eat? I'll be glad to cook you something, or I can make a quick sandwich."

Holy Moses, make her stop talking about food!

"Nothing right now. I ate on the way."

His hand went to his mouth, muffling a belch of soured gym socks.

"Are you sure?"

"I'm sure."

Head cocked her direction, expecting further discussion, his eyes remained closed, shifting his focus away from the time-capsule room.

She can be insistent when it comes to food. Hell, she can be insistent about most everything. It's her way, though. I should have remembered.

"If he says he's not hungry Lily, then he's not hungry." Pop's voice rose through the floor vent beneath Ben's shoes.

Installed to circulate heat upstairs, the opening also provided an excellent eavesdropping conduit during childhood.

Not until his grandmother and his stomach calmed did Ben head downstairs and outside to fetch Smoky. An oval sticker on the vehicle's back window caught his eye—Running Is Cheaper Than Therapy—an insight to Ben's twisted humor and frantic pastime. He *had to* run. No alternative existed when the hours began to tick down toward *berserk.*

As Ben reentered the front door, Pop turned in that direction.

"Looks more like a bobcat you're toting than a house pet."

Granny stepped from the kitchen, having heard Pop's voice.

"They Law', look at the size of that thing!" she said. Granny's euphemism skirted the Third Commandment, regarding abuse of the Lord's name. Living in a community restricted to the use of the few religiously acceptable exclamations, her favorite made the top ten.

"He's a big one alright," Ben said.

Upstairs, the cat explored its new surroundings while Ben gathered up running gear. From the suitcase he removed an unopened tube of Extra Protective Cream. The thick white paste went on the insides of his thighs to keep them from chafing during his punishing runs. Although, before the acquisition of the miracle ointment he had run until he burned through the skin, ignoring the stinging, and the rivulets of blood painting his legs.

It had required multiple sessions with Dr. Mendel before he acknowledged his frenetic running. That it was more therapeutic than the litany of medications he had tried. He forever ran solo, the same way he had arranged his life.

Giving Smoky a quick glance, Ben turned off his cell phone and placed the device on the nightstand.

"No point in taking this."

Running granted him the ability to remain on stage, to keep playing his role, until he accomplished whatever he needed to accomplish, despite having judged himself as deficient in fulfilling myriad obligations, without offering any specifics. That would be too easy for a man who viewed life as a perpetual struggle by natural design.

The same fear of inadequacy had kept his ass planted in a church pew for more than half his life—fear of the unknown, the other side, or even the existence of another side. For all his genius, all his contemplation and observation, he had never ascertained to his own satisfaction if all the fuss would be worth it in the end.

"If there's not an afterlife, some sort of reward for all this bullshit, I'm going to be really pissed off," Ben said to Smoky, careful of his decibel level.

The cat had taken residence in the half-empty suitcase, which offered the scent of home.

"Don't mess with Granny's stuff while I'm gone," Ben said, picking the cat up to familiarize it with the new litterbox arrangements.

Only the surroundings were new to the pet. His master's disappearances occurred every few days, sometimes following an escalation of manic behavior, or on other occasions after too much time abed. He went running in search of a conclusion, or a facsimile of some peace of mind, yet how should he expect it to come? Sudden epiphany? The wisdom of old age? Would he recognize it if he met it on the trail?

Consumed with the idea of being able to play the game long enough to win led Ben to consider potential interference from any number of obstacles—car wreck, terminal disease. Most likely, he decided, his mental firewall would wear too thin for even frenetic running to forestall the placement of a period at the end of an abbreviated existence.

Forget *quality* of life! He ran to exhaustion in pursuit of *quantity*. He ran in the hope that revelation or transcendence would catch up to him.

Wooded treks, he liked best. The Appalachian Trail, a few strides from his cabin atop Cut Laurel Knob, was his favorite, with only seldom witnesses to his extremism—a wild creature speeding past in day-glow shorts and Nikes. Little likelihood of people disrupting his mantra—though it was not a mantra in the true sense. Rather, a mystical trinity where the rhythm of each footfall in relation to his breathing and his heartbeat took him out of his mind, even out of his surroundings other than the fleeting blur of scenery quickly bypassed.

Changes in flora and topography amounted to nothing more than the pages in his latest chapter. Kicked up by his feet, the numbers advanced as he went deeper and deeper, to the point where a follow-up chapter could be assured. And as the mindlessness of his activity mounted, the process became a meditation, birthing a mind freed of earthly weight. Ultimately orgasmic in the liberating level of movement, pain, and bodily triumph, the high became irresistible.

Not a soul around to see him sometimes stumble, crawl the last league back home. Drag into bed. Spend a recuperative day or two.

Could he truly deny the presence of a tiny seed buried in a mostly unused corner of his brain, a seed that takes root, and kudzu-like threatens to flourish and dominate his entire being if sacrifice is not made? Eye for an eye. Bodily punishment.

OUTFITTED AND DOWNSTAIRS, HE GLANCED into the living room where the face of President George W. Bush filled the television screen as Pop and Granny watched the late news.

Probably hoping I'll join in.

"I'm going running," he shouted toward them. "Don't wait up for me."

The front door slammed on any questions.

Find out more about Ben's grandparents by subscribing to Southern Fried Karma's YouTube channel, Fugitive Views.

CHAPTER THREE

"And Jesus said unto him, 'No man, having put his hand to the plough, and looking back, is fit for the kingdom of God."
—Luke 9:62

The smell of fried bologna filled the upstairs bedroom when Ben jerked awake to Granny's forceful knocking and announcement.

"Breakfast is ready when you are."

"In a minute," he said, still in his running clothes, and having slept on top of the covers, kicked-off shoes at his bedside.

Stiff in standing, he stretched, setting off muscle spasms in both calves.

"Can't let them see me like this. Man, I'm not used to thinking about what I wear. Smoky never complains, do you, Smoky?"

At the sound of his name, the circle of fur on the bed uncoiled and stood, yawning wide, his curled pink tongue extended.

"I hope to hell I threw something in this suitcase that will work for breakfast."

"Are you up and out of bed?" Granny yelled, back downstairs.

Ben laughed.

"Damned if that doesn't bring back the memories. 'School days, school days / wonderful Golden Rule days,'" he sang from a childhood song Granny taught him. "How in the hell did I remember that?" he asked Smoky, the feline nonchalant and grown accustomed to the one-sided conversations.

"Aha!" Ben exclaimed, having uncovered his rarely worn robe, an off-to-college gift from Granny's Sunday school class. The garish orange-and-yellow plaid caused him to smile.

"Looks more suited for deer season and hunter safety."

Before putting it on, he stopped in the bathroom to apply deodorant. The thought of the previous night's toilet-hugging gave him a shiver, yet he felt a greater mastery of the stairs as he descended for a much-needed meal.

"Good morning," he said, pulling out the same chair he had forever chosen—one of four at the red-and-white enameled, 1950s dinette set. There, Granny had secretly taught a pre-school version of Ben the nuances of Maxwell House coffee.

"Hey there, young man."

Pop had waited on Ben before eating.

"Late night, huh?" he asked, without taking his eyes off the morning newspaper; he was already halfway through the scant twenty pages of *The Clarion*.

Lacking sufficient readership to publish its own periodical, Abundance got its news from Groverton, the county seat.

"Yes, sir," Ben said. To shift attention, he flicked an index finger against the backside of the fanned-out pages. "Say, folks still actually read those things?"

"'Round here they do," Pop said drolly.

"Oh yeah," Ben said. "I forgot that Abundance had opted out of stepping into the new millennium."

"Still thinks he's a comedian, Lily," Pop said toward the kitchen.

The front page bore a recognizable image.

"That Eric Rudolph is still headline news apparently."

"That's what being on the FBI's most-wanted list will get you," Pop said. "Plus, the article's about another supposed sighting of him in the parking lot for the Devil's Courthouse, up on the Blue Ridge Parkway."

"Reckon it's true, or maybe one more attention hog wanting to see their name in print?" Ben asked.

"Couldn't say. The witness claims to have seen a man rifling through the trash cans, who ran off when they pulled into the lot."

Granny, following the conversation while at the stove, stepped into the breakfast nook, coffeepot in hand, refreshing Pop's mug.

"They's folks around who see him as a hero," she said, mildly defiant.

Ben's head flew back to make eye contact with her.

"What in the world do you mean?" he asked. Without allowing her to answer he stated the obvious. "The man is responsible for two deaths and injuring more than one-hundred people. He's nothing more than a homegrown terrorist!"

Air had rushed between the seat of Ben's britches and his chair, as he rose in anger. Granny flinched not.

"He's fighting against abortion," she said, without actually indicating her feelings on the matter.

"Yeah, by killing people," Ben added. "And he's opposed to way more than abortion, like gay rights, religious freedom, even the corporate structure of our government—including free trade."

"I don't know about all that," Granny said. "I'm only passing along what I hear."

"What you hear from folks at Redeemer Baptist?" Ben asked.

"I ain't saying," she replied, turning her back on him and returning to the kitchen.

From behind his newspaper, Pop cautioned, "Best leave that one lay, boy. Ain't neither of you going to win the other over."

When Granny reappeared with a platter of food, Ben leaned to the right, allowing room for her to slide three over-easy eggs and two slices of fried bologna onto his plate.

"A fellow needs some nourishment after all that running," Granny said, casually dismissing the previous exchange. "Did you sleep okay?" she asked as she placed a tray of homemade biscuits in the middle of the table and set down a cup of coffee for Ben with her other hand.

"Yes, ma'am, I did."

Back from the kitchen again bearing a stick of butter,

Granny sat down. Pop had his head bowed, eyes closed, as he spoke in a quiet, deferential tone.

"Father in heaven, we thank you for this day and for the food set before us. Thank you for bringing Ben home safely. And Father, we pray for your healing of Jason's broken body. Please restore him to health, along with so many others who need your healing. Forgive us of our sins. Thank you for our many blessings. In the name of Jesus, we pray. Amen."

"Amen," responded Granny.

As if he were a kid again, Ben heard himself add, "Amen."

"Somebody pass me one of those biscuits," Pop said. "You know, boy, these eat right where you hold them."

Ben nodded over his cup of coffee, smiling as he drank. He never tired of Pop's extensive list of enigmatic sayings. Long ago he determined not to ask for clarification, preferring to simply enjoy the colorful expressions.

"What time are we leaving for the hospital?" Ben asked. "I have to shower."

"Soon as we can all get ready," Pop answered.

"Don't figure on me taking much time," Granny said, "as long as I can get some help cleaning up with breakfast."

"Well, if y'all want to leave right away I can drive over separately."

"No need for that," Granny said. "No sense in us taking two cars, wasting gas. We'll ride together."

Ben chewed slowly on the last of the bologna. All flavor had fled when he realized his entrapment.

Later, dragging out his shower, he tried to anticipate his reaction to seeing Daddy for the second time in fourteen years—the last ten, consecutive in his absence. Pop and Granny would be present, eyeballing him.

He might have stayed out the day under the showerhead, but the arrival of frigid well water ejected him from the stall.

Shivering, he dressed.

"Wish me luck, Smoky."

His furry friend took interest as his master gathered wallet, keys, some breath mints, and a tattered copy of *The Gulag Archipelago*. The book had lain atop his old desk, condemning Ben over a high-school book report he faked without completing the reading assignment.

Lastly, Ben picked up Cowboy, slipping the toy into his front pocket.

With a final word to Smoky, "Be a good kitty, and don't shred any of Granny's stuff," he drew a deep breath and headed downstairs.

"All aboard! I'm driving, and the train is about to leave the station," he said in the direction of his grandparents' bedroom, reasoning that being in the driver's seat offered him some measure of control.

"We can take our car," Granny said, appearing in the living room adjusting the belt that accentuated her tiny waist. The fashionable dress and shoes implied a cheerier destination.

"Too many gray-haired drivers on the road already," Ben pushed, "especially adding all the leaf-lookers in town for the October colors. Besides, whose reflexes do you trust more— mine, or those of the old gentleman emerging from your bedroom?"

Pop and Granny both smiled at the act, the way he had enlivened their home for so many years.

"I reckon that train will wait long enough for me to get my hat," Pop said, removing his felt fedora from the coat rack in the hallway. The straw version beside it he kept on reserve for the warm months. "My old, bald head can't take too much sun, nor airishness."

As the three stepped out the front door, Ben asked, "Aren't you going to lock it?"

"Naw," Pop said. "We ain't got nothing worth stealing, and if somebody needs it worse than us then God bless them. They can have it."

Tweet, tweet.

Pop's last syllable ended with Ben pushing the unlock button on his key ring.

"My, what a nice car!" Granny said, eyeing the Acura MDX.

"It's an SUV. A sport utility vehicle," Ben said, opening the door for her.

"Well, whatever you call it, it sure is fancy. Are these seats real leather?"

"Yes, ma'am. They came that way." Avoidance of ostentation had been a primary directive of his youth, taught both at church and home. "I bought it because it has the highest rating for driving in the snow, of which there's aplenty up my way."

"How much did this set you back?" Pop asked, settling into the co-pilot position and fighting with the seat belt.

Money not an issue for him, Ben only purchased the best, primarily on the grounds of equipment breakdown being incompatible with remote living, but also in spite of his grandparents' Depression-era frugality.

Next he'll give me the 'buy American' argument, and I don't want to explain that Honda makes Acura, but that there has been a Honda assembly plant in Ohio since 1989, and another opened last year in Alabama.

"I'd be embarrassed to say," Ben said, capitulating to change the subject. "Too much, but I got a good deal."

He stressed the words that had to inexorably accompany any Bramley purchase—"good deal."

Their family values encompassed many rules, and finances had its own subset: 1. Don't talk about money, whether you have it, or you don't. 2. Pay your tithe and give extra offerings. 3. Never pay retail or shop at the big mall in Asheville. 4. Don't buy anything you don't need, especially if it's showy. 5. Always pay the lowest price possible and don't buy anything unless it's a good deal. 6. Save your receipt.

More rules followed, though the first few dictated the majority of financial transactions. Ben's vehicle violated those principles. He slumped a bit in his seat with the weight of the infraction.

"Back roads or interstate?" he asked, pulling onto River Road.

"Let's go the back way," Granny said. "I can't abide that fast traffic. Dangerous."

Happily veering away from the Unolama River, Ben refreshed himself to the natural wonders that attracted the constant influx of tourists.

From the first settler to unhitch a wagon, that section of earth came to be referred to as Abundance. Perhaps the name was chosen to inspire optimism, or it could have been selected in homage to the plentiful trees, the numerous streams, or the gently laying mountain plateau, surrounded by soaring ridgelines.

The name stuck and so did the settlement. By the time Ben came along eight generations had passed, with few families budging from their original claims. The Etter farm, owned by his mother's clan, even boasted a few stalwart apple trees from the inception of the community.

"If anybody needs to stop for anything, holler."

Any excuse to pull over would do, giving him a chance to stretch his sore legs lest they cramp up while driving.

The first houses they passed, the ones whose owners claimed Abundance as their citizenship, were utilitarian, well kept, though small. The few exceptions were the occasional two-story farmhouses, the white clapboard kind, with wraparound porches shading assemblages of chairs, mainly employed for passing Sunday afternoons, allowing mountains of fried chicken and potato salad to digest in comfort. Those same farmhouses occasionally boasted gingerbread trim, an appealing yet unnecessary feature and, by local Puritanical standards, considered "showy."

To the last house, remnants of flourishing summer gardens could be seen in the side yards. The custom was to have one's vegetable garden most visible from the road, as proof of participation in the work-intensive ritual. Residents employed home gardens to establish levels of diligence. A patch taken over by weeds nullified all possibility of positive assessment, while the largest gardens garnered widespread public admiration for the owners' sizeable time commitment.

The passage of years had not dimmed Ben's memory of countless hours pulling weeds from Bramley-family gardens. Without effort he could still feel the sensation of the final tug of resistance as pesky roots yielded to his pull.

The exhaustive summer tradition became part of the collective consciousness, spawning an oral history: "The Dovers lay out the straightest, longest rows;" "Looks like Ed Newton has added cantaloupes this year;" "Old Granny Henfield had to use a walker to hobble around once she turned ninety, and never missed putting in a garden, right up until she died. God rest her soul."

Though much of the autumn season remained, every yard along the route had its leaves raked.

"Don't know why anyone would rake with so many leaves yet to fall." With the last word out of his mouth, Ben knew he had stepped in it.

"They'll kill the grass off if you let 'em pile up," Granny said. "Besides, it's trifling to let your yard look a mess. Cleanliness is next to Godliness," she ended.

Ben dropped his head slightly so that Granny could not see in the rearview mirror the smile he couldn't repress.

Damn, how I'd love to tell her that old cleanliness and Godliness saying isn't anywhere in the Bible.

His Folklore and Religion class at Duke had exposed him to the true origins of many Christian customs and beliefs, often rooted in paganism, pre-dating the Holy Bible.

That one class, freshman year, allowed him to feel his world expanding to include concepts never voiced in Abundance—concepts leading him to sections of the library he had overlooked, checking out books on philosophy, metaphysics, the supernatural, reincarnation, quantum physics, and Eastern religions: all inseminating a new mindset.

He became the possessor of an eclectic philosophy that bore no resemblance to the Redeemer Baptist, Sunday-school-boy who amazed teachers with his scriptural prowess. The newfound understanding he kept from his grandparents, with its threat to their tightrope relationship.

Inflexible members of the community would label him heretical, or worse.

'I was a boy of blind faith. Now I'm a man of science and reason.' That's what I would like to tell them if I could work up the courage to expose my truest self.

Ben shifted his thoughts back to fallen leaves and relentless raking jobs with Granny. She would rake while he walked the smaller piles into a central heap for burning.

"No way to forget all those leaves, Granny. I can smell that wispy smoke, see the flames gobbling up those rusty-brown piles. And when I got too close to the fire you'd say, 'If you play in the fire, you'll pee in your bed tonight.'"

That humorous memory set the whole vehicle in an uproar, the subject of fastidious raking dying with the laughter.

Talk inside the cab shifted to inquiries about his latest happenings, which limited conversation given a life which could be Cliff's note-d into four words: computer, eat, sleep, run.

His absence of talk about his dad resonated in the quiet pauses.

I'll be damned if I'm going to pretend to give a shit. His accident changes nothing.

Close to Asheville they passed a Presbyterian church, with a stately iron fence encompassing the graveyard.

"The older you get, the more Death touches you," Granny said absently, watching the blurred snapshot of grayed headstones.

"Any ideas why Death started so early with me?"

The irritability in Ben's voice cut the closeness. That same tone, the one that hinted to the disturbance within, had warned people away since age eight.

Pop fielded the volatile question.

"The Bible tells us that the Lord works in mysterious ways."

When Ben failed to comment, Pop continued.

"It also says that all must die, but with the promise of living again . . . forever. The promise is real. You just ain't found the way yet."

"I hope you're right, Pop. I sure hope you're right."

I doubt it, though. How's a Bible promise supposed to apply to a lapsed Christian? And back then, when I was being devout as I knew how, the shit storm still came.

Silent seconds later, Granny changed the subject.

"The doctor is going to meet us soon as we get to the hospital."

Mission Hospital, the regional center for healthcare, offered the best-available staff and technology for the entire western portion of North Carolina.

Pulling up to the imposing facility, Ben said, "I'm going to let you two out at the main entrance. I'll catch up after I find a spot in the parking deck."

"You don't need to go to any trouble," Pop voiced.

"What trouble? We're here right now."

He stopped within feet of the entrance, jumping out to assist Granny.

"You reckon I've become some kind of invalid since you saw me last?" she asked.

"No, ma'am. Just doing my civic duty."

"I'm still getting around well enough to keep that old man fed and the house cleaned."

She took the hand Ben offered and kissed the back of it.

"Do you want me to meet you in the lobby or at the ICU?"

"Maybe we could use a little head start. How about the ICU?" she answered.

"You got it," he said, waiting until both were inside before driving to the parking deck.

"Damn. How tempting to drive off, swing by their house, pick up Smoky and my stuff! They'd have no trouble finding a ride home between all those folks at Redeemer Baptist Church anxious to play Good Samaritan . . . given the guarantee of public recognition. Of course I could never face Pop and Granny again."

He made eye contact with himself in the rearview mirror.

"Nor could I face myself. What am I saying? I can't believe I'm even thinking along this line. I could never abandon my grandparents, though I guess, in a way, that's what I've been doing these many years. God, I suck!"

He pulled into an open space on the lowest level, checked his cell phone for service, and speed-dialed Dr. Mendel's office.

"I'm at the hospital."

"Good morning to you, too, Benjamin. Care to share details?"

"I'm about to go in and see him for the first time. That, or drive off and leave my grandparents stranded."

"Are those two options your only available choices?"

Feeling trapped, he evacuated the SUV, pacing about the parking structure. Footfalls echoed off the concrete deck in a twenty-yard circuit.

"I can't think. I mean I can't think of other options."

"That's alright," she said. "Let's back up a bit. What is your father's condition?"

"Essentially comatose, whether medically induced or not, I'm not sure."

"Perspective, Ben. Perspective."

"Okay. And by, okay, I mean, 'What?'"

"The reality of your perceived crisis is that your potential interaction with your dad will be limited. No direct communication. You do get that? Right? Or do you find his bodily presence too objectionable?"

"I get it, Doc. Still, I'm spooked. Plain spooked."

"In what way?"

"In the way that the mere sight of him is going to stir up all the old shit I've tried to repress or forget."

"Don't you think you might be endowing him with more power than is likely? His voiceless body lying in a hospital bed doesn't have the ability to conjure every negative experience of yours, unless of course you give him that power." She paused. "Make sense?"

"That makes sense, but when have I claimed to be a sensible client?"

The observation made him laugh at himself.

"I feel you can handle this first step. However, if you decide otherwise, I strongly advise that you explain yourself to your grandparents rather than vanish. Your tie to them is too crucial to sacrifice. Agree?"

"Agreed. And thanks, for now. Don't be surprised to hear from me again."

"Anytime, as I said before. Good-bye, Ben."

"Bye, Doc."

Up the parking-deck elevator, through the crosswalk, and into the lobby, he checked the hospital map for directions, taking a hallway which ended at locked double doors. To the right, Pop and Granny sat in the family waiting area. Ben noticed some sleeping bags and pillows tossed in a back corner and pointed to them. Pop explained.

"Some folks are from so far off, they sleep here overnight. One couple have a little boy hit by a car. They've been here going on a week. Talked to them yesterday while we waited in line to get in."

"Where are all these folks now?" Ben asked.

"Inside." Pop nodded at the ICU entrance. "The line forms here, with folks waiting to get in soon as visiting hours begin. Most of them have jobs to head off to, so they want to see their people as long as possible before having to leave."

Adjacent to the shut doors, Ben noticed a black sign with white lettering, spelling out the hours for visitation.

How did I make it to my age without any hint this kind of thing went on? And, I reckon, at every ICU in every hospital in the country. Hell, around the world.

You're a privileged white boy, with money and good health.

Ben ignored Moses's observation as Granny stepped forward and pushed a red button below the sign.

"Yes?"

The voice came from a small speaker attached to the wall.

"Bramley family to see Jason Bramley."

Her voice tremored, setting off constriction in Ben's chest.

"One moment. I'll check and see if it's okay."

"What does she mean she'll check?" he asked.

Though having avoided his dad, the notion of being prevented from entering by the whim of an anonymous voice galled Ben.

Pop spoke up. "It's all right, son. They don't want us coming in if they're doing some procedure or if he's out for more tests."

At the sound of an obnoxious *buzz*, the doors swung open. Granny and Pop entered, stopping at the scrub station inside. Ben made it in as the doors closed against his backside.

"This is too real," he whispered, before imitating his grandparents' example of hand-washing followed by donning a bright-yellow disposable gown along with head and foot covers.

Why didn't someone point out how ridiculous they all looked? Squash the tension with a good laugh?

The solemnity of the place would not allow it. Everything about the giant room, its sanitized scent, low-lit cubicles festooned with tubes, wires, blinking lights, beeping alarms, high-tech equipment surrounding patient bedsides: all the hardware flatly stated that within those confines, life and death coexisted across the thinnest of lines.

Trying to look straight ahead, he failed, eyes drawn to the sideshow of suffering.

Please don't let me see the little boy hit by the car. Please don't let me see him.

A few hours earlier, when running had exhausted his body, his mind refused to disengage. He turned to *The Gulag Archipelago*. Its hundreds of pages peppered with Russian characters and unpronounceable places had looked like a giant sleeping pill.

Walking the ICU corridor he thought about another little boy, unnamed, from the book: the son of Inushin, a harmless locomotive engineer.

When the Ministry of Internal Affairs jurists came to arrest Inushin, a tiny coffin stood in the room containing the body of his newly dead son. The agents dumped the child's body out of the coffin, leaving it on the floor as they pulled the father to prison.

The image Ben's mind had framed popped in and out of his consciousness.

Granny looked over her shoulder at him.

"Your daddy's in room 129."

The information seemed unnecessary since Ben trailed closely behind them.

She's more worried than she's letting on, he figured.

Within seconds they stopped outside a room where a dry-erase sign read, "Jason B." The drawn curtain muffled a woman's voice.

"I think you've got company," she said.

What the hell? Is he conscious?

A hand extended from behind the draped material, unveiling the interior. Muted by crisscrossed emotions, Ben could only register the clacking sound of the curtain hooks in the metal track.

"Looks like family," the nurse beamed.

Another setting, and the man in the hospital bed would have gone unrecognized. Coal hair had been replaced by total gray, and the sun which once burnished the skin had exacted a toll, carving deep crevices that forked out from the corners of closed eyes. Other erosions of time began at the nose, tracing down past the sides of his mouth.

The Jason Bramley of Ben's youth amounted to six feet of tanned skin and ropey farm muscles, crowned with a shock of hair so black that it had a bluish-green sheen in bright sunlight. The only child of Sam and Lily Bramley, he had evolved into a stereotype, modeling textbook only-child behavior, spoiled by his mother, never fully maturing, not venturing from home, and lacking his own dream, he stayed with the family business.

The upside of Daddy's stunted development manifested in his eagerness to play hide-and-seek; occasionally fill a grocery bag with steaming popcorn and haul a pajama-clad Ben to the drive-in theater in Groverton; or usher the family off on trips to county fairs and amusement parks.

"He's completely out," said the young nurse, a little too cheery. "We have to keep him that way."

Granny moved close to the bed, taking her son's hand. Pop stood behind her so closely that they formed an image of one person, their utmost attention unified.

They look like figures from a nativity scene beatifically gazing on baby Jesus.

Suddenly fearless with his father unable to awaken, Ben determined to express interest, however insincere. "What's that in his mouth?"

"It's a breathing tube. We had to intubate him."

The nurse stopped, as if that concluded matters.

"Why?"

"His injuries are making breathing difficult. That's a ventilator behind you."

She pointed at one of the many devices in the room. From it, Ben heard *whoosh, whoosh* sounds, keeping time with Daddy's chest falls.

EVAN WILLIAMS 37

"How is he, overall?"

"It's really not my place to tell you. Dr. Berner will be with you soon."

Chart in hand, she exited.

"It doesn't sound good." Granny's heavy words settled to the floor, where she and Pop remained frozen.

Relieved at not being eye-to-eye with them, Ben countered, "We don't know for sure. The doctor may tell us it looks worse than it is."

In Ben's hierarchy of hatred, nothing exceeded loathsome hypocrites. The frequency of encountering them in Abundance served as reason enough for avoidance of the area, in his harsh assessment of the place. And churchgoing hypocrites—the worst kind by his reckoning—occupied significant pew space at Redeemer Baptist, "the only Jesus show in town."

Appearance-wise, Daddy looked morgue bound. That observation bounced around inside Ben's head. What would he feel? How would he react, and to specifics, how should he react to suit Granny and Pop?

Better figure it out ahead of time if I'm to sound and look genuine.

He slammed the brakes on his mind.

God! How screwed up am I?

A voice from behind startled him.

"Hello, I'm Dr. Berner. You must be the Bramleys."

Tall, with an all-but-bald head, his dark eyeglass frames pushed against pale, indoor skin.

Obviously not straight out of med school.

Dr. Berner moved to the opposite side of the bed, facing the family.

"I'm afraid the news is rather grim," he began.

From Granny, a faint sigh escaped. She let go of Daddy's hand to extract a tissue from her purse.

"His back is broken in three places. Two of the breaks are higher up in the cervical and thoracic regions. The lower damage has likely paralyzed his legs, though we can't know if that's a permanent condition. The upper cracked vertebrae are in the region where nerves control respiratory function and heartbeat. The resulting paralysis of the breathing muscles is the reason for the need of the ventilator."

He pointed to the machine.

"Will you have to operate?" Granny asked.

"Any surgery to fuse the broken vertebrae is out of the question for now. Swelling from the trauma extends the length of his back, pressing on the spinal cord. To reduce that we're giving him corticosteroids. The goal is to keep him immobilized using Propofol, a hypnotic agent which some people call the 'twilight drug.' It puts him in an extra-deep sleep state. Opioids, in this case Fentanyl, are being administered to handle the pain. You may notice excessive sweating. That's a common symptom of cervical injuries, and if you're watching the monitors, fluctuations are normal."

"How long before there's some change?" Ben and Pop let Granny ask the questions.

"No way of knowing, but I have to tell you . . ."

His pause shrunk the room into a white-hot ball.

"As the swelling recedes most anything can occur."

Ben felt hope suck past him on its way out, leaving the room a vacuum.

Still, the doctor continued to speak.

"We assume spinal-cord damage due to the quantity of blood and fluid which showed up on the MRI. With less swelling comes movement of the cord, effected nerves, and the damaged vertebrae. The result could be loss of all respiratory function, a severe drop in blood pressure, or even loss of heartbeat."

A steaming heap of bad, yet Dr. Berner would not state the obvious.

"You mean he could die?"

"Yes, ma'am. That is a possibility."

"How much of a possibility?"

"I can't give you credible numbers."

"Do you *think* he's going to die?"

"The MRI showed massive trauma, internal bleeding. Yes, to be blunt."

Pop squeezed Granny's shaking shoulders. She held the tissue to her nose.

"Does he have a DNR on file, or a living will?"

Pop spoke up for Granny. "Not that we know of."

"You are his parents? Right?"

Pop nodded.

"Is there a spouse who might know?"

"No," Pop said simply.

"In that case I would like you to consider some difficult decisions that may arise. I can't say when. Still, it's best to have a plan in mind ahead of time."

His directive added another pebble to the weight of the world.

"If you don't have any more questions . . ." and he walked out on the devastation.

Before any family discussion could ensue, the perky nurse bounced in with a clipboard and a throwaway Bic pen.

"This is the standard *Do Not Resuscitate* form. Dr. Berner said you might need it. I'll leave it here. If you have any questions I'll be at the desk."

No one picked up the clipboard angled atop the adjustable bedside table.

"We're not about to have this talk in front of him," Granny said, looking at Daddy.

She took the lead out of the room, down the hallway, stopping at the hand-wash station to discard the disposable scrubs. Pop and Ben followed her beyond the heavy doors of the ICU, wandering without destination.

"How about a cup of coffee?" Pop suggested, interrupting the beat of their march.

"It's a little after eleven now. ICU visiting hours end at noon and reopen at two. Plenty of time. Might as well go to the cafeteria," Granny concluded.

Upon arrival, she turned to Pop and Ben. "I don't much feel like eating right now. Can we get some coffee and find a table off in a quiet corner?"

"Sure we can, Sugar Babe. You go find the spot, and I'll get your coffee. Ben, what do you want?" Pop caught Ben's eye and nodded toward Granny, not wanting her left alone.

"Coffee's fine with me. Black."

Granny zigzagged between the tables of early eaters. Ben followed.

Surrounded by a buffer of unoccupied tables, she set her purse on the farthest-removed one and dropped into a seat. Ben took the chair directly across, waiting for her to speak first, but she held silence until Pop arrived with a tray bearing three blue foam cups featuring the Maxwell House label.

"Look," he said. "They're serving our brand."

Granny gave a hint of smile.

Ben removed his lid and blew on the murky surface, creating tiny ripples and a small cloud of steam. He planned to occupy himself with the cup until his grandparents mixed their cream and sugar. Better that one of them open the sticky dialogue.

Miles beyond the glass wall behind Granny rose five distinct ridgelines, each one higher than the previous. He squinted to make out the narrow ribbon that delineated the Blue Ridge Parkway.

Not the time to be acting like some swivel-headed tourist, he decided after a moment.

Granny led with the hard question. "What are we going to do?"

"Not anything we can do other than continue praying for God's mercy. That, and wait," Pop answered.

"I mean what are we going to do about that awful paper?"

Pop's coffee needed tending. More stirring. Minutes ached by.

The Gulag Archipelago rested beside Ben's cup, offering immediate escape. The bookmark provided proof of previous time invested.

They have no idea how hard I had to resist bringing my laptop. Heroin withdrawal would be less of a problem. The book's a compromise. Why do I have to be bored to death because my screwed-up dad fell out of a damn tree?

Granny's head lowered into the circle her arms had formed on the Formica surface. Her words had the effect of someone trapped in a confined space. "They're asking us to sign his death sentence."

"That's not so," Pop said with gentle assurance. His hand found the middle of her back. "They're giving us the opportunity to let him go be with the Lord if it's God's will that he go."

Her shoulders heaved at the words.

"I reckon you're right," she agreed. "When the Lord calls us, we've got no choice but to go."

The cumulative mention of God's name and God's will rankled Ben, having spent more time with Pop and Granny in the last few hours than he had over the past fourteen years.

Why can't they see it for what it is? Nothing more than an injury caused by a fall, that's all. Like God really gives a shit about the individual day-to-day goings on with the six-billion people on this planet, especially some apple growers in Abundance.

A few sips of coffee amidst the tableau of their suffering softened his view. No one could accuse his grandparents of not practicing their beliefs, and though he could list a few of their flaws neither of them had claimed to be perfect. Nor were they stingy when it came to forgiveness.

Back when I used to eavesdrop at the gap under my bedroom door, I couldn't have been more than six the night Granny came over to the house carrying a note from Pop: 'Gone fishing. Back in a few days.' Crying to Mama and Daddy, though she knew he was most likely off playing poker and drinking with some of his old buddies, yet she worried it might have been another woman.

Reckon I forgave Pop somewhere along the way for lying to Granny, much as I knew he hurt her. All pretty minor when you think about the crap millions of other couples squabble and break up over.

Pop spoke.

"This is the way I see it—and I ain't saying it's the right way or the only way—but signing that paper may not mean a thing."

"What are you getting at?" Granny asked.

"Well, I figure what's going to happen is going to happen, and it may not come down to some writing on some paper."

She stared at him, looking confused.

He added, "The final say may be out of our hands. Isn't it pretty much that way right now?"

Ben grasped Pop's reasoning and broke silence to join rank.

"Pop's making a good point. No use fretting over nothing. Y'all used to tell me that all the time."

Both waited for Granny to weigh their words.

"The notion still pains me."

"Hon, you and I have talked about this where each other's concerned."

She nodded *yes* with a slight drop of her chin.

"And we both agreed neither one of us want to be left hanging on hooked up to some machine. So don't you think Jason would want the same?"

"You're right. My heart tells me you're right. I just hate that it's come to this."

"We all hate it."

Pop wisely changed the subject.

"How about we grab something to eat before the noon crowd gets here?"

"I want to have a word with Ben first."

Pop eased back into his chair, having already risen to pursue lunch.

*What now? I don't like the sound of this. She's got that solemn
tone she saves for dire pronouncements. Even Pop looks concerned.*

"There's been a world of hurt since things fell apart at
home. We've all suffered, likely you most. Your Pop and I
don't bring it up in front of you, even though it's plain for us
to see. And we ain't no different from any other parents or
grandparents who can't abide seeing their children or grandchildren
hurting. Lord knows we would do anything to make your world a
happier place. That's why your Pop and me, we don't let a day
pass without praying for you. Whether that means anything
to you or not, we ain't given up."

She looked at Ben, who immediately returned to the view
out the window, intent on holding his composure.

"When your daddy retreated into his own little world it left
you crushed, and that's a grudge you've kept alive ever since.
But Ben," she paused, "did you ever stop to think how it hit
your Pop and me? You and him at odds in addition to us pretty
much losing our only son?"

He recognized his cue to answer, and though ever-respectful
of them Ben acted as if he sat alone at the table, refusing to
allow her few words to undo a lifetime of perceived wrongs.

She continued.

"Our only child has been living right next door, but a million
miles away. That's a hurt that we have to wake up to every day.
Never coming over to our house. Never a meal together."

Ben's hands involuntarily went to either side of his bowed
head. His eyes squeezed shut to hold back the hot tears.

Granny's words had flung a bigger rock into the water,
causing the circle of hurt to swell in size. She and Pop were
trapped inside it as well.

Ben felt the anguish of his cluelessness. The years of
entanglement in self-pity had obscured the deeper truth.

And all that time Granny nor Pop never taking it out on me.

Pop spoke up.

"We have a good idea how you feel about your daddy. While

you're entitled to your feelings, you have to see the whole mess. It's sunk a wedge that's split us apart like dried kindling."

Pop's hand on Ben's shoulder brought no relief—an anvil pressing down.

"Your granny says we lost our son, but we also lost our grandson."

Pop paused, his voice unsteady.

"And son . . ." Ben loved it when Pop called him that. "Your granny and me likely don't have much time, few years left to waste."

After a heavy pause, Pop broke the awkwardness. "What say we get something to eat?"

"I'll catch up to y'all in a little bit," Ben mumbled.

"What do you mean?" Pop asked.

"I need some fresh air to clear my head."

His chair emitted a screeching sound as it scraped across the tiles. Quick-stepping toward the exit, he left his grandparents behind without giving them the opportunity to debate his avoidance tactic.

Shoving through the lobby's main doors, momentum took him outside and well into the crosswalk zone, where an oncoming Corvette braked with a jerk. Ben ignored the near miss, dashing the remaining distance to the parking deck and the SUV.

A shaking hand sought the elusive unlock button on the keychain. Raising the rear hatch, he pulled a small bag from the spare-tire storage space. Both Ben and bag plunged into the vehicle's cargo area, where he undressed, emerging in the running shorts, tee shirt, and shoes he kept stowed for emergencies.

He remembered to retrieve the cellphone from the pocket of his pants.

Pop and Granny's curiosity will kick in before too long.

Clop, clop, clop, went the Nikes, pounding the concrete deck until he emerged on the open road leading across Biltmore

Avenue. Facing a hillside neighborhood of tree-lined streets and remodeled classical architecture, he waited for the traffic light to change.

"Too much. Too much," he chanted, running in place, anxious for the long light to reverse itself.

First Corinthians, chapter ten, verse thirteen, Moses interjected.

"What the hell are you talking about?" Ben shouted at the voice, attracting strange looks from fellow pedestrians at the intersection.

"There hath no temptation taken you but such as is common to man: but God is faithful, who will not suffer you to be tempted above that ye are able; but will with the temptation also make a way to escape, that ye may be able to bear." The voice paused. Don't you remember what you claimed to be your favorite verse during the childhood years?

Planting both feet, Ben pondered the observation, stung that his lack of progress should be such easy fodder.

"Who wouldn't want to escape? Grandparents tag-teaming me and Moses jumping in too."

The *Don't Walk* sign had changed to show a rudimentary human figure traversing the crosswalk. Taking a step, Ben felt the cellphone shift in his pocket. Dr. Mendel might be available to make him feel better about himself.

Hungry traffic whizzed within four feet of where he stood. Unconcerned, he dialed her private number.

"Dr. Joyce Mendel speaking. How may I help you?"

"It's Ben."

"Are you alright?"

"I see how this works, Doc. You assume the worst when I call."

"Pardon me if I don't recall the two of us simply exchanging pleasantries."

"Point made and taken. Here's the scoop. I made it in to see my unconscious dad. Add in extremely tense shit about filing a

Do Not Resuscitate order. Then I had it pointed out to me how my role in our family trauma hasn't helped the situation where my grandparents are concerned, vis-a-vis, their only son."

He stopped, awaiting sympathy mixed with validation.

"Where are you now?"

"Standing along Biltmore Avenue wearing my running clothes."

Dr. Mendel didn't immediately respond. Ben began running in place once more.

"Okay. So I'm a shit. Tell me something we don't both already know."

"Ben. Ben," she interrupted. "I'm not judging you. I'm merely trying to assess the situation and process the information you've given me. Understand?"

"Got it. Sorry to be so defensive. By the way, my laptop is useless for e-mailing, and I can only reach you by cell phone when I'm in Asheville at the hospital. I'm not going to risk calling on my grandparents' land-line. Too little privacy and too many nosy ears. You know, the ever-watchful Jesus police."

He ceased jogging in place.

"It's astounding how effortlessly you manage to work in your digs at religion, especially the Southern Baptist variety," she observed. "Yet you protested when I pointed out how your Southern Baptist grandmother essentially demanded that you lie to your mother. How she taught you to keep secrets. Insisted she *must* have been doing the right thing."

"Yeah, I did go a little Stockholm syndrome on you there."

"Though you have heard me say this before, it bears repeating. One of the fundamental attributes of guilt-based religions is the assignment of blame. You decided to blame yourself for instigating family troubles, despite the fact that you also blame your dad. And it sounds like your grandparents are also wanting to also place some of the fallout on you."

"Got that right," he interjected.

"However, your actions based on all that you experienced are no more than that—your actions. Over and done with. Blame, guilt, right, wrong, none of those elements should apply to what happened and what continued over the years. In other words, Ben, the entire Bramley family dynamic is not your sole responsibility."

"That helps to hear, again."

"There's a book I planned to recommend to you, by Don Miguel Ruiz. It's entitled *The Four Agreements: A Practical Guide to Personal Freedom*. I think you would find it beneficial. In fact, one of the agreements is applicable to your current frustration. That is, 'Don't Take It Personally.' When you learn that lesson people around you can make all types of ridiculous assertions about you, while you are able to listen without incorporating their judgments into your self-image."

"Sort of like the old 'sticks and stones may break my bones' thing?"

"Somewhat, though to a higher degree. Another saying of letting something 'roll off you, like water off a duck's back,' is also getting to the point. Easier said than accomplished, I know, because we all have opinions which we delight in sharing—so many, that they can't all be accurate, right?"

"True."

"When you are fully capable of not taking things personally you will have granted yourself a freedom that is life-changing. And it would seem that you have the perfect opportunity to start practicing. I'll help you get started. Say aloud for me, 'My family's problems are not my fault.'"

He hesitated.

"Say it for me. For *you*. 'My family's problems are not my fault.'"

"My family's problems are not my fault."

"Again. Louder."

"I feel ridiculous and people are staring."

"Do it!"

"My family's problems are not my fault!"

"Better. Now yell it."

"You've got to be kidding."

"No kidding. All the decibels you can muster. Blow a hole in my eardrum."

"Okay. Here goes." He pulled in air to full capacity. *"My family's problems are not my fault."*

Heads in passing cars turned at the outburst.

"That's more like it. Now believe it. Repeat that while you return to your vehicle, where you will change your clothes and then rejoin your grandparents. That's a professional prescription, not a suggestion."

"Will do."

"One other thought for you to mull over—and it deals with the lying during your childhood. When people teach you to lie at an early age it changes you forever. I'm including not only telling lies, also living lies. That's how some members of close groups deal with conflict and many other difficulties they encounter. Those lies then become part of the fabric of family secrets, the unspoken tensions that bind us together, which, if ever verbalized, would rip us apart. And secrets rarely travel alone."

"Kinda like sardines."

"What?" she asked.

"You start out with one sardine, which eventually becomes a giant swirling bait-ball of sardines. At least that's what they called it in a nature show the other night. In the Bramley family's case the individual lies became a giant bait-ball of lies—perpetual motion in support of the initial secret. And my personal bait-ball stinks of sardines having hung around for twenty-four years."

"I like it. The bait-ball reference is insightful. Lies foster lies. Every family has their share, some more harmful than others. When lying becomes the go-to solution for handling uncomfortable situations, suffering is certain to follow—for the person lying and all those in close contact."

"Tell me about it. I'm already exhausted from trying to act normal, and my tongue is a bloodied mess from biting it constantly. My experience has shown me that most people aren't big fans of the truth. Smooth, polished lies go down better than hard, uncomfortable facts."

"Amen, brother. Testify." She began laughing at herself. "Did I phrase that correctly?"

"Like a native Southerner, Doc. We'll convert you yet."

"Unlikely. Now get back to your family."

REUNITED WITH HIS GRANDPARENTS, THE earlier tension got glossed over by the reopening of ICU visiting hours.

"Bramley family," Ben told the speaker box. The three entered when the doors parted.

In room 129, Pop and Granny spent the afternoon in mud-brown chairs situated between Daddy's bed and the window—the one location where they could be out of the way of the host of monitors, IV stands, and the traffic of staff drawing blood, checking vitals, and silencing the frequent equipment alarms. Each irksome beep launched Granny into panic mode.

Pacing or staring out the window, Ben altered his routine by checking the red LED glow of Daddy's critical numbers, trying to atone for his outburst by being the vigilant eyes for his grandparents.

"His blood pressure's low like the doctor said."

"Too bad he can't see the view."

Granny refused comment on the numbers.

"The air sure is clear today. I can even make out the tower on Mount Pisgah. Your Daddy loves the mountains. He used to go hiking Sunday afternoons once church let out, even when he and your mama started dating."

Granny must be losing it. She never mentions Mama.

Amelia Suzanne Etter Bramley—"Amy Sue," Daddy called her. No one else dared.

Ben had heard the story of her first day in school. When the teacher read the roll, saying, "Amelia Suzanne Etter," some wiseass boy spouted, "Amy Sue," and laughed.

Mama rose from her seat, walked over to him, punched him in the nose, and announced to her bloodied tormentor, "I'm Amelia." And she remained Amelia throughout her school years.

Around Ben's childhood home, Daddy's voice rang, "Where are my black socks, Amy Sue?" Or, "Where are the car keys, Amy Sue?" He had a special power over the fiery redhead who stole his heart that first day of school.

No easy feat. Mama was tough—farm-girl tough, and then some.

ICU HOURS SLOGGED BY. GIVEN the threesome's infrequent get-togethers they had endless catching up available for them, but that would violate the somber tone imposed by Pop and Granny.

This damn vigil is becoming a wake. Guess we have to be stoic so God will see we're taking it seriously. Sympathetic magic at work here.

On occasion Granny approached the bed to hold Daddy's hand. After mouthing a few inaudible words, she would return to her seat. She also kept herself occupied with quizzing anyone who ventured into the room.

"Is he doing any better? When will the doctor be back by?" she pried, with slight variations of the same basic questions.

Pop closed his eyes. His moving mouth led Ben to surmise a silent prayer was in progress until his grandad's head snapped backward and he awakened with a snort.

"Sam, wake up. You're snoring. They can probably hear you all the way to the nurses' station."

"Sorry, Sugar Babe. Reckon I ought not have eaten so much

down at the cafeteria."

He rubbed his eyes only to close them again.

"This dang apron thing is making me hot."

He tugged at the narrow neck of the scrub outfit.

A speaker in the ceiling announced, "Visiting hours will be over in ten minutes."

"We haven't seen the doctor this afternoon."

The pitiable tone of Granny's voice reminded Ben of his first movie-theater experience—the scene where Bambi's mother got shot by a hunter and the frightened fawn wailed, "Mother. Mother."

"Looks like we'll have to wait until tomorrow," Ben suggested, more than ready to be gone.

"They let visitors back in from seven to nine tonight," she said.

Pop had also reached his limit.

"That's a two-hour wait to get in, and it puts us back home after ten o'clock. If something changes overnight they'll call us."

"Maybe I ought to stay the night. I can sleep in this chair or in the waiting room if need be."

"Hon, you won't get any good rest. Let's get on home and come back fresh tomorrow. Okay?"

Her forehead furrowed at the idea. Both hands held her purse close in front of her; she looked like an abandoned child.

"It'll be fine. I promise."

Pop took her by the elbow, gently nudging her forward until her shoes released from the resilient tile flooring.

Subscribe to Southern Fried Karma's YouTube channel, Fugitive Views, for a peek into the family's longstanding dysfunction.

CHAPTER FOUR

"... for I the LORD thy God am a jealous God, visiting the iniquity of the fathers upon the children unto the third and fourth generation of them that hate me; and shewing mercy unto thousands of them that love me, and keep my commandments."
—*Exodus 20:5*

B en stopped the Acura at the hospital entrance to pick up his waiting grandparents.

"What happened to the '66 Chevy pickup?" Pop asked, working his way into the cab.

"Still got it and not letting go of it. Seemed time to treat myself to a few creature comforts, air conditioning being high on the list."

"Well, I sure enjoy this new-car smell," Pop said. "There ain't many things in this old world that can make a feller sit up straight and feel better than the smell of his own new car."

Ben felt the full-body release of leaving misery behind, thankful that his grandparents had also rejoined the greater world.

"You were about the only young fellow that had a car back in the day on Bare Top Mountain, if I'm remembering my stories correctly," Ben said, earning a wide smile from his grandfather, as the vehicle nosed out onto Biltmore Avenue.

"He had his pick of all the girls around for miles," Granny said from the back seat. "Any girl in her right mind would have rather gone dating in a car instead of some old wagon with a smelly horse, or worse—a mule!"

"First time I saw your grandmother, she was working in the office at her daddy's saw mill." Pop reminisced. "My daddy and uncles had been cutting timber up above Brevard, in the Pink

Beds, and I got wrangled into hauling the logs in that rickety faded-to-pink GMC truck. That was our family vehicle too, the one I learned to drive in around age twelve. Couldn't even see over the hood until Mom gave me a couple of Sears and Roebuck catalogs to sit on."

He chuckled.

"The brake pedal on that old contraption went all the way to the floorboard. It's a wonder I didn't get killed driving on all them winding, mountain roads."

"And that's what you drove when you came to pick me up on our first date," Granny added. "Tell Ben, what I had to say about that."

"I remember," Pop said. "That truck's engine had a bunch of seals needed replacing. Probably cracked fuel lines too. You had to drive with both windows rolled down or it would gas you out of the cab. So, at the end of our evening, Lily said she'd soon stay home as to have her hair in wind-blown knots and her dress smelling like Hi-Test."

Transformative laughter filled the vehicle's interior.

Pop added, "That's when I figured I needed a car, and she was a beauty—a 1939 Chevrolet Master DeLuxe Sport Coupe, lots of chrome."

He slipped into reverie.

"A fellow never forgets his first car."

"How could you afford a car during a time when the country was at war and barely out of the Depression? I know you said cash was hard to come by around here," Ben asked.

"I know the answer to that one," Granny said. "And Sam ain't likely to let on about it for reason of being prideful, so I'll tell it."

Nobody could beat Granny for telling stories. Whether true or fanciful, she had filled Ben's ears with tales innumerable. Her natural gift was augmented by uncanny mimicry. Dozens of people whom Ben knew and didn't know paraded across her stage in the form of exaggerated voices, sure to draw a laugh and imprint on his eager mind.

"Your Pop missed being old enough for World War II by a couple of years. Course that didn't stop him from trying to sign up underage. He got caught at it, and his Paw wouldn't sign for him to go in early. They needed Sam home, instead of off in Europe or somewhere, because he had no brothers to help out on the family farm. Back then with mules or horses, maybe oxen for farming, everything took ten times as long to do as it does nowadays, with tractors, electricity, and plumbing. Sam had little male help, his Paw off timbering for weeks at a time. When *you* was a boy, Ben, you could turn on a faucet at the sink or the spigot at the shed and there's water. You needed firewood, so you cranked the chainsaw and filled a pickup bed in an hour or two. Got a field needs plowing? Hitch the plow to the tractor, and you're done before noon. Not back then."

She could go on forever talking if it was left up to Ben.

"Picture a house where the only way to heat it came from a fireplace and a wood cookstove, both of them gobbling up wood fast as you could cut it. Then figure on each drop of water that came in that house being hauled by the bucketful from some far-off spring."

Ben fought the urge to tell Granny that that was how he lived on Cut Laurel Knob.

That'll bring up too many questions of where I live, and other details they don't need to know. It's just ego anyway, wanting to tell them about my self-imposed hardships.

He rejoined her story.

"Those chores don't begin to cover the farming, gardening, tending livestock, general repairs, or hunting to put meat on the table. So during your grandpa's fourth-grade year of school his parents yanked him out to work on the farm."

Cutting his eyes, Ben could see Pop gone serious.

"That didn't mean he stopped learning, and you know how he's reading if he's not out in the orchard, but he had to learn things other than books at that time, like plowing for one. You tell this part Sam."

She leaned forward to tap her husband on the shoulder. He drew a breath.

"We had two mules, Dove and Coal. Dove was the best-natured of the two, and we used her most for plowing. Coal was bigger and stronger, and when we got to clearing land he could pull a stump out of the ground like no other mule on the mountain. Course I'd seen Daddy plow a hundred times and he'd let me practice a mite. I'd never done it on my own until he told me to plow a new patch for our garden while he was gone. Reckon I must have been eight or nine. Hitching up the mule, that came easy from having done it. The plow, well, I had to reach over my head to grab the handles, and the only thing I could see in front of me was Dove's rear end and head."

"What did you do?" Ben asked, engrossed in the story, trying to picture a boyhood Pop.

A full head of dark hair didn't appear easily in the image.

"Well, Mama had come out of the house, watching me, doing her best at trying not to act nervous. She kept knotting up that apron with her hands, not saying anything. So I got Dove over to where I needed to start, and I picked me out the tallest poplar tree I could see that was higher than Dove's head. I lined up with that tree top to lay out the first row. Then I took the reins—they seemed about a mile long—and wrapped the extra length around my chest and belly, and told Dove to take off."

He laughed at the recollection.

"That first try we didn't plow a lick. The old plow skidded across the top of the ground with me drug along behind it. Course I couldn't let go, reined in to Dove as I was. Now that did get Mom's Irish up. More scared than mad.

"I spittered and sputtered around long enough until I finally figured it out, and got the field plowed before Daddy got back home."

Granny jumped in.

"And he got so good at plowing that it wasn't long before he started plowing other folks' fields by day, for cash money, and his own fields at night. He hung a kerosene lantern on the plow handle to light his way. That's how he earned enough to buy a nice car and court me. And look, here you are today on account of that."

She patted Ben's shoulder over the seat.

Happy in spite of himself, Ben considered what a host of timely events had aligned to bring about his existence and place him in the car at that moment with the people who loved him most. Then his stomach moaned, terminating the introspection.

"I don't know about y'all, but this talk about hard work has got me hungry. How about I pull into Bojangles' and get some chicken to take home?"

"There's food at home. We don't have to stop."

Granny had been helping feed family for close to seventy years. It became her language of love.

"No cooking tonight. It's on me," Ben said. Soon the vehicle's interior smelled of hot, greasy chicken, dirty rice, and biscuits. "I have eaten chicken and driven at the same time. Don't worry. I won't try it now and risk giving anybody the nerves."

Pop and Granny loved his use of old-timey phrases, which they took as evidence he had perhaps paid more attention to them than they often thought.

"Tell me what's going on in the orchard?" Ben asked.

"We've not finished with the Rome Beauties or started the Arkansas Blacks or the few Limbertwigs either. After your Daddy's fall I strung out enough boxes for the pickers today. They'll need more tomorrow. Juan, the crew leader, knows how to use the tractor and move bin boxes around. But he's not the best at using the forklift to load the truck, and our insurance won't cover him to haul apples to the packing house."

With River Road a short distance ahead of them, Ben schemed to avoid another hospital visit without coming across as a callous derelict.

"How about tomorrow you and Granny go on over to Mission, and I'll run the crew and haul a few loads?"

"You don't need to do that."

According to Granny, Ben didn't need to do anything once he had made it plain he wouldn't be returning.

"Somebody needs to tend to the picking," he said, adding, "with all that's going on."

He didn't want to be interpreted as slighting Pop.

"He's right," Pop agreed. "Too many apples left to let them go to waste. Too much money."

"Settled then."

Ben hurried to end the matter.

"I can come to the hospital later if we get caught up or it rains."

No way am I going back to that ICU tomorrow. Plenty of excuses even if it does rain.

"Then you'd best get to bed early," Granny said, as they pulled into the driveway.

CHAPTER FIVE

"For even when we were with you, this we commanded you, that if any would not work, neither should he eat."
—*II Thessalonians 3:10*

The next morning over breakfast Granny announced, "Your Pop and me will be back before it gets too late of the evening."

"Y'all not trust me with run of the help and orchard?" Ben asked, chuckling at any question of his capabilities.

"Not that."

Her words aroused Ben's suspicions, remembering how Granny liked to spring her private-agenda plans on short notice, reducing chance of refusal.

"The Wednesday Prayer Meeting service tonight at church is going to be a prayer vigil for Jason."

Silence.

Aware that she had to be staring at the back of his head, a pot of hot coffee in her hand, Ben looked resolutely across the table. Pop's newspaper had lowered to the degree that allowed blue eyes to peer above the bifocal rims at the pair of them.

Ben had his speech ready. "This is a classic case of sympathetic magic. Let me explain with a simple example. A fortressed city, long under enemy siege, is about to be defeated. The king, certain of his people's imminent destruction, must act quickly and extraordinarily. Therefore, he and his son, the crown prince, scale the highest wall, in clear view of the citizens within, and the invading army outside. All eyes upon them, the king draws a dagger, slitting his son's throat. Before the blood can dry on the stone wall, the invaders have begun retreating. Aware that the king has made the supreme sacrifice of his son's life, the city's gods are obligated to mercifully grant the city victory over its enemies. The defeated army retreats before the local gods exact a deadly toll on them. But the gods did nothing to defeat them. In the case of this prayer meeting, you think if enough hopefuls assemble and pray fervently, for whatever amount of time is the magical number of minutes or hours, then God has little choice but to reward your open submission and worship by granting your collective petition. But a spinal injury doesn't know it's supposed to be afraid of God."

More than he wanted anything, practically any unimaginable windfall, Ben wanted to utter those exact words. He could feel his entire being tingling with the mere thought. But he couldn't.

"Did you know that one of the primary purposes in establishing mid-week prayer meetings was to inform the public of recent news prior to the days of electronic mass communication?" Ben said, absolutely unable to avoid some comment.

"You could meet us there," Granny unflappably said.

"We'll see," he said, using learned experience at sidestepping her.

Diverting to Pop, he added another layer of deflection. "Which one is Juan? And does he speak English?"

"He speaks enough to get by. No need to worry. I'm going with you, and I'll introduce you to him before Lily and I head to the hospital."

"I get it. Got to let the crew leader know the new kid is in charge."

Pop and Granny nodded in unison.

"Of course this isn't the first time I've had to ride herd. Y'all remember the Jamaican crew we had one season?"

They both assented.

"That one Friday night they pitched a big one and didn't feel like picking Saturday morning. As I recall, it was you that sent me across the road to roust them out of the old house."

Pop laughed at the memory as Ben continued.

"Man, the looks I got from a bunch of hungover pickers. They were not happy with me, speaking the Queen's English so fast I couldn't understand a word. What was that all about anyway?"

"That was good for you. Gave you a different taste of what the business involves. If you can handle the help the rest is easy. Treat them with respect, pay them well, and everybody gets along. Besides, these Mexicans are way better workers than the local good-for-nothing whites, and the niggers, pretending to look for day work, hanging out in front of the Homeless Mission in Groverton."

"Sam Bramley!" Granny snapped, smacking his arm. "You know better than to talk like that."

"Like what? It's the truth. Waiting around until the shelter serves up the next free meal. Don't any of them know the Bible says, 'if any would not work, neither should he eat?' Ever since they built that cheap public housing all the no-accounts moved in there, lazing on the front porch, waiting for the mailman to deliver their welfare checks. We wouldn't have got another apple picked if it was not for the migrant labor that showed up."

"We don't say *nigger* in this house. You know that." Granny cut her eyes at Ben and looked down, embarrassed.

"Tarnation, Lilly. I can't keep up with all the newfangled changes."

"Well, you better learn that one or you'll find yourself in a heap of trouble one of these days."

The exchange jolted Ben back to childhood remembrances: Granny reading from the books *Little Black Sambo* and *The Adventures of Huckleberry Finn*. Maybe she had learned something since then and maybe she hadn't. Either way his childhood was littered with uses of the awful word. Boys on the playground, whenever two sided against one it led to the inevitable cry of, "Two against one's / nigger fun." Then there was that section of houses on the south side of Groverton, that everybody called "niggertown." None of this had seemed questionable behavior in that all-white world of Abundance when people of color mostly kept to the big city of Asheville. Ben had to leave to see the damage and the violence those words could do.

Granny ought not be embarrassed of Pop's language on account of me. He's been making his true feelings known all my life. And the ideas are just as awful without the words. She's acting like I was company instead of family. She can't act like those prejudices have gone away here. Not when I know they're just blended into a more politically correct woodwork.

Mouth shut and eyes on his plate, Ben gobbled the last of his breakfast.

I reckon sorely needed change still has a fight on its hands in Abundance.

With that topic still running through his head, Ben later met Juan, and acknowledged the rest of the crew with a wave.

The harvest continued.

"Want me to give you a refresher course on the tractor and forklift?" Pop asked with a smirk.

"Hey, old-timer, I was practically born on that tractor, and as I recall it was me that gave you an introductory tour to the forklift."

He grabbed Pop by the shoulder good-naturedly, both glad of the other's company, working together once again.

"Take good care of Granny today for me. I feel like she's close to coming unglued."

"She's not far from it I figure. Come over if you can."

"I'll try."

He guessed Pop knew better.

"I can do more good here than there, especially with him unconscious."

Ben's use of "him," rather than "Daddy," voiced evidence of the ancient wound that would likely fester forever.

"Alright then. I leave the family business in your capable hands."

As Pop pulled away in the pickup, Ben thought about the "family business" and how it all hinged on Daddy's outcome.

"Three possibilities: 1. He gets better, and everything returns to normal around here. 2. He survives, paralyzed, and can't run the operation. 3. He dies, and no outcome is certain."

For the first time since receiving the news, Ben faced the near future through the lens of those directly affected.

"That's one chance in three of status quo. Pop can't run the entire business by himself any more than I could tolerate it around here with Daddy in the picture."

Extending the timeline of possible outcomes brought further realizations.

"In all three possibilities, Pop and Granny advance in age. What becomes of them? Daddy can't be counted on to step up and do right by them. He's not doing right by them now, for God's sake."

Mental images of the beloved duo moving feebly about their day raised a lump in Ben's throat.

"Probably shove them off to an old folk's home if he hasn't drunk up all the money. Likely I would have to pay, which is no big deal, though they deserve way better—dignity and respect along with the option of living out their days in their own home. Guess I could hire an in-home nurse."

He paused to ask himself the most difficult question.

"Am I prepared to settle for a few minutes a year with them as their time winds down?"

The rumble of Juan passing by on the tractor jogged Ben back to immediate matters—loading the truck and delivering the apples picked from yesterday. He could foresee a day of catch up; he was already planning to hustle and make a good impression on Pop. The unnecessary gesture was symptomatic of both Ben's need to please others, particularly his family, and the added community-wide pressure in Abundance to perform to one's best at all times.

"Onward Christian Soldiers, and all that gung-ho zealotry," he admonished himself, smiling at the open admission of his motivators.

Abundance ran on pressure, from keeping up appearances of homes, lawns, vehicles, and the orchards, to endless self-imposed standards, impossible for each resident to simultaneously remember and keep. The result: a hyper-sense of pride, with families judging themselves and others, each certain that their own virtues were the best.

Ben grew up inoculated with "The Bramley Way." And, like every other family's "Way," each inflexible ideology imposed a black-and-white interpretation on a multi-colored world.

"If you'll keep count of the bin boxes each picker gets today, you can bring the full ones straight here to the loading area and save us some time," Ben told Juan early on.

"Si," Juan said with a nod, and, throughout the breezy day, he kept the tractor in high gear, shuttling boxes as the pickers progressed down the rows, placing empty ones ahead, and roaring back toward Ben when each became full.

Soon the grass in high-traffic areas was flattened, going from green to almost black. The process took on a game-like quality as Juan and Ben waved to each other with the deposit of each new bin of just-picked Rome Beauties, and each time Ben returned from the packing house with a load of empties on board, he'd smile at the neat row of full boxes Juan had lined under the shade of adjacent trees.

With the sun close to setting and Ben securing the last binder chain on his fifth load, Juan parked the tractor, shutting it off for the first time since lunch.

"We done?" he asked.

"Yes, sir," Ben said, shaking Juan's hand. "Tell the crew I said gracias, muy bueno. Mañana amigos."

Juan smiled at the rustic attempted Spanish as he waved good-bye.

The sudden quiet in the orchard—no machinery running, no radios playing, and no workers shouting across the rows—had Ben reflecting again. The good feeling he'd had all day kept growing. The more tired he got, the better he felt on the inside.

It had been a day of reawakening, reawakened proof of being no less rooted to the soil than the trees surrounding him. All the money from his other career could never buy the awareness of *belonging* he experienced at that moment.

"One more load," he said aloud, wondering why he didn't feel that depth of being all the time.

Across the highway from the packing house, Ben could not miss Redeemer Baptist, nor its parking lot, pregnant with vehicles.

"Bet a bunch of them have got 'God Is My Co-Pilot' plates on their front bumpers."

Before he could cackle at his cynical observation, he caught sight of Pop and Granny's old Impala, or the little of it visible within a swarm of locals. No caption was needed for him to interpret the frenzy that accompanied bad news—somebody else's bad news.

"It's a show of their relief that the proverbial Death Angel has passed over their houses, leaving them safe from harm for the moment."

Dead certain of that particular element of human nature, he afforded himself a wry smile.

"Didn't y'all hear? That angel's occupied at the Bramley place for the time being."

With truck windows rolled up, keeping the cool evening air off his sweaty body, he took opportunity to shout his mind. "You fucking hypocrites! Y'all haven't given a shit about Daddy in forever."

He punctuated his ire with a lengthy blast of the truck's horn, gleefully watching church members jump.

"They claim to be Baptists, but it looks like they're Quakers."

Hardly able to steer the truck while hee-hawing at his denominational joke, one hand waved wildly but innocently, as if he had been greeting his grandparents.

"I'm still on the job. Don't expect me to join in your nonsense," he said in ventriloquist fashion, without moving his lower jaw.

THE LINE OF TRUCKS AT the packing house proved short, with Ben unloaded by the outset of nightfall.

"What a day," he said, as he walked across the concrete platform toward the loading dock. His fifth receipt ticket of the day in hand, he would remember to grab the other four out of the glovebox in the truck and give them to Pop when he got back.

He slapped the ticket against the open palm of his other hand. "That's 1,440 bushels of apples that wouldn't have made it in today."

Settling back into the driver's seat, he bounced around the potholed rear yard of the building. Before pulling out onto the highway, he checked both side-view mirrors to make sure the chains securing the empty boxes remained taut.

Funny, he thought, *every nuance of today's work has been automatic, reflexive.*

The sight of Redeemer Baptist Church across the road marred the moment.

"Son of a bitch."

The message sign out front had changed to, "No man having put his hand to the plow, and looking back, is fit for the Kingdom of God—Luke 9:62."

"Son of a bitch," Ben said again. "Reckon that's another direct zing at me. Pop's plowing message hits home. Ben Bramley looked back. Still looks back, zigging and zagging all over the place, and won't ever be back inside that damn building again."

Foot off the brake, he eased the truck forward.

"So Hell it is for me," he concluded, trying to focus instead about how refreshing his upcoming shower would feel.

Caught up in the sensation of hot water and clean skin, he nearly missed seeing the Abundance Café, its red neon OPEN sign aglow.

"Granny's not home, and lacking a microwave oven I'm left facing a cold meal. Damned if that is going to do after busting my ass all day!"

Ben rose up from the seat, almost standing on the brake pedal before the aging pads grabbed. He guided the flatbed alongside the restaurant, the side-view mirror inches from touching the eave of the porch roof.

Doing his best to shake errant apple leaves and twigs from his hair, he stepped into the cozy cafe.

"Anybody home?" he yelled down the row of booths.

Every seat was empty—and hadn't he deep-down distrusted that sign anyway?

Grill's turned off, and they're cleaning up to go, he decided.

Preparing to leave, his hand worked the worn, brass knob he had touched a hundred times before.

"May I help you?"

Inches from a clean getaway. Now I'll have to explain, and she'll explain. Meanwhile the clock's still ticking. My stomach's collapsed in on itself, and I'm no closer to getting my cheeseburger.

He turned.

"Oh my God! Ben!"

Her hand went to her mouth, muffling what he heard to be a tiny whimper. A coal-black pile of curls rebelled against an attempted ponytail, framing the face he had fought to push out of his head.

One answer. "Silk."

The reunion halted in a been-so-long-I'm-unsure-what-to-do pause.

So much for avoiding all contact with the indigenous. Now I'm standing here like a cliché from a spaghetti Western. Somebody cue the tumbleweed to roll by before we draw our six-shooters. And no doubt about it, I'm the outlaw, drifted into town, helpless to dodge this bullet.

Half a second proved that the years had not managed to steal her unofficial title—Prettiest Girl In Class.

Prettiest 'woman,' he mentally edited, *and if she plans to slap the shit out of me, she has the right. At least I can enjoy the view for a moment.*

But the stark absence of every other person in the world tripped rusty synapses inside Ben. Reflections on "what might have been" were shoved aside by thoughts of "what might could be."

The elation had but a second to register before she rushed him, arms encircling his neck. Hints of perfume combined with cooking oil rose to his nostrils at the same moment his brain acknowledged the glimpse of a diamond ring and wedding band.

Hug her back! Moses interjected.

A delicious warmth clung to his clothes when she released enough pressure from around his ribcage to create space between them.

"What-in-the-world?" she said, in a startled staccato. "You are the last person I ever expected to see around here."

Her wide smile made his own face hurt.

"Graduation day, when you walked across that stage, I yelled your name—though I doubt you heard. And then you were gone. What happened, Ben?"

He twisted his head, checking the windows for late customers or a jealous husband come to pick up his wife at closing time.

"Where did you go after college?" she insisted.

"I had to get away."

"But never return? Not even a phone call. Why?"

Allowing himself a quick examination of her face, he could not deny she had been his first love, his *only* love. It took her questioning expression to jog him back into the moment.

"All my family crap from way back," he said. "You remember the story of the little kid. broken beyond repair."

Damn! Why am I talking like this is a therapy session with Mendel? Quit self-disclosing. "A fool uttereth all his mind." What?

Where the hell did that come from?

The book of Proverbs.

Ignoring the reminder from Moses, Ben continued.

"And I wanted to get far from my dad. That's another family tale best left in the closet."

She took his chin by the hand, forcing him to look at her.

"Then why are you here now?"

Her arctic-blue eyes held both compassion and caution. He capitulated.

"The man fell and broke his back a couple of days ago."

"Oh, my! How is he?"

"In Mission ICU. May not make it."

"I'm so sorry," she offered, her sincerity ringing deeper than mannerly Southern courtesy.

"Don't be. And here's an insight into what a shitty son I am. I've not been able to muster an ounce of sorrow for the man. Instead, I'm more concerned about a cheeseburger and a hot shower."

His pulse jumped visibly in taut neck muscles.

"If you're trying to shock me, somehow push me away again, it's not happening. I'm not stupid. You worshipped your grand-parents. And clearly the boy caught up in all those fights at school didn't go looking for trouble."

Appreciative of a sympathetic listener, he mused, "Other kids sure made growing up look easy."

"Don't expect a lot of pity from the only Jewish kid growing up in this Baptist paradise, although you had it a thousand times worse—except for the nose."

"I must have missed something."

Silk turned her head sideways to give him a profile view.

"In Abundance this proboscis is more uncommon than a bigfoot sighting. And while my nose may not be famous like Barbara Streisand's—for sheer size, well, hers looks Protestant compared to my beak."

"Wait a minute. Have you forgotten my childhood crush?"

He hastened to tack on his near omission, "Other than you?"

"Raquel Welch? All the guys went nuts over her. Oh, I've got it! Farah Fawcett. Her red swimsuit poster must have been in every boy's bedroom in America."

"Wrong on both counts. The correct answer is Cher."

"Cher? Really?"

"Oh, hell yeah! The long dark hair, almond-shaped face, the sultry voice, and most of all, her nose."

"Why?"

"Hers, like yours, is distinctive, with pronounced variations, not the redundant, rounded, blob of cartilage that sits on everyone else's face around here. The bridge of *your* nose reminds me of the mountain ridgelines I could never leave."

Silk hugged him again, with less urgency than the surprised greeting, and the hairs raised on the back of his neck.

"Welcome home, Ben Bramley. I was about to give up on ever seeing you again."

Her breath on his skin left him unnerved, but diffused of anger. Without forethought he told her, "Your husband is one lucky man."

In response Silk threw back her head and laughed, banging into his jaw.

"How is that funny?" he asked, rubbing the point of impact and wearing a quizzical expression.

She twitched her ring finger in his face.

"Are you referring to this?"

"Yes," he said.

Between laughs she finally blurted, "Cubic zirconia and gold electroplate. My twenty-dollar insurance policy against the young bucks in rut and the old goats on Viagra."

"You mean?"

"Strictly for show. Not married. Never have been. Too busy manifesting my dream. You?"

"Not even close."

"Well sir, have a seat and place your order, now that we have established our mutual status as single folk."

"What?"

"You came through that door having no idea as to my whereabouts. Therefore, you must have intended to eat. What'll it be?"

"Is that cheeseburger possible? And fries?"

"No problem."

"Hold on," Ben urged. "I'm coming with you. I can't eat out anywhere until I've inspected the rear of the restaurant and verified the Health Department grade."

Short of the kitchen entrance she looked back over her shoulder, catching him mid ogle.

"Grade A, right?"

Lacking a comeback, he cursed the heat erupting from his face.

I'd like to say, '100%. Grade A.' Too provocative though. Don't want to shift this reunion into overdrive. But damn if she isn't more attractive than ever! And why did I make the retarded decision to kill what we had? Oh yeah, I'm a weirdo. She had me confusing myself for a normal person there for a second. Must have been the hugs.

Attempting to save face, he tried to be casual.

"There's that quick wit that I've missed."

She whipped about.

"Have you, Ben? Have you really missed my quick wit? Have you given me a second's thought?"

"I, uh."

"Wrong answer! Friendship like we had as kids, it's priceless. We watched out for each other when neither of us had anybody else. And you can run away if that's how you choose to deal with adversity, but you don't get to flip a switch and decide when *I* quit being *your* friend."

Pools threatened to spill over her lower eyelids.

"Please don't cry."

"These are angry tears. I can't control it."

She sniffled and wiped her face with a corner of her apron. When she looked up, his right hand held a wallet.

"What?" she asked.

Without replying he flipped it open and dug deep beneath credit cards, extracting several small white rectangles. Flipping them over, he handed the items to Silk.

"Oh my god! You didn't!"

"I most certainly did."

"What's this, like all of my elementary-school pictures?"

"Yes, ma'am. That's not all."

A lumpy wad of folded paper appeared from beneath his driver's license. Each crease was rounded and softened as only time could have achieved.

Their heads almost touched as they looked down on the ceremonious opening of the artifact.

"How did you get this?" Silk gasped. "That's from my commencement program at Chapel Hill."

Ben offered only silence.

"Who gave this to you?"

"No one."

"Well, someone did. I didn't send you an invitation, and it was an invitation-only event."

"I was there."

"You were not."

"I slipped one of the class marshals a twenty-dollar bill to get in. NBC newscaster, David Brinkley gave the commencement address."

He paused to give her a challenging look.

"I only saved the page with your name on it. See? Right there you are."

His finger hovered above her name.

"Why are you shaking?" she asked.

Without thinking, "New meds," he admitted, moving on. "Honestly, I haven't unfolded this since that day, but it's been in every wallet I've owned."

Real tears choked her response.

"Why didn't you at least say hello? Let me know you were there?"

He shook his head.

"Couldn't. Didn't know how to any more than I could figure out how to get in touch with you without risking falling apart. I'm like an old sweater with a lot of loose threads. You go pulling on one, and the whole thing could unravel."

"Sorry I doubted you."

"Based on my actions, what other conclusion could you draw?"

A raucous growl from his stomach punctuated the question.

"Sounds like we have a gastronomical emergency on our hands. To the kitchen!"

They passed behind the counter and through stainless-steel double doors. Scattered across one work surface, the washed components of a coffee urn were laid out to dry. Close by, an industrial-sized can of coffee advertised, "Maxwell House, Good to the Last Drop."

There's Pop and Granny's perennial brand. Wonder if they know she serves it? Come to think of it, why didn't either of them mention Silk being here at the restaurant?

"So, how did you end up with this place?"

Safer he figured, to be the one asking the questions.

She talked as she worked.

"Halfway through grad school my dad's congestive heart disease knocked him out of work. The money dried up, and the erstwhile Dr. Silk, psychologist extraordinaire, slinked back home. Got a job. Saved my nickels. Ended up in the culinary program at A-B Tech—Princeton for Poor Folk, we liked to call the place. Throw in a heavy guilt complex about my aging parents, only child and all, and I stayed after graduation, working crazy restaurant hours to earn my own place. I live in the apartment upstairs. Not an exquisite tale."

"Exquisite enough for me," he said, snake-bit by regret for getting caught up in the allure of a legitimate conversation with a female his age.

"Better watch it with that smooth talk, mister. I'm sensing a Romeo side you haven't met yet."

Ben ignored the comment, pretending to be transfixed by three thick patties popping on the grill.

"One burger for me. Two for you. My guess is you're starving."

She moved to lift the basket from the fryer. With the contents dumped under a heat lamp, a generous application of salt followed.

"Hope you don't have high blood pressure."

"Just the right amount," he cooed, self-control having given way to the vanity of cleverness.

"Now you're catching on. I'll have you writing your own column for *Penthouse* before you know it."

The reference to the skin magazine stirred ancient guilt. He recalled the day childhood curiosity led him to Daddy's boat and a hidden grocery bag full of magazines. In between fishing trips, the boat became a ready repository for items for that lacked a designated space. Given a family business where pressing work never ceased, often a year would pass before Daddy backed his truck up to the boat and hitched its trailer to the truck bumper.

A worthy treasure hunter, that day young Ben dug through the surface junk, determined to investigate the contents until he got to the bottom of the boat. Whatever he pulled out, he simply stacked atop a heap, working his way around the boat, leaving anthills of uninteresting items in clockwise fashion. He found and discarded a box half-full with tubes of grease, a couple of torn picksacks, a loose bundle of tomato stakes, and a host of smaller miscellaneous intruders, which had been wedged in to fill the entirety of the space. Reaching the rear of the boat, close to the shed's back wall, his excavation led to an unrelated oddity. Buried at the bottom of a bunch of useless clutter, a folded, brown, paper grocery bag, which held several magazines.

TORMENT, EXOTIQUE, BONDS OF PLEASURE, and *BONDAGE DIGEST.* Strangest of all, at the bottom of the stack a grossly different cover pictured a naked boy and girl not much older than him standing alongside each other. A ball of nausea had wrenched Ben's stomach as he dropped that magazine back into the bag.

Silk didn't notice Ben's lapsed attention as she loaded a giant tray with the burgers, fries, and assorted condiments, parting the kitchen doors with her hip.

Selecting a booth, Ben slid to the center of the bench seat. Silk stopped to remove her apron, throwing it on the counter. Her tight jeans caught his attention as she bent over the booth. Lingering, she didn't sit. Both hands on the table, her torso bent low, she afforded him a view down her half-opened blouse. The lacey bra arrested his eyeballs.

"Do you want to tell me why you're so uncomfortable in the world of people?"

"Do I?" he asked, distracted and stalling.

Quit staring at her boobs before she catches you, Ben!

He leaned back into the seat.

Do I?

Escaping into the food, he let the question disintegrate.

"From my Folklore and Religion class, I recall Jewish dietary law about strict avoidance of eating meat together with any milk products."

Wiping a napkin across her grin, she swallowed before replying. "I can acknowledge my Jewish heritage without feeling guilty for not eating kosher. Anyway, Jews don't have hell."

"Lucky," he said, regretful of interjecting religion into pleasant conversation.

She kept her eyes on the vinyl, gingham tablecloth.

"I want you to think about why you insist on being so hard on yourself."

Pausing, she allowed her request to register before continuing.

"You did it all through school. Had to make all *A's*. Top of the class."

Balling both hands into fists, she extended her arms forward and growled in her best Hulk imitation, "Must go to Duke University," to which, he smiled.

"No time for Ben to socialize or have fun. Whether school or farm work, you always had something that needed doing, and only you could do it. You never let up except to blow off steam by smashing some guy's face."

"You're right."

"Yeah, I'm right, and there's more. You made the choice to push yourself, a choice that had outside influences. My guess, the farm, the family business with a reputation to keep up in the community, and church, of course, dangling heaven just out of your reach, while threatening your ass with hellfire. Am I right so far?"

"Dead on. I used to tell myself my three favorite words were, God, family, and church. So where are you keeping your crystal ball?"

"Psychology 101. Wasn't that a requirement at Duke?"

"It was on the electives list. Usually avoided by computer geeks who didn't have a lot of personal encounters. Waking hours we stayed isolated in the computer lab, hanging out with our kind. Not much practical need for the social sciences."

"I see. That explains a lot."

Their catching up extended way beyond the hearty fare and continued as he helped clean for closing. While Silk washed dishes, Ben hauled giant trash bags outside. Passing her on one trip, he noticed white suds about to crest the sink where she stood.

"Where's the automatic dishwasher?" he asked.

"Looking at her," Silk said. "This place opened mostly on dreams. Not enough cash to afford one of those nice Hobart machines. Still adding coinage to that jar."

"Must be the soap I'm smelling. Really familiar," Ben said.

A sudsy hand reached overhead, grabbing a plastic bottle labelled "Ivory Dishwashing Detergent, Classic Scent."

"Those industrial grade detergents tear up my skin," Silk said. "Plus, I grew up with my mom using nothing else."

"Granny used Palmolive, that unmistakable green."

Mysteries could not go unanswered for Ben, his brow furrowed over dish detergent.

"Now I know. Mama used Ivory for dishes, and at my bath time when I was really young. Mountains of suds. Smart on her part, getting me to stay in longer. Odd though . . ."

"What's that Sherlock?"

"My stomach went queasy while thinking about it."

"Don't go tourist on me and start blaming the food. I've got a reputation to uphold. And if you're going to throw up, do it in the bushes out back when you take out those last two bags."

When he returned from his final trip to the dumpster, she stood framed by the door opening. In her hand an order ticket waved with the breeze.

"How much do I owe you?"

"On the house. Feel free to take advantage of that arrangement during your stay."

"Never know, I may make you regret that offer. The food's great, and the view is to die for."

From the height of the stoop, she bent down and kissed the top of his head.

"Well aren't you sweet," she said. Placing the ticket in his shirt pocket, she patted his chest.

"What's this? A souvenir for the tourist?"

"The café phone number and my upstairs phone. Don't worry," she added. "No expectations. You've got too much going on with your family. If you want to keep in touch, refer to my 'business card.'"

She laughed and tossed a stray curl back from her face. And for a quick second, he lost himself. Immersed in the scene—her smile, her face, the organic ease of her company—he swore that beneath the note folded in his breast pocket, his heart paused for a beat, maybe two.

Get back into the conversation. She's talking about her phone number.

"Oh, yeah. That would be land-line only," he said.

"Unless you want to hike the vertical trail to the top of Bobcat Mountain and try your cellular thingy there."

She nodded to the left, where the faintest outline of a dark mass loomed above Abundance.

"Any ideas about the closest cell reception?"

"Parts of Groverton, I hear. Definitely Asheville."

"Internet?"

"Groverton is the closest, for sure. The library, specifically."

Scores of occasions Pop and Granny had deposited boyhood Ben at that same library, leaving him alone while they tended to boring business. As the main source of his worldly knowledge, the shelves of books fed a famished mind, and were especially handy on the subject of human anatomy.

In the reference section, he located close-up photos of reproductive organs, arrows leading from proper names to each mysterious part, and text to explain how humans made baby humans—information he never received in the form of "the talk" from either grandparent.

Silk continued, "To the right of the card catalog they've got a couple of computers you can sign up for. Thirty minutes per session. One session per day. No exceptions."

Her words had him shaking his head, right hand resting on the spot she had kissed.

"We're not a preferred techy vacation spot," she tossed in.

"Damn it!"

"Ooh. Language there, mister. And within hearing distance of Redeemer. That could get you impeached, or whatever it is those people do."

Silk lacked the experience to detect the onset of a mental tailspin once Ben realized the helpline to Dr. Mendel was anything less than automatic.

"Tell me something that will make me stay."

"What are you talking about?" she asked.

Without knowing, he had captured both her hands within his. In a voice bordering on manic, he implored, "Tell me something that will keep me from racing away from here this minute."

Occupants of any passing cars would have seen the silhouette of an apparent marriage proposal in progress—hands clasped, faces close in the greenish glow of the security light.

"There *is* cable available."

"No. No. Not that."

Fear had climbed from the recesses of his gut up to his full belly. Cheeseburgers churned.

"Tell me why I should put myself through the family drama around the corner."

Over his shoulder, a jumpy index finger pointed in the direction of River Road.

Drawing a deep breath, Silk began, "I could flatter you with praise about your integrity, or the power of supreme love, though that plays right into the Baptist bullshit that got you into this mess, all their jibber-jabber about putting the rest of the world ahead of your own, evil self-interests."

She broke from his gaze to direct her attention to the church's hulking presence, the parking lot restored to its normal emptiness.

"Screw that nonsense!" she yelled at the edifice and then redirected her words to him in a tender tone. "You come first. And treating yourself with love supersedes everything else."

Ben released her hands as tension in free-fall cascaded out of his body, harmlessly flooding the pavement. A contorted expression had given way to that of a pardoned man.

"However, you and I are not recess playmates anymore, and one of the sucky parts of being an adult is unavoidable obligation. You know what your gut is telling you, or you wouldn't have made it to this point."

He didn't interrupt to divulge.

"Hard choices like these require getting out of your head. Go with what your body intuits."

When he failed to respond, she dropped the F-bomb.

"We all have to do what the situation demands when *family* is involved."

The strength of her advice seemed compounded by her position standing above him. Looking the part of classic authority figure, her freed hands encircled a narrow waist.

His own body language signified defeat.

"Not the answer I wanted to hear."

"No doubt."

"Nor can I refute your conclusion without coming off looking like a colossal ass."

"So get out of here and head back to your grandparents."

The growl of a large truck pulling away from the packing house accented the moment.

"They need you, Ben."

Her words rode the crest of grinding gears, punctuating his resolved acceptance.

"You're right. It's not their fault that they feature in the grotesque portrait of my past. I love them more than anyone."

He hesitated.

"I'm not sure I can be around them for any length of time."

"Go! Now!"

Her words defied questioning and set his body in motion.

A few reluctant steps and he turned back. "Thanks. See you," hand up in a feeble good-bye.

"One can always hope," she said to herself.

Had he looked back a second time, he would have seen her, eyes still locked on him, tears twinkling in the narrow cone of light.

What's the story behind Silk? Subscribe to Southern Fried Karma's YouTube channel, Fugitive Views, to find out.

CHAPTER SIX

"He that loveth father or mother more than me is not worthy of me: and he that loveth son or daughter more than me is not worthy of me."
—*Matthew 10:37*

"I'm drowning in myself."

Rolling down River Road in the cab of the flatbed, Ben tried to lasso a mind gone maverick. The reintroduction of Silk Mayer in his life propelled him into swirling unfamiliarity.

"Didn't foresee a reunion, ever. What am I supposed to do now? Bad timing, not that there could ever be good timing. Based on history, me, plus any female on the planet, equals failure."

The harsh verdict had much to do with his lack of female interaction, minimal to the point of not having a "history." He gave up all social life when he was focusing on his escape plans.

Silk became a casualty of that strategy. He figured her parents didn't want her associated with the kid from the screwed up Bramley family. Nor could he picture her living estranged from her own folks in whatever vagabond lifestyle lay in store for him. Cutting ties with her as he did with the rest of the student body, he thought he did her a favor.

Lost in thought, the present grabbed him in the form of an opossum's glowing eyes, as it waddled across River Road—make that a 'possum, never "an opossum" in those environs. The sighting reminded Ben of the queer notions mountain folk arrived at from daily exposure to the interplay of nature.

"Possum sightings are a sure sign the economy's doing good," Pop had often postulated. "When times is tough, more 'possums in a pot on the stove, than out on the highway."

Ben smiled at the country wisdom as the truck's high-beams swung across the gravel work yard between the big and little sheds.

Setting the parking brake, he put the engine to sleep. Lights from Pop and Granny's reflected in the side-view mirrors.

"Back from the church and still awake."

The thought caused him to linger in the quiet cab.

"Can't sit here too long. Granny will figure something's wrong. Times like this I wish I smoked. A cigarette sounds good right now."

He pushed back in the seat. Sore fingers intertwined behind his head.

"I'm letting myself get caught up in an ego-stroking mind-mess. Not one dateable attribute do I bring to the table. Pick from any number of flaws. Soon as she finds out about my running, for instance, she'll run too."

That detail he had omitted from her.

"Damn, damn, damn."

He resorted to his old stand-by of beating out his frustration on the steering wheel.

Pop's voice halted the outburst. His bald head glowed a dim orange from his pipe. Ben hadn't noticed him, barely visible below the open window of the cab.

"You alright?" Pop asked.

"Yes, sir."

Ben stepped out onto the running board before reaching the ground.

"Rough day?"

"Actually, I had a great day. That back there," pointing toward the cab with his thumb, "that was a completely different matter."

Pop didn't pry.

"You know there'll be no peace until your Granny sees your face."

They headed toward the house.

Ben remembered his manners.

"How was *your* day?" he asked.

"More of the same. No change according to the doctor. Made for a long wait. Like the good book says, in Ecclesiastes, '. . . remember the days of darkness; for they shall be many.'"

"Pop."

They stood on the centerline of the road. Ben tried to focus on the shadowed face.

"I probably wouldn't be alive if it weren't for you and Granny." Before objection could be raised, he added, "Whatever part of me is good, the credit goes to y'all."

Pop locked him in a bear hug.

"We likely wouldn't be here without you, son."

CHAPTER SEVEN

"For whom the Lord loveth he chasteneth, and scourgeth every son whom he receiveth."
—Hebrews 12:6

At breakfast the next morning, Pop surprised Ben by saying, "Let's switch off today, and you go to Mission Hospital with your grandmother."

Ben recognized Pop's subtle way of handing down orders disguised as suggestions.

"Yes, sir."

After Ben finished the last bite of grits, he went back upstairs to switch from work clothes to citywear.

"Well, Smoky, it seems my plans have been changed for me."

The cat had joined him on the bed as Ben removed shoes and socks.

"Ben, are you talking to me?" Granny asked, having heard him through the floor grate.

"No. Be right down," he hollered back.

He found her standing at the foot of the stairs, wearing a heavy purple cape, purse in hand.

She must stay cold every second of winter with her zero-percent body fat.

"Didn't mean to hold you up," he said.

"Oh, you didn't hold me up. I just now finished getting ready."

Right. She can't admit how worried she is. Guess I'm worried too, for a different set of reasons.

"Let's get on down the road."

"You're the driver," she said.

Ben closed the house door behind her and hurried ahead to open her car door.

"I feel like royalty the way you treat me."

"As royal as they come."

He could see loving appreciation in her eyes as he closed the door with a soft *thunk*. The difference between the sounds of this new car and those of his old Chevy truck registered deeply on a mind in constant observational mode.

The family oak tree beside the driveway had begun losing its leaves. The rattle of kicking them up with his feet brought back memories of hunting trips with Pop. Canned sardines and soda crackers from the deep pockets of their field coats served as the standard picnic lunch far into the forest. A sunny patch of pine needles made for a soft bed and nap afterward.

He settled in behind the steering wheel, smiling broadly.

"Somebody's in a good mood."

"Happy thoughts, Granny."

Slipping the transmission into reverse, he backed onto River Road.

"That's the secret to my vitality—good, clean living and happy thoughts."

If only that were true.

The drive to the hospital became a question-and-answer session as she plied him for personal information. Without much to tell, he gave her succinct responses: "I'm eating enough; I live alone, unless you count Smoky; it's a house, not an apartment; not renting, I own it; outside of town, way back in the woods; I'm not dating; no, I haven't thought about marriage."

She's not going to ask the hard questions about my mental state, how often I'm running, or if I'm ever moving back here. It's that Southern thing. We fill the air with trivial crap and put off addressing important matters—genteel to the grave.

When Ben's limited personal information had been exhausted, Granny switched topics.

"It's a blessing that we don't have to drive further into

downtown Asheville to see your daddy."

Accustomed to her and Pop prefacing innumerable comments with "It's a blessing," Ben waited for an explanation, but one was not forthcoming.

"Why is that?" he asked, smiling at her wily, yet transparent, old tactic.

"You know, all those strange people on the streets playing their weird music, looking for a handout. It ought to be illegal."

"Well, they do have to get permits from the city in order to play."

She ignored his factual response.

"And if *they* aren't bad enough, decent folks can't use the sidewalk without running into all those hippie types, their raggedy clothes, and that long, twisted hair. What do you call it?"

"Dreadlocks?" Ben offered.

"That sounds about right."

She says 'hippie' with the same disgust she usually reserves for 'liquor.'

For the next few miles, he did nothing more than listen as Granny maligned Asheville culture, concluding with, "It's a regular Sodom and Gomorrah, if you ask me."

His favorite city, Asheville had provided endless enjoyment during Ben's teenage years, on those occasions when the farm freed him. If possible, he would have taken up residence at the old Pack Square Library. With its narrow aisles and crowded shelves, the ornate architecture gave the setting a fairytale quality, perfect for settling in on a rainy afternoon with a good book.

The antithesis of Abundance, the colorful city had exemplified his dream for, not only a different way of life, but an enhanced, better life than that which he had endured.

No point in arguing with conservative, evangelical entrenchment. Once they decide Jesus is the answer to every question, and a 3,000 year-old book is mankind's instruction manual, all evidence to the contrary is a device of Satan's. Scary part is, that's the same dead-end rut I was carving for myself until I opened my eyes to realize that my religion didn't comply with my real life experiences.

Thankful to see the turn-off sign for Mission Hospital, he slowed to avoid a group of protesters filling the sidewalk and spilling out into the street. Some took advantage of the slowed traffic to tap on the windows of vehicles, mouthing messages and extending pamphlets in outstretched hands.

"Holy Moses! What the hell do we have here?" Ben said, unused to censoring his language.

In automatic answer, he caught the gist of the gathering, the messages painted on homemade signs—*Save the Unborn, America Must Repent!, Abortion Is Murder.*

"So much for peaceful demonstration," Ben observed. Placards pumped in the autumn air, the anger a veritable cloud.

"That's the Planned Parenthood clinic there," said Granny, pointing to a low structure barely visible through the crowd.

"Eric Rudolph disciples?" Ben asked, thinking of yesterday's breakfast.

"Some, maybe," Granny said.

"Reckon anybody from Abundance is to be found in that mob?"

"Can't say."

After miles of her judgmental comments, he could not resist pushing back, convinced that his views reflected the moral high ground, and those rabid people were representative of every external objection he had to religion.

"Because I think I recognize some faces from back in my Redeemer days," he said. "And if there are any Eric Rudolph sympathizers in that gang, they left out one important message amongst their signs."

"Which would be?" Granny asked.

"*Murder Is Murder.* Their poster boy is a killer, randomly murdering and maiming anyone who happens to be within the vicinity when his bombs explode."

"Eye for an eye, and tooth for tooth," she said.

He took advantage of the stopped traffic to turn on her.

"Are we really going there? That's your best justification?"

Granny squeezed tighter on the purse in her lap, muting herself until they reached the hospital's main entrance.

"I'll drop you at the front. Save you the long walk from the parking structure," he said to her, his tone without anger, though flat.

And it will be 'a blessing' to get you and your self-righteous judgments out of the car.

"No, no don't do that." She emphatically disagreed. "I'd rather not be left alone for who-knows-telling how long it'll take you to find a parking spot."

She unclutched her purse and pulled out a handicapped placard.

"Take this and hang it on your mirror. I remembered to bring it this time. It's from back when I had my knee surgery. We can park closer that way and go in together."

Woohoo! Look at Granny, breaking the law. Must be that Asheville influence taking over.

WHEN THEY ARRIVED OUTSIDE THE ICU doors, Ben noticed the waiting room overflowing.

Before he could comment, Granny said, "Bad wreck up on the Parkway yesterday. A couple of cars went over the edge. It gets too crowded up there this time of year with tourists who ain't used to mountain roads."

Five visitors ahead of them in line, Ben checked the time on his cellphone.

Seven more minutes to wait in line for the privilege of seeing that son of a bitch stretched out in bed. No. That's not right. I retract 'son of a bitch.' Granny's no bitch, and her sorry-ass son is no bad reflection on her. Bastard? No. That drags her back in it. This whole fucking fiasco is bringing up so much shit I've had walled off. It's impossible not to think about the childhood crap, with all the familiar people and surroundings queuing it up. I sense another run coming on. And what about, Silk? Not that I had plans to see her today, but Pop put an end to me casually stopping at the café after a haul. She'll be pissed if she thinks I broke my promise.

A loud *clack* signaled the opening of the ICU doors. Hopefuls and the hopeless shuffled forward. Hands were washed and adorned in yellow scrubs, and the clutch of frightened baby chicks scattered their separate ways.

Though it was only his second day as a visitor, the routine abraded Ben's patience. Nurses marched in and out to the rhythm of incessant beeping. Daddy remained oblivious. Meanwhile, Granny, waiting expectantly on Dr. Berner's words, had to settle for, "No change."

For this we fret? Torment for Granny, uproot and upheaval for me. To what end? Should have brought my laptop, though she would have thought it disrespectful.

The thought of his dad deserving respect elicited a laugh.

"What's funny?" Granny asked.

Caught. Ben had to get creative. His mind resorted to the repository that shone the brightest—childhood memories, polarized as *good* or *bad*.

"Remember that time Daddy asked me to spray the corn in the garden? He said he already had the material measured out and mixed with the water, ready to go. All I needed to do was carry the hand sprayer from the shed to the garden, shake it, pump it up good, and give those rows a good dousing."

Smiling, she took up the telling of it. "Oh, you sprayed and sprayed. Made sure to use up all of it, as I recall. Came back up to the shed telling your daddy you were done. That's when he asked why the full tank of material was still sitting where he left it."

Ben noted a twinkle had returned to her eyes, and he was pleased to see a smile.

"You had grabbed the tank we used when burning brush

piles, the one filled with diesel fuel. The summer sun hit that diesel and wilted your daddy's corn before the day was out. Ruined it, rotting every kernel to a sickly black."

Her first story led to a morning full of them. A therapeutic exercise for both parties, soon Ben's dread gave way to enjoyment. Granny had to be the one to announce it almost time for another hospital cafeteria meal.

They gravitated to the same table from two days earlier, exhibiting an inner need for a sliver of control.

In the middle of a mouthful of banana pudding, Ben's cellphone rang. He dropped the spoon and scrambled. Above the number, "Silk" appeared on the screen.

Damn! I forgot she entered it in my phone last night. Fuck. Fuck. Fuck.

He smashed the "Silent" button.

"Who called?" Granny asked, the product of a generation who risked broken limbs racing to answer each ringing phone.

Couldn't talk to her in front of Granny. Now I need a lie.

"Unknown caller. If it's someone whose number I don't have saved to my phone, it shows up as an unknown caller. Saves answering a lot of gimmicky sales calls."

Trying to sound nonchalant, he doubted she bought it, given his red face and kneejerk panic.

Minutes after they returned to ICU room 129, a stranger poked his head in, asking, "Is this a convenient time for me to join you?"

The newcomer wore the same disposable yellow-scrub outfit.

Probably a vulture from the business office wanting to know how we intend to pay for this four-star room.

Granny looked happy. "Yes. Please come on in."

Shorter and older than Ben, the visitor snaked his way around the diagnostic equipment to where Granny sat.

He extended a hand.

"It's good to see you, Mrs. Bramley, though not under these conditions."

He glanced toward Daddy and then to Ben.

"And this must be the grandson I've heard such wonderful things about."

He had to pivot to shake Ben's confused hand.

They said only immediate family could get in. Who is this character?

"Ben, this is Reverend Thomas. He's our pastor."

"Please call me Adam," the Reverend said, mid-shake.

His blue eyes and rounded features exuded kindness.

I'm not buying it. And how pissed would Granny get if I run out of here to disinfect my hand at the scrub station?

How about you quit tossing everyone on the same shit pile based on your singular experiences?

Okay. Okay. So he's not Reverend Shepard. What the hell? I figured that icon would still be preaching at Redeemer until he stroked out in the pulpit.

A Kodiak bear in a suit and tie, Reverend Shepard had commanded attention. Though his brown crewcut had grayed at the temples, he fondly spoke of his college years, having given up a possible pro-football career to join the seminary.

"Jesus is my quarterback, and the Heavenly Father is my Head Coach," he said often, forcing generations of mothers to explain basic football vernacular to their curious children.

No longer intimidating opposing offenses, the Reverend kept the fear of God stirred up in his flock with his booming, hell-fire focus. His favorite Bible verse, based on frequency of usage, was the latter half of Romans 12:19, "Vengeance is mine; I will repay, saith the Lord."

Ensconced at Redeemer for more than twenty years, he steered a community-wide flock where all but a few stray sheep attended. He had never married, though many eligible ladies had been attracted to David Shepard's broad-shouldered, six-four frame. The more brazen and educated among them whispered of his physique in comparison to another *David*—the classic sculpture by Michelangelo—amusing themselves with the possibilities of the art's anatomically accurate nudity correlating to the pastor.

"The church is my bride," he often said, fending off blatant advances and reiterating his spiritual commitment for the ears of the locals.

"WHAT HAPPENED TO REVEREND SHEPARD?" Ben asked.

"Reverend Shepard lost his eyesight, forcing his retirement."

It took bodily might for Ben to keep from bursting out laughing. *They say it will make you go blind. Should have only done it until he needed glasses.*

Granny clearly approved of the replacement. "Reverend Thomas has been with us for several years. We've watched his children grow up."

A wife and children? That's a big switch.

"That's true. Stephen starts high school this year, and Ruth moves up to middle school. But I'm here to talk about your family. How is Jason doing?"

And old Shepard's gone blind. Must be hell for him.

"No change."

Ben heard Granny say the words he imagined plastered across her mind.

"They've got him heavily medicated. All we can do is wait."

"And pray," the pastor added.

"Of course," Granny replied.

Ouch! Granny's slipping. That embarrassing omission is going to leave a scar.

"Speaking of which," Reverend Thomas said, "I would like to pray over Jason, if that's alright with the two of you."

"Please do," said Granny.

Reverend Thomas made eye contact with Ben, seeking his approval.

When did a minister ever ask permission for anything? New to me.

Ben nodded his assent.

"Do you mind if we gather around his bed and hold hands?"

Granny and Ben wordlessly complied. Physical discomfort manifested throughout his body, as a result of total abhorrence to the ritual.

It's going to take a long, hot shower to wash off the slimy feeling.

Reverend Thomas began. Unlike the bombastic Reverend Shepard, a proponent of the louder-is-better philosophy, the new guy prayed in a meek, pliant tone.

"Our Father in heaven, we come before you this day on behalf of Jason Bramley, in the midst of a critical trauma. He is in dire need of your miraculous intervention. We humbly implore you, by the power of your Holy Spirit, to heal his body, if that be your will. And to strengthen his family, who also are caught up in this trying crisis. We thank you for your love and concern in this matter. In Jesus's name we pray. Amen."

"Amen," mouthed Granny—and Ben, in spite of himself.

Short and sweet, at least. Well, maybe not sweet. He didn't lay on the syrup. I can't take the syrup.

"Thank you, Reverend." Granny squeezed his hands.

"Yeah. Thanks, Reverend." Ben forced.

"It's just Adam," he stressed again to Ben. "I also want to mention that I've spoken to those who were unable to attend Prayer Meeting last night. Now the entire congregation is aware of your need for collective prayer. I hope I didn't overstep my bounds."

"Not at all." Granny smiled at the news. "That's a comfort."

"If I can bring you anything or relieve y'all by sitting with Jason, please call me. At the moment, I have another pressing engagement. Please forgive my haste."

He waved goodbye on his way out the door.

Damned if he didn't sound sincere.

When he was out of earshot, Granny said, "He's been a real blessing to our congregation."

To Ben's delight, she didn't elaborate. He turned his

attention to time with Silk, calculating his chances of getting back to Abundance before the café's closing.

Rising to exit, he improvised on the move.

"Granny, I'm going to grab a giant cup of steaming caffeine. You want anything?"

The hike to the cafeteria provided plenty of time to return Silk's call and explain his previous lack of response.

Their conversation concluded with him saying, "Out of my control. I hope to make it back in time to see you."

After standing in line to pay for the diversionary cup of Maxwell House, he retraced his path. Alternating the hot cup from one hand to the other, he noticed a small, unoccupied seating area to the left side of the corridor. Selecting a corner chair, he situated the coffee on an end table.

"Whew! Hot cup. Hot cup."

I can tell Granny I got slowed down in a long line at the cafeteria and stopped for a bathroom break. Hell, I can pile up an hour's worth of delays if I need to.

On the verge of closing his eyes, Ben noticed a *Smithsonian* magazine resting on an adjoining chair that caught his attention. The cover, a Charles Russell painting of a Great Plains Native American on horseback, piqued Ben's love of Western lore, leading to a smile when he contemplated the resiliency of the Apache, and their code for survival in the desert: Eat when you have the chance to do so. Drink when water is available. Sleep when you can, because there is no way of knowing when those opportunities will arise again.

Cell service and privacy. My only shot today at reaching Dr. Mendel.

"Thanks, *Smithsonian*," he said.

Doris answered Ben's call. The doctor had five minutes remaining with a current patient.

"Will you ask her to call me at this number when she gets done?"

"Glad to, Mr. Bramley."

He stood to pace the time away. First ring, he answered, "Hey, Doc."

"Hello, Ben. How are you?"

"In need of hearing your voice."

"Sorry to be abrupt. My next appointment is waiting for me. Quickly, please."

"Same struggle, different day, dealing with my past and the constant reminders around here."

"Is there a question in there?" she asked.

"Yes, ma'am." He paused. "Is life kicking *everybody's* butt on a minute-to-minute basis?"

"Short answer, *yes,* in six-billion unique ways. Little comfort I'm sure, as you deal with your personal version of life."

"Oh, well," he replied.

"Don't despair," she added. "Last night I determined that you might benefit from the Four Noble Truths of Buddhism, particularly the first two."

"You know my aversion to all things religious," he began, to which she interrupted.

"Buddhism, at its fundamental teaching, is a philosophy, not a religion. Now listen."

"Yes, ma'am."

"The first noble truth is that to live, is to suffer. The second, is that the origin of suffering is attachment. Would you say that you are attached to your past?"

Without hesitation he answered, "Absolutely. The past is where I reside, living inside my head, riveted to the projection of screwed-up childhood home movies. No intermissions. No popcorn. Regret prevents escape."

"That's a sad commentary, though I'm glad to hear your admission regarding your past. Understanding that dynamic is key to the simple solution."

"Which is?"

"Let it go."

He waited for her to continue, until he could bear it no more.

"Then what?"

"Too simple for that intricate mind of yours?"

"No. I mean, what?"

"I realize it's uncommon for a psychiatric professional to be spouting Buddhist teachings. However, in this case the lesson is directly applicable to you."

"How so?"

"You are going to continue the cycle of suffering by holding onto your victim story, or your victim *status*, if that makes more sense. The lesson is also universal. All attachment is suffering. In order to end the suffering, simply let go. Break the attachment."

"You make it sound easy," he said.

"I'm not trivializing what you've been through. The letting go has to be on your terms. You have to arrive at the mechanism, or mechanisms. What I *am* certain of, is that long ago you accepted a shallow future for the opportunity to wallow in the past. Today, tomorrow, or next year, you can reverse that decision and radically change your life."

"Regret is the biggest part of my identity," he said, "when lumped together with its companions, blame and guilt. How can a new version of Ben Bramley function freed from wallowing?"

"These aren't hollow platitudes I'm giving you, Ben. If you look at life objectively, you will have to admit that no amount of guilt can solve the past, nor can living with the same frustrated mindset result in a happier future for you."

Trying to absorb her advice, he hit on a fitting analogy.

"Exactly like the computer programs I write," he said. "I design them to achieve the same predictable result. Now my internal program, my outdated thought process, needs to be rewritten if I want different results."

"Precisely! And though I can't give you a list of particulars about Ben Bramley, version 2.0, so to speak, I do know it's possible."

"Okay. I'll go along."

"Let me use a Buddhist model in another example, then

I have to leave you. Imagine a Buddhist monk isolated in a mountaintop monastery. His day consists primarily of prayer, meditation, throw in a few chants, replacing and lighting candles at the central shrine, and consuming bowls of rice. Now compare him to yourself. The present finds you back in the community you dread, forced to deal with family and a locale you've avoided. You're facing decisions that have long-term impact, choices coming at you rapid-fire in an emotionally charged environment."

She paused momentarily.

"Which of the two, you or the monk, is on the fast track for personal growth?"

"Me, I guess."

"Correct. In addition to your correct response do you understand what happened?"

"You lost me there, Doc."

"A shift occurred in your thinking. You went from victim mentality to seeing your situation as opportunity for growth. Now practice doing that until it becomes a full-time outlook. I've got to go, and you've got to *let go*. Good-bye!"

He repeated her instruction for the entirety of his journey back to room 129, and his grandmother.

ON THE DRIVE HOME, BEN used the narrow gaps of silence between their nostalgic exchanges to manufacture a reason for leaving the house once he and Granny arrived.

If I take the SUV, she'll quiz me to death about where I'm going and when I'll be back.

He hit on another option.

Running! I'll tell her I'm going for a run, change my clothes, and run the mile and a half up to the cafe. Then what? My running clothes will be an instant curiosity to Silk. Ah hell, I'll figure something out.

Zipping through yellow traffic lights, the pair made it home sooner than he'd expected.

"Headed out for a run," he said, as soon as the front door closed behind them.

"What about supper?"

"Don't worry about me. I'll make a sandwich when I get back. And tell Pop I'll switch off with him tomorrow."

"Suit yourself then."

He recognized her loaded tone—a small weapon from the vast arsenal utilized to get forward her agenda. But passive-aggressive scolding couldn't stick to a man on his way to rendezvous with a beautiful woman.

100 RIPPLES

CHAPTER EIGHT

"Thus saith the LORD of hosts, I remember that which Amalek did to Israel, how he laid wait for him in the way, when he came up from Egypt. Now go and smite Amalek, and utterly destroy all that they have, and spare them not; but slay both man and woman, infant and suckling, ox and sheep, camel and ass."
—I Samuel 15:2-3

B en's soles smacked the asphalt of River Road, heading toward more unknown.

"For a fellow who thrives on a steady diet of the predictable, I've been living way outside my comfort back here."

Halfway into the journey, he switched to the opposite lane to avoid an oncoming large truck. Its horn emitted three quick exclamations, and an arm extended from the cab, waving in long slow strokes. Binder chains rattled against the load of empty boxes as Pop whooshed by Ben.

The horizon served up a view of spotlights. Aimed at the Redeemer Baptist steeple, they converged to form a glowing column in the growing darkness.

Don't go getting all bitter and negative right before you see Silk. Nobody wants to be around that version of Ben. Run it out of your system.

He broke into a sprint that continued to the door of Abundance Café.

Hands on his knees, sucking air, he heard the bell jingling from the restaurant door. Without looking up, he sidestepped to give the exiting diners right-of-way.

"Hey Billy, check out the fag in the yellow shorts," one said, followed by mocking laughter.

"Day-Glo," said Ben, straightening up to full height. His

shadow reached out to touch them. "Ever get tired of being a dumbass, Turlock?"

Unaccustomed to being challenged, Jeff Turlock and his sidekick froze. Ben could see them trying to place him.

Some folks are incapable of change, the primary clue to the childhood bully's identity. Savoring his advantage, Ben pushed more.

"How's life on minimum wage?"

Ben grew electrified by the sight of their fists balling up and the confusion on their faces.

"I'll take that as a 'no comment.' And I'll also give you a hint."

He paused and gave them a wide grin.

"The crazy badass that whipped your butt on the grade-school playground is, right now, prepared to introduce your face to this asphalt parking lot."

He balled his own fists, the grin shifting from friendly to fierce.

A slow blink registered Turlock's comprehension.

"Bramley. What're you doing here?"

Ben noted Turlock made no counter threat, nor did he make a move.

"I'll be asking the questions, Turlock. Like why are you still standing here stinking up all outdoors? And why don't I quit talking and give you the beating you've got coming for a lifetime of picking on anybody you thought you could whip?"

Billy looked to his alpha partner for direction, seeing the back-down written on Turlock's face before the words confirmed it.

"We was just leaving."

The bully puffed out his chest, trying to save face.

"Before you run off, hear this. I may be around here for a long time, and I better not see your low-rent ass again, ever. And that goes double for at the café here."

Cocking a thumb toward the restaurant's picture window,

Ben's movement caused both ne'er-do-wells to jump.

"You and your boyfriend are going to find another place to stuff your faces. Got it?"

"Got it."

They backed up a few steps before turning to tumble into a patchwork and primer sedan.

"Where did *that* come from?"

The words spun him around. Silk stood half outside the restaurant door. He hadn't heard the warning bell on the door. Nor could he discern the intent behind her expression.

"I'm confused," she finally said.

"About what?"

"When I saw you through the front window, out here in a stand-off with yahoo one and yahoo two, I eased up behind the curtain to get a closer view of the drama. And out of curiosity I cracked the window."

I'm starting to understand how Turlock and Billy must have felt. Where's she going with this? Pissed that I ran off good customers?

"I heard you mention being around here for a long time. Am I right?"

CHAPTER NINE

". . . lovers of pleasures more than lovers of God; having a form of godliness, but denying the power thereof: from such turn away. For of this sort are they which creep into houses, and lead captive silly women laden with sins, led away with divers lusts, ever learning, and never able to come to the knowledge of the truth."
—*II Timothy 3:4-7*

"So when were you going to tell me about staying—or had you decided to keep quiet, since I don't figure into your plans?" Silk asked.

"You want the truth?"

"I'm a big fan."

"It surprised the hell out of me, and I know that's going to make you skeptical, but I swear, I don't know where it came from."

Silk didn't comment.

"As much as it would make me look like an idiot, drive me to my grandparents' house, and you can ask both of them if I've even hinted at the idea."

After a few seconds of consideration, "Alright, I believe you."

Yet he noticed the clarification didn't seem to sit well.

"Can we go inside and talk?"

"Do we need to?" she asked, unable to mask her hurt.

"Do you think I ended up at your door by accident?"

"No telling where you were going dressed like that."

She laughed a little.

"Well, ma'am, you see, these here is my courting clothes."

He gave it his best hillbilly drawl, hoping humor could make up for some of the ground he'd lost with her.

"Courting? Oh my! And I didn't know I was receiving."

She laughed a little more, took his hand, and pulled him inside.

"Food first, or talk?"

"I choose *c*, all of the above."

"Why is it you show up at closing time, again?"

She walked toward the kitchen.

"Trying to avoid a public appearance? Don't want to get caught catting around?"

"More like divine intervention, I suppose, with thugs like those around and you alone all the time."

"I hate to deflate your protector side. If you came any time before closing, you could meet my staff. I'm too cheap to pay them to clean when I can do it."

"Good to know you're not alone. I would come earlier if my schedule didn't revolve around the whim of grandparents. You want the truth?"

"The truth again? Why not?"

Frozen onion rings dropped in the fryer, and hotdogs landed on the grill.

"I'm a novice at female-male interactions. I have no game, as in, not a player."

"I think I follow."

Looking away from him, pretending to be engrossed in cooking, she smiled.

"Therefore, I have no filters and no choice other than to blurt my mind when I'm around you. Perhaps you're familiar with Homer Simpson—can't contain his thoughts, spontaneously narrating whatever he sees, even when it's just road signs? Especially billboards for doughnuts or burgers."

He waited.

She out-waited.

"I've been thinking about getting back here all day," he said.

"Which one am I, the doughnut or the burger?"

He stepped forward to kiss her. She pushed him away.

"The hotdogs are burning," she said.

A convenient excuse, she rolled them charred side up, cold side to the heat, as the alarm beeped on the fryer, keeping her busy and away from him. Assembling their meal, she carried it out to the dining area. Ben selected the table from the night before.

"I see a pattern emerging," she said, then caught herself. "That wasn't cool."

"What do you mean?" he asked.

"Talking about patterns emerging, kissing you when I please. That's presumptuous. You came back because of your folks, not me. And I go acting like I might be able to alter the course of things, no matter what The Universe has ordained."

She looked down at her plate.

"And here I'm still talking too much."

"We agreed to talk, didn't we? Out there in the parking lot?" He aimed an onion ring in that direction.

"More like a Wild West scene than a conversation, with all that action."

"You're not mad at me for telling two paying customers to get the hell out of Dodge?"

"Shoot no. They were bad for business."

She talked through a hearty bite of burnt hotdog while wiping a glob of chili from the corner of her mouth.

"Their days were numbered. You did me a favor, which brings us back to topic. Shall we call it a Freudian slip regarding the subject of your return to Abundance—I mean Dodge, Marshal Bramley?"

When he finished laughing, he said, "I'm more of a Jungian. And I won't refer to you as Miss Kitty, or we might waste the night with nonsense. Fact is, I don't have an answer, only a bunch of questions based on possible outcomes with my dad. Any of them could require my direct involvement, if I can get over my past and be a stand-up guy. Or maybe my past will win, and I'll simply throw money at the home-front problems from a safe distance."

The vinyl tablecloth made a small whirring sound from the friction of her hand sliding across to take his.

He continued.

"Never have I considered moving back to Abundance. It's the place to eternally avoid, my kryptonite."

He noticed her hand flinch at those words.

"I've told myself thousands of times that the one way to preserve my sanity is to stay away. This setting and the collective negativity from my personal history are synonymous."

"Does it have to be that way? Forever, I mean?"

Her eyes spoke more than sympathy and concern.

Is that love? Is that what it looks like? Or is it infatuation, rekindling a childhood flame in the context of crisis? God, this is all too new, too soon, too everything. I've walked into something maybe serious, and I've got not a clue. Play it safe? Try to fake 'normal'? Risk it all and self-disclose even more?

He decided in an instant.

"You saw what happened out there with Turlock and Numbnuts. It came automatically. I *wanted* them to jump me. I *wanted* to feel the sensation of my knuckles smashing his jaw. I wanted blood, mayhem. That's the real me since third grade. The anger, no, the rage, if I'm being honest, is a millisecond below the surface. It rockets out. So many triggers. Kinda like your Dr. Bruce Banner reference the other night, when he transforms into the Hulk."

He paused, and placed a hand atop hers.

"All teasing aside, I'm not that hero, not any kind of hero. Just a screwed-up guy with serious problems, walking around with a long list of complaints I'd like to shout into God's ear, if there is a God."

Letting go of her hand, he held out both of his, open palms up—a guilty man pleading his case.

"Best I can figure, that whole avalanche of James, then Mama, then my dad, my grieving process. . . . I got stuck in anger and haven't moved on to the next steps."

Head hung, he fell silent, awaiting her verdict.

"Maybe a lot of the anger is rooted in that church."

She nodded in the direction of Redeemer.

"That had to screw you up, seriously screw you up. All the rules, right?"

"Too many to juggle, and all of them still ping-pong-ing in my cranium all day, even though I renounced my membership as soon as I left for college."

He shook his head, as if trying to shake some of them out, before continuing.

"It may not sound like a big deal. You know, Abundance is tiny. There is no gene pool, only a gene puddle. And so damn painfully close, as in everybody knows everybody else, and all their business. No privacy. Word spreads. And contrary to the saying about sticks and stones, words *can* hurt you.

"And sure, I'm bitter, though I'm way more pissed off at myself than all the hypocrites combined, because that shit is so ingrained in me. I mean, I literally have dozens of Bible verses ringing in my ears, and I haven't cracked a Bible in almost twenty years."

"What a load you're carrying around," Silk said, "along with more rules at home and your self-imposed rules!"

She let that settle a bit. He had his eyes closed, nodding to the affirmative.

"And I'd say lots of guilt for not keeping all those rules."

"Bingo. Dr. Mendel says that forcing religion on kids is the worst form of child abuse, and that putting the fear of God into them amounts to bullying."

"I would agree, especially that God-is-going-to-get-you bullshit."

"You're on a roll. How do you know all this? I thought you didn't go to church."

"Didn't and don't. Being Jewish, I'm familiar with *that* religion's version of rules and regulations. Ever see how much bookshelf the Talmud takes up?"

She spread her arms wide as she could.

"Thirty-eight volumes, more than ten-million words, and that bunch across the road think they've got it rough. Lucky for me, I grew up with agnostic-leaning parents, but I've lived around the local religious fanatics all my life. And Redeemer's message board out front spells out more Baptist beliefs than I care to know."

She paused to remove her hair tie, using both hands to flip out her hair to its full length and volume. Mesmerized by the simple act, Ben mentally put a bold check mark in all the boxes on his hair-fetish wish list.

If she noticed his enraptured expression, she gave no indication.

"By the way, who comes up with all those weekly sayings for the sign, like: 'Turn or burn; If you died tonight would you go to heaven or hell; Jesus is the only way?' Some of them have such goofy plays on words. I swear, I've thought about photographing them for some sort of offbeat book or album. Probably get tarred and feathered if it made the bestseller list and word wormed its way back here by stagecoach."

"So you figured out my background from secondary evidence?"

"Guess I'd have to include televangelists. Not that I sit through an entire program. You can get the gist in a minute or two. It's funny how I find them hysterically entertaining and simultaneously nauseating."

On that note she pushed the last stub of hotdog into her mouth.

"Sorta like a car wreck, you can't help but gawk. Know what I mean?"

"Yeah, maybe," he said. "I can't stomach five seconds of that shit. And you can't write it off as just some megalomaniac foaming about his version of religious dedication. They're not aberrations. Every single one of them has a wide audience of followers donating wheelbarrow-loads of money to pay for that expensive air time." He paused to look eye-to-eye. "That's the really scary part; the woods are full of those nut jobs."

His composure came close to dissolving when he noted that his ideal of beauty wore globs of chili at each corner of her mouth.

"Remember a year ago, after 9/11, the newspaper articles quoting some of your most esteemed Protestant leaders?" she asked.

"I can't say that I do. It's best for me to pretend I don't see the captions to anything religious or right-wing, and quickly move on."

"These supposed men of God had only vile condemnations, calling our nation sinful, singled out by God for punishment. Ranting against everyone who doesn't see the world as they do, or follow their archaic rules. And that's part of your background. That's part of you."

"Am I that transparent?"

"Not transparent. My observations are from the perspective of someone who grew up alongside you, yet way outside the norm. You are, or were, a zealot, Ben. The pressure to perform brings out the best and worst in you. And where can you find more peer pressure than in little, old Abundance?"

"Got that right."

"Think about it. Your inner need to please people found all these venues to satisfy that compulsion. And purists, who are broken by the realities of life, are capable of crazy things."

She paused to be certain of his full attention.

"Consider this: Can you understand how brave you had to be to walk away from your childhood religion? How you literally defied hellfire to quit worshipping the Southern Baptist God? I don't know anyone around here that has had that kind of nerve. That takes balls mister, water-melon-sized balls."

"So you *do* think I'm crazy?"

"That's what you got out of what I told you?"

She shook an index finger at him, stopping short of scolding.

"I think we're all crazy. My personal philosophy and unusual ideas we'll save for another time. Point is, maybe you *are* stuck in anger mode. And that could be at the heart of your problems, though it doesn't have to be the finality."

"Hey, I'm a certifiable nut job. Do you disagree?"

"What I'm saying isn't meant to downplay your situation. We're looking at your reaction in light of the five stages of grief. The model has been dumbed down. It's not so simple as one, two, three, four, five. No rule says you have to grieve in order. Nor do you have to experience all five steps. Stuck in anger, number two on the list, does not mean that you have to experience three and four, 'Bargaining' and 'Depression,' before you can end up at five, 'Acceptance.' And it's out there for you. Somewhere, somehow, acceptance is available. You might not even have to find it. It may find you, in unexpected fashion. Can you say *epiphany?*"

She squeezed his hands tighter.

"That's it? That's all?" he asked in disbelief.

"Is that all? Were you listening?"

"Yeah. Sure. Just summarize what I should have heard."

Exasperated, she took a breath and recapped.

"What you should have heard is that you aren't walking around with a terminal condition. 'Screwed up' today does not have to mean, 'screwed up' tomorrow."

"What you aren't taking into account is the level of screwed up I am."

"Tell me."

Releasing his hands, she folded her arms on the table top.

Is this a dare? Does she want to know so she can help, or know to get ammunition?

When he hesitated, she said, "Go ahead and blurt. I'm not here to judge."

"I've got quirks."

He could see her fighting laughter.

"I thought you weren't going to judge?"

A small laugh did escape before she could cover her mouth to stop its neighbors spilling out.

"Everybody has quirks."

"Not like mine. I put the psycho in psychoanalysis."

She held up an open hand, palm forward, to stop him.

"Did you hear what you said? Really?"

"What?"

She launched into song.

"No-bo-dy knows the troub-le I see. / No-bo-dy knows my sor-row."

Only a slight amount of effect was lost by her not being an elderly man singing in a tremolo bass.

"And your point?"

"Point is: you're not a victim unless you decide to be a victim. Those things happened *around* you, not *to* you. They didn't leave you homeless, starving, or peg-legged and rotting from syphilis in a Turkish prison."

Ben's mind immediately went to *The Gulag Archipelago,* and Solzhenitsyn's statements regarding the tens of millions of Russians arrested and imprisoned for life.

Tens of millions! That puts things in perspective.

"See these clothes?"

"Is this a trick question?"

"I'm dressed like this because I've been running."

"Now you *are* starting to sound psycho. You are wearing running clothes because you've been running. Ooh, you're freaking me out here."

"You don't get it. I don't just run, I run like some wild maniac to total exhaustion."

"Whatever works for you."

She remained unshaken and refused to participate in his charged emotion.

"What I do is crazy!"

"Says who?"

"What do you means 'says who'?"

"Look, you've decided this manic running of yours is crazy. Give me a break. Labelling it as crazy, because you decided that? Come on, Ben, you're smarter than that. It's circular reasoning to arbitrarily call something crazy, then by virtue of your association with it, conclude you're crazy. Follow me?"

"I suppose."

"Do you *want* to be crazy?"

"Well, no. Of course not. You're still not getting it."

He paused to weigh his next words.

"I hear voices inside my head."

She burst out with laughter, slapping the table repeatedly, as the red of his face grew in intensity.

"I divulged something I've not shared with another human, and you make light of it?"

Trying to rein in her glee, she said, "Everybody hears voices. It's called self-talk."

"Mine goes beyond that. Sometimes I talk to myself, aloud or silently. Then I may argue with the talk."

Seeing her about to laugh further, he became more defensive.

"I have *my* talk in here. Maybe there's more than one voice." The tip of his index finger was fixed to his temple.

All control fled her, turning herself parallel to the bench seat so she could double up in uncontrolled spasms of hilarity.

Having steeled himself for rejection, objection, or perhaps sympathy at his confession, Ben was unprepared for that response. He got up to leave.

"No. Wait. Come back and sit down," she spoke through continued laughter, as happy tears involuntarily streaked down her face.

"Why should I?"

"I need to ask you something."

The asking had to wait a minute as she made several attempts to look serious.

"Has this voice ever told you to hurt someone, or say, hurt yourself?"

"No."

"Has this voice ever convinced you to do anything you wouldn't have done on your own?"

Starting to feel like he sat in a witness stand, he answered, "No." When she nodded slightly, he continued, "What does that mean?"

"Schizophrenics often have auditory hallucination. However, the illness goes way beyond that, with serious symptoms, none of which you exhibit. Not even PPD, paranoid personality disorder. You're way too together to have a mental illness, my professional opinion."

She couldn't resist being tickled with herself, and at her first major opportunity to use her college training.

"Look, I've seen firsthand what you think you have . . . you don't. Not anywhere close."

"Then how do you explain the voice?"

"I don't deny the voice, even voices. What you must understand, is that it's really *your* voice."

"No way."

"Yes. Way. It's essentially a remembrance, an assimilation of all the standards for behavior you've heard, especially in church. It's *you*, reasoning with *you*, arguing as to how your beliefs and actions *now*, are in conflict with what you were taught as a kid. Once you rejected Baptist ideology, and the Bible too, I'm guessing?"

Ben nodded.

"You created a compartmentalized voice, a voice diametrically opposite to the adult Ben you want to be. That way, you can view the voice as totally unrelated to you, and the inner voice you accept as truly *you* can engage in dialogue that includes theology the new *you* finds abhorrent."

She challenged Ben with, "What does the voice say to that?"

"Nothing at the moment. It'll wait until I'm alone to quote King James Bible verses at me about men being led astray by women, a line or two dealing with liars and false prophets, then probably conclude with a discourse on the Devil's snares."

"See?"

She was exuberant.

"You already know what's coming. How could you have any inkling if it weren't you writing those lines?"

"I'm at a loss. More like overwhelmed. I've sat here and listened to you logically trivialize my delusions. And you make it sound simple, which also kind of pisses me off. Even when you're making fun, I can't picture me without them. They've been part of me for so long I'm wanting to lash out in their defense."

"When you're faced with truth which you can't accept, the technical term is *cognitive dissonance*. And the lashing out over feeling threatened, even the good Dr. Jung, whom you advocate, would call that nothing more than *ego*."

He sighed, "Damn! That's encouraging. You do know it's going to take time getting beyond thinking of myself as broken beyond repair."

"You're not FUBAR. Get that through your head. Acceptance and peace of mind are on the way, and what a great meeting that will be."

She gave her best encouraging smile, melting further resistance.

"We have a shit-ton more to talk about, and I've hit you pretty hard. Now what?" she asked.

"Now what, what?"

"Now that you've continued to bare your soul, and I'm still sitting here, what's next . . . for us?"

"Is there an 'us?' I figured a glimpse of my twisted soul would end much chance of that."

"If I didn't think there was an 'us,' why would I give you my number, essentially begging you to come back? Then when you do show up, stay open late to feed you? Or throw my arms around you and kiss you like you're headed off to war?"

He hesitated a second before answering.

"I don't know. Maybe feeling sorry for me? Throwing me a bone."

"Ooooh!" she growled through gritted teeth.

He failed to notice her left arm draw back. Nor did he give much thought when she leaned toward him, across the table.

The side of his face caught fire before it registered he'd been slapped, the fury in her expression daring him to keep talking in the same vein.

Her next words came as a direct order.

"Get out."

"What?"

His innocent act had no traction.

"You heard me. Get—out—now!"

Her outstretched arm directed him to the door.

Unmoved, he stared at her, confused as to whether she joked, or presented him with some pivotal test.

When she held her pose, he got up and headed out the door, the bell jingling "goodbye."

Why did I say that? Couldn't keep my mouth shut. I told her I had no game with women. Then I proved it.

In the darkness, Ben's eyes adjusted. The white stripe on the asphalt edge shone enough to keep him on the road. With families homebound at the late hour, the lack of traffic noise allowed the roar of the Unolama River to dominate, pounding into his skull its power to transform life.

She's right about that victim shit. I'm only a victim as much as I allow myself to be. It's not like I'm Aleksandr Solzhenitsyn, rotting away in some Russian prison cell. My grandparents love me. I've got money, my health. So why do I stay stuck in the past?

The river muted the sound of his footfalls as his mind raced to untangle the mess of his life. Deep in thought, when he did stop to take in his location, he found himself at the old bus-stop crossroads, the holly tree standing atop the knoll, silhouetted against Pisces and Pegasus.

No need to check the root he used to tightrope walk as a kid. It would be there, grown bigger, same as him, attached to the tree that had weathered each day he had, and more.

Life goes on, popped into his stream of thought, and the words hanging there, pressing on his prefrontal cortex.

Struck with clarity, he turned back and ran in the opposite direction. Minutes later, he knocked on the café door. The curtain in the front window parted, revealing a slice of Silk's face.

"Please let me in. I'm sorry. Please."

His hands assumed the penitent, prayerful union, as he pleaded loud enough to be heard for half a mile. The desperation magnified given her indifferent expression on the opposite side of the pane.

When she vanished from view, he dropped his head, defeated.

"My big chance at real happiness and I screwed it up."

Click. He thought he heard the sound, maybe the deadbolt sliding open, or maybe closed. He couldn't be sure.

Lady or tiger? Lady or tiger?

His trembling hand tested the door knob.

When he stepped inside, Silk stood by the counter, feet wide apart and hands on her hips.

Tiger?

"I will overlook that supreme indiscretion, only owing to your naiveté with women."

She drew breath slowly, her seething visible. Not until calm returned did she continue to speak.

"In spite of your foolishness, I want there to be an 'us.' Do you?"

He felt his legs give beneath him with the shift of fate.

"Scared as hell, but yes. You get me. I can be myself, weird as I am, and it seems like you can handle it. Corny as it may sound, I get so caught up with you that all the head games go silent."

"There's the first hint at the Romeo I mentioned before."

She stepped forward, pulling him into her.

"Though it may sound romance-novel corny too. . . . I think you are worth the wait."

"Me, like I am now? That's what you want?"

"That's all I want."

She squeezed his slapped cheek until he winced, though he didn't need the reminder. Smiling at his pain, she asked, "What about you? What expectations do you have in a relationship?"

"Since I felt I wouldn't have one, I guess the answer is: none."

"There must be something."

"Sure, I guess. What about distance? Are you assuming I'm going to be around, or thinking about me living up Boone way?"

"You want the truth? Life, according to Silk?"

She laughed, and at that moment it hit him how much he loved her spirit. This woman didn't waste time throwing coins in fountains—too small of a wishing pool for her sprawling dreams. Instead, she horded her lucky pennies until she could fling them into the ocean.

"I think it's better to learn from the past than live in it," she said. "Besides, it's nothing more than a story we keep alive. It isn't real, in the truest sense of the word, not any more than you and I, here in this moment are real. The illusion of reality, this whole energetic experience we share, you know," she said offhandedly, as he shook his head to indicate total bewilderment, which did nothing to deter her enthusiasm for her subject.

"The essence of what we call 'life' is, of course, the first law of thermodynamics, and the law of conservation of energy. You and I are living proof of the validity of quantum entanglement. Wouldn't you agree?"

She perhaps took his stunned silence as a reasonable response to what she viewed as a rhetorical question.

"I'll give you my take on quantum physics and how it relates to the human existence when we have plenty of discussion time."

From the breathless, manic speech, he inferred her lack of

available human contact to share such heady thoughts.

She raced on.

"As for the future, the future isn't here yet, and I'm not going to be paralyzed by any fear of it. The present is where I choose to live, and here we are, together in it. Now help me clean this place so we can enjoy the present in a different location."

"Glad to help, and by the way, my grandparents are home. I want you to come meet them. Tonight."

Surprised by his own bravery, he puffed up, as he'd seen assertive actors do in the movies, unwilling to accept "no" for an answer.

She reached to put a hand on his chest. Her palm covered his heartbeat.

"You sure about this?"

"Absolutely," he said, Bogart and Clooney rolled into one.

"Then let's get this place cleaned, and I'll rush upstairs to wash."

Fifteen minutes later they entered her apartment.

"I'm going to grab a quick shower. There's beer in the fridge, if you want one."

Ben drank in the décor. The word *Bohemian* came to mind. Assorted candles sprouted from every horizontal surface. Eclectic artwork covered the walls, from Grandma Moses, to a depiction of the elephant God, Ganesha. And what could only be classified as a shrine, had a smiling, brass Buddha as its feature. Plump fertility goddesses, fairies, gnomes, and a couple of exquisite porcelain pieces rounded out the colorful display.

He carefully inspected the underside of the porcelain figurines for the maker's mark.

Lladro. The real deal.

"See anything you like?" she yelled through the open bathroom door.

Yeah. Behind the shower curtain, for sure.

"I'm cracking up at the Buddha and other idols being across the road from Redeemer Baptist, and their strict, 'Thou shalt have no other gods before me, or make any graven images' policy."

That drew a laugh from Silk.

"Suppose they would put me in stocks in the public square?"

"That, or burn you at the stake to keep the heresy from spreading. I especially like the picture of Ganesha."

"What if no one is watching?" Silk asked Ben.

"What do you mean?" he asked, stepping closer to the bathroom.

"Have you ever considered that maybe there is no God? That maybe our biggest collective mistake is in thinking that we are special? That mentality leads to all kinds of trouble. Once we decide that we matter, you know, standout as individuals to some Creator who made us, life takes on a meaning that can be both false and self-destructive."

The sound of running water ceased while he framed an answer.

"If a child's sincere prayers cannot stop sexual abuse at the hands of a recognized 'man of God,' what does that say about God?" he asked.

"You've entertained the idea, I gather," she responded.

Considering a world without the Christian version of God, Ben subconsciously returned to her shrine, staring at suggested alternatives.

When he looked up, she had entered the room, her hair up in a towel, and another wrapped around her torso.

"Funny you should single out the Ganesha painting, the God of wisdom, knowledge, and new beginnings. Rather apropos, don't you think?"

Silence.

She turned from the picture to find a stupefied look stamped on his face.

"First time being alone with a woman wearing only a towel?"

He stood mute, which delighted her extremely. The hand which held the towel at her breast line, shifted to her mouth as she laughed.

Ben gasped, stepping back, though the wrap remained in place, drawing more laughter from Silk.

"What are you afraid of?" she teased.

When it became obvious that no answer was forthcoming, she pushed further.

"Would you like a sneak peek at what you're getting into, so to speak?"

Without waiting, the towel opened wide, along with his eyes.

Pleased at the response, she concluded, "There'll be plenty more time for that. Right now we better hurry on to your grandparents' before it gets too late."

CHAPTER TEN

"And we know that all things work together for good to them that love God, to them who are called according to his purpose."
—Romans 8:28

"If you're not sure about this, I can let you out on the road, so your grandparents can't see my truck in the driveway," Silk said.

Ben awaited a sarcastic follow-up. When none came, he got it, got it fully that she cared for him, enough to be thoughtful in even a small way, enough to care about his privacy. That's when a tiny *click* occurred within him. A little piece of the mechanism that had made Ben the best version of his former self moved after decades of being frozen in place.

"Positive. I want you to meet them. Really more like I want them to meet you."

"This isn't so you don't have to take the heat for being out too long?" she asked.

"I want to move forward, like you said."

"Great. Now do something about that I've-recently-seen-this-woman-naked look plastered all over you face."

"Got it. I'll think about something else, like pickled eggs in that pink juice, sitting on convenience-store check-out counters, in the gallon-size jars."

"You dialed that image up in a hurry. Any backstory in there you'd like to share?"

Pulling in the driveway, she cut off the ignition.

"It's not too late to change your mind."

"The only thing I'm changing is me. 'Fucked up' today does not have to mean, 'fucked up' tomorrow," he said.

"Somebody's been listening. Although, your attempt at a

confident tone sounded more like a kid trying to convince himself the monster under the bed wasn't going to grab him by the ankles if he got up to go to the bathroom in the dark."

Her door half open, she had one foot on the ground.

"Ben, is that you?"

Granny stood on the porch, before they could get out, calling into the night.

"It's me."

"Who's that with you?"

"You'll see in a second." He looked over his shoulder to Silk, her face framed by the cab's dome light. "I'm sorry."

"No problem. She worries about you. Not everybody has a grandmother around who cares so much. You're lucky."

"Right now I'm feeling treated more like that little kid you mentioned."

"You can put a stop to that. My guess is you will."

Granny made no attempt to mask her impatience.

"I can't see you."

"Coming," he said.

Side-by-side they walked across musty-smelling oak leaves. Surprising them both, he took her hand, half out of affection, half daring Granny to comment. Stepping up to her boldly, he did formal introductions in the diffuse porch light.

"Granny, this is Silk Mayer. Silk, this is my grandmother, Lily Bramley."

"So nice to meet you Mrs. Bramley."

Silk extended her free right hand to shake. Granny clasped it instead, holding on.

"Ben's elementary-school girlfriend, my, what a lovely woman you've become! I told him it was a mistake to break up with you. Come on inside."

"I really should be going."

"Nonsense, it's not late. Come on in and sit a spell. Sam's in the living room with the TV going. I'll make some coffee."

Accustomed to being heeded, she turned and walked into

the house without further discussion.

"You *can* see me standing here?" Ben asked. "Because I felt invisible while you two made all nicey, nicey. And who would have guessed what I figured to be a bombshell didn't even amount to a firecracker?"

"Maybe you underestimate your grandmother. Don't you think she might be happy for you to bring such a lovely woman home?"

Inside, Pop rose from his recliner as Ben made introductions again.

"Y'all sit down and I'll be right back with the coffee," Granny insisted.

"Isn't it a little late for coffee, Hon?" Pop asked.

Granny gave him her best shut-up-you're-interfering-look.

"I'm going to make decaf Sam. Why don't you come help me?"

Long before, Ben had deemed her the master at issuing commands enfolded within a question. He could accurately assume that Pop's time in the kitchen would include both correction and instruction for appropriate behavior during Silk's visit.

"You know we've caused a commotion," Ben said, once his grandparents left the room.

"Well, it's not every day that their grandson brings home a lady friend."

"It's not *any* day," he corrected. "Don't feel like you have to stay."

"Of course I have to stay. They're your grandparents and more. Practically your parents. This is their chance to get to know me, and for me to make a good impression."

"It's hardly planned, though."

"I imagine if it hadn't happened this way, it would be a year from now and you would still be putting it off. Right?"

She looked at him knowingly and tugged the hand that hadn't let go of hers since they arrived.

"To deny it would be folly," he said.

Granny returned with a tray in each hand.

"Here's a few snacks while the coffee's making. It's not much."

She couldn't omit her lifelong habit of apologizing for anything she served.

Pop came in with fixings for the coffee, noticeably closemouthed.

"How long have you been running the café?" Granny asked.

"A little less than two years," Silk said.

"You plan on keeping the place open long?"

This is becoming an interview, Ben thought.

Checking Silk's expression, she seemed not-at-all put off.

"I'll probably keep at it until I get married and children come along."

Damn, she's laying it on thick. Is Granny buying any of this?

"My, what a sensible young woman," Granny said.

"Thank you, ma'am."

Ben, nor Pop, had spoken since the trays of cookies, crackers and cheese had appeared. The men occupied themselves with eating, except for when Pop got up to fetch the coffee. Granny hadn't mentioned it since engaging Silk.

CHAPTER ELEVEN

"For God shall bring every work into judgment, with every secret thing, whether it be good, or whether it be evil."
—Ecclesiastes 12:14

The following morning, with the last stack of empty bin boxes unloaded from the flatbed truck, Pop and Ben shared a quiet moment.

"Do me a big favor," Pop asked.

Still seated on the forklift, Ben assumed that some unforeseen work instigated the request. Reaching down to turn the ignition key, he saw the palm-side of Pop's hand shoot skyward.

"Not that," Pop said.

Paused, the elder man scanned the surrounding area before speaking further.

"Don't go thinking ill of me," he said.

Pop's low voice, out of place outside unless they were stalking deer in tandem, forced Ben to lean way forward in the seat, ears piqued to gather every word of what was shaping up to be a conspiratorial message.

"It's been days now, with no change in your daddy's situation."

Ben nodded his assent.

"Point is, sitting in that ICU room all day and evening makes me feel helpless. The message being that I can't do one iota to change a thing. Meanwhile, back here they's loads of things I *can* do. And you know I can't abide watching hard-earned apples hit the ground."

"Yes, sir," Ben said.

"More than the money, and even with all your help, I can't keep sitting on my hands all day."

"What can I do?" Ben asked.

"A team of stout mules couldn't drag your granny from his bedside. No use in heading down that road. This evening, over supper, I'm going to tell her that going forward, either you or me will drop her off at the hospital, and go back to get her, as late as she wants to stay."

Feet planted wide, and both hands on his hips, Pop peered hard into Ben's eyes.

"You figure that makes me some kind of heartless son-of-a-bitch?"

Exposing more of his inner nature than customary, Pop's obvious man-to-man question grabbed Ben by the heart. Matching his grandfather's penetrating gaze, he replied.

"No, sir. I reckon if anything it proves you have a great big heart that can't take being torn apart, bit by bit, day by day."

"So you'll back me up then? Talk reason to your grandmother? She'll listen to you."

"Sure will, and I'll never let on that we had this conversation."

Bounding off the forklift, Ben wrapped his grandfather in a bear hug.

GRANNY TOOK TO THE PLAN like a tomcat to bath time. Unable to surmount the male solidarity, she switched to playing the *hurt* card, careful, however, not to insinuate that either of the two men cared less for her son.

Defeated in emotionally manipulating either of them into her daily waiting game, and herself never in possession of a driver's license, Granny had no choice other than to accept the new arrangement. Ben offered to take on chauffeuring duties to gain a smidgen more freedom of movement, a plan which took additional advantage of Pop's greater skill in managing the labor.

The second morning of the new terms, Ben deposited Granny at the hospital entrance and detoured by way of the Groverton Public Library. In search of the computers, he remembered Silk's directions.

"To the right of the card catalog," he said aloud, customarily talking to himself, or Smoky, absent of any human voice around his Cut Laurel Knob cabin.

He shook his head in amazement at the lack of change in the library's floor plan since his childhood.

"Like some *Twilight Zone* episode, again. Stuck in a time capsule."

Rounding the corner, he found one of the two computers already occupied.

"What the hell?"

The long-haired occupant spun around in her seat.

"Again with the strong language," Silk smirked. "Did that liberal element at Duke erode your manners?" Smiling at his surprised pause, she added, "And it appears that I may have picked up a stalker."

"Don't flatter yourself," he said, returning the smile. "Consider this meeting an inevitability of small-town existence."

She ran out her lower lip in mock disappointment. "I live in a world where there are no accidents or coincidences," she said.

When Ben didn't engage on that pearl of wisdom, she turned back to her screen.

"What's my favorite restauranteur doing away from the kitchen?"

"Well," she said, typing as she spoke, "by the time the library administration got around to blocking all my favorite porn sites, I had also developed an addiction for Amazon. It's a shopping site, big on books."

"I'm quite familiar," he said.

Too much of that know-it-all-tone. Reign in the ego. This is Silk, not some client. And what's up with another porn reference?

"Oh, I forgot that I was in the presence of the techie Jedi master. Forgive me, great one!"

For three seconds she had him hoofing it on a hotplate, but she couldn't contain her amusement longer.

"You are so funny," he said.

What is funny—funny strange—is how long it's been without anyone teasing me. Another one of life's simple pleasures in payment for solitude.

Silk is still talking. Get out of your head, and back to her, Moses said.

"I accept your apology," she told Ben. "Especially since you interrupted my limited 'me time.'"

"What?"

"Open for lunch and dinner at the café . . . oops, I mean dinner and supper. Pardon my uppity terminology. Open for dinner and supper makes for a long day. Mornings are my designated time for getting out and away from Abundance. It's worth paying my staff a few extra hours to go in and begin prepping without my dazzling presence required."

"Okay. I'm shutting up now, and jumping on my allotted thirty minutes of electronic getaway."

"No, no, no," she scolded. "Before proceeding further you will have to register with Mrs. Potts, over at the Reference Desk, to get computer access. Use your grandparents' address, because these babies are strictly for locals, whose tax dollars funded this frivolous enterprise. Though, she might waive the requirements given your celebrity status. Need me to come with you, verify your identity?"

"For the Special of the Day, we're serving heaps of sarcasm, I take it."

"I'm dishing it. The question being, 'Can you take it?'"

Without responding, he marched toward the paperwork, returning three minutes later.

"Look at you," she said. "Slumming it computer-style with the local yokels."

"Checking my email. That's all. Ever heard of it?"

Her turn to ignore him, until almost banging heads, with him inspecting her screen.

"Hey! Privacy mister. Didn't you read the etiquette section which you signed over there?"

"What's the Amazon fascination?" he asked.

"Goes to what I mentioned the other night, my thirst for all-things woo-woo."

"What the hell is *woo-woo*?"

"My word for that mixture of mysticism and cutting-edge quantum physics. And stop making that face at me. You know, lots of the major names in physics were students of the Indian Vedas and other texts—Bohr, Schrodinger, Einstein, Tesla. Robert Oppenheimer learned Sanskrit so he could read directly from the ancient Indian texts. We're talking the framework for the seminal thought that led to modern quantum physics, instigated by Indian wisdom thousands of years old."

"And Amazon fits in how?"

"I've read about everything from here to Malaprop's on the subjects."

Ben smiled at the mention of his favorite bookstore, a blueprint for his ideal heaven, and a perennial stop when visiting Asheville, as far back as his high-school days. Silk's reference, without pausing to explain, with her knowing that he knew, struck him as too wonderful for words.

"Now Amazon, my Amazon, is the window to the latest and greatest. Kinda my personal version of a savior. Not that I need saving."

Returning attention to her search, the two of them conversed above the *clickety-clack* of veteran keyboard usage.

"Abundance doesn't deserve to be the recipient of the likes of you," Ben said.

"More sarcasm, mister?"

"Not at all."

Neither could keep quiet more than a minute.

"Damn!" Ben exclaimed.

"What?"

"Just saw the day listed in the corner of my screen. Saturday."

"Yeah. So?"

"When you live off the grid, days of the week all run together. This realization means tomorrow is Sunday. Thought I'd be out of here by now. Instead, Pop and Granny are going to try to drag me to church tomorrow, soak up all that loving concern regarding my dad."

"What's one Sunday? No big deal."

"Big fucking deal," he said too loudly. "Do you like The Three Stooges?"

"What non sequitur madness is this?" she asked.

"Indulge me," he said.

"Very well. I cannot bring myself to watch them perform, though it pains me to turn my back on three fellow Jews, including Shemp. Slapstick comedy is an oxymoron. The mere thought of watching them makes my sensibilities recoil."

"Bingo!" Ben said. "Now take that same aversion to idiocy and multiply it to the power of nausea. That's me where church service is concerned. I couldn't make it through the opening prayer, hell, the opening hymn. Every aspect of it screams *RUN*, before any additional experience can attach itself to my memory banks—memory banks which I already wrestle with to scrub clean, or avoid accessing."

"I can see you all in major dither mode simply contemplating the topic. How about I give you a convenient excuse, a scheduling conflict, if you like?"

"Better make it good and ironclad. Granny will worm her way through any exposed flesh."

"Take me on a picnic tomorrow morning. Brunch on me."

What I wouldn't give to brunch all over her.

"I'll bring the food. You pick the spot."

"Best deal I've heard since getting here. See you at, shall we say, nine? That eclipses Sunday school too."

"Deal," she said, offering her hand to shake on it.

PICKING UP GRANNY THAT EVENING, Ben determined to avoid the subject of church until they were back in the presence of Pop, figuring safety in numbers, and hoping to garner some payback for standing strong on the new hospital-visitation routine.

As anticipated, her litany of the day matched every other day since Ben had driven her.

"You want to stop and get something to eat?" she asked.

"Nah. Pop said he would wait on us. He's working late to try and get in another load to the packing house."

"Makes sense, what with them being closed tomorrow, Sunday, and all."

I just stepped in a steaming pile of road apples. Change the subject. Change the subject, and make it fast.

"Anything good to eat at the cafeteria today?"

The topic was successfully dodged for the remainder of the trip, but back home Ben ate little supper, his stomach a knot of Granny-instigated dread.

Dessert came served with her agenda.

"Sunday school, or only preaching tomorrow, Sam?"

No third choice—none of the above.

Certain of the upcoming debate, Ben took the driver's seat.

"I've got plans tomorrow," he said.

Parsing his information, he hoped Granny would be put off enough to end the matter. Plans? Him? It sounded bogus enough to piss her off and send her stomping back into the kitchen.

"May I ask?" she inquired, with the guile of a coiled copperhead.

"I got invited to brunch."

"Brunch. My, how cosmopolitan for you!"

She left those words hanging in the air. Let the prey speak next.

"Yes, ma'am. I guess."

More tense silence as he tried to find something interesting on the table at which to stare.

"I bumped into Silk Mayer today."

When he dared look up, Granny's face had untwisted.

"My, yes! Lovely girl. So nice of her to stop by the other night. Are you sweet on her? You seemed to be."

"Lily, quit quizzing the boy. Can't you see you're making him uncomfortable?" Pop said.

The interrogation proved brief. Ben passed on dessert to escape up the stairs.

"Wow! Less painful than I expected, Smoky."

The cat jumped from the bed to make figure eights between Ben's ankles, rubbing whiskered cheeks against his shins.

Want to know why?

"What insight can you share, Moses?"

Silk is Granny's golden ticket.

"Cut the movie analogy and speak plainly."

The first time you drove Granny to the hospital, without Pop along, she quizzed you about girlfriends and dating.

"Yeah. So?"

A romance between you and Silk could plant you back in Abundance, back in Granny's world. Outside of your dad recovering, that's her greatest hope, her urgent prayer.

FITFUL SLEEP DOMINATED BEN'S NIGHT. Moses's revelation had sparked the desire to grab his Nikes and run a few miles, though he didn't think it prudent to show up at Silk's place looking like roadkill.

Showered, shaved, and out the door without a word, he drove wearing a satisfied smile until he caught sight of the Unolama

River. Fog rose along its course, softening the sun's early rays. Postcard worthy, the image irritated Ben.

"Hard enough to push it out of my head without flashing a visual reminder."

Proximity saved him, as he arrived at her parking lot still short of full-blown agitation.

Across the road, Redeemer Baptist stood empty, without hint at the flurry of worshippers from miles around, awake, fed, and staring at mirrors to perfect their hairdo, or adjust the Windsor knot on their favorite K-Mart tie.

"This entire place is a gigantic reminder, an ever-present flashback. And the bad far outweighs whatever good I try to muster. All I can figure is try to override the old with some megabytes of new memories during my stay here. Maybe start today with a focus on stockpiling positive replacements."

His right hand, poised midair above the horn, elicited a warning from Moses.

Are you really going to sit out here and honk the horn for her to come running, like some undereducated oaf?

Cutting the engine, Ben walked the few feet to an exterior set of steps that led upstairs to her door. A welcoming hug enveloped him as he noticed how seductively she could make a faded, plaid, flannel shirt come alive.

"Let me grab that for you," he said, noticing the wicker picnic basket on the floor behind her. "Anything else?"

"Let me run get a blanket. You can grab the small ice chest off the kitchen counter if you want. Otherwise, that's it."

Unavoidably, the scent of incense reached his nose. Though he couldn't name it, the pleasant aroma smelt familiar.

Returning with a Navajo print blanket folded in her arms, she caught him smiling.

"Why the big grin?"

"Oh, I couldn't help compare the polar differences between this place, and what's about to transpire less than a hundred yards across the road. Like an alternate universe."

"Alternate universe theory is one I could talk about for hours. Later, though. Where are we headed?"

Ben dropped the smile.

"Wherever you want to go," he said, hoping magnanimity might save him the indignity of admitting his forgetfulness.

"No dice. You pick," she said, edging past him, down the stairs and buckled in the passenger seat before he could reach the parking lot.

Key in the ignition, he paused, prepared to admit his failure, when Silk intervened.

"Say, doesn't your family have a pond?"

"Now how would you know about that?"

"People like to fish, hang out. Pretty soon word gets around."

"Guess I forgot all about Pop or Daddy pretty much running folks off from there every time we turned around. Most people seemed harmless enough. I do remember asking Daddy one time as to why we couldn't leave them be. His answer involved a word I'd never heard—liability. He tried to explain it in terms a kid could understand, saying if something bad happened to someone at the pond, that in a roundabout way we would be held accountable, and as a result, we could lose the farm."

He started the engine.

"Reckon I got it after that. Made more sense than thinking of Pop or Daddy acting out of meanness of selfishness."

"Sounds like you dad isn't all bad," Silk said.

Rather than address the topic, Ben vacantly stared ahead at nothing, flexing jaw muscles, and white-knuckle gripping the steering wheel. He drew in his lower lip, to bite on it.

"Why does that make you mad?" Silk asked.

"You don't know him. There's much I'm not sure I can bring myself to say out loud. Sinister shit. Shit that might make you question it being passed on to me."

Silk put her hand to his chin, forcing him to face her.

"You love your grandparents, right?"

"Sure, to whatever capability I have. At least in terms of how

I see love portrayed."

"A little obtuse of an answer. My point is, do you think your grandparents are flawless?"

"Oh, hell no!"

"Then why can't you extend that same latitude to your dad? Not perfect, just human, even though his flaws may be more obvious, or worse, by your rulebook."

Other than Dr. Mendel, for no other person on the planet, outside of Silk, would he have extended a receptive ear when discussing long-held opinions of his dad.

"More likely the Baptist rulebook, when you put it that way," he said after quick deliberation. "All those Bible stories that illustrate the consequences of breaking God's laws, they end up totally villainizing the sinner. As in, your culture worships idols, you all must be exterminated. Or, you lied about the offering you gave. Boom, drop dead on the spot as an example for all to see. No one speaking up and saying 'You fucked up majorly. Don't do it again.'"

"Sounds like you found your answer," she said.

"Maybe so. What disturbs me is realizing how I'm still applying narrow-minded judgments—black or white, right or wrong—after thinking I had outgrown that stupid shit."

"Baby steps are better than *no* steps," she said, in cheerful tone. "Your story, too, needs a villain, and from what you *have* told me, your dad made some bad decisions when put into situations he never expected. We all do. Heroes and public icons are no more than people whose screw-ups haven't come to light. Or, in some cases, their good deeds stack up greater than their worst. Pick some well-known whom you admire," she said.

"What?"

"Pick some respected public figure, and I can probably give you major dirt on them."

"Is that so?" he asked.

"Better believe it, from George Washington on through to Ghandi. The more revered they are, the greater probability of irreverent behavior in their lives. A personal theory of mine."

She chuckled before continuing.

"They aren't bad guys, simply imperfect humans. The problem I see, is that more than your dad, down deep, you think of yourself as the bad guy also."

Quieted by her words, he sat motionless.

"One bad guy at a time," he finally said. "I'm determined to make some better memories today."

"To the pond then!" she proclaimed, arm outstretched as if leading a charge.

BACKTRACKING DOWN RIVER ROAD, BEN stayed intent on Silk to avoid letting the Unolama drag him down.

Prior to reaching his grandparents' house, he turned left onto an unmarked route which the family had unimaginatively dubbed "The Pond Road." Mostly bare, sandy soil, the lack of gravel perhaps discouraged curiosity seekers from taking a tour.

"Never been down here," Silk said.

"This is a main artery for our apple operation. We've gotten by without a need for much maintenance what with all the heavy machinery and truck traffic keeping it compacted."

"Are we about to cross a creek?" she asked, looking ahead at the twisting line of brush and trash trees, out of place with productive land use.

"Yep, Blossom Creek, though technically it's nothing more than a rivulet off of the Unolama. It rejoins the main river close to the far corner of our property."

"You said *our* property. Thought you had given up your claim, so to speak."

"Old habits again. When you grow up in the thick of a family business, everything becomes *our*. Part of the acknowledgement that the workload is a shared enterprise, and by taking the 'our' approach, the ultimate success."

"You're proud of all this, aren't you?"

"Damn straight," he said. "The apple business has fed my family for multiple generations, and we in turn, feed the world. For instance, on an average year, we pick around 45,000 bushels of apples. That equates to around four-million apples for public consumption, all because of Bramley long hours and teamwork."

Her open-mouthed response delighted him.

"I had no idea."

"Few folks do," he said. "You're aware of America's love affair with the image of a small family farm, autumn colors in the background, a Holstein or two in the rolling, green pasture, fence-lined lane leading to the humble house and red barn?"

He hesitated for a response that didn't come.

"Hell, we get hordes of tourists around here, cameras in hand to take that picture back to their urban asphalt mazes. Well, that's what the farm is, nothing more than an image, a nostalgic backdrop that makes the city folks feel all warm and tingly. Not two people out of a hundred live on a farm these days. They know *nada* when it comes to farm life, as in nada damn inkling, no idea how dysfunctional the people in the barn, the house, the field can be."

"I'm going to stick with the Norman Rockwell image," she said. "Portrayals of people's best sides."

Socially stunted, though not to the point of oblivion, Ben ended the negative narrative, also realizing his penchant for cynical tangents, tangents which escalated in animation and volume. Whether they served to make his points, he cared little, simply taking pleasure in hurling opinionated salvos.

Ben contented himself with a recollection of farm life also unbeknownst to tourists—ever-present danger. Before he could read, Daddy had indulged Ben with rides on the Massey Ferguson tractor. Careful not to step on any pedals, or Daddy's feet, he would sit atop the fender, fingers gripping the underside of the stamped metal. Huge knobby tires rotating within inches of his unprotected hands could have permanently disabled Ben's fingers, or worse, had he let his mind wander for a second.

Elementary school classmates, those who didn't live on farms, the ones who boasted of spending after-school hours munching on potato chips in front of the television, had no hint how disciplined a young farmhand could be when necessity demanded.

Silk did not notice him smiling as she absorbed the fresh scenery. His amusement came from the horde of dark secrets, the questions of a child recognizing his proximity to death on a speeding tractor fender. Wondering, if he fell off, crushed to death under the spinning tire, would he find himself swiftly reunited with family members already in heaven? Or would he emerge in hell having lied?

Still waiting on that answer.

Don't share your gruesome side with Silk, Moses advised.

The adults in Ben's family had begun early with their warnings against accidents, often reciting the community collection of retold stories of death and dismemberment. Ben had kept caution at the edge of his mind when close to machinery or working with sharp tools, all of which stayed surgically sharp with Pop's penchant for using the electric grinding stone.

"That hoe'll take off a toe," he told Ben one day in the garden. Ben had shed his shoes while cutting weeds from between tomato plants, tired of dirt getting inside and scratching his un-socked feet.

Without realizing it, perhaps he had enjoyed the specter of danger. Maybe those other kids didn't have to work, but neither did they get to speed around acres of family land on a tractor with their dad.

SECONDS LATER THE BLACK SUV crossed the creek and came within sight of their destination. As proof, shards of twinkling light sprung from tiny openings in the dense foliage guarding the pond.

Skirting the sizable oval body, they watched cirrus cloud

formations reflect on the wavy surface. Ben guided the vehicle to his former favorite fishing spot. Without a word, he stopped, opened the door, and strode to the water's edge where cattails and willows gave way.

Several juvenile sunfish swirled around last spring's nesting areas, punchbowl-sized hollows in the muddy bottom.

Ben spoke to the water.

"Milestones . . . that's what we call the scared-as-hell times when we can look back on them from the passage of years, and within the safety of the present. These waters have captured thousands of sunsets since that secret fishing trip with Granny.

"More millstone than milestone, pulling me under."

The haunting declaration surfaced from some muddy bottom within him—a response to time and place. Intended for no one's hearing in particular, the ode demanded vocal tribute, reverential tribute to the sacredness of events witnessed.

"What are you talking about?" she asked the back of his head, having followed along behind her odd date.

Rather than sit, he more so collapsed onto the sloping bank, tan broom straw shooting up between his feet and legs, palms pushing against the ground behind him for support.

"Ever hear of the butterfly effect?" he asked, his voice detached.

"Sure, the idea that some simple, random act becomes the impetus for a succession of actions, and then the chain of reactions, when spread across time, and/or distance, can become significantly impactful."

Having proven her understanding on the subject, she hushed. His cue to speak passed. Silk filled the gap, lest he drift further.

"Any number of examples. Kid on a snowy mountaintop makes a large snowball, rolls it downhill. Picking up speed and size, it reaches the lift line at a ski lodge, crushing dozens of skiers."

She gave a short laugh at her cartoonish example. He didn't respond, so she kept talking.

"Or maybe a more subtle example. . . ."

He cut her off.

"This place marks the beginning of my misery," he said.

"What should have been a carefree summer, an eight-year-old's summer, I spent keeping an eye on James, my four-year-old baby brother. Momma dumped him on me, saying I was a big boy, quite responsible for my age. Of course that's pretty well true of any farm kid. Not that Mama had it anywhere near easy, working the farm as hard as Pop or Daddy did, and taking care of everything at home. I mean everything—writing paychecks out of that notebook-sized checkbook, cooking every meal, cleaning (which spoiled, only-child Daddy never did), grocery shopping, laundry, you name it.

"Still, it pissed me off. James curious as a cat, running about all day, and the questions, never-ending questions of me. Now, looking back, I should have been flattered by the admiration, but by summer's end, my frustration had come to a boil. Four years as the only grandchild, the sole focus of both sets of grandparents, and content with my own company, the big brother role came as a *big* sacrifice."

A pair of migrating mallards swooped in low, the mates landing on the far-left corner of the pond, close enough for the human intruders to see the sun reflect off the male's iridescent-green head. Ben, ever observant, took note.

"Same green as the Zebco reel on my rod from back then," he said.

"I determined to squeeze at least an ounce of fun out of that last Saturday, convincing Granny to take me fishing, only me. Not telling Mama, I timed it during our afternoon nap. She often fell asleep in bed with us, telling stories until we gave up the fight with slumber."

He closed his eyes and leaned his head back.

"The picture is clear as spring water. Me, sneaking out of bed, tiptoeing to the kitchen, seeing Granny's outline through the door—her voice, sweet as honey, as it slipped through the screen's tiny squares. 'Are you there, Ben?' she whispered, unable to see inside, what with the afternoon shade.

"I eased outside, stirring the flies perched on the crisscross wires, holding onto the handle until the door fully closed, to keep that long spring from snapping it shut with the usual *bang*.

"Granny had on her typical outfit—white blouse, tan slacks, and slip-on white tennis shoes, the ones with pointed toes. She already had her rod. I'd left mine propped against the house, by the back steps.

"Up the driveway, crossing the road (it was gravel back then, soaked with our burnt motor oil to cut the dust), I remember looking back over my shoulder, half expecting to see Mama in my bedroom window, hollering for me to get back to the house."

He drew a ragged breath and paused.

"Damn how I wish she had. My whole life could have been re-written in that instant."

"Then you might not be here with me, *this* instant," Silk said, a little too chipper for Ben's liking, peeved at the long list of bystanders who had casually dismissed his circumstances over the years.

After a long bite of his tongue, he continued.

"We dug some redworms from alongside the old chicken coop, until our recycled Van Camp's Pork and Beans can about overflowed. Then we walked down here, here, to this exact spot. Man, the fish were biting that day, so well that I wanted to set a family record, and beat Granny's total in the process.

"We pulled so many fish out of the water, this bank got soaked. Granny caught an especially big bluegill, and decided to keep it. As usual, we put the keepers on a stringer, floating in the water's edge until we got ready to go home.

"That's when her shoes lost traction on the wet grass. She pitched headfirst into the pond, rolled to her back, and tried to stand, fighting the slippery clay bottom. Each attempt at standing took her farther from the edge, into deeper water.

"I had no idea that she had never learned to swim. Had

Mama known, she would have never allowed James and me alone with Granny at the pond."

"Oh, Ben!" Silk said, hand to her mouth.

"Her yelling for help, nobody working in the orchard behind us, home a half-mile away, and the closest neighbors in those pea-sized houses you can see on the far sides of that field."

He pointed in the direction as proof of his words.

"In her panic, she backpedaled further out, thrashing rather than swimming. Until only her head remained above water. Seconds later, she went all the way under."

Tremor took over his voice.

"I reckon even a kid can recognize when options tumble down to one, so I shucked my shoes and shirt, and jumped in. Dogpaddling I could do, but no more.

"Forever is what it felt like before rising back up to the surface, though Granny had come back up when I did. Reckon her sinking got her scared enough to thrash a little harder, at least until I could reach her. Just about pulled me under until I talked to her.

"Talked? Hell, I had to have been screaming, telling her to hold onto my belt, knowing I needed both feet to kick if we were to make it out. And trouble on top of trouble, I'd almost worn myself out reaching her. Good thing I'm a natural floater, and good thing she's pint-sized. We stayed above water long enough for me to catch my breath.

"A few inches at a time, we moved, with me giving it everything my body could do. For at least the final half of the distance, I had my eyes closed, terrified we wouldn't make it. That I would give out."

He allowed himself a slight chuckle.

"No telling how long we laid flopped out on the bank, sucking air. I saw a hawk glide past, way overhead, and wondered what it might be making of the crazy folks on the ground, arms and legs spread wide. That stood out. And one additional detail. Other than the racket from our oxygen replenishment, lurking in the background I could hear waves lapping against the edge of the pond. Like listening to death's serenade."

Eager to learn more about the Unolama River and its significance in Ben's life? Subscribe to Southern Fried Karma's YouTube channel, Fugitive Views.

CHAPTER TWELVE

"If a man have a stubborn and rebellious son, which will not obey the voice of his father, or the voice of his mother, and that, when they have chastened him, will not harken unto them: Then shall his father and his mother lay hold on him, and bring him out unto the elders of his city, and unto the gate of his place; And they shall say unto the elders of his city, This our son is stubborn and rebellious, he will not obey our voice; he is a glutton and a drunkard. And all the men of his city shall stone him with stones, that he die: so shalt thou put evil away from among you; and all Israel shall hear, and fear."
—*Deuteronomy 21:18–21*

Silk crammed the remnants of their meal back into the picnic basket and shook the Navajo blanket clean. The popping sound attracted Ben's attention from a few yards away, where he stood staring at the glistening waters of the pond.

"Fantastic food," he said. "I didn't think anyone could beat Granny's cooking, though she's stuck with country fare. Yours, now that's right up there with the Grove Park Inn."

"A fan of Grove Park, are we?"

"Not only the food, the architecture, the view, the history. In fact, the lobby, with those walk-in-sized fireplaces, is one of my favorite places on earth," he said.

Silk stowed the basket in the rear of the SUV and returned to the blanket with the small cooler.

"Come join me for some champagne," she said.

His eyes had fixated back on the pond until the crunching rumble of ice and the clinking of crystal stemware dragged him back to her.

"Maybe a smackerel," he said, resuming his previous spot alongside her.

"Somebody's been watching Winnie the Pooh," she said.

"Guilty," he said. "Pooh Bear better not get between me and my honey. Pop has been keeping bees since before my time, and he's generous with honey, especially as repayment for the dangerous job of helping him transport the hives at bloom time. Few things, if any, can top Pop's sourwood honey. As for the champagne, I haven't tried alcohol with my latest meds. But I suppose a little can't hurt."

Not since the abrupt ending to his recounting of the near-drowning incident with Granny, had the subject been broached. Too pretty of a day, too rare of an occasion to risk marring it all, until the cawing of crows, circling above a distant stand of white pines, evoked enough foreboding to revisit the tale.

"What did your mom say? I mean about the accident, when you and Granny showed up back home?" Silk asked, lowering her line of sight to take a long pull of champagne.

"We didn't tell her. *I* didn't tell her."

"Why? What about your wet clothes?"

Unable to mask her shock, Silk's expression of bewilderment had frozen on her face.

"Okay," Ben said, in tacit acceptance of the storyteller's role.

"After . . ." He hesitated. "After, we waited until our clothes dried. On the walk back, Granny made me promise not to tell, reasoning how we would not get to go fishing together again, how Mama would be mad, and so on. She even threw in a recent sermon topic about loyalty, with the example of Jesus's disciples abandoning him when the Romans came to haul him off for crucifixion."

"How awful to lay all that on a little boy," Silk said.

"Oh, it gets worse. When we got within sight of the house, Mama sat waiting on the front porch and James played in the yard. When he saw our stringer of fish he commenced to begging to go fishing. He loved nothing better. So he's jumping around, asking over and over to go fishing, while Mama's boring a hole through me with her eyeballs. Meanwhile, Granny walks off to her house, leaving me to face the consequences alone."

Silk couldn't contain her abhorrence.

"Let me say, I know you're nuts about your grandmother, but that level of manipulation goes way beyond mere child abuse. That's screwing with someone's psyche. How could she do that? What did your mother say whenever you eventually got around to telling her what happened?"

"Other than Dr. Mendel, my therapist up in Boone, you're the only other person to hear the story."

"Oh, Ben!"

"Kinda funny how for all my religious zealotry, nearly drowning with Granny was as close as I ever came to a baptism."

Her arms had encircled his neck. He could feel her tears touch his throat where his shirt opened.

"What a load to carry around," she said.

"Tip of the Bramley iceberg."

150 RIPPLES

CHAPTER THIRTEEN

"Even so it is not the will of your Father which is in heaven, that one of these little ones should perish."
—*Matthew 18:14*

AUGUST 1978

Long dark eyelashes twitched as James opened a single brown eye, shifting it to Mama. She slept.

"How about you and I get some rest before Ben gets home from school?" she had said, fifteen minutes earlier.

He opened a second eye and raised his head a few inches above the pillow. She didn't move. He began to separate his body from the crumpled cowboy sheet, twisting around until both feet touched the floor. With no sign of her being alerted, he stood up straight, a smile forming. He had wasted no time implementing his plan, it being Ben's first day of returning to school, and only two days since Granny and Ben had gone fishing without taking him.

Crossing the room in a few breathless steps, he paused in the doorway for one last look back at his sleeping mother.

In the kitchen, he opened the refrigerator, looking for the container which held leftover worms from recent fishing trips. Not there, and no time to dig for any without getting spotted by Granny, Pop, or Daddy. However, on the middle shelf sat a bowl of whole-kernel corn from last night's supper. The fish in the pond liked red worms, but the trout in the Unolama River loved corn.

Opening a drawer to the right of the stove, he removed a plastic sandwich bag. Holding it open with one hand, James used the other to scoop corn from the bowl, dumping most of it into the bag.

Ignoring his mess, he slid a kitchen chair to the screen door, climbed up, and released the latch from the eyehook. Then he and the bag of corn stepped outside.

Frayed and stained play shoes waited for him on the concrete patio. The cool surface soothed his feet as he checked inside the shoes for spiders, like Granny had taught him.

"They may look like nothing more than shoes to you James, but to spiders, they look like a safe, dry home," she warned. "And spider bites aren't good for little boys."

No laces for him to have to struggle with as he slid on the right shoe, then the left. Peeking around the house corner, the sharp edge of the brickwork pushed into his cheek—no one up at the shed, or in Granny's yard. Moving to the opposite end of the house, the same held true, and his little legs motored across the yard, stopping to hide behind a large oak near the road.

On the other side of River Road, he continued to run in the open for as long as he dared. Then he paused under the cover of some apple-tree limbs. No one called out for him, so he continued in that stealthy manner, making his way down the length of the Pond Road and over the bridge.

On the hill above the pond, he heard the tractor. Pickers shouted to have their boxes moved as they progressed down the rows. A high bank protected him from their view. He ran beyond the sounds until he reached the last row of apples, drawing quick breaths through a widespread smile.

James had reached the strip of woods that snaked its way between the orchard and Unolama River. Within sight, an obvious trail cut through a rhododendron thicket. He followed it until reaching the familiar sycamore where his cane fishing pole stood propped against the flaking gray bark. The family's favorite fishing hole lay a few yards beyond the tree. There the churning water sounded like the bellowing of the angry giant in James's favorite book, *Jack and the Beanstalk*.

The shoes of the four-year old made shallow indentations in the wet sand at water's edge. With the sun's afternoon arc reduced by the high ridgeline on the opposite bank, long shadows already extended across the river, darkening much of it to black.

"That's where the biggest trout like to hide, in the shady spots," Pop had often told James and Ben.

At the end of his pole, several yards of five-pound-test line were wound to form a silvery cocoon. James raised the cane to a steep angle, rolling it clockwise in his hands, extending the line out to a manageable length. Setting it on the ground, he pulled the bag of corn from the back pocket of his cut-off blue jeans and carefully pushed two kernels over the barb of the hook.

When he swung his bait out over the river it plopped under the water, much too close to shore. Trying again, he managed to place it farther out, where it landed in the fast current, which stripped the corn and washed the empty hook ashore a short distance downstream. In the clear shallow water, he could see the corn float away. After several more attempts, it became apparent that he couldn't reach the slow eddies where trout awaited from shore.

Midstream stood the boulder from which the whole family liked to fish. A massive granite triangle, flat at the peak, it sloped sharply on the upstream and downstream sides. There the water's flow stymied as it turned back on its course, swirling to create slow pools, irresistible to trout tired of fighting the constant pull of the river. Mama, Daddy, and Pop had often used the trail of smaller stones that led from the bank to step their way out to the fishing rock. Granny wouldn't try it.

"They may make it look easy James," she had answered when he questioned her, "But those rocks are covered with slippery moss, and I ain't about to chance falling in."

The series of stones resembled the path that led from Granny's front porch to her driveway, nothing nearly as dangerous as she made it sound.

The first spacing between rocks was a short one. With a half-step James made it onto the closest one. The next gap was larger, though he had no problem. Looking into the water, it hardly seemed more than knee deep.

Third rock, and his soles slid on the slimy landing. Wobbling, he plunged the handle of his rod into the water, using the riverbed to steady himself. When he pulled the pole up, he didn't notice that most of its length was wet. On to rock four and rock five, which proved easy enough. Rock six, the one closest to his destination, was too far ahead for his short stride. No wonder Daddy picked him up and carried him across when the family came fishing.

Looking back at his starting point on the bank, he'd made great progress. One rock to go, then a half-step onto the boulder and good fishing would be his. He needed only to jump. Not even a best-jump-ever. Just an average jump like he'd done many times before, playing in the yard, jumping ditches along the fields.

"Mama'll be mad," he reasoned aloud, barely able to hear his voice over Unolama's roar. "Not so mad when I got fish."

He took the leap.

In a second of disbelief he watched the toe portion of his left foot touch the rock, knowing that not enough sole made contact to propel him forward. The reality flashed across neural connections milliseconds before he felt his center of gravity jerk him in reverse. His next thought registered the total immersion and loud gurgling as the river thrummed against his eardrums.

While being pushed forward, he simultaneously sank.

Though it was an eighty-degree summer day, the mountain river ran at a cold fifty degrees. James' extremities began to go numb before he could orient himself. His body responded automatically, restricting blood flow to protect its core.

When his back slammed into a boulder, a large bubble of air escaped him. Sharp pain ran up his spine as he slid off the rounded edge of the rock and continued downstream.

Eyes open, urgent to return to the surface, he couldn't distinguish up from down. His one chance: that the air remaining in his lungs would float him upward. Releasing his grip on the cane pole, he used both hands to claw at the water in the direction his body seemed to want to move.

Carbon dioxide levels in his bloodstream rose, urging him to exhale, though he remained below the surface. Flapping his arms, using up the last reserves of oxygen, his chest reached bursting point, overriding the fight to hold his breath a little longer, just as his head popped above the water's surface.

Glassy-eyed and unable to focus, he bobbed low in the flow, mouth at water level. With the current propelling him, and powerless to fight it, he tried rolling over onto his back. He'd heard Daddy preach the floating technique during swimming lessons at the pond.

James succeeded. Floating feet-first down the river, he fought for the air his body craved.

Through the blur of water and movement he could make out a twisted tree limb ahead, extending well out across the river. If his direction held true, he'd travel under it, where low-hanging branches offered an anchor.

Timing. One chance to make his grab as he seemed destined to meet up with the limb.

Closer. He was sure to pass under it.

Ready. He pulled his arms out of the water. It took huge effort, numbed from the cold. Grab. His arms flailed, slamming into the limb. *Grab. Grab. Grab*, his mind commanded.

Neither arm could respond in time, as the limb pushed them back over the top of his head.

Slower water along each bank slid by in his limited vision. But the central current had claimed him. Paddling proved useless. He amounted to an over-sized cork, short on buoyancy.

Both feet hit the next rock, pushing them to the river bottom. One became wedged in a narrow crevice where two boulders met.

Stuck. Before he could comprehend the danger, the water forced his body forward. Facedown, the urge to breathe became irresistible. Oxygen depleted, lungs on fire, and consciousness fading, the breath-hold barrier broke.

The Unolama rushed into his nose, causing him to cough. Vocal cords constricted, sealing the air tube, preventing water from entering his lungs. It bypassed to his stomach. Mercifully, he lost consciousness before cardiac arrest occurred.

Six minutes to brain death.

Tick. Tick. Tick.

But the water was cold enough to extend the window of rescue and recovery to possibly an hour.

CHAPTER FOURTEEN

"Withhold not correction from the child: for if thou beatest him with the rod, he shall not die."
—*Proverbs 23:13*

"Unforgiving land that exacts payment for the crops it brings. Hard to be a Bramley and not feel that way. Our family chain of heartbreak, linked in succession."

Silk used her shirttail to wipe a face wet with tears.

"You already know the conclusion to that tragedy. Front-page material in *The Clarion* newspaper for days," Ben said. "It took place the first day of third-grade year, the day I first saw you."

Without effort, Silk recalled the day.

"For me, much of that time is little more than a blur of cardboard boxes. My parents hadn't finished unpacking from our cross-country move," she said. "Other than the terror of a new school, what stands out is my mom's frantic search for my dresses and shoes, along with the box containing my school supplies."

Her slight laugh, combined with a corner of her shirt dabbing an eye, stirred Ben's heart. Pulling her back in, the intense hug he gave her was more for his benefit than hers.

"Navy blue dress with white trim," he said, speaking to the curls waving at the back of her head, "though guys aren't supposed to pay attention to fashion at that age. Any age, for that matter."

She leaned back to look him in the eye.

"Oh, my god! You've been holding onto that detail all these years?"

"My instant favorite of all your outfits and no great feat of recall when the girl in the dress is the most beautiful you've ever seen."

His last word still hanging midair, she kissed him, like no one before, like he wanted it to never end.

"Tell me more," she said, the look in her eyes suggestive of *more* to come.

Beneath her hands, she felt his body go rigid.

"The *after* school happening is the conclusion I meant, the one where I ran all the way home from the bus stop to share my exciting news, and found Granny at my parents' kitchen table, the phone at her elbow, its cord coiled up on the linoleum, and her expression—stoic, yet unable to mask bottomless dread.

"Holy fucking Moses! How many years did it take for me to erase the image of that expression every time I saw her face?"

The setting, the timing, and Silk's concern combined to make her the unlucky recipient of undue bottled-up hurt, yet she made no effort to stop him. Nor could he have left it untold, once uncorked.

"James missing. Half the community searching for him. Granny and me, knees to the floor, praying. Never more afraid, before *or since*. Surprisingly, I didn't suffer a brain aneurysm, bearing down with such prolonged intensity, trying to strike any possible bargain with God. All those hours in extreme panic mode, only to have Mama come flying through the screen door, screaming that her angel was dead. Soon followed by Daddy and Pop with their horrific recounting of the massive search, divers discovering his body underwater in the Unolama, and Mama clawing at the back doors of the departing ambulance, streaking it with her own blood."

He paused.

"That gigantic heap of ugliness, while my head yelled at me, 'Your fault. Your fault.'"

"How could you possibly have believed that?" Silk asked.

Ignoring her befuddled look, Ben uttered his verdict.

"I set it all in motion. He wouldn't have taken off on his own if I hadn't left him to go fishing with Granny."

When Silk started to speak again, he put up a trembling hand.

"Thanks. Don't bother. Plenty of others have logically exonerated me, attacking my assignment of blame from every possible angle. I have to free myself."

He forced a smile.

"You do realize I only served up the appetizer? Right?"

She nodded to the affirmative.

"Because that event became the catalyst for a succession of bad shit."

160 RIPPLES

Chapter Fifteen

"Behold, how good and how pleasant it is for brethren to dwell together in unity!"
—*Psalm 133:1*

Granny waited under the bus-stop holly tree shielding her face from the dust cloud which engulfed the entire intersection. Ben emerged from the growling vehicle, swatting his way through the airborne grit.

Maybe Mama sent Granny in her place.

He ran to receive the much-needed hug Granny freely offered, giving no thought to the faces watching from the bus windows.

"So, how did school go?"

Seeing her smile again fortified his own improved mood.

"Okay, I guess. Mrs. Hazelton said I've got a lot of catching up to do. Maybe Mama will help me with my homework."

"I don't know, Ben. Haven't seen her all day."

Her words settled with the falling dust.

"Say, if there's no rush on your homework, why don't you change into your work clothes and come over to my house for a snack? I promised Pop I'd be along directly to help pick up the drop apples. We've about got a full load ready to haul to the juice plant in Groverton. Maybe you could help us out until supper time."

"Won't Mama worry where I'm at?"

"I'll write a note for you to stick on the refrigerator. Ain't that where your dad and mom leave messages for one another?"

"Okay."

He didn't want to disappoint Granny by not going along, nor did he want to upset Mama *by* going along, who would then fuss at Daddy, who, in turn, would fuss at or spank him. The new lists of 'What to Do,' and 'What Not to Do' concerning family members left him pulled in a number of ways at once.

They're all giving me the nerves—his way of expressing the dilemma to himself, using phrasing he'd heard from the adults.

Maybe like Pop says, I got to 'go along, to get along.'

Granny veered toward the garden before they got within sight of the houses.

"I'm going to step down to the garden and pick some tomatoes for supper. I promised your Pop."

In Ben's ideal scenario, Mama would be waiting on the front porch. A few more strides up the road, he found disappointment.

No Mama inside either, at least no visible Mama, her bedroom door closed.

Before the most-awful day, doors in the house would be open wide. Cross breezes helped tame the summer heat in a house without the luxury of central air conditioning. In the winter, open doors allowed woodstove warmth to radiate to each chilly room.

The strange house of closed doors proclaimed a message: *There's been a change. There's been a change. What is the change? James is dead. James is dead.*

Hand on the knob of his bedroom door, he heard voices floating in through the back screen. Easing around the kitchen counter, the source remained unseen. Moving closer, his silhouette in the door opening betrayed him.

"James, I mean Ben, come on out here."

Daddy scratched at an unseen annoyance at the back of his neck.

"Sorry, Ben. We were just talking about James, and how our family's doing."

Seated beside Daddy at the picnic table was another man, wearing a blue suit, sweaty at the pits. His left arm draped across Daddy's shoulders—Reverend Shepard.

"Hey Ben. How you *been?*"

He laughed mildly at his own pun.

"No, really son, come over here and join your father and me. I stopped by to check on one of my favorite families in their time of need."

The Reverend turned to look at Daddy, pulling him in close with a linebacker arm. Daddy wore an uncomfortable smile.

Trying to keep his thoughts from showing, Ben took a seat on the picnic bench across from them.

Reverend Shepard looked directly at Ben.

"I had hoped to bring some comfort to your dear mother. It turns out she is not inclined to speak to me. Oh, don't get me wrong. I understand how the travails of this world can wear us down. You know the Devil uses life's difficulties to try and separate us from the love of God."

Ben half listened. He wondered if Granny would come looking for him.

"Ben, do you know the Lord?"

Snapping to attention, Ben guessed an answer was expected from him.

The Reverend repeated, "Do you know the Lord, son?"

Ben nodded *yes*, and uttered a semblance of affirmation.

"Daddy, I promised Pop I'd help him pick up apples this afternoon." Quick lie. "He's counting on me."

Ben rose to leave.

"Okay," Daddy managed.

"That sure is a fine boy the Lord's blessed you with, Jason."

Ben heard the compliment behind his back. Without taking time to change from his school clothes, he rushed around the corner of the house.

What's he doing here? Mama won't come out at all if she gets wind of him.

Angling across the yard toward Granny's house, he tried to squelch the uncomfortable encounter with thoughts of food.

Given the lunch at school and Mama's distraught menu of cold cereal and sour milk for breakfast, he found plenty of appetite for the hot snack Granny served. Her fried bologna, grits, and scrambled eggs improved his disposition, along with a cup of Maxwell House.

"Hadn't you best go home and change your clothes before we go out to work?"

"No," Ben answered. "It'll be alright."

"We best get to the orchard then. Your grandpa will be expecting us."

Pop will be expecting Mama too. Please be there, Mama. Don't make Pop and Granny mad. Don't make me have to lie again. Please, please, please be there.

Ben crossed the fingers on both hands as he walked along with Granny. He searched the ground for a four-leaf clover, needing all the luck he could get—luck that Mama had come out of her bedroom to help the rest of the family.

The flight patterns of grasshoppers taking off from the tall grass, typically entertaining, went ignored by a boy who felt that his luck had run thin, and maybe forever vanished.

Their business had been a family business for generations, with everyone expected to contribute long hours. Labor costs ran high, Ben had overheard. And he knew for sure that on Friday afternoons Daddy pulled money out of his pocket and handed it to the workers, or wrote them checks from the big binder that looked like a three-ring notebook.

He had heard Daddy tell Mama many times, "I swear, the pickers are making more money than we are." So instead of paying laborers to gather up and box apples left on the ground from the picking process, the Bramley family took on the menial chore themselves. The work resulted in a lot of back pain, sore knees, and thorn-poked fingers.

If any family member dared to openly gripe about the task, Pop would address the complaint with dollars and common sense. "The apples sent to the packing house pay the bills. The ones going to the juice plant put money in our pockets."

An unmistakable trail of orchard grass worn flat by tractor

tires directed Granny and Ben to their destination. His crossed fingers ached, but he wouldn't uncross them until he saw that Mama had joined Pop ahead of them.

She can whip me if she wants, wearing my school clothes to the orchard, but it'll be worth it to see her outside. Maybe she'll just fuss instead of spanking me in front of Pop and Granny.

To the right, he heard the muffled rumble of apples exiting picksacks, bumping their way into eighteen-bushel bin boxes. Nor could he mistake the whishing sound of errant apples zipping through the leaves, thumping on the ground. He winced a little at each individual *thump*, knowing that what should have been a high-dollar apple, had slipped from a picker's grasp, struck the ground, and bruised in the process, becoming a cheapened juice apple.

"That's the sound of money lost," he'd heard Pop say a gazillion times.

The host of crucial factors leading to a profitable crop had reached all the way down to touch Ben's eight-year-old thinking. Along with the adults, he fretted through the bloom season, with the fear of frost browning the delicate flowers, leaving them unable to produce fruit. He prayed for summer rains to stave off drought, then sweated through each answered prayer when towering, purple thunderheads threatened to dump hail and ruin an entire crop. Until the apples were picked, delivered to the packing house, and sold at a good price, his young nerves remained frayed from a business with frequent opportunity for failure.

As Granny and Ben closed in on Pop's pickup truck, a deep voice spoke from under a nearby tree.

"Grab a bucket and come join the fun."

"Are you trying to spook us Sam? Not a good idea for a man who will expect supper later."

"Aw, Sugar Babe, I was just funning you. I see you brought help."

He smiled at Ben from a narrow opening between two limbs. Incapable of further patience, Ben poked his head through the hedge of leaves to see if Mama worked alongside Pop.

"Just me in here, Ben. And I'm lonely. I could use the company of a hardworking grandson."

At least Pop didn't come right out and say it. Mama's not here. Mama's not going to be here. Not today. Maybe not whenever. She wouldn't let me get out of work. So why's she making us all work harder? It ain't fair.

On his hands and knees, scouring the grass for hidden fruit, Pop had a five-gallon bucket, dragging it along the ground as he filled it one apple at a time. Granny and Ben used smaller ten-quart galvanized buckets, the same ones used come winter for hand-spreading fertilizer and lime around the same trees.

It didn't escape Ben that the previous picking season five family members had worked under a tree, and the number was now reduced to three. The ugly difference urged him to flee. Ingrained loyalty kept him in place. He would not disappoint Pop nor Granny.

I can work faster. Make up for Mama and James.

With a fury, he began clawing at every apple in sight.

"Whoa there, boy." Pop watched Ben scrambling like the grass was on fire. "Slow and steady wins the race."

He slowed, a little, hoping to satisfy Pop, though still expending extra effort.

An approaching tractor rumbled closer—Daddy, on the red Massey Ferguson. The diesel smoke burned Ben's nose, though he liked the powerful odor, associating it with work getting done by his family.

Daddy's appearance should have meant the Reverend had left. Making sure, Ben pivoted all the way around, looking beneath the limbs for a set of legs in suit pants.

All clear.

Using heavy metal forks attached to its rear, the Massey Ferguson moved the juice apple box farther down the row. All business, Daddy didn't speak. The machine's tires stirred up a buzz of yellow jackets and hornets, feeding off the juice from squashed apples which littered the worn grass between the trees. Ben gave them plenty of space as he headed to the box to dump his bruised fruit.

Reckon how many buckets it takes to fill that box? Maybe a hundred I bet. Pop might know, but if I ask him, he might think I was whining.

The flying pests could be found in the box, as well as crawling on most of the apples under the trees. Ben had been stung enough to figure out how to keep from upsetting them, their presence unable to scare him or slow his progress.

When Pop declared it quitting time, Granny suggested Ben join them for supper.

"Your Daddy won't be in for a long time. He's got three loads to haul to the packing house this evening."

"I can't Granny. Mrs. Hazelton sent that work home for me to make up."

A half-lie—his teacher had told him to take his time.

The new Ben, out of necessity, had begun making excuses if it meant protecting himself and keeping the peace.

After saying his goodbyes, he ran for the house, with, *Don't upset Mama*, being the dominant message playing in his head. *Mama's already upset.* He paused in revelation on the back porch, hand on the screen-door handle. *What's the word Daddy uses? Don't upset Mama 'further.'*

Tiptoeing inside, he changed out of his school clothes and took a seat at the kitchen table, where he nibbled at a cold meal, alone.

MAMA'S ABSENCE KEPT THE LOSS of James raw and itching. She became a series of blurred snapshots, darting from her bedroom sanctum, shutting the bathroom door behind her. A few times, when Ben would have normally been outside, his presence indoors startled her.

A jumped rabbit, she would wordlessly rush for cover.

Suppers waited in pots on the stove without the cook in sight—family mealtime dissolved.

"Daddy, I'm tired of eating by myself. Why can't I eat supper at Granny's?"

"Because you live here, and your mother has food fixed for you. Do you want to upset her by not eating her food?"

"You always work late in the orchard. I'm by myself. The food is cold."

"What do you mean by yourself? Your mother's always here."

"She never comes out of the bedroom."

Ben awaited Daddy's wrath.

"Look Ben, I'm not going to say that things are alright around here. It *will* get better with time."

Seconds before Ben could blurt out the questions he burned to let fly—*Why don't I count, Daddy? James is gone, but I'm still here. What's wrong with me? Doesn't Mama love me?*—Daddy walked away, leaving the shadowed boy behind the screen door shaking at the thought of hearing the answers to his unspoken questions.

Returning to his bedroom, little knees pressed the hard floor. He prayed through folded hands, "God, please make me brave, like Daniel Boone."

BEN BEGAN PIECING TOGETHER THE new world on River Road.

Mama hides in the bedroom. Daddy hides in the orchard.

Nowhere could Ben hide. After school, with Daddy in the orchard, the silent house spooked Ben, especially his bedroom. He used it for sleeping, reverting to the Mickey Mouse night light, even though Daddy teased him about it. Also absent from bedtime prayers, Daddy hauled apples while Ben put himself to bed alone.

Maybe I'm the ghost, he told himself, on the many occasions when he got to feeling invisible.

Home alone, while not really alone, he sought the company of Pop and Granny, in spite of its own set of troubles.

Aware that eating next door fueled the silent war between Mama and Granny, Ben could not bring himself to resist, even when Mama's behavior made her the target of Granny's uncomfortable observations.

She took frequent opportunity to quiz Ben about his mother.

"How's your mama today, Ben?"

"She's fine," he lied. The lies and half-truths came easier since Granny taught him to keep things from Mama. He figured he could also keep a few things from Granny.

"Haven't seen her today," she pressed, her tone casual, her motivation unmistakably predatory. "And I couldn't help but notice your daddy left work early. Drove off in the car. Saw him come back, unloading groceries from it. Funny that your mama would slow down the harvesting, not getting out to help us all, then have him do the grocery shopping to boot."

She could act as if her words were harmless, meant only to pass the time, but to a boy who devoted all his willpower to making his world and those in it harmonious, Granny's charged language dropped like bombs on his plane of existence.

He had to defend Mama.

"Come to think of it, she said she had a bellyache."

Granny didn't acknowledge the fabrication. It hung in the sticky September evening air until it floated off to wherever lies reside.

Why can't Granny quit picking on Mama? An answer came. *If Mama would help us work, Granny would stop. We have to make money even with James dead. Don't Mama know that? Daddy ought to tell her. We're all working. She ought to too.*

That same debate he had daily, with nothing changing, other than his growing confusion and resentment.

Granny and Pop are old, and they still pick up juice apples. They don't use James as an excuse. And like Pop says, the apples are rotting faster than we can pick them up.

Was Mama taking advantage of them, as Granny all but said aloud? Was he mad at Mama? Mad at Granny? Mostly he was upset about the contradictions in his world. Lying awake at night, balling the sheet up with his fists, he tested the limits of the cotton fabric, straining against the terms the new life pressed upon him.

The source of all the change came down to one word—James.

Why did he have to run off and get drownded? Somebody would've taken him fishing. But he couldn't wait. Couldn't mind Mama. And see what it got us. It ain't never going to be the same, he concluded.

His frustration grew when he spoke in loud whispers to shadows on the ceiling. "Dang it, James! Why'd you have to do it?" Then, ashamed at his outburst of blaming James, another night would pass as he cried in his pillow to keep Mama from hearing, hoping for the deliverance of sleep.

Too soon, sleep brought no sanctuary as the nightmare began—the same basic details each occasion:

Ben hears the screen door slam shut. He jumps out of bed, searching for James, room by room—nowhere. Ben is yelling to no avail, stumbling forward at a dead run. His cries are being swallowed up by an increasing roar—the river. He comes to a halt at the bank, his shoes plowing up the wet sand at water's edge.

James is walking on a dam made of stacked stones, stretching out into the Unolama. Rocks are sliding and splashing into the water, the dam disintegrating into the rapids. Pole in one hand, the other arm outstretched to help his balance, James is tight-rope walking to the midpoint of the river where the current is most swift.

The dam has evaporated behind him, and the collapse has caught up to him. The dam is gone. Whitewater reaches James's knees, flipping his body into the air. Ben is screaming a protracted, 'NO!'

Less than a second. Less than a second and James is lost to the torrent.

Ben is yelling James's name. He wants to jump in, like he did to save Granny, but this isn't the same as the pond. This will cost his life. A question leaps to his mind, 'Do I love Granny more than James?'

Guilt joins the terror. He struggles to justify his inaction with the thought, 'I can't beat the river. I can't beat the river.' Instead, he runs downstream, hollering while watching for James to pop up. Faster, afraid that the rapids have surged James ahead of him. Along the bank, he stumbles in soft sand, slowing his progress, and then fearing he may have overrun James's momentum, he runs back upstream.

"James! James!" the name reverberating between the corridor of trees.

172 RIPPLES

Chapter Sixteen

"And further, by these, my son, be admonished: of making many books there is no end; and much study is a weariness of the flesh."
—*Ecclesiastes 12:12*

To quiet the telling of more misery, Silk kissed him as before. Rather than pull away, she held fast until he went pliant. Watching her lips part with each word, he heard her say, "If I remember correctly, when we set out from my parking lot, you said that you wanted to make some good memories today."

He was enveloped by her seductive voice, and she had undone the third button on her shirt before he comprehended the extent of memory making which she had in mind.

"How LONG HAVE I BEEN asleep?" he asked, quickly sitting up from the blanket. "And where are my clothes?"

"Worry not," Silk said. "You slept for an hour or so. Your clothes are folded, and right behind you. I made you a pillow while I stood guard. More like *sat* guard, while you rested."

He yanked on clothes with house-afire immediacy. A fully dressed Silk couldn't resist laughing.

"And now you are overcome with modesty?" she joked. "Why the need to hide that handsome body? With you asleep, I had plenty of time to commit to memory every bulging muscle. Flawlessly made."

"Wonderfully made," Ben said, correcting her.

"Is that so?" she asked.

"I will praise thee; for I am fearfully and wonderfully made . . . from Psalm 139, the fourteenth verse. Surprised you didn't know that. It's also in y'all's Bible, the Ketuvim, or Writings, section of the Tanakh."

"Fascinating," she said. "That might get you laid at Hebrew University in Jerusalem, with one of your undergrad students, but not around here so much, Rabbi Bramley."

"I know. Too much sharing," he said. "Hard to keep quiet after long spells with only a cat for company."

Both enjoyed the moment, Ben able to do so in spite of his proclivity to quote scripture.

Outwardly, Silk's evaluation of his body appeared correct. However, if judgment and self-talk translated into scars, every inch of Ben's back would be disfigured from flagellating his conscience with ingrained Bible commands. The former penitent Protestant had physically escaped church credos, but could not erase indoctrination.

Hitching his belt, he watched her staring at him.

"Easy for you to poke fun, dressed ahead of me."

"Would you prefer I take mine off again?" She reached to undo her pants.

"Yes. I mean, no," he said. "Are you in a rush to get back to the café?"

"Closed Sundays. My one day off."

"What about feeding that ready-made crowd across the highway from you? After they've been counted 'present' by God and neighbors they can't miss seeing the Abundance Café. They're set up for you like a hunting trip to the zoo."

"I tried that for a while, but something about watching a gang straight from church, in hats, heels, and suit clothes gobbling burgers and fries, totally turned my stomach. And public praying over my food became a competition, with longer thanks-givings evidently earning higher marks."

Her expression of disgust, combined with a guttural sound and shaking her hands as if to discard something vile, pre-empted debate on the matter. "Not worth the money."

"Where to, then?"

"What's that mean?" she asked.

"Pop and Granny will head straight to Mission Hospital, and they may be expecting me there, but I gave them no indication I was coming. So if you're free, let's make a day of it."

Silk's expression lost its carefree quality. She drew in a deep breath before speaking.

"Listen," she said. "Don't go making assumptions."

"Like what?" he asked, completely flummoxed.

"Like my time is yours. Like I'm going to follow along at your whim."

"Whoa! Where is this coming from? I *asked* you. Maybe without advance notice, but I did ask."

She dropped her head, and spoke looking down at the blanket.

"My defensiveness is because I don't want you thinking I'm easy pickings for you." Her head jerked up. "Because I'm not. Easy that is. Except with you."

"The thought never occurred to me," he said.

A distant cawing of crows underscored a long pause before she spoke again.

"It's not cricket, as the English would say, for me to go piling more guilt on top of the misery you've shared with me today, but I've got to tell you."

"Tell me what?"

"For all my bravado, all my Miss Independent persona, I'm damaged too."

Before he could speak, she stopped him.

"Let me finish this," she said. "When you're tallying up the casualties of your family tragedy, you need to include me." She rushed to add, "Nothing like you suffered, of course, but still deeply wounded. That cutting yourself off from me hurt. Still hurts. My only friend, my ally, shunned me, and until I left for college, no one else my age around here stepped up to fill that gap. Not your fault. Just my reality. And now, these many years later, I'm given this glimmer of hope."

She grasped both his hands and met his eyes. "Don't hurt me again, Ben Bramley."

As she searched his eyes for assurance, he struggled.

But before he could voice his jumbled thoughts, she found her answer articulated perfectly in the window which opened to reveal his soul.

When the words to his preamble finally came, they did so with the hesitancy of a first grader called upon to read aloud in class.

"I-want-to-say-the-right-thing-in-the-right-way-using-the-right-words-here," he began, verbalizing his stream of consciousness.

"You don't need to say any more," she said. "I got my answer."

"What?"

"More than any words, I saw you, the uncensored you. And now I know that you are incapable of willfully hurting me, or anyone."

"You got all that without me saying anything?"

"Without a doubt."

"Okay. Good for me, I guess. But I *was* going to tell you that I never trivialize anything you say, do, or stand for. My complete respect and admiration for you. I won't take advantage of you. And your willingness to let me back into your life is a precious gift, not to be taken lightly."

The return of her smile, her face aglow, shoved his collected darkness into a far corner.

"Truth is, since puberty I've fantasized about being intimate with you. That amounts to around twenty years of foreplay prior to consummation. Hardly a rush job, wouldn't you say? Maybe technically a first date, but a first date a mighty long time in coming. And my asking for more of your free time was because I don't want today to end."

"Well, when you put it that way," she said. "Truth is, I've wanted the same, and the realization not only matched, it exceeded the anticipation."

Her seductive smile morphed into a long kiss.

"If we're going anywhere, we have to stop by my place first, and let me change."

BEN PULLED INTO HIS GRANDPARENTS' driveway.

"Too early for church to have let out. I'll put a note on Granny's refrigerator door."

Leaving Silk in the Acura, he soon returned.

"What did you say on the note?"

"Out on the town with local hussy."

He couldn't escape grinning widely at his idea of humor.

"That's one," Silk said, holding up an index finger.

"One what?"

"The first one of only three strikes you get before you're out."

"Tough date," he said. "No, I kept the message generic—'Back later, Ben.'"

"Generic? More like vague and suspicious."

"Let's go with *all-purpose*, serving the situation no matter how their schedule plays out, or if we run late. No muss. No fuss. No details."

Backing out onto River Road, and soon zipping past the Unolama for the third time that morning, Ben's mind had shifted to Silk. The sight of her in the passenger seat, and the scent of fading perfume, enhanced the remembrance of her hands moving across his skin from before—soothing hands, that even in a short time had begun to restore flow to his constricted body.

"What is that perfume? It's new to me."

Before she could answer, he laughed roundly for no apparent reason.

"Good thing you can so easily amuse yourself, there. What's the inside joke?" she asked.

Through the hysterics he got out, "The 'it's new to me' part. Like I know any perfume by scent other than the White

Shoulders which Granny likes me to get for her. I am such a damn novice at much of the everyday stuff."

"Mine is in a lower price range than Granny's. It's called Skin Musk."

"Okay. Noted. What I do know is that most of them make my eyes water and nose run like a firehose. Yours is an earthy, sweet, primal, yet delicate sort of scent, delicious enough to eat. Makes me want to roll around in it, like one wild animal encountering the scent of another."

"Like a potential mate?" she asked, staring innocently out the side window.

At his silence, she turned to witness red-faced Ben, bursting out with her own laughter.

"Why do you take such delight in my embarrassment?" he asked.

"Because I've got a feeling that you've been riding the gravy train where teasing and sarcasm are involved, as in being the dish-er, not the dish-ee."

She had her left hand on his shoulder.

"That train has run out of track when you're around me."

Feeling the warmth of her hand through his green-checked shirt, Ben decided, *What's a little embarrassment, if it means feeling her touch?*

Before making the turn into the café parking lot, Silk suggested, "Pull around back in case your folks get out and recognize your vehicle. It's probably already the talk of the town. We can go in through the rear door of the restaurant."

"Brilliant *and* beautiful," Ben said.

She squeezed his hand and smiled before hopping out, the two of them soon inside and upstairs.

"Where are we going?" she asked. "So I know how to dress."

"Maybe I said you pick. Maybe I didn't. Either way, I have a destination in mind that dictates casual wear."

"Casual how? Slacks? Jeans? Skirt?"

"I thought I had nailed it with the *casual* nomenclature."

He paused, returning her questioning look. "You see how I'm dressed."

"Yeah. Izod jeans. Ralph Lauren shirt. Topsiders. Just tell me where were going."

"Not going to happen. My first opportunity to surprise a woman my own age and I will not be deprived of the moment."

"Understand then, what you get is what you get."

The final words trailed behind as she moved to get ready.

"What I just got was a semantically null sentence," he yelled toward her bedroom, seconds before the sound of shower water.

Man how I would love to strip down and join her for some shower sex. Be bold and seize the day? Be balanced and exhibit restraint?

The back-and-forth debate continued. The final vote called for boldness. Head down and bulling forward, he nearly bowled her over as she appeared, dressed, and toweling her head.

"Where were you headed?" she asked.

Lacking a quick lie, he stood stupefied, silent, and revisiting red-faced.

Working the towel into each ear, she intuited, "Ah, I think I get it. Smooth, but too slow."

She placed cooling hands against his cheeks and jaw, applying a quick kiss. "Is it hot in here? Or is it just you?" she joked, her enthusiastic smile inches close.

"Your laughter is music to me," he said.

Silk encircled him. "You are the kindest man."

EN ROUTE TO THE MYSTERY location, he capitulated minimally by answering a few questions—though little was revealed.

Silk entertained herself with the discovery of his "Stand-Bys" CD in the dashboard player. The black Sharpie title had faded from frequent use.

"Let's take a listen to hermit man's musical inspiration," she said.

When "Losing My Religion" began playing, she nodded in agreement. "Makes sense."

Deeper down, when Barry Manilow's "Copa Cabana" began, she lost all composure, releasing her seatbelt in order to lean forward with intense exuberance.

"You're making a strong case for my *hermit man* lifestyle," he said.

Their speed reduced as the SUV angled up an exit ramp off of Interstate 26, diverting her attention as to their whereabouts. Clustered convenience stores and corporate fast-food joints offered no clues.

Frustrated over her inability to guess his chosen location, she commented, "Must think you're some kind of Boy Scout, that 'Always Be Prepared' motto they love."

"I suppose that their organization has it merits." He paused to allow her to get the pun. If she did, she ignored it. "Country boys, particularly farm boys, chew up and spit out Boy Scouts like Skoal dipping tobacco. I prefer the wisdom of our thirteenth president, 'I will prepare and my opportunity will come.'"

With the final word, he turned left into a graveled parking lot abounding with cars. The sign above the door said *Crystal Visions*, hand-painted in crystalline-shaped script. Silk had to crane her neck to read it through the tinted portion of the windshield.

"Wait a minute. I think I've heard of this. Remind me."

"This is Western North Carolina's version of Mecca, for all things *woo-woo*, to use your parlance."

"What the holy hell?" She literally bounced in her seat. "How did you find this?"

"You're not the only one who knows their way around a search engine. Type *woo-woo books* into the query bar, and voila!" He extended both arms, presenting his find. "Thank you Groverton Library, and of course, the county's taxpayers."

"Why are we waiting?" she asked.

"This is conditional," he said to her quizzical face, "like my relationship with broccoli."

She's not laughing. Cut the attempt at cuteness.

"You sprang for brunch, and champagne to boot. Now, we are going to step inside that store, and buy absolutely everything that delights your heart."

"But. . . ."

"And a shapely one it is, may I say?" he said, satisfied to turn the squirm on her. "Save your but's, and please do not force me to whip out my American Express Gold Card in a tacky display of my financial prowess."

Her skeptical look compelled him to ask, "Deal?"

"Deal," she said, with noticeable reluctance.

"Wait," he said, grabbing the crook of her arm, already halfway out the door. "This isn't some macho, misogynist move here. Nor a commentary on you. Hell, I'm a goddamn feminist, if we're going with labels. It's so seldom I get to use my money for anyone else's benefit. Not showing off. Not buying affection. Have I left out any other possible misunderstandings?"

"You thoroughly state your case. This discomfort is mine, classic PSYCH 101 material—unfamiliarity and awkwardness with being a recipient."

"So we're cool?" he asked, nodding his head subconsciously, determined not to come across as a colossal ass.

"We're cool," she said. "I hope they have gigantic shopping carts."

THE ACURA'S BACK END LOADED with books aplenty and Buddhas of numerous sizes, body types, poses, and colors, Ben pulled into a nearby Bojangles' drive-through line.

"Now you get to enjoy *my* best attempt at cooking," he said.

"Any reason why we can't eat inside, rather than grease up your new car?" Silk asked.

Before he could answer she added, "It's that people phobia

thing of yours isn't it? Exceeded recommended exposure to human life forms back at the bookstore. Right?"

"You have to agree, life wouldn't suck so much without all the damn people."

"Well."

"What do you mean, *well?* Have you forgotten what shits those grade-school kids were to you and me?"

Silk Mayer, third grader, had stood as Ben's singular point of grace. With Abundance School having one class per grade, the two enjoyed entire days together.

Silk had accepted the role of outsider easily. Being Jewish in a nest of Southern Baptists automatically marked her. Both parents had spoken often of their people's necessary social adaptations as soon as she could begin to comprehend.

"What's Jewish?" Ben had asked her at recess. The two stood alone alongside the ladder leading up to the big slide.

"Nothing like everybody else around here, I can tell you that. For starters, we don't believe in Jesus."

"Don't believe in Jesus," he had said excitedly, looking around for any audience. "Don't believe in Jesus?" he asked again, in a close whisper.

"And lots of other stuff," she said. "Does that make you not want to be my friend?"

He had studied on that question, in the moment, and for many thereafter.

"Everybody I know believes in Jesus—everybody in school, all my family, everyone around here. But the way they're treating me, treating you, I might as well be Jewish too."

"I could teach you," she interjected.

He had twisted about, unable to look her in the eye, his deepest emotions having risen.

"What I mean is, I ain't got any other friends," he admitted. "Why would I go and get rid of the only one I got?"

She threw her arms around his neck and kissed a cheek. Immediately he turned, checking for witnesses.

They'll tease me even more, now.

"You're my best friend forever," Silk said.

The feelings he had fought to push down, threatened to spill out.

"Just don't kiss me no more."

"REMEMBER HOW JEFF TURLOCK DECIDED that you were his girlfriend?" Ben asked.

"Without ever having spoken to me," Silk said. "Yeah, I remember him being one of those guys who lacked the courtesy to remember or call anyone by name. 'Red' he called you, until after that day by the monkey bars. Later he avoided you like it was his job."

"Most of that incident didn't register. Reckon I went some kind of berserk."

"Berserk, and then some," she said. "You tried to ignore him, until he got up in your face, and you landed one to his jaw." Hesitating, she continued. "That probably would have ended the matter, him laid out on the ground. That's when you threw yourself on top of him, and used his face like a tether ball."

Both of them let those disturbing facts settle in for a moment.

"After that first punch, my next fully aware moment didn't come until being in the school nurse's office, her tending a crying, bloodied Jeff Turlock. Must have been Mrs. Hazelton who jarred me back to reality, pouring that damned stinging mercurochrome on my knuckles, gashed by Turlock's teeth."

Ben looked her straight in the eyes, not seeking clemency or sympathy, simply making his point clear.

"He didn't figure, along with everybody else, that I had bottled up a devil's dose of rage."

The unburdening process had reached therapeutic levels due to his trust and newfound closeness with Silk.

"You know, not even a paddling for me. Either they all knew about Turlock's bullying, or they felt sorry for me on account of James. Another case of an adult ignoring my glaring problem, rather than offering real help."

"I do know how that fight earned Ben Bramley a reputation as the fellow to beat, and that afterward, you practically had boys lining up, trying to prove their mettle against you—even some quite a bit older than us."

Mixed emotions surged through Ben, disinclined to revisit childhood events that directly related to what he had termed, "that most-awful day." Pop and Granny had ushered him out the screen door, scurrying to shield him, while Mama's tormented wailing faded behind them.

"Reckon I released frustration by pummeling school mates. I can see it now in light of our longstanding Southern practices. We go to extremes to avoid dealings which pose the potential for public stigma. Don't discuss taboo matters, especially mental illness or emotional imbalances. Preserve the family name and all that posturing nonsense. Better to beat up kids at school than get a mental health diagnosis and risk having the entire community learn that your child is going to a shrink, maybe even taking happy pills."

Carrot-colored curls swayed with his head's disgust at ingrained stupidity.

His simple admission lacked defensiveness or justification. It also lacked school-wide views on his emotional stability. Silk didn't offer to fill in the gaps.

"What you probably don't know about is me getting called out of class to meet with the county's school psychologist. She had a bunch of questions about home life, my anger issues, how I felt about James's death. Most answers, I lied. Telling the truth to any question would have made the mess worse."

"How could you know that?" Silk asked.

"Easy. She smelled like a lie."

Silk laughed.

"Really. Think about it. Here's this stranger, with an imitation I-care-about-you expression, going through the motions, checking off the boxes: 'Would you say that your parents spend enough time with you?', 'Do you sleep through the night?', 'Any bad dreams?'

"Two sessions with Miss Mental Health Lady, and I was declared fit to move about unsupervised in public—NO DANGER TO HIMSELF OR OTHERS. Big red letters at the bottom of the last page of my file. Signed. Dated. Hell, go ahead and notarize it."

"Now you're making stuff up," she said.

"Maybe, but you have to admit, the sympathy I had been getting flipped to treating me like I had cooties after the mess with Mama and Reverend Shepard, then Daddy's shenanigans."

What Ben didn't deduce was that many parents had warned their children away from him. Around community supper tables, the Bramley family shortcomings came up often. Mothers determined that such un-Christian-like behavior not jump off onto their own brood.

On that topic, Silk knew much more than Ben.

"Thank you for choosing Bojangles'. How may I help you?"

"Yeah," Silk said before ordering. "I guess they were some brat-ass monsters."

CHAPTER SEVENTEEN

"And the LORD said unto Cain, Where is Abel thy brother? And he said, I know not: Am I my brother's keeper? And he said, What hast thou done? the voice of thy brother's blood crieth unto me from the ground. And now art thou cursed from the earth, which hath opened her mouth to receive thy brother's blood from thy hand; When thou tillest the ground, it shall not henceforth yield unto thee her strength; a fugitive and a vagabond shalt thou be in the earth. And Cain said unto the LORD, My punishment is greater than I can bear."
—Genesis 4:9–13

"How do you plan to eat fried chicken and drive?" Silk asked.

"Hard to resist the temptation, but I can hang on for ten minutes or so," Ben said. Back on the interstate, the SUV weaved in and out of Sunday tourist traffic. "By the way, I have on many an occasion made a major dent in a bucket of chicken while driving. Back in the old Chevy pickup days."

"Plan on stopping at the rest area up ahead? Got in mind a romantic concrete table with a view of the tractor-trailer pullover lane?" she asked.

"Something like that," he said.

Minutes later they flew past the busy rest area to take the next exit.

"Somebody enjoys being in control a little too much," Silk said.

"My guess is that it's more like two somebodies, based on the reaction from the passenger side. Grown accustomed to being in the driver seat, Miss Mayer?"

"That's Ms. Mayer, as any true feminist would know. And yes, Ben Bramley, man of mystery, I *have* had to take the wheel

... to a much greater extent since Dad's death."

"What? How did I miss that?"

"You didn't. I saw no point in heaping more on you. Two years ago, the congestive heart failure exacted its toll. The upside—if you call it that—was that his illness gave Mom time to grasp her coming reality.

"Maybe I should have moved back in with her, but after the first couple of months following his passing, and lots of mother-daughter time, she decided to live alone." Silk paused. "She told me, 'I'll not be penalizing you for my misfortune.'"

When Silk said no more, a glance from Ben revealed her right hand, crushing the armrest opening. Allowing for a moment of respectful silence, he fumbled for words in response.

"I don't know what to say. *Sorry* doesn't cut it. No one your age should have to lose a loving parent."

A single tear tracked down her left cheek for him to see. No more did she allow, though she avoided the risk of speaking. Such evident emotional turmoil compelled Ben to fill the quiet quarters, concerned for her and his own awkwardness.

"Since I got back, I've wasted no opportunity to trash my dad, and that subject matter turns out to be ill timed and insensitive. You should have shut me down from grinding salt into your wounds."

Sensible enough to not push further when she failed to respond, he drove well beyond the Asheville Airport terminal and took the first right-hand turn. A few-hundred yards ahead, he slowed, searching until he spotted his target.

A semblance of a road penetrated the trees bordering the highway. Following the route for no more than a minute of bumpiness, the woods disappeared. Before them lay the clear expanse of airport runways.

"This is why I asked you to leave the blanket in the back," he said. "Picnic 2.0."

He finished the sentence a second ahead of a departing Boeing 727. The roaring engines eliminated all possibility of communication until the plane became airborne, and several-hundred yards distant, fading into the blueness.

"There must be a story."

Relieved by her return to the present, Ben responded, "There's always a story. This one is about a teenager with a driver's license, lying about his whereabouts. Not researching for a paper at the Pack Square Library—in fact, there is no paper. Instead, he's here, stretched out in the bed of a pickup, watching planes come and go. The ones taking off are focal to his escape plans. And if he can push enough of the ugly memories aside for a moment, he can see himself riding high, having a window seat, from which he looks down at that truck, only difference being, there's no longer anyone in the back of it."

CHAPTER EIGHTEEN

"For whom the Lord loveth he chasteneth, and scourgeth every son whom he receiveth."
—Hebrews 12:6

With the last of Silk's bookstore purchases upstairs, the two of them stood in her living room, hands on hips, both perspiring from carting heavy loads.

Shifting a hand to fan her face, Silk acknowledged, "I seem to be glistening a bit. Perhaps you'll get a second chance at that shower, although it's rather small in there. We would have to stay close together."

The most desirable woman in my world, my lifelong fantasy, stands before me inviting to get naked together in her shower, to have sex with her for the second time today. My life is unrecognizable at this point.

"Silk . . . without any exaggeration, today is the best day of my life. Magical." He had taken both her hands in his. "Not a single other comes close, except maybe our first time on the playground. You introduced yourself, 'Hi,' you said. Not *hey*, like us locals. 'I'm Silk. Like the cloth.' You probably thought this country kid had no clue, but I knew. I knew from when Mama drug me along to the fabric store in Groverton. Those bolts of gorgeous silk begged me to touch them, a different, special fabric. Paltry, however, compared to the skin my hands traced today."

Though little of the evening's last light reached inside her apartment, the flickering candles she had lit to enshrine her new Buddhas glimmered in the tears pooling up along her lower eyelids.

"Your suggestion, the shower, immediately had my blood surging."

She smiled gently, and leaned back, pulling him in the direction.

"Nothing more I would rather do."

More of her body weight went into directing him.

He hadn't budged.

"A million thanks. No. . . . I can't believe I'm saying that, though with good reason."

She had ceased trying to force him.

"If I stay here another minute, there's a good chance I might never leave. And like you said the other night, we're no longer kids on that playground. Adult life with adult responsibilities to family, no matter how sucky or hard. Today, however . . . today you showed me a world which I had given up on ever experiencing."

Shattered by his own words, he reached out, burying his face in her hair, lest she see him lose control.

"I understand *alone*, maybe better than you realize." On tiptoe to rest her chin above his strong shoulder, she continued. "I'm surrounded by people every day, staff, customers, yet I feel so terribly alone. You get that? Right?"

"I do. It's never about the numbers." He sniffled. "A single, like-minded other can provide more than a roomful of well-wishers," Ben said, thinking back to the community members that paraded through Pop and Granny's house following the drowning of James. How *he* felt like the invisible ghost, with no one noticing him, how his parents had shoved him off onto his grandparents while Mama caterwauled for days next door, how they barred him from the funeral, how he had felt invisible ever since the death of his brother.

DURING THE RETURN TO HIS grandparents', Ben thought about his limited sexual experiences, the list of those that could also be cataloged as part of a *relationship* consisting of a single name— Amber. She also majored in computer programming at Duke. They had met freshman year, before his troubles levelled out. Her peanut-farm background appealed to him as much as their shared computer interests. Most weekends they ended up in bed when Ben's roommate, Jake, went home to Highpoint.

On one of those occasions, Ben woke up, disoriented, standing on the bed. In quick sentences Amber explained as she rushed to get dressed. His night-terror screaming had jolted her awake. Non-stop screaming, and based on the commotion and loud complaints from the dormitory hallway, he had cut loose with some serious decibels. The incident ended their intimate relationship, making even friendship sketchy.

Recollections of Amber's stricken face, led to his assessment of being unfit for female companionship, an assessment later extended to companionship in general. By design, his work could be done from home, allowing him to become a shadow man in a world of limited acquaintances.

"What am I doing?" he hollered above the October air, rushing in all four fully opened windows. The faster he drove, the more sensational the sting of numbness, spreading across his face and hands, became. Numb was a mindset with which he could relate. Numb had served him well throughout the years.

CHAPTER NINETEEN

"Judge not, that ye be not judged."
—Matthew 7:1

"Don't forget to stop at the grocery on the way home, and get me two pounds of butter. That is, if you still want me to make you that shortbread."

"Why not get it after I pick you up from the hospital?" Ben asked Granny.

"It has to have time to soften, not melt, to blend it in with the other ingredients. So don't put it in the refrigerator when you get home with it. Leave it set out."

A teenage Ben, out on one of his solo forays, had discovered that the Winn-Dixie in Groverton sold rotisserie chickens, hot and ready to eat. And a whole one about satisfied his farm-hand appetite.

While looking for something sweet to chase the chicken, his eyes had fallen upon a display of bright-red wrappers, unusually small packaging compared to the other bags and trays of cookies on the same aisle.

Must be something special, he had decided, and his inclination proved correct once he had tasted Walker Shortbread. Special, for miles, but pricey. Thus began his search for a recipe to match the few ingredients listed on the back.

Granny's culinary genius found little challenge in duplicating the Scottish-made goodies. She even began saving other cookie tins to refill them with her shortbread, presenting at least one each time she and Pop met up with Ben.

Across the breakfast table, Pop also had an assignment for Ben.

"Right after you drop the first load at the packing house, gas up the truck. That fuel gauge can't be trusted."

"Got it," Ben said.

Pop reached a hand back, signifying he sought his wallet.

"Don't worry. Gas is on me today," Ben said, quickly adding, "Y'all have been feeding me like company for days. I owe you. Groceries too."

"Mighty generous of you," Pop said, though he would have likely refused had Ben not framed the offer in certain words.

"When it comes to generosity, where do you reckon I learned it?"

Pop sat his coffee down to face Ben, a trace of steam on the lower section of his glasses.

Ben continued. "Every summer visit, from friends or family, none of them leaving without grocery bags heaped with whatever our garden had ready. Same with apples, even when those folks only came visiting at harvest time, their motives clear as a fall day. And what about customers from every corner, other states, pulling up to the shed for a bushel, or a trunk load? They couldn't leave what you didn't give them extra. Yes, sir, y'all taught me well."

To see Pop's face beaming gave Ben's day an extra-hopeful start.

"It's better to give, than to receive. That came straight from Jesus," Pop said. "Does my old heart good, knowing you carry on that lesson. 'Course, we wouldn't figure on anything less from the finest grandson around."

The weight of that title, *finest grandson*, conflicted with Ben's self-assessment. Overcome with unworthiness, he lowered his eyes, piecing together a realistic response.

"Pop," he said, beginning slowly, "another big lesson you taught me was to always do my best, no matter how inconvenient it might be." The thought incomplete, Ben took his time to expound upon it. "What I want you to understand, is that no matter how it may look, no matter how my words, my actions, my absence are giving evidence to the contrary, every minute of every day, I am one-hundred percent doing the absolute best I can, fighting all the way. Unfortunately, that effort doesn't always materialize in ways other people want it to appear, or in ways which they can recognize."

Only then could he look up, hoping, searching for any sign of recognition and acceptance from Pop.

"We know that, your Granny and me. Never a doubt about it, son."

ON THE DRIVE TO THE hospital, Granny interrogated Ben regarding his brunch date with Silk.

"We haven't set a wedding date yet. However, we have picked out our colors."

Ben's overt sarcasm, on many occasions, had saved him the outright disrespect of telling her to shut up.

Her last words, before closing the vehicle door and heading toward the ICU—"Don't forget the butter, and don't forget to leave it out on the kitchen counter to soften."—reminded Ben that he had indeed forgotten.

THE NECESSITY OF AN EXTRA stop led Ben to forego his usual morning visit to the Groverton Public Library.

"Hope I'm not sacrificing a chance to see Silk. And how does one follow up on the perfection of yesterday? Maybe she'll take the lead on that one. Save me the risk of over-thinking myself into screwing up."

Searching for the quickest locale for butter on the way back to work with Pop, found Ben outside the Winn-Dixie Grocery store. Grabbing a cart from the rack in the parking lot, he looked up at the faded giant sign.

"Man, this place is ancient!" And in that instant he froze. "Winn-Dixie day," he said, dazed.

The reference—his own—he had long ago attached to Mama's first venture in public following weeks of secluded grieving. Little more than a shadow at home. Never present for mealtime with Ben. No churchgoing. No family togetherness.

"Ben, will you get us a shopping cart?"

The voice in his mind is hers, but she looks different, wearing a scarf on her head, and sunglasses which she keeps on inside the store.

He follows her to the second aisle, with bagged candy on one side and chips on the other, selecting a tray of Reese's Cups, Ben's favorite. That's when they hear a vocal exchange from around the corner, on aisle three.

A strident voice in a know-it-all tone is saying, "Well, if anybody asks me, what kind of a mother lets a four-year old slip out of the house?"

Mama freezes. Her hand holds the candy mid-air, and she's eavesdropping in spite of the threat.

Then a second voice affirms, "In my day, I never took my eyes off the children. Not for a single, solitary second."

"Too young to know better, or too selfish to care, I suppose," the first voice adds. "Now that poor child's blood is on her hands, God forgive her."

At those final words, a loud *splat* launches Ben's body backward. His wide eyes fixate on the tray of candy, abandoned on the glossy floor. Mama has his hand, dragging him out of the store.

No groceries. No Reese's Cups. Homeward bound, she sheds not a single tear, instead, drawing in breath like all the air has gone out of the world.

No BUTTER. No shortbread, on River Road.

CHAPTER TWENTY

"For he shall give his angels charge over thee, to keep thee in all thy ways. For they shall bear thee up in their hands, lest thou dash thy foot against a stone."
—Psalm 91:11–12

Despite expectations of an abbreviated stay in Abundance, his sojourn reached day eight, with routine regularity settling in, as if to stay. Daddy's ICU limbo fueled the situation. The singular abbreviated aspect of the marathon-like visit applied to Ben's running, ironically cut short. Apple harvesting work, which often extended late into the night, and two trips daily chauffeuring Granny back and forth to Mission Hospital, accounted for much of each twenty-four hour period, leaving little time for his mental health regimen.

The blast of Winn-Dixie Day images dictated imperative need for feet-on-pavement time, but Pop awaited on the farm.

"Don't forget to gas her up," he yelled as Ben inched the loaded truck forward.

What few Rome Beauties remained would be picked complete that day, leaving a small number of Arkansas Blacks and Limbertwigs left to harvest. Neither of those varieties had a niche in the commercial market, leaving them to be stored in the big shed for individual sales to those repeat customers who craved the particular qualities of each.

At the packing house, competition for waiting-line positions had dwindled with the season skidding toward a halt. Unloaded swiftly, Ben aimed the flatbed toward Uncle Stan's gas station, pulling barely off the road and up to a pump likely older than himself.

In full-service fashion, Uncle Stan stepped from the shadow

of the store's open door, prepared to check oil and windshield wipers while the fill-up took place.

"Whoa there! How the heck are you, nephew?"

Stan's grease-stained hands made an audible *thwack* sound against Ben's back in a bear-hug-worthy reunion. Two years younger than Ben's mother, his resemblance to her was profound, starting with the carrot hair and emerald eyes, the same uncommon DNA prevalent in Ben.

"Heard you was back in these parts. Sorry about your dad, and all. Still think the world of Sam and Lily. We keep up. They wouldn't have let you skip town without telling me. Just figured you had a plateful without an old uncle interfering."

"You couldn't interfere if you tried. One of the few bright spots around here, for me," Ben said, in truth, and grinning widely.

When cancer claimed Grandma Etter, during Ben's first-grade year, Grandpa Etter chose to divorce himself of the family farm and all local reminders, fleeing to early retirement in Florida. Stan and Mama stayed on, he at his dream job, the extra bay of the station used for rebuilding classic cars. He still occupied the family home, while Mama and the Bramleys took over the Etter orchard.

"What'll you have?" Stan asked, turning to business.

"Fill her up, please, sir," Ben said, checking his wallet and jeans pockets for cash.

"Reckon I should go electronic," Stan said, "but long as I can walk out here, I'll keep pumping by hand. Otherwise I wouldn't get to visit with anyone. By that, I mean all the tourists, not the same tired-faced residents."

He laughed at himself.

"Only ATM we got is over there at the end of the café," he said, likely for the ten-thousandth time, though the first to his nephew.

"Back in a minute," Ben said over his shoulder, one foot already across the road's white-striped borderline.

He smiled at the continued absence of a wedding ring on Stan's hand, remembering his uncle's comment on the topic, from who knew when: "Reckon they's not a female around here who appreciates the pleasing aroma of forty-weight burnt motor oil, smeared on greasy coveralls."

Stan's bachelorhood wasn't all that set him apart in a sea of mundane folks. With no progeny from him, the Etter name—around since the founding of Abundance—would cease to appear on any new gravestones once he departed. And like Ben, he opted out of church attendance permanently, content with his own understanding—a philosophy which needed no weekly prodding, nor required attendance.

"I'm home-churched," he enjoyed telling the nosiest of the local lot. "God and me, we've got an arrangement."

For all his gregariousness, Stan maintained personal privacy. Not a soul in Abundance new of his love for poetry, both reading and writing it. The shock of having numerous of his pieces published in various poetry anthologies would have reverberated for years of gossip fodder, maybe adding further to the false rumor that he was gay—rather, "an old queer"—in a community immune to political correctness and modern social awareness.

Ben utilized each stride closer to the café in debate about entering. Short on time, he wanted to keep neither Uncle Stan, nor Pop, waiting on him.

"She's busy," became excuse number one.

"And a slam-bam-thank-you-ma'am-hi-and-bye wouldn't be cool," excuse number two.

Angling to the ATM, he withdrew the maximum amount, still counting the twenties when an odd voice behind him demanded, "Your money, or your life!"

His feet were barely back to earth after a startled jump, when cackling laughter reached his ears.

"On the high-strung side today, are we Mister Bramley?"

"Rrrrr!" he growled, turning. "What if I had taken a swing

at my assailant?" he asked Silk.

"Too quick for you," she said, going into a weaving-and-bobbing pantomime.

As he pushed the cash into a front pocket, she explained.

"Standing at the cash register, I saw you through the front glass. When you didn't come in, I figured you were dodging me."

"Never, and can we agree to delete the growl back there. Poor taste, but an indicator of a day gone to crap before the noon hour."

"Well, maybe I can bring some cheer. Step inside for a surprise."

When she saw his expression, she clarified. "Not that kind of surprise, you hound dog. Come see."

Her hand waved him inside to the sight of bustling tables that he had not seen occupied since his return.

"Back this way," she instructed, stopping at a table with a solitary patron—a bespectacled, elderly lady, nursing a cup of coffee, a knoll of empty sugar packets neatly centered on the tabletop.

"Tah dah!" Silk exclaimed, both arms outstretched.

The lady looked up, her blurred eyeballs twice their size through her thick lenses.

"Any guesses?" Silk asked. "Either one of you."

Nipping any potential awkwardness, Ben put out a hand to shake.

"You haven't changed a wink, Mrs. Hazelton. Ben Bramley here. How have you been since we last saw each other?"

"Well, aren't you the sweetest thing. And I've been healthy and happy. What about my favorite student?"

"You're going to make me blush."

Her expression of delight reminded him of the dominant memory he associated with her.

His first day returning to her class, following James's death and the funeral he had been kept from. Though his family all assured him that he could handle it, the chalkboard up front, with his name B-E-N in tall lettering, covered with thoughtful messages from classmates and teachers throughout the school, overwhelmed him. Being the object of attention proved too much, his already-queasy stomach unable to handle the stress. Racing to the boys' bathroom he dropped to the floor, embracing the first toilet. The heaving sounds echoed in the high-ceilinged room.

When he heard the restroom door open, followed by tight clicks on the tiled floor, he tried to finish throwing up quietly in his stall, hoping to go unnoticed.

"Ben, are you okay?"

Once he got over the confusion of Mrs. Hazelton in the boys' bathroom, he replied, "Yes, ma'am."

Wiping his mouth with toilet paper and flushing his cornflakes, he stepped out to face her. She appeared unruffled at being in the wrong bathroom.

"I'm sorry." Shame heated his face.

"Sorry for what Ben? For being naturally upset after all you've been through? For having to face a classroom full of students staring at you? Please look at me, and listen closely."

Lifting his eyes from the patterned black and white tiles, he saw the concern on her face, enough that he recognized in her a sincere ally.

"You're hurting, but somehow through all of that, you're brave enough to come back to school, to a place where everyone knows about your family's loss. You're brave for being willing to face all the questions from students and teachers who want to help." She paused. "Do you know what folks mean when they say *guts*?"

His head nodded.

"Well, you've got more guts than anybody I know."

He smiled at her comforting words, the most encouraging message he had received since James's death. He also smiled, thinking about how his *guts* had betrayed him in the bathroom stall.

Seeing her smiling at him from the safety of Silk's restaurant prompted him to gush, though he sidestepped questions regarding his wellbeing.

"Hands down, my favorite teacher," he said, and before she could play modest, he added, "One day we must sit down together, so that I may tell you how you turned my life around. Just not today. I have multiple people I'm neglecting by standing here."

"You got it," she said. "Given my age, don't take too long in making good on that invite." Her right index finger stood aloft.

"Soon," he said, leaning toward the door, yet taking a second to blow her a kiss, which she pretend-caught, and applied to her cheek.

"Right back," Silk said to her former teacher.

Following Ben to the door, Silk's rubber soles squeaked on the floor when he wheeled around suddenly.

"Thanks," he said, "Really. Thanks."

"You okay?" she asked, needing to know, while also hyper-aware of eyes on the two of them, in a crowd parched for fresh news.

"Not sure," he said, switching to whisper level. Without betrayal of emotion, he straight-faced told her, "I would be much better if I could kiss you this moment."

"Thanks for stopping by. Come back when you can," she said, instantly. Louder than necessary, she stopped barely shy of shaking his hand.

Recognizing his cue, Ben exited with the bell on the door in mid-jingle.

Returning to the gas station, he found Uncle Stan washing the truck windshield.

"Helps to do this every few years, whether it needs it or not," Uncle Stan said, grinning at his own humor.

Finding a ray of clarity in the moment, Ben asked, "How's Grandpa Etter? I haven't talked to him in a few months."

Long stretches slipped by without face-to-face time with

Grandpa Etter. The lapses Ben supplemented with telephone calls, which provided some comfort, reconnecting to the man, who was not that much unlike Pop. Maybe they shared generational attributes, maybe the character passed down from courageous, independent settlers who stepped off a ship from the other side of the Atlantic and kept moving forward into an unknown wilderness without any guarantee of survival. Whatever the source, Ben recognized an unshakable depth which he found enviable.

"He's doing fine," Stan said. "The two of us are making plans for another deep-sea fishing trip, soon as the leaf-looker dollars slow down for me."

"Man, how that sounds fun!" Ben said.

"He'd like nothing better than for you to join us. 'Course you can't figure on him coming up to see us."

"He and I share that Abundance aversion thing," Ben said, looking at the dollar total on the gas pump.

Taking the cash from Ben, his uncle said, "Right back with your change."

When Stan reappeared he had money in one hand and a cold Cheerwine in the other.

"Reckon you're still guzzling these," he said.

"You never fail to have my favorite on hand, even back when no one else around here kept them in stock. What do I owe you for the drink?"

"You're kidding? Right?"

Stan slapped him on the back for the second time as Ben climbed up into the cab.

Easing out into "lunch-hour rush," Ben soon took the right onto River Road. Windows down, the crisp air felt great, a definite improvement over muggy summers, which made him think again about Grandpa Etter.

"Don't know how he can take that Florida heat, and worse, the humidity. The air's so heavy with moisture, it makes me feel like my lungs can't assimilate enough oxygen."

At the word *oxygen,* a creature jumped into the road a short ways ahead. *Puppy,* registered in Ben's head, causing his foot to find the brake. He thought he had enough time to slow since the creature's speed should take it across the road before the truck arrived. Then there was more movement, a blur of blue coming out of the trees to the right, and without thought, Ben's left foot found the clutch pedal.

"Goddamn it!" he yelled, realizing the blue belonged to a denim jacket, and inside was a young boy, no doubt in pursuit of the runaway pup.

The half-empty Cheerwine bottle dropped to the floorboard. With both hands freed to grip the steering wheel, Ben had risen up off the seat, pulling on the wheel, pushing on the pedals, and mentally willing the truck to quit rolling. The boy hadn't noticed anything other than the puppy's direction, a singular focus that fearfully omitted all other goings on, even the grotesque noises emitting from Ben's shuddering vehicle.

Feeling as though his stomach had climbed up his throat far enough to turn itself inside out, Ben's driving experience and mind did the math, calculating if he could grind to a halt in time, or if he should ditch the truck. Left ditch, not an option, the boy's path. Left ditch not an option, the Unolama River!

Panicked, with necessity dictating he reach a conclusion, Ben and the truck agreed that stopping could be achieved. The little boy's feet had barely crossed the left lane as the truck jerked to a halt.

The next danger immediate, Ben reacted with swiftness, switching off the ignition, throwing the parking brake, and activating the hazard lights. There was enough straight highway in both directions for the truck to be seen.

If they hit it, I don't care, flashed across his mind. *Save the boy.*

Guilty of not checking traffic either, Ben launched himself down from the cab, bounding across the road, and in the direction of the churning water.

"Hey! Hey! Hey!" he yelled repeatedly without having sighted the child, reasoning that he might distract the boy from blindly pitching into the river.

Three strides had Ben standing at the top of the bank, staring at granite boulders amidst whitewater. Rather than completely vertical, the bank sloped, gradual enough to descend without tumbling headfirst. Halfway down, a past rain-swollen river had belched out several large rocks. Between a cluster of them sat the boy, puppy in his lap.

AFTER RESTORING THE TWO RUNAWAYS to their home and a frenzied babysitter, Ben returned to the truck's cab.

"Damn! Damn! Damn!" he screamed, beating all hell out of the innocent steering wheel. "Couldn't have been any older than James!"

Tick. Tick. Tick, he heard at the end of his tirade. The sound came in sequence with the warning lights, still flashing.

He cut the lights. Eliminate all reminders. But he couldn't cut the sweaty stench of fear that hung in the cab.

CHAPTER TWENTY-ONE

"Then Herod, when he saw that he was mocked of the wise men, was exceeding wroth, and sent forth, and slew all the children that were in Bethlehem, and in all the coasts thereof, from two years old and under, according to the time which he had diligently enquired of the wise men."
—Matthew 2:16

The season's last apples bound for the packing house waited in a line to the side of the wide-open row, the regular location for using the forklift to load the truck.

The family nomenclature for the spot—"the wide balk"—owed to another of Pop's idiosyncratic words, in use nowhere but the Bramley farm. Curious enough, a high-school Ben had investigated a few choice words of Pop's, and found that *balk* had Old English usage, originating in the Norse language, and applied to a furrow left unplowed, creating a space between rows. Touché, Pop!

The absence of Pop's pickup indicated that he had retired for lunch. The pickers, finishing their own lunch, had moved across the road to the block of Arkansas Blacks, an apple deep-red enough to be classed *mahogany* in color, with flesh that was rock-hard and inedible until it had been stored for months.

Bypassing the running board, Ben jumped from the cab, doubled over, his face almost brushing the frost-burnt fescue. He had hands on hips, hunting oxygen to supplement his sprinting heart.

May as well go ahead and throw up while I'm at it, he thought, though it didn't transpire.

When his breath slowed enough to speak, he did so, feeling the need to reason matters aloud.

"Godfuckingdamn and Holy Moses!" he exclaimed, reaching for the most irreverent language he could conceive to put to his situation.

"Started out revisiting Winn-Dixie Day, and without let-up, it's become Shitstorm Day. Is there some cosmic alliance going on?"

Waiting, as if for an answer, he found that the quiet bordered on disturbing, with only autumn wind rattling the leaves.

Alone—the caption for his life—did not provide protection without price.

"Is this the part where I'm supposed to fall to my knees in prayer? My tear-streaked face begging for forgiveness?"

Raising his eyes heavenward, he despised himself for the puppet-like response.

"The error of my ways has reached an undeniable climax, and broken—my defiant human nature shattered by disappointing failure—comes the realization that I can't make it on my own. By design, life's travails prove that I was never *meant* to make it on my own. The only conclusion, the only solution, is that I need God, not simply to save me from calamity, but to save my immortal soul, to apply the redemptive blood of my slain savior, Jesus Christ, to rescue me from everlasting, hellfire punishment."

He paused to allow the clouds to part, which he assumed would be followed by a concentrated sunbeam casting a spotlight upon the hallowed ground where he stood—the prodigal son returned at last, the lost sheep back to the fold.

The silence made its own undeniable point.

"Well fuck that shit. Fuck that shit six ways from Sunday. Ain't happening. Ain't ever going to happen. Life is not like the board game. There's not some unseen, giant hand flipping the spinner, and moving the pieces along the path to achieve an optimal, pre-destined result.

"Not that I have the answers. Though what I do know for certain, is that when organized religions, *any* brand of organized religion, start claiming to have all the answers, start insisting that their way is the only one, true way, to the exclusions of all others, I call bullshit. No loving, creator god is going to permanently penalize billions of puny humans who happened to be born in the wrong country, wrong period of time, unexposed to education, circumstantially out of the loop of those my-way-or-the-highway-to-hell religions. That one is a no-brainer."

If he had had a notion that the rant would improve his outlook, he thought incorrectly. The specter of the shit day lessened not an iota. If he could clear the image of the little boy, if he could disassociate him from his memories of James.

Working backward through the morning's timeline, he sought a pleasant image upon which to focus. Thoughts of Uncle Stan improved his outlook, and immediately preceding the Cheerwine from Stan was the brief reunion with Mrs. Hazelton.

"Good times," sufficiently positive to declare it aloud. Her kindness helped him through the worst of times, making it possible to transition back into public life. Her face appeared in flip-book fashion as his mind scrolled through benevolent scenes in which she featured, extending to her role as his Sunday school teacher.

Kaboom! He flipped too far, far back to an image gone freeze-frame in his mind, the one where Mrs. Hazelton stopped him on his way out of Sunday school, early December, 1978, with James's drowning less than four-months past. She's smiling profoundly, bent at the waist, their faces inches apart, overjoyed to share her news.

"Ben, you've been chosen to play one of the wise men in our Christmas pageant."

He could see his tiny reflection in her glasses, the ones with the sparkly chain that kept them around her neck.

Those parts usually went to the older children, except for newborn Jesus, played by the most docile baby in the congregation at the time.

Why would they pick me? It's not my turn to be in the play. Will Mama say I can? Did I say I would? Within seconds the answer came. *Oh, it's on account of James. Feeling sorry for me, like some Christmas play's gonna make me forget.*

Out of respect for Mrs. Hazelton, he hid his anger and resentment.

He mounted the steps, slipping into the pew beside his dad and grandparents. After Reverend Shepard's final amen, Ben spilled the news to his family, minus his mother, who never came to church anymore.

"I'm going to be a wise man in the Christmas play."

"At school?" Granny asked.

"No. Here at church. Mrs. Hazelton asked me right before the preaching. I figure she didn't want the others in class to hear, making them jealous and all."

The adults all hesitated at Ben's news, until Daddy finally said, "That's great buddy."

"GATHER UP ALL YOUR BELONGINGS class. I don't want to be getting calls from your mothers about forgotten coats or gloves left behind at school over Christmas break."

Mrs. Hazelton realized she had no control over the exuberant chaos.

"Don't forget to take home all the artwork you made for your families. It would be a shame to disappoint them."

Ben held a fistful of glittered stars, Santas, and Christmas tree cut-outs.

Maybe Mama will let me hang them on the tree.

"I won't see some of you again until the second of January, so Merry Christmas and Happy New Year to you all," she shouted to the backs of thirty third-graders, piled up at the door. "Oh, and Happy Hanukkah, Silk."

The bell rang. Ben emerged from the coat closet, shifting the artwork in his hands to don his coat. Silk waited by the classroom door.

"Merry Christmas, Ben. Here. I made a card for you."

Flustered, he added the card to his hand without looking at it.

"Thanks. I don't have nothing to give *you*."

"That's okay," she said. "I won't be seeing you for a long time, so I wanted you to have the card."

Surprised by the card, and confused by Silk's comment about not seeing him for a long time, Ben tried to make sense of it.

Oh yeah, her family doesn't go to Redeemer. I won't see her until school starts back.

"Merry Christmas to you too," he said, unaware that anyone would not celebrate the Christian holiday. In his closeness to her, their differences had lost significance to him, but that meant that he sometimes did not understand her.

When she stepped up and hugged him, he nearly dropped his belongings.

"I'll miss you," she said, low and unhurried.

"Uh huh," he said, appreciative of the tender contact, while also thankful that they were the last ones in the room.

Finding an empty seat on the bus, he checked to make sure no one looked over his shoulder as he pulled out her card. On the green glitter Christmas tree she had made several small, red hearts. Opening his treasure, a single large heart on the left page glittered gold. The words underneath captured his attention:

To Ben
From
Silk
Your Girlfriend

"My girlfriend! My girlfriend," he said in an excited whisper.

He repeated the words scores of times on the bus ride home, staring out the window as a different Abundance passed by.

Most houses had some form of decoration, whether that was reindeer grazing in the yard, or deep-green wreaths hanging on doors, highlighted with crimson bows. Even the front of Redeemer Baptist Church caught his eye for the first time. Its elaborate nativity scene sparked more hope than he had felt since the most-awful day. He would enjoy the holidays, with the promise of returning to school and a girlfriend.

Running from the bus stop all the way home, he burst through the front door, gasping as he asked Mama, "Can we go looking at Christmas lights tonight?"

"Isn't tonight your rehearsal for the Christmas pageant?"

"Aw shoot!" He'd forgotten. "Can we ride around after and look at lights?"

"I suppose so. We'll have to check with your dad to see if he's up for it."

"Oh thank you. Thank you."

He squeezed her waist. The newfound Christmas spirit had his world shifting to the better.

Running to his room, he hid the special card between two books on his shelf before Mama could see it, and then ran back to the kitchen with his handmade decorations.

"Look at these, Mama. I made them at school."

He extended his creations to her, hoping she would like them.

"My goodness, Ben. Did you really make these?"

He smiled and nodded, happy with her response.

"These are wonderful. I didn't know you had such artistic talent."

Her *oohing* and *aahing* nourished a heart too-long underfed.

"Can we hang some on the tree?"

His pure enthusiasm touched her heart as well. She struggled to keep from falling to her knees and holding him close for a long cry.

"We can hang them on the tree, on the walls, in the windows . . . anywhere you want."

"Let's get out the rest of the decorations, like you promised we'd do when I got out of school," he said.

"We can do that. I'll meet you in the spare bedroom after I check the oven."

Ben had the storage-closet door open when she arrived. He leaned back at the waist, trying to see the contents of the top shelf.

"I can't reach."

"Watch out. Let me."

Mama reached above her head, removing a cardboard box partially hanging over the edge of the unpainted pine shelf. Ben rushed to inspect it.

"Look at the candles with glitter on them. What are those red flowers on that big plate?"

"Poinsettias."

She pulled down a second box, overflowing with tinsel streamers. The muffled clink of colored light bulbs came from underneath the tinsel. Ben abandoned the original box to examine the second.

The third and biggest box remained.

"Run to the broom closet and get the stepstool. The last one's too far back for me to grab," she told him.

It took him mere seconds, excited by the treasure hunt.

"Stay back. This is heavy. Make a spot on the bed for me to put it."

Ben slid the first two boxes closer to the head of the bed.

"Whoo!" Mama set it down. The flaps were folded crossways to seal the contents.

"Reckon what all's in there?"

Mama laughed. "This is like Christmas day for you already, with all the surprises inside."

She unfolded the box top.

"Christmas placemats and hand towels," she said, pulling a stack of fabric out.

"Aw!" Ben exclaimed.

"Wait a minute." Mama recaptured the moment. "Stockings."

She held them aloft, then began to separate them across the foot of the bed.

"Where's mine? Where's mine?"

He grabbed for them, as Mama fended him off with her elbow.

"Hold your horses, mister. Here's yours."

When she removed Ben's from the stack, James's stocking stared at her, his name embroidered across the top, and below, a little elf in red and green, holding a toy train.

"Mama. Mama, can I hang mine up right now?" He waited a few seconds before speaking again. "Mama?"

His words weren't reaching her.

She locked on the object in her hands, unable to breathe. The image of standing on a high desert mesa filled her mind.

Wind funnels up the cliff face. Her red curls are lifting skyward. Two bare feet, ten toes flirting with the edge, freeing a tiny avalanche of sand, grains falling, reaching for the desert floor far below. The drop is exquisitely high. Arms out to her side, floating. Leaning her weight forward, another inch forward, and she can have that incredible feeling of flying—a bird loosed from its cage. She can be free. The letting go, the not fighting is sweetly tempting. Oh, to finally unravel, and there comes the first tug.

Ben pulled on her wrist, "Can I, Mama? Can I?"

"What?" She caught her breath, heart rhythm erratic.

"Can I hang my stocking right now?"

PRIOR TO SUPPER, BEN WATCHED television as he threaded popcorn onto a slowly growing garland. Mostly he merely listened to the programs, having learned that taking his eyes off his work led to a needle in the fingers. However, he glanced up often to watch the colored lights on the seven-foot Frasier fir.

"Now it smells like Christmas in our house."

In the kitchen, Mama spoke to Daddy.

"I'll take him to rehearsal if you don't have time. And drop him off. No going in," Mama said. "We can both pick him up and drive around to look at lights, like he asked. Okay?"

"Sounds good to me," Daddy said, chipper enough, a fresh biscuit in hand swiped from the tray. The bread still hot, he alternated it between hands as he approached Ben.

"Say, that's some mighty-fine artwork there, buddy. Your mom told me it was really good."

"Thanks. I'm making this too." Ben held up a couple of feet of stringed popcorn for his dad to inspect. "It'll go on the tree."

"Absolutely. You're being a big helper with the decorating. I'm sure mom appreciates that."

Daddy chomped on the cooled biscuit.

"Supper," Mama called.

"Can we eat over here, by the tree?" Ben asked.

Though it violated the Saturday-night-only rule for eating in the living room, neither parent could refuse his few simple requests.

"What are you going to do with all your time away from school?" Daddy asked, as he settled into his favorite chair, his plate on a TV tray.

"I'm going to eat a lot of candy, and Mama says I can help her bake more cookies."

Ben had his own biscuit. He used it to sop up the beef drippings on his plate.

"And help in the orchard too," he hurried to add, lest he sound "trifling," as Pop and Granny often said. He hadn't forgotten their condemnatory explanation of the word.

After supper Mama reminded Ben, "Get ready. We're leaving for church in five minutes. Where's your coat?"

"Right here." He held it up for her to see.

In the Abundance Post Office parking lot, a safe distance from the church, she gave Ben his instructions.

"I'll stay here until I see you get inside the door. When you get finished, come straight out. Your dad and I will be parked over here. Got it?"

"Yes, ma'am."

"I mean it, Ben. I won't come inside looking for you."

He grasped her seriousness, without understanding the reason.

"Okay. I will."

"Will what?"

"Will come outside when I'm done."

"That's my boy. Now off with you."

Two hours later, Ben emerged from the steepled building, spotting the family car immediately, the only one parked far from the church. The outlines of his parents' heads rose above the front seat.

"How did it go?" his mother asked before he could get inside.

"Lots of fun. I got to wear my costume. It's neat."

"Do you have any lines?" his dad asked.

"Lines?"

Rephrasing, "Any speaking parts?" Daddy asked.

"No, but I have to remember when to move and where to go. It's not too hard."

"I'm sure you'll do fine," his mother assured him. "Still want to go looking at lights?"

"Yes, ma'am," Ben replied, energized by the opportunity to have fun together.

"Well, your dad thought you might enjoy looking at the decorations even more if you had a chocolate milkshake from the Cardinal Drive-In."

She passed a tall shake over the seat.

The cold cup felt good in his grasp.

"Thanks a bunch!"

Within the next second he could be heard pulling on the straw.

Daddy shifted gears, and the Country Squire station wagon turned onto the highway in search of illuminated beauty. It was a simple search, as if all the community had an agreed upon plan. Rarely did one house's decorations duplicate those of the neighbors.

The car radio, tuned to an all-Christmas-music station, intensified the holiday spirit. When "The Little Drummer Boy" played, Ben accompanied the *pa-rumpa-pum-pum* parts by squeaking his straw up and down in the cup's plastic lid.

Hesitant to end the fun, Mama finally checked her watch by the radio's glow.

"Oh Ben, it's way past your bedtime. I had no idea it could be this late."

"Just a little more, please, Mama."

"Maybe your dad will take the long way home. After that, it's straight to bed."

PAGEANT TIME ARRIVED TWO NIGHTS later. Adorable in the wise man outfit he had brought home, Ben voiced his impatience to Daddy over Mama's absence.

"Where's Mama? My play's tonight."

"I know your play is tonight, and your mother knows that. She'll be home soon, and we can all go."

Daddy's reply lacked conviction. Ben knew for certain that Mama had gone shopping, which could last forever by Ben's timeframe.

"Are you ready to go soon as your mother gets here?"

"Yes, sir. I'm ready. I want to go. I have to be there early. Mrs. Hazelton said so."

"If she's not here soon, we'll have to go on," Daddy said.

"Mama has to be there. I don't want to do the play if she's not there to see me."

"She'll be here son. I promise. Do you want a snack, or something to drink?"

"No. I just want Mama here so we can go together. Daddy, what are we going to do?"

"Maybe your grandparents haven't left yet. You could ride with them if you're worried about being late."

"You could come too, if you leave Mama a note on the refrigerator."

He reasoned, *If Mama's too late, Daddy may not come either.*

"Alright then. Grab your things while I leave her a message."

GRANNY MADE MATTERS WORSE FOR Ben, insisting on photographing him in his costume.

"Quit fidgeting so I can get a decent picture."

Aggravation wouldn't let Ben cooperate, as Granny tried again and again to capture the moment on Kodak film.

Daddy intervened.

"Let's go Mama. You can take more pictures at the church."

Five minutes later, Granny, Pop, and Daddy sat in their regular family pew. Ben waited behind the curtain, his fingers crossed.

"Mama don't miss the play. At least don't miss seeing my parts."

The organist began setting the mood with a variety of classic Christmas carols. Backstage, the many children couldn't be quiet and contained indefinitely. After a couple of collisions with the maroon stage curtain, the lights lowered and Reverend Shepard stepped into a spotlight, stage left.

"Please bow your heads as we give thanks to the *true* star of this production. . . ."

When Reverend Shepard ended his prayer, the curtains parted. From the dark backstage, Ben could make out Daddy, Granny, and Pop. No Mama.

Shortly into the play, and seconds before stepping onstage, he saw her arrive, sliding in next to Daddy.

The production progressed without major disaster. Lines came close to script, and the participants navigated without collision.

After the final scene, Ben beamed, lined up with the entire cast. His smile widened when he saw his family, all standing, clapping, and smiling back at him. He did wonder why Mama broke off before the applause ended, working her way to the end of the pew, and turning up the aisle toward the main exit.

He went flying down off the stage, exactly like Mrs. Hazelton had said not to do, racing to his mother, whose progress had been halted short of the door by Reverend Shepard's massive frame.

"Mama, Mama, did you see me? Did you see me?"

Standing behind her, he yanked on her skirt.

She turned and leaned down to face him. "Not now," and resumed talking to the minister.

Ben edged around, squeezing himself between them.

"Amelia, you have been missed by our congregation," Reverend Shepard said.

"That's nice to hear."

Ben could see the minister's feet moving in time and direction with Mama's. He spoke quickly and excitedly.

"When can we expect your return? Soon I pray."

Mama took a wide step to the left, almost tripping Ben.

"Reverend, you'll know as soon as I do."

"There must be some way I can help," he continued. "What's it been, more than three months now?"

Mama's feet stopped shuffling. Her voice grew loud.

"I didn't know there was a time limit on grieving the loss of a child!"

Ben noticed the church members gone quiet around him.

"You can't continue to forsake God and be angry with Him over your loss."

The Reverend's voice reverberated throughout the sanctuary.

If Mama knew that all eyes rested on her, she gave no indication in her manner, nor her words, as she not only matched Reverend Shepard's volume and the authority in his voice, she raised it considerably.

"You have no knowledge of my relationship with God. That's personal, and frankly, none of your business. And for your information, my issue is not with God. My issue is with those in this congregation who choose to judge me, see fit to gossip about me, stare at me in public like I'm some kind of leper, or worse. That's what keeping me out of church, all the goddamn hypocrites!"

She grabbed Ben's hand, shoving past a stunned Reverend Shepard and out the double doors.

In the tumult, Ben feared he would fall down the front steps, until Mama paused on the landing and scooped him up. Over her shoulder, the last thing he saw was every eye in the building locked on the two of them.

Straight to the car, parked across the road, she deposited Ben in the driver seat.

"Scoot over."

He could see her red face, her mouth closed tightly, and a fierceness about her that startled him. This went far beyond any anger he had ever seen at his misbehavior.

Throwing her purse in the back seat, she started the car.

Before she could shift into gear, Daddy had run up beside the car. Without looking directly at him, she reached over and locked her door, and the door behind her, as his wide-eyed face filled her window. His knuckles pounded the glass. Ben feared that the window would break and there would be blood.

"What was that all about?" Daddy shouted.

The dual hysteria made Ben want to run back in the church to the calm of Pop and Granny. But fearing that a move might worsen the situation, he stayed.

Mama kept her gaze front, a vicious grip on the steering wheel, until a quick left hand moved to crack the driver window an inch. Through the narrow gap she yelled to Daddy, "See you at home!"

Loose gravel flew from behind the car. Ben turned to look over his seat and saw Daddy's astonished expression flash by in the station wagon's gallery of windows. Above and well-back-of his father, church members had spilled out of the building like swarming hornets. In the front of the crowd, at the top of the stairs, stood Pop and Granny, with the Reverend beside them.

Halfway home, Mama spoke for the first time.

"That monster!"

Then she scream-growled, like the panther Ben had heard back in the mountains with Pop one evening after hunting. That was the closest possible association he could make, watching her pound the steering wheel with one hand.

She assured him, "I'm not mad at you, Ben. And I did see you, from the very beginning. The traffic with all the Christmas shoppers slowed me way down."

She omitted being delayed from shopping two cities away to avoid accidental contact with any folks from Abundance.

"That's okay. You made it."

Her calmness did nothing to change what he witnessed at church.

"Did Reverend Shepard do something wrong?"

"That depends on what you call *wrong*. Let's just say he upset me with what he said."

"About James?"

"Sort of about James, and also about me."

"Mama, I'm sorry."

He was particularly sorry that Mama, who had at long last returned to acting like old Mama, might now be in danger of acting again like she did following James's death.

"That's sweet of you," she said, as they pulled into their driveway. "Did you have fun doing the play?"

"Yes, ma'am."

Something about Mama's tone of voice disturbed Ben. She began rushing him around as soon as they got in the house.

"Take off your costume. Hang it over your desk chair. Brush your teeth, and get in bed. I'll see you in the morning."

He had more questions about the incident, but no time. The

screen door slammed shut, followed by the main door. Mama exited his room in the direction of the ruckus.

Hardly a second passed before Ben heard, "What is wrong with you? Have you lost your mind?"

Daddy yelled, but it was not like his in-the-orchard yelling, to see if the pickers needed boxes moved, or yelling so Ben could find him.

"Not out here," Mama said.

Ben heard their bedroom door shut angrily.

The thin two walls between his bed and his parents' room did little to muffle Daddy's roar. Easily making out the heated words, Ben listened for a moment, and then covered his head with the pillow. That eliminated Mama's comments. Daddy's still penetrated clearly. More than simply loud, they were ugly. Ben couldn't take it. For a moment he considered bursting into their room and taking up for Mama.

"O lit-tle town of Beth-le-hem / how still we see thee lie . . ." escaped from under the pillow as Ben sang with volume, trying to drown out Daddy's attack.

Which is the worst of Ben's childhood tragedies? Find out by subscribing to Southern Fried Karma's YouTube channel, Fugitive Views.

CHAPTER TWENTY-TWO

"A virtuous woman is a crown to her husband: but she that maketh ashamed is as rottenness in his bones."
—Proverbs 12:4

The next morning when Ben awoke, he remained in bed. Though he needed to use the bathroom, he dismissed the thought.

I'll play astronaut instead.

He had invented the game, one in which he sealed the covers around his body, leaving no openings. The bed and covers become his space capsule, and any air leaks could be deadly. Even his space suit wouldn't protect him. As far as he knew, astronauts couldn't go to the bathroom when they wore their space suits. Nor would he allow himself to scratch anywhere his body itched, because the suit would prevent contact between his fingers and any itchy spot.

That morning his elaborate and demanding undertaking became less of a game, and more of a stalling tactic. The fight between his parents had rushed back the second he awoke.

If I stay in bed long enough, Daddy will be gone to the orchard. Maybe Mama too.

He extended the space mission until his bladder insisted the capsule splashdown.

After the bathroom, where he didn't flush, he dressed quietly. He cracked the bedroom door an inch, and one green eye looked side to side. No Daddy or Mama in sight. One foot into the living room and still nothing, so he dared expose his entire body, stopping and listening to the quiet.

Maybe I can make it to Granny's for breakfast.

He tiptoed to the back door and slipped out undetected. Observing an empty carport where the yellow station wagon should be parked, his second observation was that of a Deputy Sheriff's car parked in Pop and Granny's driveway.

Curiosity and a hungry belly overrode misgivings of walking into an unknown situation.

Neither grandparent acknowledged his entry. Pop could be heard in conversation in the living room. Ben headed for the kitchen, expecting to find Granny and some answers.

Breakfast dishes sat on the counter, but she wasn't there. Retracing his steps put him in the dining room, near the entryway into the living room.

Pop spoke in the adjoining room.

"What are you saying Clyde?"

Clyde remained anonymous until *deputy* popped into Ben's head.

"I'm saying if she left in the middle of the night, she could be two, three states away by now. Impossible to apprehend."

"Impossible?"

Daddy's voice, sounding almost as mad as the night before. "She took my car and $1,000.00 emergency money I kept hidden in my sock drawer, and you're telling me impossible?"

"Quit flying off the handle," Granny said. "She might have took the money and gone Christmas shopping."

Instant revelation had Ben's knees betraying him. Fingertips tried to catch a groove between the knotty pine wall boards for support.

"Oh," he whimpered, before collapsing on the tile floor.

Granny rushed around the corner.

"Good gracious! Ben!" she exclaimed, alerting the men in the next room.

When he looked up, she had knelt down, her face close to his. Behind her, with concerned expressions, stood Pop, Daddy, and a man in uniform.

"What's happened? Where's Mama?" Ben pleaded.

Granny had him, squeezing hard, her anguish undisguised.

"Let me help you up," she said.

Pop assisted with getting Ben up from the floor. They sat him at the dining table. Granny pulled another chair up to his, practically sitting in his lap, encircling him with her arms. She looked over her shoulder at the trio of men.

"Y'all need to do your talking outside." She added, "A goodly distance from the house."

Regaining her calm, Granny spoke to Ben.

"Your daddy's upset that your mama's gone and he doesn't know where she went. She didn't say anything about leaving in the car. That about sums it up."

She tried to avert hard questions before he got a chance to formulate them.

"Now let's get in the kitchen and fix you something to eat. This mess will sort itself out on its own."

Too bewildered to look at her, too shocked to speak, Ben sat, motionless.

Granny continued, "Can you stand up?"

Without waiting, she lifted him to his feet, guiding him to the breakfast nook and *his* chair at the dinette table.

"Want me to get you some Maxwell House?"

His silence continued.

"I'm going to get you a cup. Be right back."

Through the picture window in front of him, Ben watched a mated pair of mourning doves flit around Granny's mimosa tree.

'They mate for life,' Pop had told him, explaining the birds' arrangement in terms of loyalty and faithfulness.

Landing on a twig, skipping to another, one flying off, but soon returning, they seemed to be playing a game. More than anything, Ben's love of nature correlated to his trust and belief in God. In silent desperation he launched into prayer.

Father in heaven, this is Ben Bramley. Something has happened to Mama. She's gone, and we don't know where. Please,

please help her to be okay, and make her come back home right away. In Jesus's name, amen.

Returning with the coffee, Granny placed the cup in front of him. The aroma, combined with the hopefulness of the sent prayer, revived him enough to speak.

"Granny, what do you think Mama's doing right now?"

"I can't say for sure. She'll be alright. Maybe back here faster than you can say Jack Robinson."

Her silly expressions usually earned a smile from Ben. But not that time, trying to comfort and convince him, when she needed convincing too. So little evidence. So many scenarios.

"How about I fry up some red rounder, as Pop calls it, and eggs to go with it?"

"My stomach doesn't feel so good, not even for fried bologna."

"I reckon it might get to feeling better once you give it some food. There's a biscuit or two left from mine and Pop's breakfast. You can nibble on those while the rest is cooking. I'll bring you some butter and honey and jelly to go with them."

She got him to eat—food that couldn't touch his pain.

"I want to see Daddy," he said with the last bite.

"That's not a good idea right now."

"Why not? Why can't I see him?"

"Your Daddy's busy dealing with the sheriff's department, trying to find your mother. Besides, he and Pop planned to go drive around looking for her once they finished up with Clyde, I mean Deputy Ponder."

"I want to go too!"

"They've left already. I'm sure."

"I want to go find Mama."

"Then sit here and finish your juice while I check outside."

When she turned to go back inside from the porch, Ben stood behind her.

"Where are they?"

"Gone, like I said. How about we have us a swing? It's not too chilly today. We can take a trip to Florida, where it'll be a lot warmer."

"I don't want to swing. When will Pop and Daddy be back?"

"That, I can't say. Truth of the matter, Ben, I don't have any answers myself. You and I are in this not-knowing thing together. Still, that don't mean we can't hope and pray for the best."

"I've already been praying."

"Good for you. Now let's get back inside and get busy."

"With what?"

"Well, I was of a notion to bake Christmas cookies today, and I sure could use an assistant."

"Mama said I could make cookies with her."

"You can still help her. But what about me? Maybe I need a chief taste tester?"

"Okay," he said.

Four-dozen cookies later, Ben went running when he heard the back door open.

"Hey there, partner," Pop said, removing his wool-lined cap and red plaid coat.

"Did you find Mama? Where's Daddy?"

Granny entered the room after the same news.

"Whoa, there. One question at a time."

Pop tried to lighten the mood. Glancing up at Granny, the message on his face read *no good news*. In exaggerated fashion, he made a point of sniffing the air.

"Smells like somebody's been doing some cooking. Am I right?"

"I helped Granny make Christmas cookies. Bells and reindeer and Christmas trees."

"Well then, I can't wait to taste them."

"Did you find Mama?"

"No. I'm afraid we didn't, but that don't mean a thing. I figure she'll be home directly," Pop said.

"Where's Daddy?" Ben asked.

"He's out looking for your mama."

"Can you and me and Granny go looking too?"

Pop dropped to one knee and placed his hands on Ben's shoulders.

"Son, not only is your daddy out looking, so are a bunch of officers from the sheriff's department, in this county and all around Asheville. Even the State Highway Patrol is trying to find your mother. I don't see how we could make much more of a difference."

Before the sadness on Ben's face could deepen further, Pop added, "We'd be better off staying here in case somebody calls with information, or be here when your mama comes driving back. You wouldn't want to be gone for that, would you?"

"No, sir," Ben admitted.

"Good. Now let's see if Granny's got something to eat other than cookies."

Circumvented questions and a silent phone highlighted the afternoon. Pop and Granny employed a host of tricks to keep Ben distracted with activity.

Late in the day, Pop asked him, "How about you run get the mail for us? It should have come by now. Save me a few steps. And get y'all's mail while you're at it."

"Watch for traffic crossing the road," Granny hollered as Ben went out the door.

When he reentered the house, he heard his grandparents in conversation. They hadn't noticed the sound of the door, as Ben waited in the next room, listening.

"What's going on, Sam?"

"Not much more than you heard me tell Ben. When we left here, we went by the sheriff's office for Jason to file a *Missing Person's Report*. Then they asked him more of the same questions that Clyde asked him here. He gave them tag number, description of the car, and a photo of Amelia."

"Do you think she ran off?"

"Jason said a couple of their suitcases were gone, along with some shoes, clothes, and toiletries."

"Was that all?" she asked.

"He didn't take much time to look. The bedside picture of her mom and dad is missing, and one of Ben and James. And of course, the money."

"Don't sound like a shopping trip."

"Nosiree. What I can't figure is why?"

"After last night's episode at the church, I suppose she's capable of about anything if she's not in her right mind."

Before their suspicions could arise, Ben slammed the door from the inside. Running into the living room, he held a handful of mail, mostly colorful envelopes indicating Christmas cards.

"Sorry about slamming the door. Look! This one don't have a stamp, and that's Daddy's name on the back. Isn't that Mama's writing?"

Granny took it from him. "Where did you find this?"

"In our mailbox," Ben said.

"That *is* your mother's handwriting." Granny said.

She cast a quizzical look toward Pop.

"Can we open it?" Ben asked.

He knew adults took mail seriously, having taught him to be careful when retrieving it, and to never open a thing apart from their presence.

"It's addressed to your daddy. What do you think Sam?"

Without hesitation, "Open it."

"How can you be so sure of yourself?"

"We need answers," he said.

Granny opened the letter, unfolding the single page:

Dear Jason,

In the space of two years I've struggled with the loss of Mother and James. I still struggle. Everywhere I look and in everybody's face, I'm reminded of them. Maybe it's driven me crazy. Most days

I'm sure of it. Now Christmas comes, a happy time, but I can't be happy, and I'm tired of faking it. If I don't go, it will be more misery for you and Ben. Much more. Tell him I love him always, and that I hope someday he can understand and forgive me. Leaving him and you may be the death of me. Staying surely will.

So sorry,

Amelia

"Read it out loud," Ben demanded.

Granny stammered a moment, shocked, while also trying to decide what to do.

"Read it!"

He grew impatient.

Granny did all she could think of, paraphrasing, "Your mama mentions Christmas and it being a happy time. She says she loves you."

Then Granny stopped.

"What else?"

Granny looked at him with troubled eyes.

"The rest is for your daddy. Private. Between him and your mama."

She folded the letter, returning it to the envelope, and placed it high on the mantle.

"Now come on in the kitchen and help me with washing some dishes."

Ben obeyed. When he and Granny finished, he noted Pop's absence.

"Where's Pop?"

"He had to run out. Forgot something. Let's see about getting some supper ready."

An hour later, Granny pulled a cast-iron skillet of cornbread from the oven. In the living room, Ben stood on a chair by the mantle, discovering that the letter from Mama was gone.

Looking out the window, he saw the sheriff's car again, parked in Daddy and Mama's driveway.

When he went running out the back door, Granny caught sight of him, and followed.

"What's going on?" she asked as soon as she entered her daughter-in-law's kitchen.

Pop, Deputy Ponder, and Ben turned to look at her. Pop spoke.

"I encouraged the sheriff's department to get a search warrant, so they could come inside and see for themselves," Pop said.

As Granny tried to process the idea, he asked her, "Where would you figure on looking for a handwriting sample?"

The whole family knew Mama kept the business checkbook in the kitchen drawer by the back door. Fascinated by the size of it, Ben often watched both his parents and grandparents write checks to workers and pay other farm expenses. He liked the sound of the paper slip being carefully torn from the others in the spiral-notebook binder. Each check left a stub behind as record of its purpose, signed by the family member writing the check. "Serious business," they often told him, the paper equating to money, he learned.

"Does she have any immediate family we can contact?" Deputy Ponder asked.

"Her father, Mitchell Etter. He'll be in her address book. I'll show you," Granny said.

She fetched a flower-printed journal from the hutch where Mama kept stamps and stationary.

"He's lives in Marsh Bay, Florida. Her brother, Stan Etter, he runs the gas station in Abundance. I'll call both of them," she said.

"Our office will call her father and brother as well. Make it official and all," said the deputy. "We'll question the dad and likely ask the Marsh Bay Police Department to send a car to his place."

"Where's Jason?" she asked Pop.

"Far as we know, still out searching for Amelia. I took it on myself to get the writing samples once the sheriff's office saw the letter," he told her.

"So Jason hasn't seen the note, right?"

"That's correct ma'am," Deputy Ponder said. "We kept it to include as evidence and gave Sam a copy for Jason to see when he returns."

"Evidence?" Granny asked.

"We generate a file when someone goes missing. Make it a matter of record and gather whatever evidence is relevant. Not only does that assist in the search, it also provides information that's often later requested."

His explanation seemed to soothe her.

"For instance, that checkbook in your hand, in order to close a joint account, the bank's going to want official word from us that the other account holder's whereabouts is unknown. It can get complicated."

"Then I'm glad you're here," she decided.

"Is that a real gun?" Ben asked the deputy.

Most of the adult talk had become too official for his complete interpretation. The large revolver, however, was right at eye level with Ben.

"It sure is. You know guns are dangerous, right?"

"Yes, sir. Daddy has one that looks a lot like that. I'm not allowed to touch it."

"Lily, why don't you and Ben go get supper on the table? I'll be over in a few minutes," Pop said.

True to his word, Pop arrived as Granny set the last bowl on the table.

"Ben, you say the prayer for us."

"God, thank you for this food and for all our blessings. Please bring Mama and Daddy home right away. In Jesus's name, amen."

Halfway through the meal, Ben looked out and saw headlight beams next door.

"Somebody's home!" he shouted. "May I be excused?"

Up and on the move, he hollered back over his shoulder without slowing.

"Wait," Pop said. "We'll come with you."

Daddy hadn't fully made it out of the truck when Ben appeared.

"Where's Mama? Did you find her?"

Pop and Granny walked up on the two, anxious for news.

"I've driven all over creation today, looking in shopping-center parking lots in probably a hundred mile circle, downtown areas, even bus stops. Nothing. No sign of her."

Dejected, Ben asked, "What are we going to do?"

"Not much we can do other than wait for her to come back or some of the law officers to find her. By the way," Daddy looked at his parents, "I stopped by the sheriff's office on the way home. They filled me in." He looked down at Ben, hesitating. "Thanks for getting the sheriff involved Dad. You did the right thing."

"You're welcome, son," Pop said. "I figured anything I could do to take away suspicion was worth doing. Did they tell you they checked her closet?"

"Yes, sir. I know how they rush to assign blame. Makes me glad to be living in a small town, where you know people in the department that'll give you the benefit of the doubt."

Granny nodded, "Amen to that, and thank the Lord."

"What's *suspicion*?" Ben asked.

"Oh, that's nothing more than big people talk," Granny replied. "Big words they have to use at places like the sheriff's department," she said. "We're just glad your Daddy's back safe, right?"

"I want Mama, too."

"We all do," she said. "For now, let's go finish our supper. Your daddy's probably starving."

"I'm too upset to eat," Daddy said.

Pop and Ben began walking toward their unfinished meal. Granny lagged behind. Realizing it, Ben slowed, bending down to pretend his shoe needed tying. He figured that neither Pop nor Granny would notice with darkness to shield him.

"You've been drinking," he heard Granny say to Daddy. "There's no answer to any problem in a bottle. And that little boy is counting on you to be both parents if she don't come back."

"She ain't coming back Mama. Didn't you read the note?"

"I read it. Lord help us. We're in one hell of fix."

Granny said 'hell.' She don't ever cuss. Maybe cause Daddy said Mama ain't coming back. Ben could feel tears coming on. *He don't know. She'll probably be back tonight with a car full of presents and good stuff to eat.* He mounted determination as to her return, keeping hope alive and damming up any crying. *Wish I could get ahold of that letter.*

Before he could be detected, Ben sped off, catching up to Pop as he stepped into the porch light.

FIVE DAYS EXPIRED WITHOUT MAMA's return. No news from the sheriff's department. Ben passed most of his time with Granny. She consoled his bouts of sobbing, wiped his nose and prayed with him for Mama's return, offering her own silent prayers for the time when Ben would heal and move on.

What little time he spent with Daddy, the report from Ben was the same.

"Daddy's different and he always smells funny."

Over meals, Pop often complained that Daddy showed up late for pruning.

"Staying out most of the night. Not sleeping. It ain't good for him, and it ain't going to fix a thing."

Evenings, Daddy's truck was gone. When it rumbled in late, Barker the dog went wild, waking Pop, Granny, and Ben, who spent the nights with his grandparents.

In an attempt to reverse the tragic turn, the Bramleys rallied together to plan a big Christmas Eve. Granny made Daddy promise to come over for supper, marshmallows in the fireplace, and perhaps the opening of a few gifts.

Reluctantly, they began the meal without him. Ben had lots of questions, mostly about Daddy.

"What you reckon's keeping Daddy?"

"Can't say," Granny said without looking up from her plate.

"Pop?"

"What, son?"

"Did Daddy say anything about work he had to take care of this evening?"

"Not a word."

The short answers disturbed Ben, aware of how grown-ups spoke little when they didn't want to talk.

At the beginning of dessert, Granny's once-a-year fruitcake, a commotion arose on the back porch.

"I'll get it," Pop said, opening the door to reveal a shining stack of presents. The indoor light spilled out onto green, red, and gold foil wrapping, topped with bows.

Pop stepped aside so Granny and Ben could get a better view from the dining table.

"No one here. Must be Santa Claus," Pop said. "He couldn't come down the chimney on account of the fire in the fireplace."

"Wait up."

Daddy's voice penetrated the wall of black beyond the porch light.

"Not done yet."

When he made it up the steps to the porch, he pushed a new bicycle with ribbons streaming off the handlebars.

"Can y'all get these boxes inside?" He passed the bike off to Pop. "One more thing. Be right back," Daddy said.

"Ohhh!" Ben squealed. "I got a bike. I got a bike. Do you see it Granny?" He rolled it back and forth across the dining-room tiles. "I wanted a bike, and I got one!"

Daddy soon returned. Standing in the open doorway, he held two suitcases and a few overstuffed bags in his hands.

"Here."

He held the baggage forward, beckoning someone to take them. Granny had risen from the table. She took a step forward into a blast of whiskey fumes.

In a shaky voice she asked for an answer she didn't want to hear.

"What's all this?"

Daddy, done with waiting, dropped the armload to the floor.

"He's yours now."

Turning, he stumbled back into darkness. The door of his idling truck slammed. Gravel flew. Gone. Gone down River Road.

CHAPTER TWENTY-THREE

"It is a fearful thing to fall into the hands of the living God."
—Hebrews 10:31

Time wounded all healing. And in the aftermath of those losses, family and faith cannibalized Ben's future. Those closest to him, those tasked to love and protect the child, abandoned him in crisis, busily throwing up walls to fortify their own safe realities. That collective betrayal left him walking the earth openly injured.

"I worry about him," Granny had said a few times, only to be dismissed by Pop.

"Why, that boy's tough as shoe leather. You know that."

Truly, Ben looked fine on the outside, working hard as ever on the farm, making good grades in school. Precocious, his relatives and the general community tended to think of him as a miniature adult, rather than the broken little boy he had become.

Both parents fell from his life in the space of days—one vanished, and the other, worse, living forty yards beyond Ben's new bedroom window. Mama's betrayal drifted to the back corners of his mind, out of sight. Daddy's refusal stung without end.

Never a word about his turmoil to anyone, primarily because no one asked. In the Puritanical workaday world he inhabited, feelings fell way behind the never-ending labor. They couldn't afford to get emotional and bogged down. Onward, Christian soldiers!

"Don't want Pop or Granny getting fed up with me too."

Pop formulated a practical-sounding approach to dealing with Ben.

"Nothing good can come of digging up old bones, Lily. Best let troubles lie where they fall, die a natural death instead of keeping them alive and fresh."

Granny didn't fully agree with the don't-ask-don't-tell policy.

"Reckon we'll see."

Advancing in years, neither of them had sufficient physical or emotional reserves to be optimal full-time parents to an inquisitive and active eight-year-old.

The one adult to make Ben a special priority came in the person of Reverend Shepard. The first Sunday after Christmas the minister approached Ben.

"Hey there, young man."

He extended a hand for Ben to shake. Seconds passed before Ben collected his thoughts and shook it.

"Hey."

"Ben, I spoke to your grandparents about lending you out to help me. That is, if you agree. You know we have evening services Sunday nights, and I have nobody to help me straighten up after Sunday school and preaching. Nothing hard, putting hymnals and Bibles back in the pew racks, sweeping, and picking up trash, inside and in the parking lot. What do you say?"

"Will I be done in time for dinner at home?"

"Thirty minutes, tops, with you helping me. And I'll make you a promise. If I'm ever the cause of you missing one of your grandmother's fine dinners, I will straightaway take you to the Cardinal Drive-In for anything you want."

The minister chuckled as he watched Ben's eyes widen to twice their normal size.

"Yes, sir. You've got a deal!" Ben stuck out *his* hand to seal the arrangement.

"In fact, maybe we'll do that today if your folks say it's okay."

"No kidding?"

"No kidding. Now, let's get started."

At the Cardinal, Ben ordered a double cheeseburger, fries *and* onion rings, plus a chocolate milkshake.

"You going to be able to eat all that?"

"Yes, sir. It's been a long time since breakfast."

"I suppose it has."

Funny how Ben found Reverend Shepard not so scary—nothing like during his sermons, when he was all red-faced, with a big vein popping up on his forehead. He even turned on the car radio and let Ben pick the station on the way back to River Road.

"See you Wednesday at Prayer Meeting." The Reverend yelled from the driveway, with Ben already halfway to the front door.

Pop and Granny seldom went to Sunday evening service, and they never did during picking season.

"I figure the good Lord can look on our hearts, seeing we're well-intentioned of course, and He knows we need all the rest we can get before back to picking on Mondays," Pop reasoned.

At school, Ben poured angry energy into being the smartest student in class. The quest became a competition that fueled his need for validation and recompense, even if no one knew he was competing against them.

At home, his upstairs bedroom provided more privacy than was best for a young boy. Racing through his homework left him idle time to explore avenues beyond his years, whether it be old newspaper clippings Granny had collected, headlining his family's tragedy, or reading mature-themed books which he slipped out of the Groverton Public Library.

Reverend Shepard made visits to the Bramley home for no apparent reason other than to spend time with Ben. They sat under the oak tree and played fetch with Barker, hunted for arrowheads with the bean field laid bare, and fished in the family pond on occasion.

"It's mighty good of you to come and spend time with Ben," Granny had mentioned to Reverend Shephard.

"Growing up in a military family, my dad wasn't around for me. Of course I know that you all spend tremendous amount of time with him. It's that he reminds me of myself at that age in several ways, and it's also my Christian duty. You're well aware of the Apostle James's instruction: 'Pure religion and undefiled before God and the Father is this, To visit the fatherless and widows in their affliction, and to keep himself unspotted from the world.' Chapter one, verse twenty-seven."

"Amen," Granny said.

"I hope that Sam doesn't take offence, as in me stepping in uninvited."

"Why, no. He appreciates another man taking interest in the boy's life, especially you being our minister."

"And don't forget how much he helps me after church, saving me an hour or more every week! That adds up, and I truly appreciate his dedication."

"Benefits him too," Granny said. "Makes him feel needed by something outside of this farm."

THE SUN HAD BEGUN STRETCHING shadows across the pond on an April evening when Reverend Shepard mentioned, "Ben, I want to teach you about fly fishing. Now there's a real man's sport!"

"But I ain't got a fly rod."

"*Don't* have a fly rod."

"Don't have a fly rod," Ben repeated.

"Already taken care of. I've still got my first one, from when I was a little older than you. We should begin with the Davidson, in Pisgah Forest. It's wider than most rivers nearby. Less chance of getting tangled overhead, and it's shallow enough for wading, most places."

Two days later, Reverend Shepard arrived at the Bramley home for supper, carrying a bag in one hand.

"Hey, Ben. Do you have any old boots, like work boots you could spare?"

"I work in old tennis shoes," Ben said.

"There's an old pair that his daddy wore about the same age," Granny said.

Laughing, Pop added, "She don't ever throw anything away."

"Neither do you, Stingy," she said. "Can it wait 'til after supper, Reverend?"

"Absolutely."

Throughout the meal, Ben rushed to finish, vexed by the possible contents of the bag. When Granny rose to remove the dirty dishes, he hurried to help.

"I'll get dessert out, then go find those boots," she said to the men.

She returned with thick slices of pound cake topped with homemade chocolate sauce—"chocolate gravy," Ben called it.

"I'll go with you to look too," he said.

"Never known you to bypass dessert," she said.

After a short search, and verification of a decent fit, they rejoined Pop and Reverend Shepard. Without a word, the minister picked up the bag from the floor. Opening it, he removed two squares of a thick charcoal-colored material.

"Felt," he said to Ben, and recognizing the need for clarification, he continued. "We're going to glue this fabric to the bottom of your boots to keep you from slipping on the mossy rocks in the Davidson. Let's do this on the back porch."

Trailing along, Ben watched the pastor place each felt square on the porch tiles, then situate each shoe within the squares. With a black marker, he traced an outline of each boot onto the fabric. Using heavy scissors and a utility knife, he cut out boot-shaped pieces, took glue from his bag, and glued the felt to the boot soles.

"Leave them here, under the porch roof, so the glue won't stink up the house. And don't go trying them out in Blossom Creek. Give them a couple of days to dry."

"Wow! Thanks."

"No problem. I did it as much for myself as you. Can't have any accidents or your granny will never let us go again."

He gave Ben a conspiratorial wink.

FOLLOWING A FEW PRACTICE SESSIONS at the Bramley pond, using the borrowed rod, Ben and Reverend Shepard made a trip to Pisgah Forest, wading the Davidson River for hours. Instruction took up much of the time, though Ben enjoyed the pay-off when he reeled in a fat rainbow.

"That felt like a whale!"

"That's part of the beauty of fly fishing. The lightweight tackle makes the challenge greater. More skill than regular bait fishing."

The experience catapulted Ben out of his funk, giving him a newfound passion. He spoke of nothing but fly fishing that night to Pop and Granny over supper, during television time, and even in bed. As fresh thoughts erupted, he hollered through the bedroom floor vent, to the living room below, where the grandparents watched the late news.

"Best get on to sleep," Granny advised. "Church comes early tomorrow."

THE NEXT DECEMBER 25 FELT like it took years to arrive. It was Ben's first Christmas as a quasi-orphan.

The small trio had bypassed breakfast to indulge in hot chocolate and Granny's Christmas cookies. The floor had become a decoupage of crumpled wrapping paper. Grandparents had rained down gifts on their singular source of attention. Toys, books, and clothes occupied all the available seating space in the den.

One sizable package remained, bearing his name in unfamiliar handwriting.

"What's this?" Ben asked.

"What does it say?" Granny asked.

"It has my name."

Tearing away the candy cane wrapping revealed a brown cardboard box with an array of postage stamps. Ben's eyes widened.

"Whatever it is, it came all the way from Maine! That's way up north of here, we learned from the globe in Mrs. Patrick's class. And it's from someplace called L.L. Bean, whatever that is."

"You need my knife to open it?" Pop asked, his hand halfway into his pocket.

"Naw. I can rip it open," Ben said. Calloused hands and nimble fingers pried off the tape. "It's wrapped on the inside and there's a card on top. Granny, will you read this?"

"It says, 'Now you're outfitted for the big time—trophy fishing on the Oconaluftee River in Cherokee! Merry Christmas, Ben.' And it's signed, 'Reverend Shepard.'"

Seconds later Ben held in one hand a fishing vest, and in the other, a youth-sized pair of waders.

"They're just like Reverend Shepard's!" he said, bouncing with excitement.

"Looks like you're set for some serious fly fishing," Pop declared.

"Sure does," Granny said.

When the Reverend had approached her and Pop about fishing farther afield with Ben, and in bigger waters, they had balked at first, but due to the pastor's persistence, they finally agreed, stipulating that Ben must first demonstrate strong swimming skills. The grandparents then spent many anxious hours at the pond over the summer, until they felt him qualified.

"I still say he ain't going unless he wears a life vest," Granny said to Pop.

"That's going to be cumbersome, and he ain't going to like it."

"He can like it, or stay home."

When Reverend Shepard stopped on a pre-dawn Saturday morning for their Cherokee trip, Ben's gear included a bright-orange life vest.

Granny poked her head fully into the car, set to back out of the driveway. Nose-to-nose she commanded, "Reverend, you see to it he wears that vest."

Though not used to taking orders, the minister assured her he would.

They arrived at the reservation with half of the new-day sun peaking over a ridge. The sedan pulled off the edge of the road near a favorite fishing hole.

"This spot has been lucky for me," the Reverend told Ben.

They pulled on waders and gathered their gear. "We'll fish it upstream, then work our way back down by lunch time. Leave here whatever you don't really need."

Ben eyed the bulging brown paper sack in the front seat floorboard, wondering what Granny might have sent for him to eat.

Maybe I can leave the life jacket here too.

From behind the opened trunk lid the Reverend said, "And don't forget to put on your life vest. I'll not be trying to sneak one past your granny, or go breaking the Ninth Commandment in the process."

FOUR HOURS, AND FIVE RAINBOW trout later, Reverend Shepard waded close to Ben.

"While the sun's shining directly on the river, we may as well take a break. The fish will be spooked by our moving shadows."

Reluctant to miss a second with his fly out of the water, Ben kept silent.

"We'll eat our lunch on the way into town. Have you ever checked out the shops in Cherokee?"

"If we did, I don't remember," Ben answered.

"Lots of folks call them tourist traps, but I think you'll see some really neat stuff," the Reverend said.

Before leaving, they cleaned the fish from their creels and put them on ice in a cooler.

"You're mighty handy with that knife," the Reverend said.

"Yes, sir. Pop and Granny both gave me lessons soon as I started fishing. They said it came with the job, and if I took up the sport, I should know how to do it all."

"Wise advice."

Back inside the car, Ben worked to balance his sack lunch on his lap through the tight curves. He watched Reverend Shepard shove a bologna sandwich in his mouth while his free hand turned the wheel in swift short arcs.

"Will you pop the top on that Coke in my bag?" he asked Ben.

Needing both hands to complete the bottle opening operation, Ben released his hold on the armrest. Clinching his butt for stability, he nonetheless found his body surfing on the vinyl seat. Half the time he kept an eye on his lap as his meal slid close to tilting onto the floorboard.

A short distance later, the car had slowed for red lights, and Cherokee town traffic, allowing Ben to finish most of his meal. Granny had packed enough to serve for supper.

The minister's promise held true about the downtown shops, leaving Ben hard-pressed to decide if the endless souvenirs surpassed the trout.

Well after sunset, when the duo pulled into the driveway on River Road, Ben thanked Reverend Shepard multiple times, then rushed inside to show off his catch, along with a real Cherokee bow-and-arrow set, with a "Made in Korea" sticker on the back—a gift from the pastor.

For the finale, he exhibited a glossy photo of himself standing beside what had to be the tribal chief, in full-feathered regalia, Ben wearing an imitation raccoon-skin cap, tail and all.

"Just like Daniel Boone!" he assured his grandparents.

CHAPTER TWENTY-FOUR

"Let the elders that rule well be counted worthy of double honour, especially they who labour in the word and doctrine. . . . Against an elder receive not an accusation, but before two or three witnesses."
—*I Timothy 5:17, 19*

Within a circle of tents, campers, all nine- to twelve-year-old boys, wielded sticks armed with marshmallows. Bobbing over the dancing flames, some marshmallows caught afire, while others remained ghostly white, too far from the heat to transform into crispy-coated, melting-center treats. It was a cat-and-mouse game, causing the dark woods to echo with laughter.

Age-wise, Ben barely made the cut, having turned nine less than a month earlier. Though somewhat intimidated by the older boys, his height belied his years. Plus, he had a personal relationship with Reverend Shepard that none of the other boys could rival.

Not a fan of marshmallows, so much as the chocolate bars and graham crackers provided for s'mores, Ben hung back at the picnic table where the treats were assembled, alternately gobbling up chunks of chocolate and chasing them with crackers.

"Ben and I are going to round up more firewood to see us through the night, George." Reverend Shepard cast a huge shadow in the firelight, his voice booming off the treed enclosure. "Why don't you treat our Junior Ambassadors to a campfire story?"

"Will do, Reverend."

"Nothing too scary though. We wouldn't want these young boys afraid to sleep in the woods tonight."

"No, sir."

His wide grin betrayed open admiration. No wife or children of his own to occupy his time, George made himself available when his preacher from Redeemer Baptist asked for assistance with the young boys' Sunday school class, especially outdoor activities.

"Have you got your flashlight, Ben?" the Reverend asked.

"Yes, sir."

Once the sun set on the darkening forest, most of the youngsters had gravitated to the security of their ready light sources.

"Alright. Let's head over this way."

Ben followed behind the hulking silhouette, doing his best to duplicate the Reverend's path.

"Picking up wood in the dark requires extra care Ben. You never know what might be lying underneath."

"Like what?" Ben asked. His unsteady voice matched the shakiness of his flashlight beam on the forest floor.

"Oh, snakes for one thing, poisonous spiders, ground hornets. Things like that. But I'm not going to let anything happen to you. Your grandparents would skin me alive. No need to worry, though. Your daddy can tell you from his own experience. I haven't lost a camper in all these years of coming out here."

"How would Daddy know?"

"Has he not told you?"

"Told me what?"

A small noise behind Ben caused him to jump.

"I was already pastoring when your daddy was a little boy. He came camping too. That's hard for you to imagine, isn't it? Your daddy once being your age?"

Hyper alert for more noises outside their circles of light, Ben half-heard the question. He gave the standard, "Yes, sir."

"We had some great times together. Made of lot of memories, from those days."

In a quick look back to check for monsters approaching from

the rear, Ben could just make out the campfire, an unsteady orange dot in a wall of black.

"Speaking of woods safety, Ben, we better do a tick check."

Reverend Shepard had stopped, and Ben almost bumped into him, looking behind.

"What?" he asked.

"A tick check. You know."

Ben did. Every day of summer when he rushed in through the old screen door, Mama had halted him in the kitchen. He couldn't pass on to his bedroom until she had assured herself he was free of the tiny varmints. Granny had taken up the practice.

"Stand still."

The minister shined light on Ben's head using his free hand to move the mass of red curls about.

"What a shock of hair. Got the color from your mother. The thickness, now that's definitely from your daddy. My, he had the thickest black hair! Still does.

"You're looking okay up top. Hand me your flashlight."

Without question, Ben complied, watching the minister click off the beam and put the device in his back pocket.

"Now, off with the shirt. Raise your arms."

The inspection continued. Ben cooperated as if he were at home. Unquestioning respect for elders, especially authority figures, had been drilled into him at home and at church.

"Good so far. Now drop your pants."

While Mama never had him do that, nor Granny, he saw himself perpetually in shorts around home. And they could see his legs that way.

Unsnapped, jeans crumpled around his ankles.

Light shown up and down his legs until Reverend Shepard commanded, "Now the underwear."

Wide-eyed, Ben looked at the man, afraid to question, yet trying to do so with his expression.

Only silence, without option. No flashlight. No escape. Mama had never taken it that far. At least none of the other boys could see as he slid his small underwear down to meet his pants. Standing rigid as a soldier, he prayed for tick check to end.

Ben stared at the overhead limbs remembering doctor visits involving uncomfortable nakedness. He could bear it.

Reverend Shepard moved behind him. A massive hand fell on Ben's shoulder, and he flinched.

"It's okay."

The voice had taken on a soft quality, much unlike his resounding church voice. Ben waited as the minister lingered long, too thorough, it seemed, to be looking for ticks.

Then the man stepped around front. Ben could practically feel the flashlight directed at his privates. He shivered in the warm humid air.

Trying to remain silent, he could hear the night sounds of the woods, but over top of forest chatter, the Reverend's breathing had become heavy. When it stopped, the wet anxious voice said, "No ticks on you. Now time to check me."

Through the dismay, Ben heard the faint rasping of a zipper in motion. Unable to bear another second, he raised his underwear and pants in unison, grabbed his shirt, turned, and ran, heedless of his lack of flashlight.

The safety of the flickering campfire became his singular beacon—stumbling, limbs scratching his arms and face, tripping, landing headlong into the underbrush, then back up running, afraid to check behind him.

At the edge of the camp he paused to fasten his pants, put on the tattered shirt, and catch his breath. Unseen, he took a position at the back of the group behind two of the oldest boys. There he remained vigilant for the return of the monster that had been in front of him the whole time.

In the late 1970s world of Abundance, Sunday as the "Lord's Day" held meteoric significance. The roar of lawnmowers ceased. Businesses closed, except for a few gas stations. Farmers shut down their tractors and sprayers at midnight on Saturday, trusting their crops to God's mercy for twenty-four hours.

Sunday reached beyond being pious for one day. It steered human behavior in Abundance. It was part of the constant pressure for everyone to be God-fearing, hardworking, neighbor-helping, and law abiding, with little wiggle room in any of those areas.

Pairs of suspicious eyes spent each day locked on fellow citizens, with the old adage, "Misery loves company," in play, though better rephrased as, "If I have to be good, so do you." Or perhaps more accurately, "If I have to *pretend* to be good, so do you."

The result: an entire community helping God do His job—The Neighborhood Watch Jesus Police, on patrol, each having a Bible at the ready with which to beat sinners about the head and shoulders. Green, brown, and blue eyes watching for misbehavior, filing infractions in their memory banks for future extortion—or more often, immediate town gossip. Tainted grain for a rumor mill that never stopped grinding.

"Hurry up campers. Get your things in the church van."

Reverend Shepard stood at the apex of constant movement as the Junior Ambassadors broke camp.

"I promised y'all's parents I would have you back in time for preaching, even if you do show up in your outdoors clothes. The good Lord will make an exception for that *this* time."

George helped the process, slinging packs, tents, and sleeping bags willy-nilly into the back of the vehicle as each camper shuffled forward with their gear.

Ben had most of his things readied, making it a point to avoid eye contact with the minister, who hadn't directed any further attention Ben's way. But when he turned from handing his gear to George, he saw a pair of large boots blocking his way.

"Better not forget your flashlight," the Reverend said.

Nothing in his voice indicated any embarrassment or apology.

Ben took the flashlight without looking up at the monster's face.

Following an uneventful drive to the church, the boys stepped out into the shadow of the gleaming steeple, rubbing tired and smoke-reddened eyes.

"Leave y'all's stuff in the van and come claim it after church." Reverend Shepard said. "I've got to scoot over to the parsonage and clean up a bit before preaching."

The group disbanded, moving toward the sanctuary in search of parents. Ben stood by the van a minute longer. He had lain awake most of the night, thoughts racing. His singular hope had been envisioning the discussion that would occur with his peers once they got back to church, with the pastor and George out of range.

Short of full disclosure, he definitely expected a lot of discussion about how weird Reverend Shepard had acted in the woods. *What'd he try with the other boys?* Surely Ben's late-night encounter with the man hadn't been an isolated event.

As he watched the pack of boys move away, undeniably headed into church without the hint of a pow-wow, Ben felt dirty and alone. A sinister realization sprang into his mind. He had been singled out, chosen, in the worst way.

Impulse told him to run from the evil—an instinctual force as old as the Reverend's evil instincts. But run where? A mile and a half down the road to home? Hide in his room and never go to church again? It didn't take Ben long to exhaust the few avoidance options as untenable. He stepped toward the iconic building, determined to stay close to the protection of his grandparents.

Outwardly, evil was nowhere to be seen that glorious April day. All of Abundance smelled like a giant floral shop. Thousands of apple trees, billions of pink-white blossoms, diffused their perfume into the air, even inside the church.

The doors were still thrown open wide as Clete and Bertha Jones walked in at the last minute. Ben twisted around to see Clete's usual rumpled clothes and bed-head hair before the couple took their predictable place in the back row.

"Why does he smell funny?" Ben had asked Pop previously.

"It's from drinking, son."

"Drinking what?"

"Liquor, and lots of it. Mr. Jones is an alcoholic—what folks call a drunk."

When Granny talked about liquor, she made it clear she didn't approve. Few things sounded worse, the way she put it. And her sainted daddy, "never touched a drop," she would righteously conclude.

Another quick glance back at the Joneses and Ben could see Mr. Jones shifting, eyes on the floor, not singing along with the hymns.

Turn around, Granny's silent look said to Ben.

End of hymn, opening prayer, and the congregation took a seat. Reverend Shepard, freshly scrubbed, and hair still wet, began.

"On occasion it behooves us as a congregation to publicly acknowledge sin in our midst."

The folks within Ben's field of vision adopted super-serious faces, as the Reverend continued.

"Today it is our Christian duty to help a fallen brother by pointing out the error of his ways. Clete Jones will you please rise?"

All heads turned to the rear of the sanctuary, nowhere to hide.

Still seated, his red-faced wife jabbed her elbow in his ribs. "Get up," she said, in a too-loud whisper.

"What?" he mouthed back to her.

"The preacher said for you to stand up."

In no hurry, or unable to hurry, Mr. Jones made it to his feet, more curiosity than alarm on his face.

Reverend Shepard regained the momentum.

"Clete Jones, by virtue of your repeated drunkenness, and your disrespect to the Lord, showing up at this place of worship, reeking of alcohol, I am informing you that you are no longer welcome at Redeemer Baptist Church. We will continue to pray for the deliverance of your soul. However, until such time as you can show that the Devil's drink no longer has control over you, do not return to this fellowship."

Two deacons, who had been flanking the door, stepped forward to the pew where Mr. Jones looked from face to face, bewildered.

On Reverend Shepard's lone authority, Clete's neighbors and few friends had become his enemies.

The scene terrified Ben. A quiet, meek man had been singled out for his misdeeds, punished, and publicly shamed. Any remaining respect Ben held for Reverend Shepard plummeted. At the same time, his fear of the man intensified, imagining his own name being called and being told to stand.

Clete Jones worked his way down the pew. The congregation gawked at the back of him as he walked out, escorted by the deacons. No fist-shaking from him, no condemning his accusers, though he was undeniably cut loose from Abundance society.

Throughout her husband's ejection, Mrs. Jones held her head high, eyes fixed front on the giant stained-glass image of Jesus as the shepherd, never moving to wipe away the tears that ran down her face.

Mr. Jones's sin had been articulated in the harshest circumstances. A few pews forward, Ben sat, bewildered and ashamed. Aware that Reverend Shepard playing peekaboo with a little boy's private parts had to fall into the 'sin' category, Ben also felt guilt by association for his involvement in the woods.

Reckon God will punish me too, for going along with it?

Ignoring the sermon, he applied what theological knowledge he possessed, attempting to understand the personal significance of the past, impactful twenty-four hours.

From the expulsion, Ben deduced two options: don't sin at all; or if he did, be sure no one found out about it. Age nine, he was beginning to grasp what it took to be a "good Baptist."

Sin, once it became known, meant risking being cut off from church, which in his child-like reasoning amounted to being cut off from God, Jesus, and the oft-mentioned, dangling carrot of eternal life in heaven.

"Churched," the term he heard a few adult members mention after services, carried monumental weight.

From the episode in the woods, he decided the accusations of a little boy against the top authority figure in town would only worsen what happened.

What's done is done! That's what Granny says. Ain't nothing that can be done about it. Then Pop's advice came to mind. On those occasions when Ben hurt himself, Pop would divert attention by joking, "Well, best stay out of them places," typically causing Ben to smile and move on.

Stay out of them places. That's what I'll do—stay as far from Reverend Shepard as I can.

As soon as the final "Amen" had been uttered, Ben employed his plan.

"Pop?"

"What?"

"I can't stay after church today."

"And why not?"

Ready with an excuse, *Lying to Pop, in church. Reckon what that'll get me?* Ben proceeded, "I got lots of reading to do for school tomorrow."

"Why didn't you do it before now?" Granny joined in, keeping to her role of self-appointed homework monitor.

"I forgot," he replied. His ears caught how lame his excuse sounded.

"Seems to me that you can spare a half hour to do your job," Pop said. He employed the tone recognizable as an end to any further debate.

In the confine between the pews, Ben somehow managed to squirm to excess.

"What's eating at you, son?" Pop asked.

Without a back-up answer, Ben blurted all he safely could of the truth. "I don't want to stay after church and help, ever again. I want to quit!"

"What brought all this on?" Granny asked. "And keep your voice down, young man."

Quitting anything, especially a commitment to another person, veered completely off the chart of acceptable Bramley family behavior. Ben knew it, felt it radiating from his grandparents. Yet, he could not justify his demand without exposing what happened in the woods.

Hard as he thought in the short time allotted before a response became necessary, no answer came that would satisfy them. And much as it killed him inside to disappoint Pop or Granny, he gave the only answer he could.

"I just don't want to do it anymore. That's all."

Though he had chosen to avoid repeating the *quit* word, he knew it changed nothing.

"Is that your final answer?" Pop asked.

"Yes, sir," Ben meekly replied. He had shrunken to looking the part of a whipped dog.

"Well, sir, then there's only one thing left to do."

Ben feared to ask, awaiting Pop's verdict.

"Nothing to be done about it other than you telling the Reverend your news."

"Persecuted," flashed in Ben's head. Mrs. Hazelton had explained the Bible word in Sunday school last Easter when discussing the topic of Jesus being crucified, and how mean people had mistreated him. Best Ben could recall, Jesus kept quiet when being persecuted by his "accusers," another word that had needed explaining.

Pop pointed to the Reverend's location and stepped aside to make way for his grandson.

"Right now."

Arm extended, Pop's order could not be mistaken, and Ben mutely took the first difficult steps.

When he reached the man, already in the process of replacing hymnals in their racks, the Reverend said, "Hey, Ben."

The tone of the greeting reflected no hint of any change in their shared experiences—a just-another-regular-Sunday pleasantry—the vileness of which instantly intensified Ben's loathing and nausea.

Choosing to stare at the scalloped leather trim on the big man's wingtip shoes, Ben spoke in a minimalized voice. "Reverend Shepard?"

"Yes?"

If I tell him Pop and Granny won't let me no more, he'll find out I'm lying.

"I don't want to help no more after church."

"Anymore."

"I don't want to help *anymore*." Ben reflexively complied.

"I'm sure sorry to hear that, Ben. Have you told your grandparents?"

"Yes, sir."

"And did they agree to this sudden change?"

"Yes, sir."

The minister did a scan of the sanctuary, neither of the elder Bramleys in sight.

"I'll certainly miss you," the Reverend said, returning to his chore.

"You can have back all the stuff you gave me."

For all he had endured, Ben's offer bore no malice. The sincere words caused Reverend Shepard pause, though he did not turn to look at Ben.

"No. No. That's not necessary. They belong to you. I want you to have them," he said, continuing down the line of pews without another word.

Like a fish thrown off the hook, Ben sped straight to the

safety of his grandparents' car, mentally urging them to cease their extended fellowshipping on the church steps and remove him from the area before any other ordeal could find him.

CHAPTER TWENTY-FIVE

"If a son shall ask bread of any of you that is a father, will he give him a stone? Or if he ask a fish, will he for a fish give him a serpent?"
—*Luke 11:11*

By age thirteen, Ben knew he didn't want to grow up and become his dad, or anyone else in Abundance.

At sixteen, he realized any computer-related field offered great job opportunity, and more importantly, guaranteed exodus.

High-school bullies picked on Ben's computer-intro classmates, calling them nerds, or twerps, and physically harassed them. Ben escaped the hazing, having achieved his dad's height early, and bearing bulging farm muscles. Classmates avoided close contact, declaring him mad-dog crazy.

He made it through high school with a total of five fights, dramatically lessening his number from the primary grades. Not that his rage softened, it merely adjusted, figuring Duke University was disinclined to accept applicants with major disciplinary records. By resisting taking the first swing, his rap sheet stayed clean. The unrecorded history included a broken jaw, two broken noses, and a mild concussion—all the other guys.

Uncomfortable at home, with Daddy ghost-like next door, and the entire farm a giant reminder of the most-awful day, he found sanctuary in the solitude of the Groverton Library. His frequent forays there became an affront to Granny, given her incessant determination to provide whatever type of home life would lend peace to his troubled world. She plied endless attempts at involving Ben in substitute-family affairs.

"Ben, aren't you going to come watch television with us?"

From his upstairs bedroom, Ben yelled through the floor grate, "I've got homework to do."

He lied. The lies came easier as Christianity lost power over him.

"But it's the weekend." Her voice travelled up, on the reverse course of his.

"Try telling that to my teachers. Even if it weren't the weekend, I've got a big, ongoing project for English." To underscore his scheme he added, "You know I'm in Advanced English class, right?"

"Yes. I just hoped you could take a break."

The identical scene played out hundreds of times, Granny never getting out of her chair to walk up the stairs to his room, to a door which stayed locked.

Unconcerned with her request, he returned to reading his paperback, *The Lord of the Rings.* He had been through the volumes three times, but this moment found him immersed in *The Two Towers,* his least favorite of the trilogy. Reading speedily to get to *The Return of the King,* he felt no remorse over wanting to be alone.

"Don't stay up too late. We've got church tomorrow."

She won't give up.

The childhood plan to avoid being alone with Reverend Shepard still held. Ben would have preferred to drop church altogether, though he assumed it impossible to do while living with devout Baptists. However, with some adroit finagling on Ben's part, entire years would pass without directly speaking a word to the monster from the woods.

Granny's reminder of Sunday obligations caused him to look away from the page, eyes honed on the window. Unmistakable, in the distance, high-beam lights pointed upward, illuminating Redeemer Baptist's steeple.

They wouldn't know a phallic symbol if it poked them in the ass.

Privately cavalier, his blatant contempt couldn't erase the sense of dread he felt, looking at the lighted steeple.

The Eye of Sauron, that's what it looks like, searching Abundance for non-believers and sinners. Ought to start inside the sanctuary, with the evil under the steeple.

Creeping himself out, he broke pattern and descended to the living room, to visible shock on Granny's face.

"Well, well. Look who made it downstairs."

"Guess I could have a snack and hangout out with the senior citizens for a while."

Pop glanced away from the television where The Blue Ridge Quartet were concluding their gospel-show theme song, one which Ben grudgingly knew by heart.

"Hey, I earned these gray hairs, what few are still hanging on," Pop smiled. "And maybe us old folks could teach you a thing or two they don't offer in your advanced classes."

"I'm sure," Ben returned. "You pretty much do every day."

Pop beamed at Ben's compliment.

Ben played along for an hour with Pop and Granny, while the Great Eye remained on his mind, the notion of it watching, peeking through curtained homes, searching the community for commandment breakers.

Would the eye be watching my dad at the moment? If it could speak, maybe I'd finally get some answers as to where he spends those long hours away from us. Away from me.

Taking the analogy further, he speculated on details.

So long as folks smile in the light of day, wave to their neighbors, the Great Eye takes no action. Church attendance is the payment to ignore all the evil. Show up and worship. Show up and worship next week. Pretend everybody is acting Christ-like, twenty-four–seven.

HIGH-SCHOOL GRADUATION ARRIVED AS THE best day of Ben's altered life, though he attended under protest. Having shunned all memory-making benchmarks—dances (including proms), concerts, plays, homecoming games, senior pictures, annuals, and a class ring—he refused to send out a single graduation invitation, preferring to bypass the final event as well. The outcome required a sterner-than-usual Pop stepping in, primarily on Granny's behalf, for Ben to order a cap and gown—under duress.

"What valedictorian doesn't show up for their own ceremony?" Granny had asked of Ben, Pop, and anyone else who got within hearing distance.

Most irksome, Reverend Shepard delivered the benediction. Throughout the tediously lengthy and sickeningly sweet prayer, Ben defiantly kept his head unbowed and his eyes open, not caring who might notice.

Scanning the assemblage, he noted Silk in the same posture, caught by his gaze, extending a knowing smile.

Only person in the world who can make a cap and gown look good, and it would have to be Silk.

Afterward, standing in the smallest circle of well-wishers, Ben felt a tug on his arm as Uncle Stan requested, "Come with me a minute."

"What's up?" Ben asked. Both cap and gown had already been shed.

"Little something for the graduate," Stan answered. His good-natured grin accompanied the request.

On the way to the main parking lot, the overgrown grass in the playground swished against the cuffs of their pants. Ben couldn't avoid seeing the swing where he first met Silk.

So long playground. So long school. And go to hell, Abundance.

Granted a pardon, he toted the release paperwork in the gold-embossed certificate holder tucked under his arm. He had only June and July left to serve in the small town.

In a lot filled with sensible vehicles, Uncle Stan stopped beside a 1966 Chevy pickup truck. Sunlight glared off the bright-red paint and showroom chrome.

"Haven't seen you driving this before," Ben said.

Uncle Stan opened the driver door. "Take a look inside."

"Wow! All-original restoration?" Ben asked.

"Yep. Did all the mechanical work myself. Got a buddy over in Groverton who took care of the bodywork and paint job. A place in Asheville redid the upholstery."

"Where'd you find such a classic? It's too cool, like something straight out of *Hot Rod* magazine!"

Uncle Stan watched as Ben nosed all around the truck in open admiration of the craftsmanship and detail from an era before his birth.

"It belonged to your Grandpa Etter." Stan paused. "He left it behind."

Ben quit inspecting the pickup to give his uncle a shocked look. In the same instant, he heard the word, "Catch!"

Just in time, Ben raised his arm to snag a flying object aiming for his head. An opened hand revealed a set of keys.

"And now it belongs to you."

ARRIVING AT DUKE UNIVERSITY, a pilgrim having reached the Promised Land, he found a community of fellow brainiacs, even the jocks and preps—and best of all, the fresh start.

Not one student had a clue about his past. He could create a stigma-free self, be judged for who he was, not what happened back in Abundance.

Seldom did he mention his last name, should anyone make the association with bygone newspaper headlines. And with few *Ben*'s on campus, and none in the computer department, his first name sufficed. He felt like a *person*, rather than a walking tragedy.

In 1988, computer study was a hot field. The small number of students who understood the workings of the intricate creatures enjoyed widespread admiration. Newfound acceptance did much to bolster Ben's self-image.

When flatland friends asked about his mountain background, he supplied a pat answer.

"It was much like growing up on the television show, *The Waltons*, only I didn't have to share a bed with a bunch of siblings."

Ben managed to concoct compelling reasons for avoiding Abundance during summer breaks. The task of making computer programming sound more important than June, July, and August apple-tending came easily for him.

The four years at Duke sped by as the highlight of his life. Then a too-soon May day arrived, graduation, with a sprawling rectangle of heads baking in the afternoon sun. The University Chancellor's voice boomed, "Benjamin Edward Bramley."

The fresh diploma declared Ben a computer programmer. Pop, Granny, and Daddy stood to applaud, their faces painted with hope. Ben would wait until the celebratory dinner to stomp the life out of the dreams they carried for him.

Somewhere between main course and dessert, Pop asked the question no one else dared.

"So, Ben, I suppose we'll be seeing you back up our way soon?"

Daddy's fork, which had been tracing circles in his plate, came to a halt.

"Actually, I'm going to be hanging around here a while, staying close to the computers. Got a program I'm writing that shows a lot of promise. NASA's interested. Could mean some big bucks."

The motionless fork held Daddy's gaze. With his head bowed, Ben was deprived of seeing if the man's face registered disappointment or relief.

Most likely relief, Ben guessed.

Granny looked like she'd been slapped.

"What on earth are you talking about? We've had to do without you four years, and that's long enough."

His favorite person on the planet, and still Ben was unwilling to make the sacrifice to please her.

"Granny, our countrified community and computer programming are years apart. This shouldn't come as a shock to anyone."

She didn't chide him for dismissing the crossroads-cluster of buildings that made up Abundance. It was the truth of the observation that got in her craw.

"Well, I don't like it one bit."

"Duly noted," Ben replied, with no intention of saying, *sorry*.

The decision had been made for sanity's sake, a necessity to maintain the delicate equilibrium, possible only by time away from all things Abundance.

They said their goodbyes in that graduation-day Steak and Ale parking lot. Daddy made it a point to extend his hand to Ben, who shook it, considering the gesture the sealing of an agreement to avoid any future contact with each other.

CHAPTER TWENTY-SIX

*"There hath no temptation taken you but such as is common to man:
but God is faithful, who will not suffer you to be tempted above that
ye are able; but will with the temptation also make a way to escape,
that ye may be able to bear it."*
—I Corinthians 10:13

The hot engine and burnt brake pad odor from the flatbed
truck jarred Ben out of his transfixed state. Alone in the
wide balk, he assessed his ability to load and haul the latest
round of apples on the truck for the season's final run to the
packing house.

"Incapable," he concluded.

Neither did *load the truck, and leave it for Pop to haul,* figure
as a reasonable plan in Ben's emotional state.

The absolute least he should do—*forego loading the truck,
but drive it back to the house and sheds*—also overwhelmed him.

No truck meant no risk of flattening children on the
highway. Beyond that fundamental point, all immediate action
became a blur.

The young day's events had tapped out his meager reserve
of able-to-function-in-public. He had lost the capacity to
be responsible—the duration of this condition being as yet
indeterminate—while much of his unfortunate flashback still
made neural intrusions.

Within the disturbing mishmash of mental images, one
neon message shone—*RUN!*

Poised to break into a sprint, he glanced at the truck's driver
door, wondering if he had it within himself to grab the keys
from the ignition, and hand them off to Pop. Though he was
hesitant, the rolled-down window offered the reprieve of not

having to enter the cab of the death machine. Yanking the John Deere keychain from the steering column, he launched his body toward Pop and Granny's house.

Three minutes put him in the kitchen, where Pop applied condiments to a makeshift lunch.

"Are you starving, son?" Pop asked a breathless Ben.

"Almost ran over a boy in the road."

Spitting out the words between gasps, Ben dangled the truck keys in front of Pop as if they were plague infested.

"Everybody's okay?" Pop asked.

"Later. Sorry. Can't. Gotta run!"

In expediency, his fingers gave up their grip. Keys hit the tile floor. The metallic concussion made Ben's heart jump in his race upstairs.

Running attire on, he didn't stop to close the front door on his way out, instead instantly angling down River Road. When it hit him that his direction would intersect the scene of the near mishap, he spun in place, like a foot soldier on drill parade, reversing his route. Otherwise, as with each previous occurrence, he had no destination in mind.

The standard refusal to accept that he's running from his past, had led to the defense of, "I'm running toward something." That "something" being temporary salvation— though he avoided framing the severity of the situation with those words. Guarded, he was afraid of waking up on a psyche ward, restrained for his delusions, certain it would be the death of him, with no way to run.

From River Road, he turned onto Valley Road, following it until within sight of Abundance. Dominating the scene, Bobcat Mountain rose more than 2,000 feet above the valley floor, its impressive prominence placing it among the top-fifty peaks in the Southeast.

To Ben, the uplifted earth looked like the degree of severe punishment he deserved for his part in James's drowning, Mama's leaving, Daddy's abandonment, Pop and Granny's heartache, and his own abandonment of family.

Unlike the other mountains encircling the plateau upon which Abundance and its environs rested, Bobcat Mountain did not belong to any connecting ridgelines. It stood alone, like a giant chocolate drop plopped on a platter.

"Reckon God had some leftover meringue when he finished with all the other mountains around here, and Bobcat ended up being the last dollop He went and flung off of His spatula," Pop had postulated to a young Ben.

Unique, it earned status as a state park, complete with picnic grounds, playground equipment, plus a two-acre pond circled by a paved walking trail, level enough to entice frequent baby-stroller parades. However, the major draw, the one which brought outdoor enthusiasts from afar, was the notorious Heaven's View Trail. Winding upward to a viewing platform on the summit, it rewarded the fittest of hikers with unimpeded 360-degree scenery, extending to peaks from four different states.

Ben's shoes clopped across the parking-lot asphalt. Few cars were there on a weekday. He streaked past the trailhead information sign without a glance. Done up in the same yellow-and-black warning colors as state road signs, it spoke to the treacherousness of the trail, and the possibility of serious injury or loss of life, with blatant emphasis on the state of North Carolina being totally absolved of responsibility in any negative outcomes resulting from usage of the trail.

In a word, it was *steep*. The likelihood of added gravel being underfoot to augment the trail, decreased with distance from the parking lot. Too much sweat involved for state-maintenance crews to make the upper reaches, even the mid reaches, leaving nature charged with trail conditions, which meant anything from decaying leaves, to bare ground, to bald rock to negotiate.

Making an effort to stay out of his head, Ben focused on the ground, almost as vertical as horizontal. Well-practiced at trail running, he had logged countless hours on the section of

Appalachian Trailwhich bordered his Cut Laurel Knob home. No stranger to the hazardous potential presented by wet moss and lichens, piles of dry leaves, or roots jutting up in the path, he knew that each footfall counted. Picking his path kept bad thoughts away.

Mentally counting the switchbacks, installed to make the ascent navigable, he ultimately quit tallying when they began coming every fifty yards—a stack of serpent-like coils reaching up the face of the mountain.

Busy watching his foot placement, he summited unexpectedly, rewarding himself by taking a few minutes rest on the observation deck, with no one else around. The fall air allowed the most distant ranges to be clearly seen.

"Pop used to say, 'You can't eat the view,' spoken in true farmer practicality, but it sure does feel filling."

From distant ranges, he pulled back to locate the Bramley and Etter farms—Pop and Granny's seventy-five acres no bigger than his thumbnail from that vantage point. The Unolama, easily traceable, even where canopied by trees, reflected the sun's light as it wound across the plateau floor. Abundance itself made little impression, were it not for the white steeple rising above the height of all nearby trees.

"Damned if it doesn't look all innocent from here." He paused at the notion. "Sorry-ass bunch of fuckers!" he screamed.

His point, though both passionate and loud, dwindled ineffective in the wide space and swirling air currents. A massive red-tailed hawk, dislodged from its perch below him, impressive in size and mastery of flight, soon became a speck, until *poof,* it vanished, swallowed up by the expanse.

"Arguing with no one but myself. And nothing I have to complain about makes the least impact out here."

An awareness of insignificance crept up on him, an insignificance of his problems, an insignificance of *everything,* brought on by the magnitude of geography and a blue sky without end. He'd felt it before, long ago during the trip Pop and Granny had taken him on to Florida to visit Uncle Lucas, Granny's brother. They spent a day at the beach, Ben's first sight of the ocean, too massive to fully comprehend.

The same grasp of dimension, of his place in the order of life, had now revisited him.

Air rushed across his sweaty face and body, the cooling sensation delicious, heightening his senses. He felt old hurts begin to loosen, as he mentally urged them to be carried away with the wind. A baptism of sorts, enough air and outdoors to swallow up his pain. For perhaps the first time, he consciously began to let go. Understanding began to seep into his cranium.

"Hard for the view to make an impact when you're busy looking down at the ground."

The immediate observation had application beyond his ascent of the trail.

"Perspective. That's the word. It's all about perspective."

A forceful updraft caught him full body. Unprepared for, it nudged him back from the deck railing, bringing to mind another of his childhood memory verses, one from the book of Proverbs.

"He that troubleth his own house shall inherit the wind. . . ." Thinking on the implications momentarily, he added, "That pretty well sums what I've been up to, and what it's going to earn me."

Allowing a few more minutes for his surroundings to work their magic, he thought it best to get going before muscles tightened and cramping took hold.

"I believe I found my thin place," he said, a reference to reading he had done regarding locations where the confluence of energies improved outlook, mood, and that word again—perspective.

"I'll be back. More than just for tune-ups. I need a major overhaul, not unlike one of those junkers Uncle Stan restores."

Setting off down the mountain, it took less than a minute to notice the requirement for a different muscle group.

"Moving forward while putting on the brakes," he had termed it, though he had never tackled so steep and unrelenting a challenge as Heaven's View Trail. A single second lapse could increase speed beyond the ability to safely slow. And trying to fully stop typically resulted in total loss of control. Sand and pebbles rolling under soles would carry him in gravity's choice of direction.

Good sense. Good shoes. Eyes out for exit strategies. No shame in dropping backward to a crab position, even scooting on his rear had to be considered. There were no judges awarding style points. He just had to reach the trail end in one piece.

Flatland tourists who freaked out at the lack of guardrails on sections of the Blue Ridge Parkway, where drop-offs hundreds of feet in sheer height hugged the highway, would have found Ben's hike too outlandish for consideration.

The trail, never more than three feet wide, often shrunk, particularly where the switchbacks encountered rock face, allowing no margin for error. Novices often embraced the rock walls and sidestepped around those locations to avoid a tumble, rather than trust their balance. That, or turned back toward the parking lot.

MARTY AND YOLANDA WICKSON, FIRST-TIME visitors to the park, had made it almost halfway up the trail, with him putting on a brave face, and her erring to the side of caution.

"I can't make it around that blind curve. The trail's not wide enough," she said.

"Sure you can. You've made it this far. The brochure said the view up top is unbelievable."

"Little good that does if you die on the way there."

"Look, you go first, and I'll stay behind to hold your hand. Once you're beyond the curve, I'll come. Just stay close to the rock face. Okay?"

"So now you're Davey Crockett?" she said.

"Trust me."

Maybe if their marriage counselor, Dr. Jenny, had not been harping on trust issues last session, Yolanda would have turned back rather than accept the challenge to enhance their relationship.

Hand-in-hand, as Marty suggested, they occupied the entirety of the trail's width when Ben rounded the switchback corner.

CHAPTER TWENTY-SEVEN

"For whosoever shall keep the whole law, and yet offend in one point, he is guilty of all."
—*James 2:10*

"Don't try to move."

The strange voice came as unfamiliar as the setting and the feeling in his head.

"Where does it hurt the most?"

Too disoriented to answer, Ben had questions of his own, but his tongue refused to coordinate with his brain.

"Can you tell us your name?"

Blinking his eyes against the penlight inches from his forehead, he remained mute.

"Your pupils are dilated."

The voice continued, either assuming that Ben comprehended, or perhaps out of habit.

"Likely a concussion, and that left leg looks pretty nasty."

Vaguely aware of someone else hovering over him, a new voice spoke to the first.

"I checked with everyone here. All the cars are accounted for, so no vehicle attached to this guy, which means no help with ID. You double-check for any on him?"

"Sure did. Even looked for a name on his underwear tag," the original voice said. "Thanks for doing the leg work, Craig."

"No problem."

"Well, Mr. Mystery Man," the original voice had returned attention to Ben. "We would normally be taking you to Groverton Community Hospital, but with the possibility of concussion, you earned yourself a ride to Mission Hospital. They've got the right equipment to check you out. Meanwhile, you also earned a sizable dose of Fentanyl. That should make your ride more comfortable."

Ben heard what sounded like doors shutting in the direction of where he thought his feet to be. His eyes couldn't focus enough to identify anything, whether from the pupil exam or his head injury. It felt better to keep them closed than fight with an indistinguishable environment. To lie still and let the strangers do their thing. However, relinquishing all control brought on feelings of helplessness and fear. His health, his continued existence, had been handed over to faceless voices.

Physically, he could not resist. They had all the power. None of which made it easy to agree to those terms. Such a tremendous level of acceptance, of trust without option, went back earlier than he could recall, a powerlessness inherent with infancy.

"Worry not. That's Craig closing the doors. I'll be back here with you the whole way. Now let's get that Fentanyl started. I'm going to inject it through the IV line I put in. That'll speed it up."

He stopped talking to focus on the delivery of the powerful medication.

"There you go. You may feel a little woozy as it hits you."

Understated, Ben felt the punch of the liquid, able to track it as it entered his bloodstream, a locomotive of pain deadening. Mental acuity fled him, but he had ceased to care.

"Lucky that couple on the trail had a cellphone, and were smart enough to know that 9-1-1 can be reached from anywhere. The county rescue team hiked up and got you out. It didn't take long for their guy to rappel down to reach you. They figured you more rolled than fell. Your foot got jammed between some rocks, and likely kept you from pitching off the cliff. We got here in time to meet them part of the way down."

The last word, *down*, slurred in Ben's ears, dragging out at length until tapering to nothing. He remembered no more of the trip.

THE MOBILE NEWS TEAM FROM Asheville's WLOS television station had been at the scene when rescuers brought Ben to the waiting ambulance. Their story would air on the evening news. In addition, local law enforcement officials notified surrounding counties of the John Doe in Mission Hospital's ER.

The fact of the victim not having a vehicle at the trailhead parking lot led those involved to suspect him of being a local. However, the lack of any *Missing Person* reports filed within the past twenty-four hours suggested the possibility of a long wait before any family or friends realized his absence and came forward.

On River Road, Pop had returned to ensure that the pickers had empty boxes available and went about loading the flatbed for the final trip to the packing house.

At the Abundance Café, Silk and her staff played catch-up following the lunch rush.

And at Mission Hospital, three floors up, on a wing opposite the ER, Granny sat bedside with her comatose son, her hope ebbing, though she would not give indication of this to anyone. Nor would she give it more than a second's thought at a time, for doubt played into the Devil's plan. Doubt meant a wavering of faith in God's capabilities. Doubt meant she lacked belief in the efficacy of, not only her own prayers, but Pop's, Reverend Thomas's, and those of the collective Redeemer Baptist congregation.

While her grandson underwent a CT scan of his brain, checking for major malfunctions, Granny bolstered herself by resorting to her usual tactic, retelling her long trove of family memories. Certain that Jason could hear her and understand, she joked and laughed at appropriate points. Heedless of nurses and nursing assistants zipping in and out of the room, her monologue went on for hours.

When the time for Ben to pick her up came and passed, she grew concerned. After fifteen minutes of lateness, she opted to leave Jason and move to the ICU waiting room.

"Ben's running late, Jason. I'm going to save him the time of scrubbing up to come back here and get me. I'll see you tomorrow. Hope you have a restful night so your body can mend. I love you."

At the locked ICU entry door she removed her disposable gown, hair cover, and shoe covers, thankful to be out of them. She was also secretly thankful for the end of another stay. Each day, more of the same nothing. Each day seeming to last longer, until she felt like screaming at someone, or some deity. Still, she had to be at his side. What kind of mother would she be if she stayed home while her son's life hung by several tubes and a respirator?

In the waiting area she found an available chair which would allow her to view Ben's arrival. The wall-mounted television in the small lobby offered a chance to occupy her mind with other people's troubles. The station setting also made her feel secure, channel thirteen, based in Asheville, the one she would have been watching from home.

Local news aired, WLOS, with Darcel Grimes reporting, a long-time veteran of the program. Granny felt like she knew the newscaster personally. After a feature on a special event upcoming at the Biltmore House, Darcel introduced a field reporter with the story of a hiking accident on Bobcat Mountain. An unidentified man had gone off the trail, with injuries serious enough to send him to Mission Hospital, where he was listed in serious but stable condition. Cameras on the scene showed the accident victim on a gurney being moved into a waiting ambulance.

The injured man's face couldn't be seen, but his Day-Glo Nikes extended beyond the gurney's length—he was a tall fellow apparently. The reporter interviewed a couple who witnessed the fall. Neither had much of significance to add, other than to state that the man had been running, and almost knocked them over. The reporter concluded by saying that local authorities requested anyone having any information regarding possible identity to come forward.

"Back to you, Darcel."

The news clip had instigated a feeling in Granny's gut which began working on a message to send to her brain. Aware of the process, she turned her interest from the program, ruminating on what it could have been about the report that had aroused her intuition, maybe nothing more than her lifelong association with the mountain's unavoidable presence.

Minutes later, Pop appeared.

"Where's Ben?"

"Can't say."

"Did he come home after dropping me off this morning?"

"Yep. He hauled a load. Then around about dinner time he showed up at the house, all a mess, going on about having almost run over a boy in the road. Then said he couldn't handle it, had to go running, and that's the last I seen him."

Granny did the math. "Dinner time to now supper, that's way longer than he could be running. You figure maybe he stopped by the café to see her?"

"I swung by there on the way here. Told me she saw him around noon when he gassed up the truck, but not since. And that had to be before he brought me the keys in the kitchen and took off."

"Maybe he came home, showered, and drove somewhere."

"Nope," Pop said, his head shaking the same message. "His car is still in our driveway."

"That don't leave many options."

Short of scratching her head, she stood in the waiting area, unable to leave until she had answers. Pop stood quietly, having stated all he knew.

Less than a minute, she asked, "Did you see his tennis shoes?"

"Not today, but I have."

"What color are they?"

"I don't exactly know what you'd call it. They're some sort of bright lime-green, yellow color. Kinda like that Gatorade stuff, only brighter."

Granny snatched her purse up from the chair where she had sat. "Come with me."

"Where we headed?"

"To the Emergency Room."

PATIENT JOHN DOE SOON HAD an identity attached to him, and a room assignment on the way.

"Mild concussion," the ER doctor said. "We're keeping him overnight for observation. We did a CT scan. No hemorrhaging. All looked fine."

"But he couldn't tell you his name?" Granny asked.

"He may have tried. His speech is terribly slurred. That will improve. And with the pain medicine he's received, his coherence has been affected. You said he's staying with you?"

"For now," Granny said.

"Well, there's a lot to go over before we send him home, as far as what to expect over the next few days, what to avoid, and what to do to aid his recovery. They will cover that tomorrow when he's released. The desk has your contact information?"

"Yes, sir," Granny said to the doctor, thirty years her junior. "That don't matter. We'll be here. I'll be here."

"Also, that's a walking cast on his left leg, not that he needs to be walking at length right away. Simple fracture of the fibula, the smaller of the two lower leg bones. The nurse will give you his room number when they take him up, which should be soon."

Making his exit, a slight wave of the doctor's hand forestalled any lengthy goodbyes.

Eyes closed, Ben's sight had gone from blurry to double vision, which worsened his lack of clarity. Better to see nothing than two of everything. And being a pain-medication virgin, the earlier Fentanyl injection had also reduced his capacity to function passably.

Granny couldn't help herself, determined to communicate with him in spite of the impossibility, the same as she had been doing with another Bramley male in a hospital bed.

"They law, help my time!" she said, in her favorite euphemism, breaking the Third Commandment wholesale, though unaware of it.

"How did this happen?" she asked, yet paused not. "What were you thinking, off on that mountain, nobody knowing where you got to? What if I hadn't seen that story on the news? How would we have known what became of you?"

The potential tally of questions stopped short when Pop intervened.

"Lily, the nurse said he needs quiet. Let his brain rest. Not even TV. The more he can sleep, the better. And now that he knows we came, we best be getting on home."

"I'll do no such thing. Not leaving my grandson like this."

"Hon, you're already wore to a frazzle. If you don't get home and get some rest yourself, you ain't going to be fit to help either Ben or Jason."

Standing behind, unable to read her expression, Sam Bramley's patience had served him well over their fifty-five years of marriage. He could wait.

Lily, not so quick to admit to her husband's sensibility, took her time before agreeing, making sure to include a reluctant tone to her acceptance of his advice.

Subscribe to Southern Fried Karma's YouTube channel, Fugitive Views, to hear how the author imagined Ben's experience of falling from a steep mountain trail.

CHAPTER TWENTY-EIGHT

"And he that curseth his father, or his mother, shall surely be put to death."
—*Exodus 21:17*

Darkness had begun losing its dominance over a narrow band of sky above the Black Mountain range. Without having to stir the ache in his head, Ben could grasp the occurrence of a shift taking place out the window to his right. Whether he was seeing sunrise or sunset, he could not determine with surety. It took him another moment to recall the association between impaired eyesight and falling from precipices.

His reentry into the world came well timed, during one of the quieter periods of a typical hospital day. With corridors nearly vacant of foot traffic, and staff immobilized by paperwork to submit before shift change, the sleep-deprived patients used the lull to full advantage. A serendipitous opportunity for Ben to tackle what felt most pressing—a timeline reconstruction of the recent events—though he found that *it hurt to think.*

"That doesn't sound very medical," he said, feeling the oddity.

His vocal observation caused a stir to his left, taking him away from the window to find a sleeping Silk reclined in a bedside chair, readjusting herself from what had to be one uncomfortable position to the next.

His gaze tapped her subconscious shoulder. Opening her eyes, she met his.

"Morning, glories," she said. "Or in this case, morning, *glory.*"

She waited. When he seemed confused, she clarified.

"That's how Mrs. Hazelton used to greet our class every morning, never growing tired of the punny-ness. Anyway, that wouldn't fly these days, what with most kids being ignorant of wildflowers."

"When did you get here?"

"Last night, after visiting hours. Your grandparents called when they got home to give me the news. I made sure they didn't intend to return overnight. Wouldn't want to be accused of being a double-vigil-er, you know—stepping on family feet, shoving my giant nose in where it doesn't belong. I'll stop with the imagery."

He smiled, a little.

"Glad you came. Sorry about the chair."

"You had no clue that I sat here."

"Makes me feel better knowing," he said. Reaching a hand from under the sheet, he attempted to hold hers.

She took it gingerly, noticing his impaired coordination.

"My being here has selfish motives, as in no way would I have slept a wink at home. I had to put eyes on you. Watch you breathe. Convince myself of the best."

Unable to avoid a sniffle, she pulled a tissue from the hospital tissue box on the nightstand. Wiping her nose, she added the wadded paper to a noticeable pile. Her touching concern cut through his mental fog.

She turned to surface matters in order to rein in her fright and sorrow.

"Those are some nasty-looking scratches on top of your hand, and your face. What's the rest of you look like?"

"Haven't seen," he said.

She started to lift the sheet, then thought better.

"Not important. Wouldn't want to mar my image of your statuesque body, the one which I had my way with at the pond."

She smiled, but didn't touch, sure that his injuries must be widespread. Enough satisfaction for her that she had made a sedated man blush.

"What's today?" he asked.

"Tuesday. Tuesday morning. Your name is Ben Bramley. I'm Silk Mayer, your girlfriend. Repeat after me, 'girlfriend.'"

She had adopted a slow, serious tone, as if speaking to an imbecile. Straight-faced, she could maintain it a mere handful of seconds before guffawing at herself.

"Still amusing yourself," he said.

"I almost forgot. Your Abundance's new most-famous citizen, though technically an ex-patriot."

"What do you mean?"

"You made the TV news. I caught the eleven o'clock edition right here, bedside with the brave survivor. And now that you've been identified, they've flashed up a picture to go with the body on the gurney. Must have been taken during your Duke days. So handsome!"

She mocked a swoon, the back of her hand to her forehead.

Up from the recliner, she tried to straighten out her hair and crumpled clothes.

"What are you doing?"

"I gotta run before Granny catches me. I've violated her implied orders."

"What orders? What does she care?"

"The medical orders about you needing rest, quiet, no stimulation. And let's face it, I could be silent as a stone and still stimulate the hell out of you."

She spun around slowly, gyrated her rear for his perusal, and for a finale, raised the bottom of her blouse to chin level.

"Oooh! I forgot about rushing out without my bra," she said, innocently. "Looks like your pupils are working fine, at least. I'll catch up with you back at River Road this evening. That is if Granny opens visiting hours."

"Don't call ahead. Show up. Won't turn you away," Ben said, resorting to sentence fragments. The utterance of each word had begun a series of flashes across his brain, lightning-like hot pain.

"Deal."

Leaning over his bed, she kissed his lips like they were razors.

"You rest, mister. We've got lots more picnicking to do."

Sorry to see her back moving through the door opening, Ben heeded her advice and shut his tired eyes.

"YOUR POP'S IDEA TO BRING your car. Mighty presumptuous," Granny said, declaring herself innocent of any breech of protocol.

"All I said was that he could get in and out easier of this than the Impala," Pop said. His exasperated defense left Ben to figure he had entered in on the tail of a disagreement that had occupied their entire drive to the hospital.

Uninterested in taking sides, Ben rode up front, sporting hospital-issue sunglasses. Nothing more than wrap-around black plastic, and highly disposable, they kept outdoor brightness from following his optic nerve up to his brain.

He tuned out both grandparents, recalling Pop's affinity for Chevrolet, the man having driven no other make since his first car. One occasion Ben got to tag along to a car lot and witness Pop's dissection of a hopeful young salesman. When the purchase price dropped to Pop's liking, the wad of cash he removed from the bib of his overalls left the salesman agape. Pop then counted out the full amount, stacking it on the car's hood in the middle of the sales lot.

"Reckon that settles it," Pop had said, replacing plenty of reserve bills back in the bib. "Right on the barrelhead."

Halfway to River Road, Ben spoke his first, though talking hurt. The search for simple words to make simple sentences left him choosing silence, though that wasn't fully possible with Granny nearby.

"Granny. Go back to the ICU."

"No such doing," she said, in her mother hen voice. "We got to get you home and settled. Maybe make you a bed on the living-room couch to keep you off those stairs."

Holy Moses! Somebody shoot me in the head, quickly.

Lacking the strength to argue, he focused on marshalling his resources to mount the stairs upon arrival.

He almost fell backward in the actual attempt.

"I told you so," Granny said, caring not one whit about employing a cliché.

TUESDAY, WEDNESDAY, AND THURSDAY BECAME the epitome of *routine*. Ben's single victory amounted to Granny's return to the hospital, Pop taking over the driving.

"No problem," Pop had said, reassuring Ben. "No more trips to the packing house: all I have to do is string out empty boxes and bring full ones back to the shed. Fact is, you would have just gotten in the way."

That smile of Pop's, his steady nature, seemed better medicine than the pills.

With River Road smack in the middle of an electronically unfriendly desert, Ben had no means of contacting Dr. Mendel, other than his grandparents' land line.

"Note to self: Pay Pop and Granny's October telephone bill, and so help me, don't let this crap continue into November."

Those words he said while on hold, the first day back on River Road, thankful, at least, that his predicament bought him some privacy.

"Yes. . . . Thanks, Doris. . . . No problem. . . . I'll keep waiting," he said to the office manager.

Soon thereafter came the reward for his patience.

"Hello, Benjamin."

"Hey, Doc. Wanted to explain my absence."

"No need. You're all over the news. How are you feeling?"

Though he intended to be thorough, Ben did little more than establish a convenient call time for the days ahead. Anticipating mental upheaval as a consequence of his inability to run, he intended to rely on her counselling. Too soon, too many words spoken, and slightly shy of a headache threatening to peak, he squeezed in a condensed version of his epiphany atop Bobcat Mountain.

"That's wonderful news, Ben."

"One final thing. Please check your email. I may be able to shoot you some through a complicated system which involves limited computer use at an out-of-town library, and my girlfriend agreeing to do it before her workday begins."

The phone's earpiece silent, he asked, "Still there, Doc?"

Her shocked surprise could not be muted by the miles. "Did you say *girlfriend?*"

"Yes, ma'am. I reckon I did."

"That's quite a development, particularly for a man who dismisses his desirability. Moving fast, and may I ask her name?"

Dr. Mendel gave him no shot at answering, following up with her next question, "Is it Silk?"

"Bingo, but my brain wants me to shut up. I promise details next call. Bye, Doc."

"Ben, I am incredibly proud of you. Call back soon. Good-bye."

Handset returned to the receiver, Ben adjusted the phone to Granny's specifications.

"That went well. Don't you think so, Smoky?"

The cat had stretched out along the top of the couch.

"With near-death survival comes privileges," he said, Granny having agreed to Smoky's downstairs relocation while Ben recuperated. Her decision did not have purely altruistic motives—she had grown tired of hearing the cat loudly bemoan the loss of its owner, the sound travelling through the floor grate to the living room, and migrating throughout the house.

Another small addition to routine came in the form of Ben's determination to use his plight to complete his reading of *The Gulag Archipelago*. Pop had fetched the copy from upstairs.

Upon seeing it, Granny voiced concern.

"You figure that's a good idea after all those instructions the nurse gave us when they discharged you? Your eyesight and all?" she asked.

Aware that Granny's concern often had unspoken agendas, Ben wondered if she would have spoken up had he held a KJV Bible in hand.

"No need to worry. I'll take it easy. Not much choice, and, besides, I'll probably only read half the words. When I come up on those unpronounceable Russian names, I skip right over and keep going."

Silk had stopped by shortly after Pop and Granny returned Ben from the hospital. She took to bringing supper, which at first rankled Granny, until Silk explained that Ben had more-or-less inconvenienced his grandparents with his foolhardy behavior.

"Therefore, it's only fair of me to pitch in and help while he can't."

So the arrangement was accepted, and welcome when the grandparents got their first sampling of Silk's culinary expertise.

Startling to Ben, when meals ended, Pop and Granny went about their evening rituals as if Silk's presence dictated no need for special treatment. Not judging them as callous or rude, he soon came to see it as the greatest compliment they could pay—treating her like family.

Each night she would stay until eleven-thirty, concluding her visit with the local news programming Pop and Granny never failed to watch. Afterward, Ben would shamble behind Silk out onto the covered front porch where they would sneak a few kisses and exchange the tender words held back around Pop and Granny.

The porch setting also served for Ben to fill in gaps from his childhood narrative. Usual shields had been lowered by his regimen of pain medication and muscle relaxers, allowing him to reveal the events of his mother's leaving, and the camping trip's sexual advances from Reverend Shepard.

"Now you have all the gory highlights," he had said, in answer to her question of any more to follow.

FRIDAY MORNING, FOLLOWING BREAKFAST AND his grandparents' departure, Ben returned to the couch, only to be startled
by Silk standing in the living room.

"What are you doing?" he asked, quickly shifting to, "What
a nice surprise!"

"I'm breaking you out." She couldn't avoid a conspiratorial
whisper, though she knew them to be alone in the house. As
if it the room contained listening devices, she quietly added,
"Get dressed and come on."

He obeyed, overjoyed at his first chance at outdoor activity.

Outside, she directed him toward her pickup, parked across
the road.

"Why the hike?" he asked.

"You'll see. I couldn't risk your Granny being home, or Pop
pulling up before we could get out of here."

When they reached her vehicle, she nodded at the truck
bed. Inside, he saw a mattress of sorts in an unimaginative
taupe color.

"I give up," he said.

"Came off the futon in my spare bedroom. It may be a little
dewy. I slipped it in last night, cover of darkness and all, avoid
any nosy folks passing by."

Her pleasure with the successful accomplishment rode
plainly on her face.

"Get in the cab," she said, without explanation.

Rather than inquire, he chose to let the surprise play out,
until she took a right turn onto the pond road.

"Headed to the pond, are we?" he asked.

"Not exactly."

Bypassing the pond, they continued up the incline, parking
on the backside of the orchard. Secluded by trees all around, she
cut the engine and looked him over like an item on the buffet.

"Out of this truck," she said.

Without question he followed her direction, meeting at the
tailgate, which she opened.

"You're tall. Probably easiest if you back up, butt against the tailgate, and what you can't manage on your own, I'll do to get you in."

The effort proved less than either expected, as she helped him get centered on his back.

"Comfortable?" she asked.

"Moreso than on Granny's couch, and the sky is a pleasant change of view."

What he took to be further adjusting as he spoke, had been her undoing his belt and zipper, which became apparent when the cool air hit his genitals.

"Whoa! What the hell?"

"Here's what the hell," she said, undoing her own pants, already stripped of blouse and bra.

"You're sick-card privileges are hereby revoked. And that speechless look on your face is priceless."

Without raising his head, he recognized the slippery sound of her jeans peeling off her legs.

"You are going to lie there and let me do all the work while I rock the hell out of your world."

She paused for effect.

"All that remains is for you to choose: Cowgirl or Reverse Cowgirl?"

"What?"

"Then, both it is!"

WHEN SILK RETURNED WITH SUPPER that night, she and Ben couldn't avoid excessive eye contact, the knowing kind of exchange. Neither Granny nor Pop made mention of it.

"Got a surprise for the cooped up patient," Pop said, which elicited red ears from Ben at hearing about the second surprise of the day. "Everybody to the den."

The room doubled as a large entryway for the front door and the stairs leading up to Ben's former bedroom. At the center stood an old piano bench with an older Bell and Howell 16mm projector. Seven feet ahead of it, a movie screen waited.

Pop spoke mainly to Silk. "We have a passel of old family movies which we never watch, until tonight. Mostly Ben's younger days."

"Oh, how delightful!" Silk literally cooed at the thought of Ben's upcoming embarrassment.

"I'll make us some popcorn later," Granny said, "after supper settles."

Far more entertaining than the films' too-frequent landscape panoramas or the close-ups of apple-tree blossoms, Ben enjoyed watching Pop shine in his dual role of projectionist and narrator.

The trip to Florida featured in one reel, with the beach that Ben had recalled atop Bobcat Mountain's viewing platform. Also included was a zoo visit while there, and several feet of film from the historical fort at St. Augustine.

In another, Ben piled brush in the orchard, with Barker the dog making cameo appearances, darting on and off screen. Daddy must have held the camera while Pop gave young Ben a pruning lesson, cheering him on with each cut.

"Best grandpa a boy ever had," Ben said when the heart-warming reel ended.

Granny and Silk shuffled off to pop the corn for the second-half showing. Pop busied himself with rewinding the reel, and threading in a new one, his face practically in the machine.

"It still holds true," Ben said. On his way to the bathroom, he heard a sniffle from Pop.

THE SECOND PORTION OF FAMILY movie night travelled farther back—birthdays and Christmases, featuring both Ben and James.

"None of these is labelled." Pop's voice cut through the cone of color emitting from the blinding light.

Ben reached forward to place a hand on his grandpa's shoulder.

"It's all right. It's important to remember everything," Ben said.

Proving his point, he laughed at the antics between James and Barker.

"He loved that dog," Ben said.

"He sure did," Granny added.

The scene switched to bath time, Ben and James small enough to share a tub, bubbles cascading over the edge. A large hand reached onscreen to prevent James from eating a fistful. Ben formed a double handful into a hat, which James then sought to obliterate. In the background, resting on the corner edge of the tub, was an unmistakable bottle of Ivory Dishwashing Detergent.

Silk elbowed Ben in his side, obviously enjoying the show. Even Granny got tickled.

I can stand a world of teasing after that number she threw on me today, he thought. *So why am I suddenly uncomfortable?* And when the discomfort rose to agitation, something told him to break away, abort, pulling him by the shirt collar. *They won't understand, thinking I'm a bad sport, and I'll ruin everybody's fun, on top of it.*

He endured the scene, which left him feeling both frigid and fiery throughout the remainder of their viewing.

Something. Something buried.

"It's too late for regular Maxwell House, but not too late for decaf. I'll fix us some," Granny said. Off to the kitchen, Silk trailed, asking if she could help.

Ben disassembled the movie screen and passed it to Pop, and everything soon returned to its home in the closet under the stairs.

"That was great. Thanks y'all." Ben's blanket thanks extended to the whole group, back in their usual spots in the living room.

Along with the coffee, a tray of cookies had appeared. They got little attention due to Silk enthusiastically probing Pop and Granny for stories about boyhood Ben.

Feeling like an invisible bystander, Ben decided to force his way into the dialogue, halted by the jarring ringer from the antiquated telephone. "Awfully late for a phone call," he said.

Granny's voice had trailed off, and her face dropped, leaving Silk to face three Bramley mannequins, none moving to take the call. Seconds passed as rings mounted.

"Shall I get the phone?" she asked sheepishly.

"I'll get it."

Ben picked up the receiver within earshot of everyone. "Bramley residence. Ben speaking. . . . Yes, I'm his son . . . okay . . . I understand . . . we'll be right there."

He hung up without a good-bye, searching the room for anything other than Pop's or Granny's eyes.

All past ordeals lost significance compared to the news he had been bequeathed to dump on them. And the moment he had gleefully played in his head, scores, hundreds of times, came wrapped in gravity he couldn't have imagined.

"His breathing is failing. The ventilator can't keep up. The doctor has lowered the Propofol so he can be awake for us to say good-bye. We have to go this minute."

Silk rushed him, arms around his neck.

"I'm so sorry," over and over again.

Pop and Granny hadn't left their chairs. The inevitable conclusion had been sending out signs of its arrival, but revealed itself in surprise.

"Is there something I can do here?" Silk had broken away from Ben to ask Granny specifically. "If not, I'll get moving and get my truck out of the way."

The helplessness of a family in pain had already infected her. None of them spoke until Ben found his voice.

"Come with us, please," he said.

More to the point, *Come with me*, though he had not a clue as to the magnitude of his request for her immersion in misery.

Silk's mouth opened to speak, her head already shaking in refusal.

"It wouldn't be right," she might have planned to say, or maybe "proper," or perhaps she would have included "intruding" in her argument, but, from the chair where seconds before there had been smiling and the enjoyment of a fresh face in her home, Granny spoke ahead of Silk.

"She should come with us."

No enthusiasm in her words. More like the flat intonation of an oracle in mid-vision, stating the facts as she saw them.

Silk voiced no opposition.

"Hon, I'll get your coat and purse," Pop said.

Already witness to her lack of forward momentum, he returned from the bedroom to find her still glued to her chair. Lovingly lifting her up, he helped get her into the coat.

Silk had gone outside to move her truck across the road, freeing up the SUV.

"I'll drive," Ben said.

"No. I'll drive," Silk said. "None of us wants you behind the wheel with that cumbersome cast on your leg."

"Turn off the coffeepot." Granny's only words before they headed out the door.

"Mrs. Bramley, why don't you ride in front?" Silk said.

"No. Ben needs more room than me."

Silk wanted to be close, to take Granny's trembling hand if needed, and pass her tissues that she had retrieved from her truck.

"They're not much," Silk said, leaning back to hand them off to Granny. "Maybe they'll last you until we get there."

Backing on to River Road, Silk shifted into drive.

"Granny, we can get to Asheville in half the time if we take the interstate," Ben said.

"Fine," she replied. Hers became the only word spoken by anyone for the entirety of the heartbreaking journey.

THE VEHICLE CRAWLED UP TO the ominous building, halting at the main entrance to deposit the parents of Jason Bramley for their final visit.

Ben informed Granny, "I'm going to come along with Silk, if that's okay with you."

She gave no objection.

The young couple waited to watch the grandparents step safely inside.

Rolling toward the parking deck, Ben began with the words which he had been sitting on for miles of highway.

"I am so sorry for dragging you into this. I don't know if I can do it, and I especially don't know what to do where Pop and Granny are concerned."

"First, I came of my own choosing. Second, we're going to all get through this. Third, you have to pull yourself together. Your dad's going to die tonight. Let that start sinking in so it doesn't come as a shock to you when it happens. And while it's okay to grieve, even cry, you cannot let yourself fall to pieces around your grandmother."

She had found a close parking space due to the hour.

"Look at me," she said, demanding. "This isn't a suggestion. You're losing a dad, no matter how you feel about him, good or bad. They're losing a son, a son they still deeply love in spite of his being an ass. Are you hearing all this?"

He rubbed the heel of each hand across his eye sockets and jerked the fog out of his brain.

"I got it. I'll be strong."

"Keep thinking about them, not yourself. You've got the rest of your life to sort it all out to your satisfaction. No feeling sorry for yourself tonight. Now let's catch up."

CHAPTER TWENTY-NINE

"Know ye not that the unrighteous shall not inherit the kingdom of God? Be not deceived: neither fornicators, nor idolaters, nor adulterers, nor effeminate, nor abusers of themselves with mankind, nor thieves, nor covetous, nor drunkards, nor revilers, nor extortioners, shall inherit the kingdom of God."
—I Corinthians 6:9–10

Silk took Ben's hand as they walked toward a giant building where death didn't elicit any more of a reaction than did an employee shift change.

Pop and Granny had passed through the locked double doors by the time Ben and Silk arrived outside the ICU.

"I'm going to stay here in the waiting room," she told him.

"Are you sure?" he asked. "You could come back."

"This is too personal a moment. I'll be here for you when you come out. Now go. Be with your family."

Seconds after pushing the speaker button, the lock clicked free, and the doors began to swing open.

"Be strong."

"I will. I hope."

He looked back at her, his chance for a new life—on the other side of the doors from him now. More than anything, in that moment, he wanted to remain on the side which offered promise, but the old life still owned him, obligations pulling him away.

Alone at the scrub station, strict adherence had lost significance. He bypassed the scrubbing part and moved to gown and head covering.

"Forget the shoes."

When he walked up to room 129, Pop and Granny stood outside the door speaking to a nurse whom Ben recognized.

"As you heard on the phone, Dr. Berner has lowered the Propofol so he can be coherent enough for you all to speak to him. Don't expect him to be too lucid. He can hear you, though it's doubtful he will respond."

Granny interjected. "Can't you turn up the breathing machine to get him enough air?"

Her request had such a pitiable quality. Ben felt control slipping. The hand in his front pocket clawed into Cowboy's plastic body.

"Mrs. Bramley, the ventilator is at full capacity. Any increased pressure at this point would rupture his lungs. The issue, now that the swelling has lessened, is spinal-cord damage. The nerves that cause the breathing muscles to work are no longer doing their job. And in addition, his heart rate is critically low. I'm afraid there's nothing we can do. Dr. Berner wanted you to know before you saw your son. Do you have any other questions?"

"How . . . ?" was all Pop got out before choking up.

The nurse understood.

"I can't say for sure. Best guess, less than an hour. That's why we called you in. I'm sorry."

She put a hand to Granny's shoulder before moving on.

The three stood unmoving. The heaviness that Pop and Granny wore forced Ben to acknowledge their advanced age, rather than the changeless picture of them which he held in his mind.

Pop's movement toward Daddy's door set Ben and Granny in motion.

Most of the monitors had been removed from the room. It looked eerily like an apartment at the end of its lease, the renter all packed and ready to go, still hanging on, maybe to hand-off the key. The three formed an arc around the foot of the bed.

Strange to see Daddy's blue eyes open, making him appear in better health than their previous visits. He stared at the ceiling, interrupted by slow, infrequent blinks, until finally looking at them, not so much directly as in their general direction.

"Jason," Granny began, "can you hear me?"

Lacking definitive acknowledgement, Granny, however, took the blink following her question as a sign he could. She moved closer, taking his hand.

"Can you squeeze my hand?"

He couldn't.

"Hey, son," Pop said, and no more.

Ben realized that left him to speak now, unprepared.

"Hey, it's Ben."

The eyes had drifted back to the ceiling, saving Ben from direct contact.

How stupid was that? This is worse than I imagined.

"We're all here together to see you," Granny said, sounding almost cheerful. "We hope you're not in pain," she added.

Pop filled in.

"Jason, since your accident, your mother and I have been praying for you. The whole church has been praying for your healing."

In spite of swirling emotions, Pop drew a deep breath, and exhaled audibly, seeming determined to convey his message.

"More important than healing, I've prayed for your forgiveness. Jesus told his disciples that all sins can be forgiven. Still, we have to confess our sins and ask the Lord to wash them away. I hope you've searched your heart, and prayed for that grace. Because it's like this, and I ain't going to sugarcoat it, your time here on this old earth is up."

The bluntness of Pop's words caused Granny's shoulders to seize. Nevertheless, he concluded his urgent plea.

"If you want to see heaven's gates, admit your sins, ask for the shed blood of our Savior to cover them, and enter on in."

After he'd said his peace, he said no more.

The vocalized reality of their Baptist faith, applied to her dying son, became Granny's breaking point.

"I can't stay another second," she implored Pop.

As if on cue, Daddy's dulled eyes rolled across her.

"I'll stay," Ben offered, surprising himself. Never before in that position, never before in immediate proximity to death, he nonetheless recognized the call.

Pop and Granny ought to be spared the final act. I can at least give them an out.

"I love you," Granny said to her son. Releasing his hand, her eyes still on him, she and Pop drifted toward the door.

Ben watched them leave, Pop's arm securing Granny's trembling frame.

Then he waited. And waited longer, making certain they wouldn't return.

Pulling a long breath, he summoned the nerve to speak.

"This is an opportunity I didn't expect."

He moved to the head of the bed, sure to be heard. Daddy's eyes had returned to the ceiling panels.

"I reckon this is where I'm supposed to get all sentimental, breakdown and say I forgive you, oh, and tell you how much I love you."

He paused.

"Not going to happen. Your death doesn't earn you a 'Get Out of Jail Free' card from me. Dying won't repay a lifetime of neglect—my lifetime. So, I'm going to use our last moments together to my benefit. You can't be healed. I still have a shot, and it's past time for me to unload some of the poison that's choked my world."

Ben leaned down, lowering his volume, lest he attract the attention of the staff.

"When I needed you the most to be a grown-up, be a dad, you cut and ran. A selfish coward, that's how I came to see you. Still do. Not that all the blame falls on you. James's death. . . ."

Ben stopped, the words he never said aloud threatened to cut short his tirade. He swallowed the guilt and gave himself back over to anger.

"I still bear a lot of that for going fishing without him. I don't even blame Mama, because once he decided to go on his own, no one could have stopped him. But Mama's leaving . . . sure, she could have stayed and suffered with the rest of us—though, why would she, after the way you treated her?"

Ben had not seen the letter. Lost in the flotsam of Mama's leaving, he didn't ask Pop or Granny about the contents of the envelope withdrawn from the mailbox the day of her disappearance. It hadn't occurred to him, once an adult, to ask to see any evidence on file at the sheriff's office.

"I heard y'all fighting that night after the Christmas pageant. Unrepeatable hatefulness flew out of your mouth. Things no one should ever have to hear. You, more worried about how you looked to the folks in church, than how Mama felt being bullied by that monster of a minister. You came down on the side of a pedophile."

He caught himself on the verge of dismantling the bedrail, no recollection of latching on to it, fighting back tears of rage, determined to not appear weak or sympathetic.

"Did you figure I forgot?"

The heavy hospital bed was jerking about, Ben's adrenaline pumping.

That "something" which couldn't be placed during movie time, the cold which clutched his heart, had been the topic of his fixation on the silent drive to the hospital. The luxury of being in the passenger seat afforded him opportunity to combine hidden memories with the images of the bathtub movie scene.

Pictures from the past coalesced to form a collage of that which he had compartmentalized to hide from himself. Suppressed childhood details leapt forward, and the need to vomit seized him, that *no time to stop the car, roll down the window, I can't wait,* kind of vomiting. Finger on the window-control button the entire drive to the hospital, he had mightily fought against every internal impulse, until ultimately, as during the film, he had held it together for the sake of the group, for the death they rushed toward.

"I remember. Oh, I remember! That sick game of yours when James and I were little, you know the one."

Leaning over the side rail his nose almost touched his dad's, eyes locked on the elder man's.

"You called it 'Find the Washcloth.' Helping us with our bath when Mama wasn't around, running your hand under the soap bubbles in the tub, fondling us, molesting us. Then making us do it to each other, while all the time you were laughing and saying, 'Where's the washcloth? Where's the washcloth?'"

He saw a spare pillow in the chair where Granny had sat earlier that day.

Ought to smother the pervert.

Fixed on the potential weapon, seconds elapsed before he decided, *Too merciful. Let him keep suffering and feel death creeping closer.*

"Then you brought your Polaroid in the bathroom that time. The bright flash shining in our eyes, while you made James and me stand there naked as you photographed us playing with each other's . . ."

A swift fist slammed the mattress, an inch from his dad's head. The older man looked terrified, eyes blinking rapidly. Too enraged to appreciate the effect, Ben went on.

"Whatever became of those photos? Huh? Did Mama figure out you were a deviant? A sexual predator? Maybe rather diddle with little boys' privates than be with a woman?"

There was no response from the dying man.

Turning from the bed, Ben paced the room like a frenzied beast, fists clenched at his sides, growling, animal-like, in his body's attempt to control immeasurable pressure, before he could trust himself to return bedside.

"After James, when you dumped me off on Pop and Granny, you became a single man, no children, partying ever chance."

Ben had regained some control.

"I wonder, how many different women did you screw in that house, trying to prove to yourself that you were a real man? Or maybe it was the other way around, with you thinking of the old Reverend while they dominated you!"

The idea of his dad as a submissive got Ben chuckling, a fiendish clucking sound, overflowing with aged retribution.

"And how much booze did you piss down the toilet, using alcohol to erase the image of what a sick fuck you've been all along?"

The half-lidded eyes shifted to Ben, almost frightening him when he considered the evil mind behind the blue irises.

He had more to say.

"Almost thirty years Pop and Granny have driven up the road to Redeemer Baptist and faced the people from the community. All those people that know full well about your drinking and carousing. You never cared enough to stop hurting everyone. That's what psychopaths do."

Hovering close over the bed again, Ben asked, "Are you getting this? A tell-all episode of 'This Is Your Life'? The Jason Bramley's-a-worthless-piece-of-shit, show?"

The eyes blinked.

"I'll take that as a *yes*."

The next moment, multiple alarms blasted from the lone monitor in the room. Ben shot upright, noticing that heart rate and respiration were the culprits.

Nurses will be coming.

Before they could, he put his mouth to his father's ear. He savored the utterance of each word, slow and distinct.

"Dying is the best thing you've ever done for me."

He backed away, swollen with satisfaction.

Leaning against the far wall, he watched the red LED numbers plummet. Hands folded behind his back, he stood engulfed in calm. The nurse who entered would be aware of the *Do Not Resuscitate* order, not that they could save the old man anyway. The outcome had no options.

Ben exercised supreme effort to keep from smiling in direct view of a harried nurse, as the waves on the heartbeat graph lost all curvature.

"He's gone," she said, looking at Ben. "I'm so sorry."

"Don't be," he replied, exiting unhurried, breathing the free air.

Letting the sensation of each step linger before taking the next, in spite of the cast, he had the easygoing expression of a man who had mastered life, mastered himself.

How did the author imagine Ben's experience of coping with such a significant death? Find out by subscribing to Southern Fried Karma's YouTube channel, Fugitive Views.

CHAPTER THIRTY

". . . the LORD gave, and the LORD hath taken away; blessed be the name of the LORD."
—Job 1:21

Mid-morning following Jason Bramley's death, locals began knocking on Pop and Granny's door.

"Can't even get the breakfast dishes washed and put up."

Highly irregular for her, Granny had not changed out of her housecoat yet.

"Now Hon, go on and get dressed. I'll get the door. We both know they mean well."

"Tell them to go *mean well* somewhere else," she told Pop.

To avoid being spotted, she ducked around the corner.

Ben sipped on his third cup of coffee in the breakfast nook. When the black rotary telephone rang, he stepped into the kitchen and raised the vintage handset to his ear.

"Bramley residence. Ben speaking. How may I help you?"

The half-day spent in third grade on telephone etiquette had not left him.

"Mrs. Hazelton would be proud of you," Silk spoke from the other end. "How are you doing by now?"

"Fine, and I'm not just saying that."

"Your dad died a few hours ago. No need to put on the macho act. I can get away from the café and come over."

"That'd be great, but don't let your business suffer on my account. Saturday's got to be one of your busiest days."

"Forget Saturday. You're more important."

"I don't know about that. I'll be okay hanging out with Pop and Granny."

He lowered his voice.

"And it's not any macho act. Remember the first night I stopped by the café? How I told you I was a shitty son?"

"Stop that nonsense."

"Honestly?"

He cupped his hand around the mouthpiece, looking around to assure privacy.

"At the risk of sounding horrible, I haven't shed a tear, nor do I expect to. That's the asshole you want to be with."

He waited, half-expecting her to hang up.

"Still trying to run me off?"

She got no answer.

"Can't accept some happiness in your life? It's going to take a lot more than your version of shock talk to shake me."

Then she hung up.

A few hours' worth of maudlin visitors tried to paint his dad as a good man, while insisting that Ben knew them—practically demanding that he remember and acknowledge them. All of this made for an explosive recipe.

"I'm going out for a bit," he said to Granny.

She didn't question, which left Ben feeling like an even bigger shit.

He ended up at the Abundance Café, nursing a glass of sweet tea, watching Silk and the staff feed the masses. He'd scrounged up an old cap, pulled down low to hide what he could of his face. Telltale red curls sprung out from under the band, as he sat on the lunch-counter stool.

Sunglasses. I should have gone with sunglasses.

Opportunity to speak to Silk approached impossible, though he didn't really want to talk. When he figured it might no longer be a threat to his sanity, he returned to his grandparents' house. He had agreed to go casket shopping with them at The Good Shepherd Funeral Home in Groverton.

A FIRST FOR BEN, THE chore proved creepier than his wildest misgivings.

He found an escape corner at the far end of the casket showroom, while the sickeningly phony salesman showed Pop and Granny his top models.

Though distant, Ben continued to hear the syrupy voice drone on.

"Now this one, well, this beautiful one is our bestseller. It has many features of our most expensive model, but with a budget in mind." And without let-up, "What sort of budget are we looking at today?"

Ben had his own private comments. "The Grim Reaper's henchman, here to put a price tag on your misery. It takes a special kind of morbid fuck to pick survivors' pockets without remorse."

Reaching all he could stomach, he stepped forward.

"A minute with my grandparents, if you please."

The bloodsucker obliged, visibly unhappy to have his victims distracted from his spiel. Having mastered his delivery after hours of practice in front of his apartment's bathroom mirror, he found it difficult to pick back up if interrupted—a loss of momentum with which he couldn't smoothly contend.

Circled together, the trio's control returned, with Ben talking.

"Listen to the kid for a change." He pointed a thumb to his chest for clarification. "Pay no attention to this guy. He's an ass. Yes, Granny, I said *ass*, and that was me being polite."

Pop laughed, in spite of the setting.

"He would convey you a deed to the moon if you signed and forked over enough dough. His opinion means nothing. What matters is what you want for your only son. Exactly what you want, because I'm paying for this one."

In stereo, both grandparents raised objection. Ben knew how to make it digestible.

"I know how slow the packing house is to pay. They have the Bramley crop, along with the rest of the area apples. Their pockets aren't deep enough for all of that debt load. You won't get paid until their brokers get all those apples sold, shipped, and payment received. Meanwhile, you're stuck with a labor bill and an ocean of gas going into the truck."

The truth of his words visibly melted the resistance on their faces.

"Y'all taught me not to talk about money. Fair enough. Let's just say if I wanted to buy that casket there," he pointed to the most-expensive model, one which someone with more balls than good sense named The El Dorado, "I would write a check and not bother to enter the amount in my balance ledger."

THAT EVENING, POP, GRANNY, BEN, and Silk sat in the Bramley living room pretending to watch television, their lives on hold until the Monday-morning funeral at the Redeemer Church cemetery. Pop had suggested a return to movie night, with many reels unwatched. Granny wouldn't have it.

Though Ben understood normal protocol, or at least Bramley protocol, for death in the family, he amused himself with the mental image of The Culhanes of Cornfield County, from Saturday night episodes of the old *Hee Haw!* television show. His family's grouping bearing a too-similar tableau to not indulge the fantasy.

"I vote for skipping church tomorrow," Granny spoke up.

"Any particular reason?" Pop asked.

After more than fifty years of marriage, they had missed church only for serious illness or monumental snow.

On the red Naugahyde couch, Ben and Silk sat hand-in-hand, awaiting Granny's reasoning.

"I can't speak for y'all, but I can't take one more long-faced neighbor or church member going on and on. Most of them are fishing for gory details anyway, and I'm tired of talking about how Jason died. It hurt my heart bad enough the first time hearing it from Ben in that ICU waiting room, and I'm tired of reliving it with the whole community."

"Amen," Pop added.

They had picked a Monday-morning funeral to lessen the number of attendees.

"We shouldn't be forced to grieve publicly," Granny insisted.

"If we stay here, they'll all stop by the house after church, based on the response we've had," Ben said.

"You're right about that," Pop added.

Ben had a childhood destination in mind.

"We've got tons of food from well-wishers. How about we pack up a bunch of it and go on a Sunday drive down to Chimney Rock and Lake Lure?"

"Sounds like a great way to spend my day off," Silk said. "That is, if I can horn in."

"You're not horning in, darling," Granny assured her. "After all we've gone through together these last days, you're family."

"Thank you Mrs. Bramley."

"So how about it? Family drive tomorrow?"

Ben pushed. All agreed.

THEY SPREAD THEIR LUNCH ON a picnic table at Lake Lure Park, flanked by high ridgelines topped with rounded granite. To their right, the lake reached out to the foot of the mountains. Left, they had a full view up Hickory Nut Gorge. The lush panorama had gone from green to an explosion of fall colors.

When eating subsided, Granny spoke up. "Now let's get down to business."

No joking in her tone.

"I'm an old woman who's going to bury her son tomorrow. None of us saw that coming. It just did, and I don't need any more surprises at my age, so will somebody please tell me what's going to happen after the funeral?"

First she looked to Pop, moved on to Silk, settling on Ben, her arms folded, waiting.

"Should I go for a walk?" Silk asked.

"No, ma'am," Granny answered her. "I figure you play into this."

"What do you want to know?" Ben asked.

"I want to know what's going to become of your Pop and me? Are you going to leave us on our own with the orchard until we get so run down you have to put us in an old folk's home? Sell off the place?"

"Whoa, whoa, whoa!" Ben had risen from the bench.

"Sit right back down."

Granny's order included an index finger aimed at his seat.

Plainly not backing off, she shed whatever degree of Southern Belle-ness that could be attributed to her, becoming business-strict, the Chairwoman of the Bramley Board.

"You're our only heir. Now how does that hit you?"

Without waiting, she continued.

"Decisions are going to be made right now, this day. And going forward, you're the one who'll be making most of them. That's the way it works in a family. Our individual actions and decisions affect the rest, to the good or the bad. It's like some of them equations you learn in school—action and reaction. Simple as that."

She paused, took a breath, and asked again, "So what's going to become of your Pop and me? I've got a right to know."

She looked determined to sit on the bench until she got her answer.

"What's that verse, Pop, the one that begins, 'For I reckon . . .'?" Ben asked.

Pop had no problem quoting, "For I reckon that the sufferings of this present time are not worthy to be compared with the glory which shall be revealed in us. Romans 8:18."

He smiled at Ben.

"You used to say that was your second-favorite verse."

"Still is, I guess. I repeated it a lot growing up when I got to feeling sorry for myself."

He had his head down, looking at the table top.

"The word 'reckon' in it felt familiar, like it was personalized for a sad, Southern boy, a boy who grew up to be an angry man. And in one of our great Southern traditions, I'm guilty of not speaking my truth, biting my tongue when I should speak up. Maybe I'm not the person any of y'all think I am. Maybe I'll never come close to being the person y'all might like me to be."

He stopped to let his words sink in.

"I'm trying to convey the likelihood of future disappointment with me. That's what happens when folks are playing out of different rulebooks, and I don't even have one. I know, better than y'all, I'm a mess, a work in progress, but still a mess. In fact, I wouldn't wish me on anyone, nor would I wish my life experiences on my worst enemy. The question each of you has to answer to your truest inner satisfaction is, do you love me for who I am this moment, even with my secret sins, or is that love based on expectations of a future, much-improved version of me?"

Allowing no more than a second for them to consider, yet not interrupt, he continued.

"That said, I've been formulating a proposition."

"And what might that be?" Granny asked.

"I thought about holding on to my place at Boone, while I live here for a trial period, if y'all will have me." He paused. "Does your lack of objection mean 'yes,'?"

Silk leaned over and kissed him. When she pulled back, he looked at his grandparents.

"Did you really think I'd leave you alone, or pack you off to a nursing home?"

"We figured you'd never come back here," Pop said.

Granny had a response born of firsthand experience.

"Family matters may look to be running slick as goose grease, until tragedy strikes. Whether death, or plain old age, settling business and property affairs can bring out the worst in the best of folks. Praise the Lord, we have had us a longstanding mess to deal with, yet we've made it to this point."

Her tone, a Duke's mixture of both happy and somber, gave Ben his first full glimpse of life's toll on her.

"I've had a change of perspective, Granny. Maybe it's from not having to eat my own cooking," he said, drawing smiles and chuckles. When the levity subsided, sober words took hold.

"Our family history, this family . . ." His right hand made a circular motion to encompass their small group. "Our history may not be one for a Hallmark movie, but what we have is a shared history. None of us immune from what gets labelled as bad. We've all suffered in our own private hell, and in our own private ways of dealing with that. Me, I've chosen to run, literally. Now I see that's not been working too swell for me. I'm tired of running. I'm so tired."

Swallowing the lump arising in his throat, he went on.

"I also see that this return trip, never one I would have chosen, may be the most therapeutic event ever, a true lifesaver, in every sense of the word. And I've come to understand that the past only has control over me if I let it. A screwed-up past doesn't have to dictate a screwed-up future. Though I don't pretend to speak for anyone other than myself, going forward, I'm determined to heap up happy memories."

When it became apparent that he had concluded, a Bramley group hug ensued.

The family joy continued on the ride home and into the evening, until one-by-one the reality of the next day's demands returned to each of them.

With the thrilling news of his more-permanent return put on hold, Ben walked Silk to her truck.

"When were you going to share your plans with me?"

She was leaning against the driver door with Ben's shirtfront in her fist, pulling him in close.

He could feel her body heat cutting the cool, night air.

"After the funeral seemed fitting. Granny blew that idea."

He took a moment to appreciate her body melded into his.

"So, you're happy with the news?" he asked.

"That's an understatement."

She planted a deep kiss on him, and when their lips reluctantly parted, she asked, "Does this mean there's an 'us,' or is the move only for your grandparents' benefit?"

Seconds dropped before he answered.

"I would not have neglected my family responsibilities. As for moving back, let's say you're the change of perspective I mentioned at the picnic."

Pushing his shoulders back, she served up an enticing look.

"What about living arrangements?"

"Oh, no, no, if I'm reading that seductive expression right in this poor light. Pop and Granny love me, and you too, it's plain to see, but don't mistake them for the progressive types. Though they will never run my life, I'd be a fool to invite trouble from the outset. Does that make me some kind of Grandma's boy in your eyes?"

She gave him a mock frown, as he explained further.

"Given the anonymity of a big city, no relatives, no peer pressure, I'm all about cohabitation without benefit of clergy," he said, reversing her frown. "What's still too fresh is how Daddy's flagrant misconduct ended up biting Pop and Granny."

"You're right, though I want the record to indicate that I said so under both duress and protest," she said.

"So noted, which the minutes of this meeting will reflect. I'll move back in with Pop and Granny for the time being, if they approve, of course. And if my new life keeps moving in the current direction, I'll be picking out a house site somewhere on the property, with your input, if you agree."

Trying to sound matter-of-fact, she asked, "What about your dad's place?"

Her head turned in that direction, assessing it with a new interest.

"Nope," Ben said, not needing to look, the building's outline the backdrop to his former night terrors.

She could hear the vacancy in his voice.

"Give it a few months and I'll likely go all Forrest Gump on it. Hire a dozer to flatten it. Too much of a billboard for pain."

"How do you know about Forrest Gump?"

"Even hermits go to the movies now and then."

"Sounds reasonable. I'll see you in the morning. I'd better scoot before Granny comes out to check on us."

"How do you feel about cats? Cat, actually?" he asked.

"Uh. . . ." she stumbled, "I'm both a cat and a dog person. In between pets at the moment."

"Cool."

She froze. "Why do you ask?"

"Getting to know more about you."

His smile looked more mischievous than innocent.

"Oh no, you don't get off that easily." Her urging did no good. "Guess I'll have to tickle it out of you."

Silk grabbed for his ribcage, both of them teetering until they collapsed onto the grass, chilly dew penetrating their clothes as they rolled in laughter.

"Oh, your hurt head!" she said, remembering.

"I'm fine," he said. "If that romp in the back of your truck the other day did no damage, this won't."

Pinned on his back, lost in the moment, his eyes caught the glint of porchlight in hers. Unmistakable poignancy. Silence. Staring.

"I love you," she half said. The three words sounded as much a realization as a declaration.

Maybe the shock was apparently mutual, as crucial seconds passed.

Earth to Ben! This is what they call 'a defining moment.' If you're going to have any chance at a decent future, say something. Don't leave her hanging.

"Listen, I should tell you, I don't throw words around."

Immediate disappointment etched her face.

"No, no, no. Wait a minute," he begged as she pushed off

his chest, separating to stand. "I'm not sure I know true love."

Continuing to lie on the ground, he knew that his defense sounded like a million other chicken-shit male cop-outs, yet he kept talking.

"Daddy and Mama fought a lot. She left him. He left me. Pop's been deceptive with Granny, and Granny played favorites with her love. What I've seen, even at best, is sadly conditional, a tit-for-tat stipulation, a selfish, tentative detente."

He paused, shy of dismissing love altogether.

"Maybe I haven't witnessed real love. So how can I know what it is?"

She stood over him, listening, her body language screaming, *'About to leave!'*

He fought for the combination of words to best express his neglected heart.

"That day on the playground, third grade, when you told me your name, asked me to push you on the swing, I know it sounds crazy as hell, only eight years old, I felt this instant connection, something deep. Now, a few days back here, and I've got that same feeling, this time multiplied to the power of infinity."

She took a visible sigh of relief.

"The thought of doing life without you now that I know you is a worse scenario than the total of all I've been through."

He paused to get up and stand beside her.

"If that's what you mean by *love,* then I love you too."

Before the final syllable faded, she had him locked in a vise-like embrace. He felt her trembling.

"Are you okay? Are you crying?"

"I've never been better. Now quit talking you idiot, and hold me."

CHAPTER THIRTY-ONE

"For to him that is joined to all the living there is hope: for a living dog is better than a dead lion. For the living know that they shall die: but the dead know not anything, neither have they any more a reward; for the memory of them is forgotten."
—*Ecclesiastes 9:4–5*

Ben wore one of his dad's old suits—charcoal, with a solid-maroon tie. Granny had insisted, and though he found it, "Bat-shit morbid to be dressed in clothes belonging to the corpse in the waiting casket," as he told Silk, lacking any dress clothes of his own, he capitulated.

Clutching a queasy stomach, he waited for Pop and Granny to come into the living room. The short ride to the cemetery topped their itinerary.

Granny had been the one to go next door to fetch the clothes, shoes too, though he had no need for the left, only one week into wearing the walking cast.

Pop had wrapped the half-Windsor knot for Ben's necktie.

"Good thing apple growers aren't expected to wear ties to work," Ben had remarked. The reference to his renewed calling visibly pleased Pop.

As he continued to wait for his grandparents, his right hand was buried in his front pants' pocket. Burnt-sienna Cowboy had gotten extra attention over the course of the emotional weeks.

Pop and Granny walked out of their bedroom with no evidence of the previous day's glee. With both dressed in black, the white of Pop's shirt and of Granny's ivory-lace trim showed in bold relief.

They look so dignified. And old, at the moment.

"Let's get this over with," Granny said, sleepless nights of worry evident.

FROM THE INSTANT THEY PULLED onto the grounds of Redeemer Baptist Church, an attendant directed them where to park, with others telling them where to go, what to do.

Silk stood at the edge of the cemetery, waiting to join the Bramleys.

"You look incredible," Ben said. "Is that okay to say at a funeral?"

She overwhelmed him in a form-fitting black dress, her long, dark hair in constant concert with the October breeze.

"It's fine," she assured him.

Anxious for closure, and nervous at his first funeral, Ben headed for the gravesite.

Silk yanked back on his hand. "Stop! Wait on your grandparents."

They were moving with the dual burden of old-age and grief, sidestepping tombstones that sprung from the ground, as numerous as dandelions gone to seed.

Granny had insisted on the simplicity of a graveside service. She wouldn't be put through hearing her son's name brought up in a sanctuary where pews of members had so long sat in judgment of him.

When Ben halted, he surveyed the knot of people around the green funeral-home tent. Not a huge group. Still, too many for his liking. As Pop and Granny caught up, Ben fought the urge to again rush forward.

He leaned down and whispered to Silk, "How long will this take?"

"Think of it as a gift you're giving your grandparents. Take yourself out of the equation."

"All right. All right."

"Now stop talking. Solemn occasion. Remember that."

When the four of them approached the tent, the group already assembled parted, allowing the Bramleys access to the front row. Uncle Stan had already seated himself there. Ben nodded to him, while also noticing that the folding chairs were arranged atop a carpet of fake grass. Some ancient attendees sat in the remaining chairs, then struggling to rise at Reverend Thomas's command to do so.

With the Bramleys in place, Reverend Thomas spoke.

"At this time we'll have the opening prayer from the pastor who knew the family well, Reverend David Shepard."

Ben started to step forward, but quick to sense his movement, Silk put her left arm over his shoulder, grabbing his other arm with her right hand.

"What the hell?" Ben was whispering through gritted teeth. She fought him back.

A young man guided the aged minister from the back edge of the crowd. Once in place, Reverend Shepard began his prayer. Ben heard not a word.

"For your grandparents," Silk whispered in his ear. "Solemn occasion," she said again.

The prayer ended. With Reverend Shepard out of sight, Silk still kept Ben under lessened restraint.

"Be seated," Reverend Thomas commanded.

Ben didn't hear another word spoken. He stayed locked down until the service ended and Silk could speak to him freely, though still in whispers.

"Get yourself together. Now. Enough is enough. You're not going to be freed until you promise me that you are going to behave yourself. Understand me?"

"I promise."

Uncle Stan spoke up.

"I hear we're going to be getting a new resident in Abundance. You know anything about that?" He smiled at Ben. "I'll have Cheerwine at the station when you get thirsty, nephew."

Ben thought about being back with his uncle, also noting that Stan then left without saying anything about Daddy's death.

For the first time since Reverend Shepard's name had been mentioned, Ben looked to Pop and Granny, now standing, talking to church friends. Silk had his arm in hand, still a little tighter than normal, watching him as he scanned the group.

"What's going on?" she asked.

He had surged forward, half-dragging her with him.

"A little errand I need to attend to."

"Stop this instant Ben Bramley. Stop!"

He did.

"Listen, I promised not to cause a stink, and I won't, but you've got to let me speak to the bastard."

He saw eyes swimming in disbelief.

"Speak to him, that's all. Swear it."

He crossed his heart with an index finger—like the little-kid promises from their playground days.

Reluctant, yet aware that a physical battle to stop him would bring negative attention, she let him go on alone.

Reverend Shepard and his aide walked apart from the crowd, headed to the opposite side of the graveyard. When Ben caught up to them he spoke to the young man.

"Excuse me. May I have a private word with the Reverend? I'll only be a moment."

The assistant moved several yards away. Ben gauged the distance against the volume of his white-hot words.

"Reverend Shepard," he began. "Long time no see."

Unamused, the Reverend asked, "Who are you?"

"One of your former chosen boys. Too many for you to recall, I'm sure."

Ben wouldn't divulge more.

"I'll call Charles back over here, and we'll put a stop to this."

"Is that the name of your seeing-eye dog over there? Call him. That's not going to stop what I have to say, you old pedophile."

"Outrageous! You can't talk to me like that."

"I'll talk to you as I damn well please. That's nothing compared to all the young boys you molested, and who knows what other perversions you've spawned over the decades."

"I did no such thing!"

"You go on telling yourself that big, fat lie. Maybe I'll decide to out you when you least expect it. Or maybe I'll take it a step further and pay you a special visit one night."

"Nobody will believe you."

Denial had lost its edge as fear of Ben's threats gripped the blind man.

"Oh, I'm sure there are still plenty of fellows around who know it to be true, waiting for that first brave voice to speak up. More importantly, when you're lying in bed at night, trying to get it up by picturing some innocent kid in the woods with his underwear down around his ankles, I want you to remember the Bible verse you were so fond of using to scare us, 'Vengeance is mine. I will repay, sayeth the Lord.'"

He paused, not trusting himself to continue.

"See you in hell, Reverend."

Ben walked away, amazed at the instantaneous transition he felt. Spitting out those words had shifted his frame of mind from victim to conqueror. He had taken back some of the power his enemy had stolen, restoring a chunk of his former self.

"Hallelujah, it's a miracle!" he exclaimed. The sarcastic twang, he kept not quite loud enough for others to hear.

Both his arms were thrown skyward, his head tilted back in exultation, at which point came his first notice of the funeral canopy's border, gold letters spelling out the business name—THE GOOD SHEPHERD FUNERAL HOME.

The immediate correlation seized him as beyond funny, fueling hysterical laughter. He pointed to it, then to Reverend Shepard being helped into the passenger seat of his ride, then back to the canopy, wanting Silk in on his joke.

"This is priceless!" he yelled to her. "Are you getting this?"

She stood halfway between him and the last of the crowd, a

few of whom had turned to discern the uproar. Unsure herself, she bore a curious expression, until he smiled in advance of reaching her.

Seconds later, a different man than the one who walked to the graveside with her hugged and lifted her off the ground.

"You are spectacular!" he yelled, louder than before, carefree of any judgmental eyes. Then he gently returned her to earth.

"I've known you were meant for me since third grade," she said, pushing a red curl back from his face, letting her hand rest there.

He could see that look again in her eyes, an open pool that led right to her soul. He hoped she could see his, and notice that the wounds were healing, and maybe not as raw as before.

"Who knew a funeral and a good dressing down could be so transformative?"

Exuberant, he broke her command for solemnity, without any remorse.

"The day's not over yet," she said, wearing a self-satisfied grin.

"Is there something mandatory after the funeral service? What do families usually do?"

"Often get together and have a meal. However, you may be in for a slight variation on the traditional."

"Do I get any clues?"

Turning to the right, she raised her arm and pointed across the road.

"Okay, still clueless," he said. "You're pointing at the Abundance Community Building."

The low block structure included a playground and softball field. Ben noted a few vehicles in the parking lot.

"I'm going to need a more direct hint."

"You're about to be the guest of honor at a party in the community building. Is that direct enough for you?"

"No. I don't get it."

"Here's what's happening. Your grandparents wanted to throw you a 'Welcome Home' party."

"On the same day as the funeral?"

"Again, their idea. Your grandfather claimed Jesus said, 'Let the dead bury their dead . . .' then something about instructing the living to get on with their business."

"And Granny agreed to this?"

"Absolutely. She got on the subject of some prodigal son returning and the father killing a fatted calf in his honor. I nodded like I knew what she was talking about."

"Who all's going to be there?"

"Your grandparents, of course. Your Uncle Stan. He went over early doing some set up."

"That's why he left so soon," Ben said.

Silk continued, "Your Grandpa Etter. He drove halfway up from Florida yesterday, and started out early this morning, then got delayed by heavy rain. That's why he missed the funeral. He'll be here soon."

Ben's eyes widened. "You're kidding."

"No."

"I haven't seen him in forever."

"Mrs. Hazelton's going to be there. She'll be fun."

"Is that all? I mean, that's plenty. I don't care for a big to-do."

"Only one other." She hesitated. Shifting from side to side, she squeezed out two words, "My mother." Before he could speak, she hurried to add, "She's been dying to see you. Oops! Sorry." She put her hand to her mouth, too late to suppress the faux pas.

He laughed at her embarrassment, as she continued to justify her mother's attendance.

"She loves you already. All I've told her. No pressure. We had to get together sometime. And she's a pro at being discreet when it comes to Christian practices and so on. Lots of experience at blending in. It'll be great."

"No need to be nervous. I'm anxious to see your mom too. Here, take my keys and drive Pop and Granny over to the community building. I'll meet y'all there in a minute."

"What are you doing? Is everything okay?"

"Couldn't be better. Tending to a little closure stuff. Maybe more like catching-up stuff. That's all. See you in a few minutes."

Seeking solitude, each measured step he took had historical significance. Averting his gaze to the sky, he watched as a singular white cloud scooted across the autumn blue. It was his favorite season of the year, and life was finally looking more optimistic than enemy.

Quiet, except for some brown leaves tumbling across the ground, he surveyed the cemetery. Outwaiting the last of the attendees, he had the place to himself, other than the grave-digging crew sitting in their truck in the far corner. Cigarette smoke spiraled heavenward from an open window as they waited like jealous dogs anxious to bury a fresh bone.

"I wouldn't mind slinging a few shovelfuls on the old man's coffin. . . . Maybe take a piss on it first."

Pleased by the thought, he laughed like a lunatic on weekend asylum leave. The outburst continued until self-consciousness caused him to check to see if the digging crew had been alerted.

Between their truck, and where he stood, the field of granite and marble tombstones chronicled generations of family history. The taste of that realization—Bramleys, Etters, and more, living, belonging, dying in succession—quelled his laughter, evoking the solemnity he couldn't muster for his dad's service.

Tapping old memories, he followed the gravel drive around the edge of the graveyard, stopping mid-way, walking up the slight slope to the second row of markers. Looking left and right, he found Grandma Etter's gravestone, recalling the funeral he didn't get to attend.

"I miss you Grandma. Probably not a day has passed without me thinking about you, thinking how my life might have been different with you in it. But also figuring that maybe your death is a big part of my closeness to Granny, and for that, I thank you."

He paused.

"I'm moving back here—shock. Yeah, it is to me too. And here's another. Grandpa's driven up from Florida to see me. Hope we can find some things in common, other than our mutual pain. I guess he had a hard time hanging around, as well. I'll talk to you again soon, and let you know how things go with Grandpa. Love you."

He moved on a few rows and veered off to his left, finding a section where several stones, in various stages of weathering, bore the Bramley name. The sight of so many direct family members' graves dialed up heightened reflection, speaking in powerful undercurrents of heritage. A newfound serenity gripped him, fortifying his previous decision to stop running from his past.

Though living family waited for him across the road, he needed to find one more dark-gray marker, one flat with the ground.

After a diligent search, he discovered it, and found himself staring at the inscription:

James Mitchell Bramley
May 22, 1974-August 29, 1978
Gone Too Soon

Not since those childhood nights without James, when Ben alternated between sleeplessness and terrifying dreams, had he spoken to his brother. A huge backlog of life events to share, that conversation would have to wait for another time, a stronger time.

Ben walked on, leaving the dead behind. Crossing the road, he stood outside the community building, not entering, but instead spying through a window until he caught Silk's attention, motioning for her to join him outside.

"What's with all the lurking?" she asked.

Ben took her arm, pulling her away from the window.

"I need my keys."

Rather than comply, Silk insisted, "First, tell me why."

"Look, I trusted you with all my screwed-up past. Now you're going to have to trust me."

He held out a waiting palm.

"I'll not lose you again."

"You're not losing me. I have a fifteen-minute errand to take care of, then right back for the party. I love you, remember?"

"Alright."

She placed the keys in his hand.

"I'll be timing you."

"Stall them for me, please." And he was gone.

Three minutes later the Acura turned onto the Bramley pond road, chased by a plume of dust. The vehicle rumbled bridge boards in the crossing of Blossom Creek.

Continuing past the pond, he stopped at the back corner of the orchard, where the woods bordered the Unolama. Out of the vehicle, he searched for the old opening in the rhododendron thicket, grown over from lack of use. Pushing the tangled canopy of leaves aside he finally discovered what appeared to be a remnant of the trailhead.

Two minutes of fighting branches and undergrowth, and he spotted the unmistakable mottled bark of the giant sycamore tree that his family had used to fish by, the trunk grown thick in his twenty-four–year absence.

Standing at river's edge, conflicted, he realized how much he loved the powerful sound of the crashing water, the noonday sun glinting between the leaves, flashing mirrors here and there on the slower pools. The idyllic site had been the setting for unforgettable family outings before it had been vandalized by tragedy.

Let go, and grow beyond the past, intruded into his thoughts.

"Where did that come from?" he asked. His voice lost to the torrent. Though unwilling to indulge the slightest chance of divine inspiration, he did admit, "Sounds like good advice."

In front of him the dark current flowed around the same

grouping of stones that led to the river's center. Without hesitation, he stepped from one to the next. Paying no mind to the cumbersome walking cast, he reached the giant boulder where his family had fished.

The slick-soled dress shoe skidded on the incline, tearing a hole in the left knee of his dad's pants. But Ben crested the peak, surveying the swirling water below him, red and yellow leaves being pushed far downstream, where the river narrowed to a ribbon, a shaft of light turning it into a silver highway.

The moving water transported him back to yet another memory, a good memory, of climbing a backyard plum tree, and hidden within the tree's upper canopy, a pair of young brothers staved off the August heat with homemade popsicles. Hiding from imagined bad guys, namely Boots, the cat, and Barker, their collie, if neither animal spied the boys, they could boast of being skilled frontiersmen—Ben, a.k.a. Daniel Boone; James, a.k.a. Davey Crockett.

Through the plum tree's leaves, in the kitchen window, the one above the sink, red hair flashed—Mama.

In that moment on the river, Ben became Daniel Boone again, off on another wilderness adventure, traveling solo, no Davy Crocket along—the loss that came fresh with each sunrise.

He dug into his pocket and removed Cowboy, staring at his companion of twenty-four years, and the only physical reminder of James of which he had allowed himself the indulgence.

"So long, partner. The promise of a new life is waiting for me. The old one hasn't been working too well. I reckon it's reached that time where we part trails."

Bending down, he wedged the worn, plastic figure into a crevice, atop the boulder. Glancing up at the narrow gash of sky, Ben raised his voice above the roar.

"I'll never forget you."

AUTHOR'S NOTE

Nature or nurture? The childhood of Ben Bramley makes a strong case for both.

A long-time observer of human nature, I find the behavior of earth's supposed "highest life form" to be arguably insane. Any number of us will advocate for extreme means to save the life of an unborn fetus, only to have that fetus reach the unripe age of eighteen, and be shoved into a uniform and shipped overseas, to die while warring for peace.

Bombs to end war? In *guns* we trust? Go figure!

Yet, aren't we all at some point acting upon that inner voice from childhood? The one we inherited from parents and relatives, made up of a tiresome list of *do's* and *don't's*, all meant to guide our actions? Do we heed the voice, or fight to resist it, thus proclaiming our adult individuality?

Far from ideal, the mixed bag of nurture handed to Ben was consistent only in the aspect of confounding him. I would have to conclude he ultimately succeeded as an adult, in spite of his nurture, rather than as a credit to it.

As for nature, mine, like Ben's, is the South—or the New South as some wishful thinkers have suggested. Any insistence that the powerful culture hasn't molded me, that I have somehow risen above my raising, is a ridiculous denial of the indelible stamp of heritage.

The lack of a Confederate flag flying in my yard, does not grant me any less cumulative exposure to the prevailing mindset.

I'm infected. We're all infected, with 7.5 billion unique viruses, sourced from the parts of our pasts that stuck, and took parasitic root. Nonetheless, we're expected to show up for work each day, and perform our best at getting along with the other diversely infected. We call it *life,* and its successful navigation can be a mystery some of us never solve.

My fictional town of Abundance is true to the existing microcosms throughout mountainous Appalachia. Readers from the region likely have no stretch identifying with the prevailing culture, maybe seeing accurate reflections of their own communities. It does not require extensive demographic research to reveal key consistencies throughout the region: cultural, religious, political, racial, and ethnic ties by which residents define themselves.

Some thrive in perpetuation of their heritage. Others wither. Some rebel against it and refashion themselves. And many simply move away, convinced that the entrenched mindset is permanent.

My response to the ever-present unacceptable, to cognitive dissonance in all its regional or cultural forms, is a vigorous shaking of my head, a physical refusal of the *crazy,* the *illogical* attempting to penetrate my cranium and lodge there. That, and to tell my stories, chronicling the vicissitudes of human nature, and peering into the abyss of pain, perhaps to unlock someone else's prison.

About the Author

Evan Williams entered his first writing competition in sixth grade, a county-wide agricultural conservation essay contest, and won second place along with a nifty plaque. For Evan, writing is his repayment of gratitude to every author who has inspired him to dream beyond what his eyes can see. His memoir, *One Apple at a Time*, received the Willie Parker Peace Award for state history from the North Carolina Historical Society. Prior to America's Revolutionary War, Evan's ancestors settled in the Blue Ridge range of the Appalachians, where he remains today. *RIPPLES* draws heavily on his family's multi-generational apple-growing business. Surrounded by orchard, Evan writes from within a former apple-storage shed—the same shed where he would steal away as a boy to enjoy quality reading time.

SHARE YOUR THOUGHTS

Want to help make *RIPPLES* a bestselling novel? Consider leaving an honest review on Goodreads, your personal author website or blog, and anywhere else readers go for recommendations. It's our priority at SFK Press to publish books for readers to enjoy, and our authors appreciate and value your feedback.

OUR SOUTHERN FRIED GUARANTEE

If you wouldn't enthusiastically recommend one of our books with a 4- or 5-star rating to a friend, then the next story is on us. We believe that much in the stories we're telling. Simply email us at *pr@sfkmultimedia.com*.

You Know About Our Bi-Monthly Zine?

Would you like your unpublished prose, poetry, or visual art featured in *The New Southern Fugitives*? A bi-monthly zine that's free to readers and subscribers and pays contributors:

$100 for book reviews, essays, short stories
$40 for flash/micro fiction
$40 for poetry
$40 for photography & visual art

Visit **NewSouthernFugitives.com/Submit** for more information.

ALSO BY SFK PRESS